Unfree Associations

UNFREE ASSOCIATIONS

A PSYCHOANALYST RECOLLECTS THE HOLOCAUST

Gottfried R. Bloch, M.D.

With
Rosalyn Bloch

*Unfree Associations; Haunting And Powerful Memories That Are
Always Painfully on the Margin of Everyday Life*

Red Hen Press ❦ *Los Angeles 2004*

Unfree Associations:
A Psychoanalyst Recollects the Holocaust

Special thanks to Helen Saltman for extensive research and editing,
and Peter Pryor for his research and copy editing.

Artistic credits:
"Family Torn Apart" & details (pages *iv*, 6, 76, 102 and 164)
by Ilana Bloch, Los Angeles, California

Cover photo copyright © 2000 by Colin Leroy, Toulouse, France

Photo credits: Susan Einstein

Book and cover design by Mark E. Cull

ISBN   1-59709-011-5
Library of Congress Catalog Number : 2004113943

Second edition 2004

The City of Los Angeles Department of Cultural Affairs, California
Arts Council and the Los Angeles County Arts Commission partially
support Red Hen Press.

Red Hen Press
www.redhen.org

for

My Parents
Willy Schönfeld, Otto Heller, Nelly, Erich
and all the others . . .

CONTENTS

CONTENTS

ACKNOWLEDGEMENTS

OVER THE YEARS I have had help and encouragement at various stages for writing this book. Martin Grotjahn was my first editor, and urged me to continue. He wrote the foreword.

My second editors were James Laveck and Jennifer Stein who had hopes of becoming publishers. James, especially, felt that publishing this book was his special mission, responding deeply to its contents. He and Jennifer devoted much time, energy and creativity to the project including a beautiful book cover design and tried to interest several publishers and institutions. Although they did not bring it to completion and went on to other projects in their life, they helped me along, and in the process became good friends who are pleased about its publication.

The editor of the book as it is now, Helen Saltman, is a former history and literature professor who lives in Northern California, and was asked by the publishers to read my original longer version and, if recommending it for publication, to edit it. Her enthusiasm for the book was warming. We spent over a year working together, by mail, e-mail, and telephone. Her careful reading and cogent suggestions made the book much better conceptually and much clearer.

My friend and colleague, Dr. Max Hayman, who is no longer well, urged me to finish the book so that I might submit it for an award at one of the international psychoanalytic meetings that he was sponsoring on Holocaust studies. Another psychoanalyst who wrote about his own experiences, Dr. Louis J. Micheels, was also kind enough to read the manuscript and along with his suggestion commented that he thought it was an important book to be printed, which was most encouraging.

Another colleague and friend, Dr. Roman Anshin, after reading the manuscript had enough belief in it to send it to a friend on the East Coast who was connected to a large publishing house.

There were a few other readers who encouraged me not only by reading the manuscript but also by contacting those they knew in the publishing arena. Annette Baran, after reading a primitive version in the early eighties, sent me to Marie Brown, an agent in New York, who sent the manuscript as it was then to many publishing houses. I appreciated her efforts and enjoyed meeting her in New York. My friend and attorney, Donald King, also passed it onto someone he knew in the book business and one of our family, Marvin Zuckerman, a literature professor, writer and editor offered other publisher suggestions.

Our favorite bookman in Los Angeles, Doug Dutton, and one of his associates, Diane Leslie, herself a published writer, were also kind enough to go through the reading, as did Sam Eisenstein, a writer whose short story on the subject affected my writing. I want to thank our friend and colleague, Dr. Jane Rubin, for lending me her own paper and other books on the subject of friendship.

Without knowing how much they helped me, I want to thank my patients. They have taught me much about the healing of trauma. Some had similar experiences and I hope that my identification with them and my treatment of them helped reduce their suffering.

I started this book in 1983. It was difficult. It seemed that it would never be published and for a few years I put it away. But as it has often been in my life, at the eleventh hour comes rescue. My daughter, Ilana, who is an artist, was giving a presentation to a group of people interested in art. She wanted to use the portrait of me that she had painted and commented that probably we would not want to take the painting from our house so she asked for one of the manuscripts that had a copy of the painting as the cover. During that presentation one of her students, Marsha Barron, became intrigued with the portrait and then the contents. She asked if it were published and then asked if we would show it to the publishers that she knew, Kate Gale and Mark E. Cull of Red Hen Press, an interesting small press. I am very pleased that they were interested, and admire the quality of their workmanship.

My wife, Roz, worked with me from the very beginning. After I wrote the draft she would read, conceptualizing, clarifying and correcting. Using her literary, poetic and professional expertise we reached this version.

GRB

FOREWORD

MANY YEARS AGO, Gottfried Bloch and I met for the first time in Southern California. I knew little about him, but enough to assume that he would never trust a Gentile German again, not even one who had left Germany, because he did not wish to live under fascistic rule. So we maintained a formal collegial distant relationship for quite some time until we became good friends.

When I got sick, deadly sick, I did not expect to live and was almost destroyed by death anxiety, fear, despair and unwillingness to surrender to what seemed to be the unavoidable. Friedl saw me in the intensive care unit and said little, as is his way. The little he said, however, marked the turning point in my return to the living. He said, approximately, "When I was in situations where I was quite sure to have come to the end of the road and would not live out the next day, I trained myself to think: I am not dead yet. I am still alive. I will live now—tomorrow I will see what happens."

I cannot say how much these words helped me when my heart seemed to refuse to beat the way it was supposed to beat. I did not surrender or resign, just continued to live, day after day.

I have not experienced what destiny has brought to my friend's life. I have learned something from him about how to live, to love life, and not give in to bitterness. I have learned how not to give up, to hope, to go on and live as long as life lasts.

The fact that Gottfried Bloch survived, started a normal life again, emigrated twice, lived through great difficult times and personal tragedy and was fated to live, is for him a mystery of chance or luck. I cannot accept such an answer, but have hardly anything better to say. If I look at him and listen as an analyst, I would say: "I do not understand this life, but I will listen until it makes sense." This had happened to a small degree. It was not good luck repeatedly—that would mean to believe in a divine providence that protected him.

What was it that kept him going? It seems to have been the

acceptance, the surrender to the cruelty of the day. Not hoping for better times but waiting for them anyway. He took survival as his duty, like Job in the Bible. The Book of Job's message is that life has to be lived even when divine powers turn against us. In Gottfried Bloch's life, the powers were human and therefore impossible to deal with, to surrender to, to accept, only possible to survive them by hanging on. He suffered without calling it heroism but simply did not stop living. My friend does not want to be praised for strength or courage but understood in human terms.

Martin Grotjahn, M.D.
Professor Emeritus
University of Southern California
Department of Psychiatry
Los Angeles, Calif. 1988
(died September 1990)

UNFREE ASSOCIATIONS

Family Torn Apart

INTRODUCTION

Auschwitz-Birkenau, July 1944

A Memorable Conversation: The Beginning of This Book

ONE OF THE MOST VIVID memories of my life is of a late afternoon in the middle of July, 1944, less than one year before the end of the war, when I met with my very dear friend Willy Schönfeld behind the hospital barracks where he was a patient. We both felt that the end of the Czech family sector of Auschwitz was approaching. Men and women who were still able to work had been sent out. Only two other doctors and I remained in the camp hospital along with the patients. Thousands who were too young, too old or too weak for heavy work, mothers with their young children, were sitting in their barracks, waiting anxiously.

Willy and I sat in the ditch close to the electric fence. The guard on the tower observed us but did not respond with the usual warning shot in the air. Everyone felt the impending changes and nobody cared about rules. We both sensed that this was to be our last time together, the final one of many talks over the six years that we had worked together. Even then we asked the same question that had constantly preoccupied us: "How was it possible?" In our need to understand the horrendous events around us, we repeatedly called upon our knowledge of psychology. We speculated on what was beyond the rational and logical to find some sense in what we had been witness to, the mass destruction of people. We could find none. Was the magnetism of the nationalistic-chauvinistic German identity powerful enough as a group phenomenon, to wipe out all reasonableness, ethical and religious constraints, and above all, humane feelings?

At times, we too had felt pulled, tempted to believe in the "German right of domination" that was being proffered to a nation hungry for power and especially appealing to its average "little man" yearning for importance. We could not comprehend how mass murder could be

1

rationalized as a patriotic duty within a civilization and a culture that we both thought we understood and to which we thought we belonged. We were deeply shaken to see how easily and swiftly the intelligentsia had been converted, without protest, to a way of thinking that fit the new political climate, requiring changes of law, the reinterpretation of history and reformulating of psychological theories. Scientific achievements were easily discarded if their creators were either Jews or political enemies. Thus went Psychoanalysis, Individual Psychology and many other important contributions in our own professions.

Willy and I ached to think how any survivor could describe the events of this place. We speculated that numbers and statistics would probably be available. They would become part of the historical account of this war. We knew, from our experience in industrial psychology, how the use of statistics reduces the uniqueness of personal experience. Our discussion of the future was macabre since we were talking about a time in which we most likely would not exist.

As psychologists, we believed that a Europe of the future would need to acknowledge these recent events so that the past would not haunt the new order as a repressed, traumatic experience does with an individual who has experienced personal trauma.

How could the impact of even a part of what happened here be communicated except by the description of actual experiences of people? Would anybody ever have the capacity or the willingness to listen to the tragedy that unfolded on this piece of land that used to be a small village in the countryside?

You may understand how compelling was my memory and how obsessive was my rumination of this conversation; how pursued I felt by its obligation. That is how the seeds of this book grew. My feelings did not change since the talk with Willy, but to communicate them was a difficult task for me. I have always been a reserved person, very private about my life and my feelings. I have enjoyed the freedom of expressing myself within whatever close circle of friends I have had in the various phases of my life. As psychoanalysts, we learn to focus on the feelings of our patients without burdening them with our own. We become practiced in constantly examining our own feelings to insure that we take responsibility for them and let them assist us, hopefully without their interfering too much, in the healing process. It is our professional stance to become close to the other person, the patient, to open our own emotions in order to be responsive, to be in touch with our own reactions but to respond only when it is in harmony with the therapeutic process.

Revealing myself through writing was a new idea for me and I had to deal with my ambivalence to break through the inhibitions uneasily accompanying me since the war ended in 1945. The long silence did not diminish the power of those experiences and may have given me time to work this through. I became less reluctant and more impelled to talk. I, who spent my days helping others to resolve their conflicts, found my nights more demanding of a resolution of my own. I felt an accelerating urgency to tell about those times.

Perhaps as one moves nearer to the closing of the gates of life there is a need to complete the tasks that we believe are ours. Could I, who was accustomed and committed in my life to alleviating pain, actually write about experiences that would make others suffer? I did not want to write details that would put the reader through the hell which we had endured. On the other hand, I wanted to describe with accuracy what had actually happened to real people. As a psychoanalyst I try to feel what it is like to be in the "other person's shoes." I wanted to tell but I also wanted to protect the reader.

In 1983, I actually began to write what had been engraving itself in my mind over the years, from 1938 to 1945 when I was systematically deprived of my civil and professional rights, and incarcerated in German concentration camps, condemned to die. Those experiences have inhabited a distinct space in my memory where they have remained suspended, but unfinished, without emotional closure. Those times return as associations—painful, intense, overpowering, demanding attention, intruding into present joy, intensifying the pain of current losses. They have the power to magnify my anxieties of tomorrow; they hold me tenaciously in their grip and I think of them as "unfree" associations because they are the involuntary appearing of what has never been forgotten. They gain strength at certain times, fade away at others but are always there.

The term, "free association," is the English translation of what Freud (1913) encouraged his patients to share by telling him everything in sequence that went through their minds without censoring. A way to uncover forgotten or repressed memories.

I thought of this term when I was in a mountain forest in California and such an "unfree" association took over. The exciting experience of a storm illuminated waves of painful reliving. I was, as I had been many times, thrown back into the heaviness of a day in February 1945, when I was part of a work unit in the Thuringian woods and had observed the sunrise over the tops of the fir trees. I was hungry, freezing and exhausted from hard labor. Unprotected and exposed to the harshness of nature, I wondered if I would ever again experience the intense joy of being in the mountains, a joy that I had developed as a child from my parents' excitement on our frequent trips. Never before had it left me. It did return again after the war and now I even have a mountain retreat of my own where, most fittingly, I have completed this book.

Since the war, I have been collecting, inventorying and sorting my experiences in my head, reliving situations and conversations many times over. They have not been forgotten. Now I can view those days with more clarity and approach those unparalleled seven years with more objectivity. New understanding, in the present, of past events and feelings can occur—this is what is called insight and it comes through introspection. It serves the patient in analysis, and is the constant task of the analyst in self-analysis, but can as well serve as part of an autobiographical process.

Massive life-threatening traumas, psychological traumas like the ones I describe in the next chapters, are experienced as looming disintegration (annihilation anxiety). They interrupt one's image of self and are often dehumanizing because they literally take away one's future, the hope of the fulfillment of one's life dream.

Heinz Kohut, one of the main contributors to contemporary psychoanalysis, defined "the time axis" as the subjective inner sense of continuity of time within a person's life. Reestablishing such continuity after the kind of traumatic fragmentation I experienced was an important part of my return to a fulfilling life. The continuity of the time axis from its roots in the past connects to the future and relates to fulfilling one's earlier goals. Writing this book has for me completed the reparatory process begun in my analysis thirty years ago. It is a very personal account of my traumatic experiences during the war and the people with whom I shared them, Jews like me, as well as others who were persecuted and segregated.

Reading, writing about, and reliving those past experiences at this stage of my life is a continuation of a most important process of self-analysis that never ends in the life of a psychoanalyst. My own experiences within the history of our times are, in a sense, everyone's history. Each person needs to integrate these events into his own history and philosophy of life which is only possible now that we know that there is a life beyond the Holocaust.

GRB
Los Angeles, California

Mother and Son

1

MY EARLY LIFE

FOR MOST OF MY ADULT LIFE I have been intrigued with coincidence and have been in awe of "accidental happenings," seemingly casual, yet often connected, and sometimes even determining survival. Mathematically, fortuitous coincidences seem so unlikely in one's real life but they do occur. Only a few survived Auschwitz and Buchenwald and I am among them—the result of favorable coincidences that if written about in a novel would seem contrived, but are as real as I am today.

It is difficult to write nostalgically now about the warmth and security of my earlier life before the Holocaust, knowing what later occurred. My descriptions of life before those terrible events do not have the intensity and drama that characterize the horrors of war, humiliation and imprisonment. Nothing of ordinary life can equal the suspense of knowing whether or not one will survive. Every day experiences before that time are pale in contrast to later events, but they formed my reactions and my vulnerabilities, my coping capacities for dealing with wartime experiences. Every person's reactions to the Holocaust depends, to some degree, upon his psychological structure and experiences. Therefore, in many ways, knowing my earlier history will help to understand my later behavior.

Although I have no definite memories of my first years, I tried to make sense of fragments from hearing my grandmother and mother talking, in German of course, which became the language of my schooling and the language which I knew best. Later, when I became a citizen of the newly created Czechoslovakia, I learned Czech, my second language. I became acquainted with Latin, English and French in school. After my liberation and emigration to Israel, I needed to learn yet another language, Hebrew, and upon emigrating to the United States, I once again changed my spoken language to English, in which I am now the most comfortable. My desire to be part of one country and speak one language was not possible for me. I was forced, several times, to change my identity, my national belonging and my language. I have always wished for the opportunity to explore one language thoroughly and gain knowledge of one literature in depth but the events of my life did not allow me that privilege.

I was born in October 1914, about six weeks after the outbreak of World War I, in a house called the Villa Francesca in Teplitz-Schonau (pretty meadow), one of the four famous spas of northwest Bohemia, which was then part of the Austrian-Hungarian monarchy. The picture of this place was sentimentally with me all of my adult life. In 1994, soon after the Russians had left Bohemia, my wife, Roz, and I visited. It was an odd experience for me to stand in front of the same old iron gate and watch strangers come out of the house and walk into the garden. It was the old place but my connection to it was gone. What remains is my nostalgia for the way it was.

My father, a reserve officer in the Austrian army, had immediately reported for service, leaving his factory, after the first appeal for volunteers, and was fighting in the Balkans at the time of my birth. At seven months I was prematurely delivered into a world of three women, my mother, Herta, my grandmother, Helene, and my nurse, Frau Leube. They told me later that they all panicked when they first saw me and anxiously doted over me fearing that I might not be fit enough to survive. That was my first survival test but not my last.

Frau Leube had been the nurse to a number of babies in our family, but before my sister Hanna's birth, five years after mine, she had moved to Dresden, to live with her relatives. We visited her after the war in the year 1921, when I was six. When she saw me again she put her hands up in surprise and said in her funny Saxon dialect, "My, my, I didn't think you would ever make it." Her words have resounded at times during the course of my life, particularly when I thought I would not make it any longer. The inflation in Germany was at its peak. She was hungry. She showed us her money, which had become worthless, not even enough to buy bread. We bought her a loaf of freshly baked bread with our Czech money, she cut off a slice and after taking the first bite said, "This is better than the best cake I ever ate." This was my very first, but not my only, encounter, with hunger and the meaning of bread. At times my life was in jeopardy over a piece of bread and the memory of that experience with Frau Leube followed me to Auschwitz and beyond.

When I was three and four, during the last years of the First World War, basic food staples were rationed. There were dated stamps on my birth certificate in order for me to have weekly distributions of milk, eggs, etc. I have been told that, as a child, I was a poor eater and underweight. Food and feeding were love and attention. They were also important maternal rituals. I was weak and anxious about my health for which I compensated by having aggressive fantasies, which were more related to feelings about my father.

In my earlier years, my father, Max, occupied a double role for me, the disciplinarian, strict and distant, looking at me over a book or newspaper to answer a question, slightly irritated with me because of the interruption; and at other times, the playmate who would sit on the floor involved with my toys and me.

History was one of my father's many interests. Despite the knowledge he gained from reading history, an awareness of his own danger from the political situation was something he denied as long as possible. In our library a whole section was devoted to German sets of *Onken's Handbook of History*, a series of twenty to thirty large volumes supplemented yearly, until 1933, when Hitler seized power. In my high school years I would often randomly choose one of the volumes to read. Rulers, royalty, dictators, political misfits, all in places of great influence, were given lots of space. I noticed that the effect of changes in power on ordinary people was given little attention. Starvation, loss of life, possessions and personal degradation were tolerated in the service of great patriotic fantasies. This fed into my protesting against injustice.

When I was about four years old, my father told me the following story, probably on one of his furloughs after being injured: He was leading a group of foot soldiers defending a strategically important road near Sarajevo, stationed on both sides of an old and not so stable bridge. They received orders to withdraw but in a last courageous move they caused the enemy to flee. The pride my father expressed while describing this mini victory was in strong contrast to his frequent convincing claim that war was mainly destructive for both sides. In my childish mind his glorification of this experience seemed so contradictory to his pacifism that it stirred conflict in me about him, adding to the conflict that his return from the war caused me—he displaced me as the only male in the family, but also gave me strength in my identifying with his maleness.

My father often admitted his nostalgia for the Austrian-Hungarian Empire, in which he was proud to be a reserve officer, and which partly formed his attitude toward education and child rearing. How strange that he was killed in Auschwitz by an army of the same mentality and military organization to which thirty years earlier he had proudly belonged. His objective interest in history encompassed what he called the "great times" but often during the war he said, "I wish these times in which we live would be less great."

In spite of my father's outspoken pacifistic and democratic philosophy, he raised me with the flair of a military disciplinarian. On our weekends, when we hiked in the nearby mountains, he would not allow us a rest or a sip of water until we arrived at our destination. As we came home from one of these trips, exhausted from hiking, I chose to stand at a window in the train corridor despite having a seat, unconsciously acting out my father's ideal in an unnecessarily harsh way. This early pseudo-military training probably was instrumental in my later surviving extreme situations such as the death march at the end of the war. These early unconscious male fantasies of achieving heroic accomplishments through suffering carried me through when I found myself in critical situations.

I vaguely remember a feeling of general restlessness and insecurity in the atmosphere; the horror of the First World War was still in the air. During my years in elementary school, the first years after the war, there was a change in the national identity of my family and others around me; until 1918 we had been part of the powerful Austrian-Hungarian monarchy. Now my family and friends, who were of the mainly German population, became a minority in the new Czechoslovakia, which led some to acquire a bitter and resentful attitude. I was stunned when my musician grandmother, whom we called Oma, but whose given name was Helene, in one of our fascinating chats said, "How can I hate the Czechs? They have such beautiful music." I was often with my grandmother when my parents went on trips and we would have long conversations about music and books. My love for music began with her playing the piano, Chopin, Schumann, Brahms. It is still my favorite instrument. Oma always appeared if either Hanna or I were sick and would play for us. Her mere mentioning of hatred shook my security and my wish for a peaceful atmosphere. My parents, who were modern and progressive in their attitudes, had led me to believe that our new democratic country was fair and open to all. I was about eight or nine years old and reacted to my grandmother's surprising remark with a highly specific painful anxiety, a feeling of distress in not belonging, of being a stranger, which unfortunately foreshadowed many such experiences in my life.

Both of my parents needed to work to cope with the post war economic depression. My mother had a small boutique where she sold her own hand-knitted and woven creations, done at home. During the first years after WWI my father tried to save his textile factory, which had been ruined during his time in the service. As a little boy I used to walk among the big machines; I loved to stare at the powerful steam engine that powered all the knitting machines. My father was a hard-working man and I never knew whether it was his indefatigable energy or his discipline that kept him going. I had feared him in my early years, later admired him and certainly took on his work ethic, which became a strong, even a too-forceful trait of my personality. With the failure of the factory, my father went back to school and became a certified accountant. In those years it was not easy in a small town to build up a practice. It was far from his hopes and dreams and his extremely sharp and curious mind was capable of so much more. With war and the subsequent fall of the monarchy, he became both more disillusioned about any fulfillment of his dreams and an even more committed pacifist.

My mother was an artistic and reasonably flexible person, considering her upbringing within the structure of middle class society. For that era she was a modern woman. I remember when she cut her very long hair to be more stylish. She was devoted to my father, whose knowledge and abilities she admired, and was willing to go along with him in whatever he wanted to do. I experienced her, and my sister Hanna, as much more outgoing and social persons than either my father or me. She was well liked, interested in others and was receptive to changes. Whenever I could, I joined her and our fox terrier Uschi on the traditional afternoon walk, especially when my father was busy during the tax season. As a curious person, she listened to me with great interest when I responded to her questions about my generation. When both my parents walked I rarely went along, and if I did, I walked with Uschi, not participating much in their conversation. There were the same family dynamics on our long weekend excursions into the nearby mountains. They would ask, "Why don't you talk?" I would not know what to say and would walk on silently. In winter we went skiing together as a family. Hanna was quite open with me about her life. I was a good listener but I would not share my life with my little sister. She always came to me whenever she was in difficulty, needing help or advice and this was also true during the war, even in Auschwitz, as well as long after when we lived in California.

My parents had a good, quite close, loyal and trusting relationship but my teenage eyes saw their life as too routine, with too little excitement and surprise. Preoccupied with romantic fantasies, I considered marriage a restraining and boring institution and was full of daydreams of forging relationships with peers and potential lovers. I was actually shy. Around thirteen, I changed rather suddenly, probably because I caught up physically. The loneliness of the previous years faded and I made friends, but I have never forgotten those feelings of isolation.

During the years until puberty I deliberately separated myself from a clinging dependency on my family, mainly my mother. I was quite unsure of myself, avoiding groups. I read a lot and identified with heroic roles. My fantasies were filled with standing up for fairness and justice against odds, but in real life this proved at times to be naive, especially during the war.

Other relationships were important to me. I usually needed one best friend, which later on proved to be crucial in my fight for survival. Our classmates called Herbert Heller and me Pontius and Pilate. In junior high school I became fascinated with chemistry and physics and I thought I had discovered my field. We spent our free time experimenting with chemicals. When we were both twelve, we switched our interest to medicine. I became nearly obsessed with the wish to become a physician. We both eventually did become physicians. My fancy was inflamed by a great curiosity about the functioning of nature and the human body as well as by the idealized humane role and authoritative position of the doctor. There was only one other profession that I ever considered—that of writer. The wonderful understanding of people shown by Jack London, Sinclair Lewis and Knut Hamsun stimulated my fantasy. However, I thought the need to promote oneself, one's services, or creations utterly humiliating, while as a physician I would be needed and sought out. My daydreams encompassed fame, and acknowledgement as someone special and important. Whenever I met a new person or group, I yearned for their recognition without having to earn it by proving myself. This was overcompensation for my inhibitions. I have had to struggle with that shyness in social situations throughout my life, in different countries and in different languages.

At age fifteen I found a small book written by a German psychiatrist, Dr. Alfred Brauchle, *Psychoanalyse und Individualpsychologie* (1930) and I wondered where and how the functions of the psyche belonged in the human body. I could not wait to finish high school to go on to the university to study medicine, but I had to spend one extra year studying Latin because my school was a technical one, teaching only modern languages. That was a hard year. I was eighteen and impatient to get to my career and to end the monotony of learning only a dead language. I read a lot during that year, much about medicine, biographies of physicians and researchers, in biology and psychology, including Freud's *Psychopathology of Everyday Life* (1904) which impressed me greatly.

One of my favorite books was *The Book of San Michele*, by Axel Munthe (1934). I spent a good deal of time with another schoolmate, Ernie, who was also studying Latin in preparation for medical school. He told me he would not read anything else by Axel Munthe, despite his status as a great humanitarian, because in another book Munthe had written that the German military mistreated Serbian prisoners during World War I. Ernie was convinced that this was anti-German propaganda. Ten years later when I was in Auschwitz witnessing the slow death of Yugoslav partisans, I was reminded of my friend's credulity. Recently, I heard from another classmate, that Ernie, who always appeared so proper and moralistic, had fallen in love with his medical secretary and was accused of poisoning his wife in order to be free to marry the secretary. Ernie hung himself in prison. I still find it unbelievable. When I was told, I immediately started to hum the monotonous repetitive melody used as a pause signal by the German Broadcasting System, the first moralistic words of the song were: "üb immer Treu und Redlichkeit" (Always exercise fidelity and honesty . . .)

In 1933, when we were studying Latin in preparation for university, we still had enough in common. Sometimes the Latin literature we studied triggered political discussions about events in Germany leading to Hitler's then-current takeover and we became progressively angrier with each other. When the Germans came, Ernie, in contrast to me, could of course continue his studies and become a doctor while I had to leave the university.

The peak of *that* year's frustrations occurred the day I failed the final examination in Latin. We all had passed the written part but I was the only Jew in a group of German students who took the oral examination. Inspector L. was a German professor representing the Czechoslovakian Ministry of Education; he obviously and deliberately focused his questions to me on the most difficult areas of grammar. After he failed me he leaned back, leaving the testing of the others to the school's Latin professor, who passed them all. This was the only test I have ever failed and it delayed my entrance into medical school. As a result, my graduation from medical school was also delayed for seven years. I could not have foreseen that the consequences of such timing would also save my life eleven years later. It was one of those accidental connections. The fact that I had not completed my medical studies provided me a privileged position in a hospital. That twist of fate was an example of my grandmother's wisdom. Amidst the greatest mishap she would say, "You never know what it is good for." However, the day on which I was flunked, I felt devastated and furious. I had to wait another half year to repeat the exam and pass.

That insult was exacerbated by another incident. My Latin teacher, Professor Schübel, told me that he had mentioned to my former professor of geography, Professor Steinbichel, how painful it was for him to watch one of his students being so flagrantly discriminated against and how stunned he was when his colleague responded without seeming to care. I understand now that such negation of justice toward an individual as well as conscious deceit in the service of a "higher goal" is what makes it possible for fascist political movements to grow. I respected and admired my geography professor for his interesting lectures. In the past, he had been fair to all students although he had not hidden his sympathy for the growing Nazi movement in Germany. When my Latin teacher told me about this conversation, I was shocked, determined to prove that I could reach my goal in spite of such obstacles and slights. That kind of willfulness was new for me.

Becoming a student at the university meant leaving my hometown of Teplitz and moving to Prague. Because I failed the Latin exam, my move was postponed, which made me feel slightly depressed. At times I was in pain and our family physician, Dr. Werner, suspected a duodenal ulcer. I probably never had one and the diet I had to follow did not improve my enjoyment of that year. In my solitary walks I would circle the large county hospital, wishing that I already was part of that wonderful world of medicine.

Later, in my own psychoanalysis, I became aware of how much my professional goals in adolescence were influenced by the enormous power given to our family doctor, Dr. Werner, whose orders in our house were law, restricting me, the premature baby, from sports and group activities in order to avoid stress and contagion. It was not until my early teens that I was able to keep up with my peers in physical maturation and emotional development; Dr. Werner's over-solicitous approach did not help me in overcoming my fears. Seeking comfort in being pampered became a familiar way for me to cope. The label, "premature baby," needing special treatment and concern, lingered on into my adult life; unless I was in a position of feeling superior, I felt unequal to my friends. The powerful position and social role of the doctor was part of my unconscious striving toward a more grandiose image.

Medical school was wonderful. My excitement about natural sciences and medicine deepened; psychology was on a back burner but never disappeared from my interest. I wanted it all. Life in the big city, music, theater, everything was wonderful but restricted because of my modest economic conditions. I tried as much as I could not to be an additional burden to my father, who was under strain building his new career as an accountant.

The lack of money did not ruin my time in school in Prague, which was full of marvelous experiences, but it certainly set clear limits. I envied the lifestyle of friends and colleagues who had rich parents and I badly wanted to make money. A friend who managed his way through the university by selling books for a publishing house invited me to become a salesman. During the next year I sold only one small brochure, and that to my father. When my business career did not develop I realized I could not sell, but I did find my niche in another direction.

I started to coach students who were preparing for their examinations in biochemistry. The students were really ahead of me in their years of studies but I knew the material well since it was my favorite subject. It provided me with a modest income, for which I worked hard, frequently preparing long into the night. I wrote and made copies of a syllabus, which I gave to my students.

At that time I was living with my girlfriend, Frieda, in a small one room apartment close to the university in order to be within walking distance. Frieda had been my girlfriend on and off in high school. Her nickname from childhood was "Maus" (Mouse) because she was slender and moved quickly. When I left Teplitz she was working in a department store. We saw each other when I visited my family during vacations. Later, she came to Prague and was with me during my last two years of medical school.

It was 1934; I was a twenty-year-old medical student who had grown up in the Sudetenland, the western part of Czechoslovakia, bordering on Germany and Austria, populated mostly by Germans. The majority of Jews who were assimilated, like my family, went to German schools and felt a part of that culture. Prague, the capital of the country, had both a Czech and a German university, each considering itself the descendent of the famous Charles University. Since German was my mother tongue, I had started my studies in the German medical school, but after the war only the Czech university remained, which is where I finally finished my medical schooling. There were many renowned Jewish professors in the German University before the war and the atmosphere was democratic enough to allow the existence of different political organizations. There was no overt discrimination for those in academic positions. In 1934, only one year after Hitler's seizure of power as Chancellor of Germany, the news from Germany grew more alarming, the propaganda escalated. I could feel that my future was endangered.

2

FORESHADOWING THE FUTURE

WHEN I WAS TWENTY, in the summer of 1934, after my first year of medical school in Prague, my close friend from junior high school, Walter Bajkovsky, and I decided to take a vacation. We hitchhiked towards the Italian Alps using all modes of transportation, singly and together, but we tried to meet each evening. Just after spending the night together in Budweis, where Czech Budweiser beer originated, we were waiting on the highway to the Austrian border for someone to give us a lift when a large and luxurious Mercedes convertible stopped. A tall athletic man with a North-German accent offered us a ride but in return asked us each to carry a bundle of bank notes, explaining that he was only allowed to take a limited amount of money across the border. We were obliging, assuming that he was a German refugee who had succeeded in passing the border into Czechoslovakia and was on his way to another country. After we reached the first town on the Austrian side of the border, he asked us to leave, took his money back and, laughing boastfully, said: "You know what I have in my trunk? It is full of high-powered explosives."

Two days later when we reached Innsbruck we heard that the Austrian Chancellor, Dollfuss, had been assassinated by a group of Nazis and that more violence was expected. Bombing, killing and provoking of other political groups had kindled political unrest in Austria. Our unnamed host, who had taken us over the border, was obviously one of Hitler's emissaries on his way to Austria, the country Germany planned to occupy next.

We hiked up the Brenner Pass trying for a ride. The atmosphere was tense; we were ignored. An Austrian letter carrier who mistook our waving arms for provocative Hitler salutes came at us with his fist clenched screaming, "Get out of our country!" When we reached the Italian border, we were surprised to find large units of the Italian army

17

camped in full alert. We were ordered into a tent where we were interrogated by the Italian military. The intelligence officer wanted to know anything we might have seen of German military movements either towards or inside Austria. We understood later why we had nothing to tell them when we learned from the German newspaper that was published in Prague, the *Prager Tagblatt*. Mussolini was ready to confront Hitler should he, against all his declarations, march into Austria. The German government got the message; it continued to undermine the political situation in Austria, but postponed any occupation. Our personal adventure was exciting for us as students on vacation and provided a more personal view of what was happening in middle Europe. It added a reality to reading the papers and listening to the news.

When we returned, we continued to study in coffeehouses and libraries, particularly in winter, when our living quarters were cold and unfriendly. We would discuss the political situation whenever we could find the time. The reactionary press in many countries was favorable to Hitler's wild, fanatic and grandiose speeches, punctuated with promises of peace and declarations of non-aggression. The enormous military preparations in Germany, along with the brainwashing of its population, were never mentioned. *We* could not ignore it since the expulsion of Jewish students from the universities of Germany brought refugees to our medical school in Prague. These newcomers gave us firsthand descriptions of the oppression and harassment of Jewish and liberal students on the other side of the border. Those who succeeded in escaping, often with nothing but a briefcase or handbag, were being supported by relief organizations in neighboring countries. Prague became a refuge for many important scientists, artists and writers. Their presence enriched the cultural life of the city and provided us an antidote to the steady poisonous intrusion of Nazi propaganda.

After World War I, the economic situation in Czechoslovakia had been better than in neighboring Germany or in the splinter state of Austria. The German population in our new republic, tired from war, was content. Yet they were limited in their loyalty to a national identity and language to which they did not belong. The non-Slavic people had an ever-present undertone of bitterness. Anti-Semitism was present in each culture and was mostly expressed by exclusion from certain clubs and organizations, as well as by making some positions inaccessible to Jews.

The new Czech democracy was hampered by the passive resistance of these minorities, who felt slighted and insulted as a group. Their anger accumulated over the years, spilling into a narcissistic over-investment in national identity and mother tongue. In addition, there was a distance between the German and the Czech Jews.

My non-Jewish German friends and colleagues at the university were increasingly influenced by Nazi organizations. Some tried to convince me that the expressed anti-Semitism was only a childhood disease that would fade away with the greatness of German accomplishments.

There were discriminatory motives as well as political motives. We saw vicious joy when envied rivals fell from position, even friends erased guilt and compassion for those they formerly respected if it meant advancement for themselves. For example, my literature professor, a highly esteemed scholar, Professor Groeschel, was married to a Jewish woman and was replaced by a formerly friendly but mediocre teacher. Highly acknowledged scientists had to leave top positions at German universities and institutions either because of their Jewish origins or political orientations which triggered general insecurity among their colleagues and students. Ethnic background and chauvinistic national esteem became foremost over intellectual human values.

Injustices suffered by individual Germans, in the present as well as in the past, were used to inflame the situation, which took on a spiritual, redemptive cloak. The attempt toward unification of everything German (*gleichschaltung*—a uniform way of thinking, wishing and believing) invoked the appearance of a coherent social structure, although its foundation was based on a rage deliberately stirred up to propel the mobilization of a collective identity. National identification and idealization of Hitler's dictatorial leadership was extended to reach the rest of the world's German population. In his speeches and proclamations, Hitler expressed rage against his opponents and was able to induce an echo among followers. His odd and deluded denunciation of Jews and communists had no limits. But it served an important purpose for his propaganda machine, namely, to distract the world from his increasing militant activity.

In 1934, Hitler, supported by the close circle around him, in one quick massacre rid himself of his initially most supportive organization, the SA (*Sturmabteilung*) storm troopers, a devoted group of Nazi Party uniformed Brownshirts ready to fight at any time and any place for the new idea of a unified Germany. The SA were more socialistic, liberally supportive of workers, while the SS, which later replaced the SA, were more fascistic, militant and war-like. The massacre must have shaken all Germany. The inner split, which at that time we could not understand, caused one of my German friends to voice his first doubts. "Have we been betrayed?" (Answered affirmatively, but eleven years later.)

From 1935 to the beginning of 1938, Europe was still in the shadow of World War I, which had ended twenty years before. Countries such as England wanted to avoid another terrible war. England's Neville Chamberlain and his political party hoped that a settlement with the Nazi regime would guarantee such peace as well as be a bulwark against the Soviets. The acceptance of Hitler's terms by other countries also supported the ruthless elimination of resistance within Germany. The next step was the use of German propaganda, under Joachim von Ribbentrop, Hitler's foreign minister, to promote the "liberation" of German populations in neighboring countries, starting with Czechoslovakia (Weitz, 1997).

When my friend Walter and I were hitchhiking in Italy in 1934, we observed that Bolzano and other cities in the northern part of that country were primarily populated by Germans. When the Italian fascistic militia marched through the streets with their flags, the German population defiantly kept their heads covered; a uniformed Italian marcher would step out of the formation and knock their hats off. These Germans, under the dominance of the Italian fascists, not yet linked with Hitler, talked about their hope that Hitler would, after occupying Austria, conquer that part of Italy (Southern Tyrol) and "free" them. Nazi propaganda in Italy faded when Hitler and Mussolini became allies. Those Germans were forgotten in the wake of events. In March 1938, Hitler and his troops marched into Austria, no longer an issue with the Italians, and then they proceeded to invade the Sudets.

These many incursions brought new waves of Jews and political refugees into Czechoslovakia. Many were arrested at the border and sent to German concentration camps. Tales of these events only emphasized for me the feeling that I needed to get out, but on hearing their stories my lack of hope increased. I felt that a tide was washing over us. Those who had already been forced out of Austria and Germany were the earlier refugees and had to accept exile as a reality. We were new to the experience, still living in our homes and still hoping for Hitler to be challenged.

Jewish psychoanalysts, scientists and well-known personalities were offered visas to countries overseas or to other European states to wait for final emigration. Sigmund Freud and his family left Vienna with the help of Princess Marie Bonaparte and moved to London. But for the average middle class Jewish family, finding a new home anywhere in the world was far more difficult. Legal immigration into Palestine was light because of the restrictions imposed by the British, who ruled there. The Jewish organizations of the free world were not effective on any large scale in bringing help to an endangered population.

3

EXILED IN PRAGUE, 1938

DURING THE SUMMER of 1938 I prepared for my last semester and final examinations at the medical school of Prague's German University. Prague, the capital of the short-lived Czechoslovakian Republic, was a truly democratic state with great freedom for all its citizens, regardless of national origin, language or religion. It was considered an outstanding center of German, Czech and other European cultures, arts and sciences. The two main scholastic institutions were the Czech and the German universities, which existed side by side. A few times during each year, peace was interrupted by student demonstrations and clashes between nationalist-extremist groups from both universities.

By 1938, Nazi propaganda had constructed an extreme right wing party for the German population of the Republic (the Sudeten Germans) under the leadership of Konrad Henlein who, after first denying his connection with Nazi Germany, later became instrumental in the political and diplomatic preparation for the annexation of the Sudetenland. The German students at my university were rapidly absorbed by that movement and became increasingly belligerent and insulting towards Jewish or liberal students and teachers. The tension grew and felt explosive. The Czech defense forces were on the alert. Reassurances from our allies, especially Great Britain and France, gave us the feeling that this time, the free world *would* resist if Hitler broke his promises to respect the borders of other countries.

During that summer vacation, I worked as a medical student extern in a clinic at the Department of Psychiatry and Neurology of the German University under Dr. Gamper, a professor who, in spite of the political climate, treated his Jewish associates and students with academic respect and politeness. (Dr. Gamper and his wife were supposedly killed in a car accident while they were on a trip in the Bavarian Alps. The rumor was

22

that he had been called to examine Hitler for his frantic behavior and apparently came away with a rather compromising diagnosis. The speculation was that his accident might have been murder). The department was the legal authority of medical expertise in psychiatric-neurologic evaluation of disabilities and was where my continuing interest in traumatic neuroses was first stimulated. I had begun reading Freud and Adler in my high school days, and as a result had modified my very early decision to become a physician, leaning more and more towards the specialty of psychiatry and neurology. That summer of 1938 was one of several periods in my life in which I escaped into my work, ignoring the growing political crisis.

A few of my Jewish friends and colleagues assiduously sought opportunities to continue their studies or their research projects in foreign universities or other settings, away from the brewing political unrest. Personal connection seemed to be one way to get there, the other was by entering a foreign country as a visitor, with enough money to stay or go elsewhere.

Then came the shocking events of the later part of September 1938. British Prime Minister Chamberlain, with his emissary Runciman, had again acceded to Hitler's requests and agreed to the annexation of the Sudetenland by Germany. Did anybody in decisive diplomatic circles still believe in Hitler's assurances and guarantees? The panic of those weeks remains unforgettable. Czechs and Jews moved hastily from the lost Sudetenland to the interior of the country, which became the "Second Republic." It was only through this "announcement" that the "first" Czechoslovakian Republic, created in 1918, was given any official end.

The German University was in Prague which remained the capital of the new, "independent" state. In spite of its location, the German University came under the jurisdiction of the Nazis.

When I tried to enroll for my last semester of medical school and register for final examinations, I was asked to sign a declaration that I was not Jewish. The clerk in the university office, who had known me for five years, looked straight into my face. Our eyes met silently. I left. This was the abortive end of my years of enthusiastic academic involvement.

I walked through the university's general hospital, where I had spent years of fascinating work and study, one last time. It was hard to believe that I could be excluded from what I had considered my world. Yet, life there went on—ambulances rushed in, lines of patients waited for their turns, doctors and students in white uniforms continued their professional duties while my own professional identity was abruptly taken from me.

On that day I met one of the German students with whom I had worked in the hospital. His obvious uneasiness made him speed up, and he gazed straight ahead, passing me as if I were invisible. I knew where he went. It was the hour in which we would be sitting next to each other at our microscopes at the Institute for Histology, headed by Professor Alfred Kohn.* In the earlier part of 1938 even my close non-Jewish friends avoided me publicly and, later, even in private. Other students were openly belligerent. I was hurt by my friends' behavior and felt the threat of what was to come. Looking back on the early '30s, I now understand their inner struggle; the wish to hold on to their individuality versus the temptation to become part of the powerful mass movement of nationalistic pride.

My heavy personal grievance was soon overshadowed by the physical danger of being deported by the Czech police as an "undesirable alien" of the Second Republic to be sent back to the Sudetenland, where my family had originally lived as citizens of the first Republic. Fortunately, the Nazis would not give us permission to leave and our deportation was cancelled. My parents, who had escaped from the Sudets just before the German occupation, were kept for a day at the train depot waiting to be shipped back. They talked seriously about suicide. One of my uncles divorced his German wife to protect her. Sick and alone, he committed suicide to free his son from having a Jewish father.

I had become a foreigner in the land in which I had grown up, in the place where I thought I was secure in personal protection and justice. I became one of a growing crowd of stateless persons, refugees, apprehensive about the next day and clinging to images of a home somewhere in the world, any place, that would take us in, orphans up for adoption. I still recall the deep sadness of those rainy days; weeks interrupted by brief moments of hope, triggered by an optimistic rumor only to be dissolved in disappointment. This was the first time in my life that I felt the nearly physical pain of hopelessness, a feeling of being lost.

* Professor Kohn would later be removed from his post and replaced by his devoted assistant.

4

INSTITUTE FOR RETRAINING

I FINALLY BEGAN to explore ways of emigrating, writing endless letters and exchanging information with friends and colleagues. After awhile I became restless, discouraged, and searched for other activity. My identity was being attacked by everything around me. Who can survive psychologically only on one's own reflection? I looked for somewhere I might be acknowledged. I had heard about an expanding department at the Jewish Community Center that dealt with counseling of refugees and preparation for their emigration. The Jewish Community Center in Prague, which prior to these critical years had provided mainly cultural and religious services, now became the place for social and legal support for the refugees from Germany and Austria in assisting them for emigration to other countries.

The founder and director of the Retraining Department was Willy Schönfeld, a young psychologist, an expert in vocational guidance and scientific graphology—the psychological analysis of handwriting as an expression of personality traits. His department was connected with the State Institute for Psychotechnic, center of all psychological testing for education and industry, under Dr. Dolezal, professor of psychology at the Czech University (Charles University).

Willy Schönfeld welcomed me. He badly needed an assistant for the growing tasks of the department and wanted to prepare someone to take over when his emigration plans materialized. He was an unusual person, tall and slim, the typical leptosome-asthenic body type as described by Kretchmer in *Physique and Character* (1922). In his twenties he had suffered from tuberculosis and had spent time in one of the quiet, special sanitariums where optimal conditions and rest were the most conservative treatment, combined with compression of cavernous tissue through pneumothorax and surgery. Chemotherapy was not yet available.

In his typically constructive way, he had turned his misfortune into advantage. After collecting material, he involved himself in a research project to see if there was a connection between physiological and behavioral changes and the expressive movements of handwriting. He made the important observation that certain deviations occurred in the handwriting of patients when their breathing capacities became impaired. He also related changes in handwriting to psychological reactions to illness and hospitalization and hoped that graphology would become a technique used by professionals for diagnosis and treatment.

After his discharge from the hospital in 1934 he published his first book, *Handschrift, Tuberkulose und Character*, in collaboration with Dr. Karl Menzel, one of the physicians at the sanitarium. The book established him as a leading graphologist and he became editor of the most prominent journal of graphology of the time, *Die Schrift* (The Script), and spoke at conferences on graphology, vocational guidance and related issues.

The political changes during this period restricted his activities. His dream was to go to the United States, a land that he thought was open to new ideas in applied psychology. When we met in 1938 at the Jewish Community Center, he was intensely involved in organizing the re-education and training program for refugees in preparation for emigration. A staff of specialists was appointed to choose instructors and programs while he concentrated on consulting and selecting applicants. When I joined the department in November of 1938, I was first a volunteer and soon an employee. I participated in all courses on graphology, first as a student and later as Willy's assistant. As vocational guidance became popular, we needed to hire more co-workers and counselors. By adding Dr. Erwin Hirsch, psychiatrist and psychoanalyst, who had been a lecturer at the German university in Prague, we could include mental health consultation as well as vocational training for emotional and mentally disordered persons of all ages.

Willy was an enormously creative person. Ideas would come to him in the midst of all the chaos around us. We soon became friends and learned how to inspire each other in those frequent moments of fear and discouragement. Our most productive moments took place while we, in

26

our official capacity, inspected newly created training centers. Walking slowly through quiet old areas of Prague, discussing plans for future projects, we were soothed by a familiar environment that reflected centuries of history, until we were jolted back to the oppressive present.

Each of us hoped to find a sponsor for emigration to the United States. Willy had an idea. Petschek, a well-known Jewish banking house in Prague, had an international communication center with telephone directories of many important cities of the world. Willy went there to look for the address of any person in New York whose last name matched his, in order to appeal for an affidavit, enabling him to emigrate to the United States. He did find a namesake, a Mr. Schönfeld in New York, to whom he wrote a letter explaining his situation and promptly received an affirmative response. There were many bureaucratic hurdles to overcome before an actual departure. The limited quota of visas per year created an unrealistic waiting list. Time was heavy, painful and precious; any loss was irretrievable yet we, as a nation, were encouraged to hold on to a future. Our hope in President Eduard Benes ended in disaster. In his last speech to the press and the radio he reminded the nation not to lose faith in the future. "I have a plan," he said with a strong voice. Some listener of that tragic moment interpreted his last remark as a hint that he was ready to request help from the Soviets should Germany break their pact of Munich, even though the ink was not yet dry. A few cynics mockingly said, "Yes, he has a plan, an aeroplan." They were right. Benes flew to England and formed a Czechoslovakian government in exile.

In November of 1938, a young Jewish boy, Herschel Grynszpan, assassinated a secretary of the German embassy in Paris. The Nazi government organized a bloody pogrom throughout Germany to retaliate. In the newly acquired Austria and in the Sudetenland, synagogues were burned, stores and offices demolished and their owners attacked. The night of November 9, 1938, was mockingly called *Kristallnacht* (Night of Broken Glass) by the Nazis. It was an opportunity for civilian mobs to ravage and for the Gestapo (*Geheime Staatspolizei*, the secret state police) and the SS (*Schutzstaffel*, a quasi-military unit of the Nazi party) to demonstrate their strength. Thousands of Jews were sent to concentration camps, which originally had been established to "concentrate" political opponents.

Although we remained outside the brute force of the Nazi regime, we were in such immediate geographic proximity that each day living in Prague felt more dangerous. We had access to newspapers of the free world and followed with particular care the British and American press, hoping to read that there would be action to help us. First the free press reacted with abhorrence to the news. The German press then denied the accusations of foreign reports, calling them lies and horror stories. The western press was influenced by German propaganda that told us that the democratic world believed the German denials, wanting to allay its conscience as well as excuse its lack of action. We could expect nothing.

From first hand reports of German and Jewish refugees, it was becoming quite clear to some of us that all Jews in land controlled by Nazi Germany were in extreme danger. We knew that there were some rescue attempts by groups working feverishly to organize illegal emigration to Palestine. Other humanitarian efforts were not very effective, although some efforts allowed a few to emigrate to other countries.

Our work expanded with new waves of Jewish refugees arriving daily at the Jewish Community Center. The most important needs were for food and shelter, financial and legal advice, particularly about permits for temporary stay. The lines of impatient applicants to be screened for retraining courses became longer and more diverse with every passing week.

We could not rely on support from the Czech Jews, who thought they were in more secure positions, either as owners of well-established businesses, or as professionals such as physicians, attorneys, artists, members of the film industry, specialists in many technical fields and researchers. They were still reluctant to think of emigration or of themselves as possible refugees, even those who had already lost their jobs.

Willy organized a program to prepare people going to other countries as refugees to learn skills in occupational counseling, school employment, industry and mental health institutions. Special focus was on teaching rehabilitation of the physically handicapped and the emotionally or mentally ill. This course attracted physicians and other professionals who not only worried about their future but were also starved for some intellectual stimulation.

Willy was the main lecturer with guest instructors from the State Institute for Psychotechnic. People of various professions and various experiences took these courses. Dr. Hirsch lectured on general psychopathology and psychoanalysis—Freudian theory and techniques of treatment. Along with Willy, I taught graphology and personality testing, using a variety of tests that describe personality traits and profiles, primarily the Rorschach test, now popularly known as the "ink blot test." This test, which allows for the projection of feelings and thoughts, along with their disturbances, had just been introduced into clinical research by Dr. Herman Rorschach of Switzerland. We became so enthusiastic in this new activity that we often forgot the reality of our situation. We bought new books, accepted new co-workers and started to outline manuscripts about our experiences and findings.

So started the new year, 1939. We were somewhat embarrassed to be busily involved and able to support ourselves, while most refugees were inactive and living on welfare, except for those few who still had their own resources.

5

WATCHING THE BETRAYAL

In February 1939, there were changes in the political atmosphere. Assaults by Germany against the Czechs were renewed in speeches and newspapers. The Czech papers seemed to be rather defensive, inappropriately it seemed, since the newly created "Second Republic" had already made overtures toward a friendly coexistence with Germany. We of the Czech and Jewish populations became more nervous and frightened. Something was in the air; if we had been able to be more honest with each other and ourselves we might have known what to expect.

In the late afternoon on March 14, I was walking slowly down one of the main boulevards of Prague, Na Prikopy, from Andre's, my favorite bookstore, to the tramway that brought me home. In front of the German House, the social center for Germans living in Prague, there was a scuffle. I heard noisy insults in German and Czech, similar to the old free days of political clashes between German and Czech nationalistic groups. This was certainly untimely and could have only one meaning. It was a forerunner, an incident staged as a provocation to support the increased boisterous militancy that we now heard on German radio and read about in their newspapers. The small and harmless residue of what had been Czechoslovakia was being blamed in a propaganda campaign for mistreating the German population. It was for the world's benefit, a preparation for Hitler's next breach of his word.

Heavy snow was falling on March 15, rather late for that time of the year. Around the corner from my home was one of the main roads leading to the center of Prague. It was early in the morning. I left for work with an uneasy feeling. I turned the corner on my way to the tramway station and saw a steady caravan of German motorized military equipment moving toward the inner city. I was not prepared for this. People were standing around crying and swearing, but the Germans ignored all of us and moved steadily on. I joined the others. We stood motionless. Soon we all looked alike, snow covered figures, our eyes on the ground. A neighbor took my hand. The German vehicles moved in an uninterrupted rhythm behind a curtain of snow. The scene felt unreal.

Silently and smoothly we had become part of the German domain. There had been preparation for the takeover. The fifth column of the Gestapo and the propaganda department had done their jobs. The next day we heard of numerous arrests of important Czech political and religious personalities. The arrests of Jews started soon after. Petschek Banking House was taken over as headquarters for the Gestapo. To be called for interrogation to the "Petschek Palace" made one stiffen with panic. Many were never seen again, especially those who left in the notorious gray buses.

During the next few days the weather had changed. As if to spite us the heavy cloud of depression all over the city lifted and the skies were now blue and clear. The Germans had taken control of the press, the radio and, as it seemed, the weather. The headlines on the first page of the now-censored papers read "Herman birds on Hitler sky," meaning Herman Goering, the head of the German air force, German airplanes and the weather were all apparently favoring Hitler. The military vehicles, including some outdated tanks, would have been relatively harmless if any well-armed world power had confronted them. The invasion was effective only because there was no resistance. Although Czech borders were dead, Czech humor was alive and well; the demonstration of power was labeled "the German metal circus."

Hitler behaved as if no power, East or West, would interfere with this move. And so it was. We could not understand what the rest of Europe was waiting for. The takeover of Czech heavy industry was a substantial addition to Hitler's military machine. Could the Nazi regime have been stopped there or was it already too late? We sat discussing the situation through nights that seemed endless, wondering what further developments would come. I, as the others, was nearly convinced that Hitler would never be peacefully restrained from progressing in his conquest nor did we think that there was a strong enough internal German resistance to do this.

The Jewish Community Center continued to gain in importance since all emigration had to go through its offices. The Nazis did not object to departures, once they had confiscated possessions and bank accounts. Some of the more influential families, whose male members were imprisoned, were not allowed to leave. Special agents of the Gestapo and the SS tried to trace hidden property and valuables that people had hoped to save for the future. They even went after what had already been taken into other countries.

Anything that supported the emigration of Jews, as long as they left what they owned, was still acceptable. A special detachment of the SS and Gestapo was in charge of Jewish possessions and dealt with problems of emigration. These officers lived and worked in luxurious places, using the power they held to benefit themselves.

The Gestapo looked on our department with suspicion. We never knew when a sudden inspection would take place and what would be considered offensive or lead to the arrest of an instructor. The Gestapo, seeing that workshops could be used for their own needs, started to order repairs and products from the carpenters, electricians, watch repairers and others. We carefully hid our manuscripts, books by Jewish authors as well as those on psychoanalysis.

Willy actually received a promissory note from the American Consulate guaranteeing him a place on the list for an immigration visa as soon as the quota allowed. There was an indefinite waiting time but it did permit him to obtain a visitor's visa for England. By the middle of August 1939 he had all papers prepared for his trip. His precious library of graphological literature and some of his yet unpublished manuscripts had been sent to a well-known psychologist and graphologist in New York City, Dr. Thea Stein Lewis. Much of it is now in my possession. That was Willy's last disposition. He postponed his departure for a week in order to arrange matters for his mother, rescheduling his flight to London to September 2.

On September 1, the German army invaded Poland. The Allies declared war on Germany and all borders were closed. Willy had missed his chance to leave, by one day—and forever.

6

PANIC AND HOPE

FINALLY, THE FREE WORLD REACTED. The Czechs were elated. We foresaw a near end of Hitler. However, our great expectation of fast change in the political structure of Germany evaporated under the heat of the catastrophic blood bath in Poland. It soon became clear that it was one move to declare war on Hitler and another to finish it. The democratic powers, particularly the immediate neighbors of Germany, had waited too long. The German military had grown while the other European countries were lulled into a false feeling of security, counting on their pacts of mutual support in case of attack. In fall of 1939, they watched the force of fascist terror disregard all rules and agreements.

Even in my last years of high school, around 1930, I had found that our German classmates as well as our teachers, though employed by the Czechoslovakian government, were being progressively influenced by the "new" German political outlook. It was an academic discussion, we were assured that much of the radical talk was part of a necessary propaganda to instill enthusiasm for Hitler's promised prosperity. The brutal invasion of Poland in 1939 made us realize that those ideologies were far worse than anyone ever imagined.

The Nazis first claimed that the invasion of Poland was a defense, a police action, but later they glorified it as an historic victory of the superior race, to rationalize the mass killings which went far beyond military reasons. We were bombarded with reports from the headquarters of the German armed forces, transmitted over booming loudspeakers on the streets and in the headlines of the local newspapers. I did not think the Germans really believed them; neither did we, the Czechs, nor the Poles, who were overrun and cruelly treated. Frightening underground information came from the newly occupied parts of Poland: Jews were being massacred by special SS units, while others were being arrested and taken to unknown destinations. The fate of many Polish officers, politicians and intellectuals was critical. The news from Poland made it clear that the German armed forces, especially the Waffen-SS, were not following the rules of the 1864 Geneva Convention in its treatment of prisoners.

I remember the day we received the first clear news about the treaty between Hitler and Stalin. Five or six of our staff members were sitting in the office. There were still a couple of us who had not given up the idea that Soviet Russia with its military power would bring the German conquest to a standstill. Nobody expected these two arch enemies to become allies.

Erwin Hirsch, our brilliant mentor in psychoanalysis, a man with great sensitivity, an enthusiastic fighter for social and human justice, had until that moment held to his conviction that the rescue of Europe would come from the East. He had told us so daily. On that morning while we read about the division of Poland by Germany and Russia, he was very quiet, withdrawn and distraught. We realized then that the political situation in Europe was much more entangled than the media of the free world and the political declarations of their leaders had led us to believe.

As we heard about the fate of Jews in Poland and the conquered Poles being rendered totally powerless or massacred, we felt the utmost urgency. It was very different from the people in the western countries who were just awakening to events. Emigration of Jews from Prague continued but became much more difficult. Our institute and clinic went on with testing, retraining and counseling as if we could still prepare people for a new life in emigration. Work helped us and kept us functioning. We lived and worked as if old codes were still applicable.

The liquidation of the Polish army went faster than had been expected, even by informed sources like Radio London, to which we secretly listened. Our staff conferences became preoccupied with the daily military situation. At times we were encouraged by rumors of conflicts within the power complex around Hitler, but nothing changed.

It was amazing how fast underground connections transmitted information. However, not knowing the source often made it impossible to judge the credibility. In those days only bad news seemed to be trustworthy. I recall the intense feelings set off by the slightest hope from a favorable rumor and then, the deep distress at continuing disappointments.

During the years 1940–41, even more detailed news about cruel mass killings of Jews in Poland reached us. Long before the invasion of Poland, the alarming information from refugees fleeing from Germany and Austria should have warned us what to expect. We had been urged by these refugees to leave, even if conditions would be worse; most of them left, trying to move on as fast as possible. However, since England and France had declared war, it was nearly impossible to receive a visa to any country. Illegal transports to Palestine were still tolerated by the Germans but did not sound reliable enough for some of us. More than once I gathered information but did not make the effort to overcome the hurdles. Money was certainly one of them, but there must have been other, inner reasons for me to delay or postpone my exit. I was not then aware of all the deeper levels of reluctance to leave.

The strong bond with my parents and other members of the family played an important role in my not trying to escape. Contemplating loss of possessions, loss of one's country and of one's home, as insecure and alien as it may have become, were inhibiting factors. Separation anxiety and guilt for leaving others behind slowed down the search for escape. Lovers often chose to remain together. Although believing that we needed to take any risk possible, we heard how escape drained some of our friends of their last means and often ended in bitter disappointment.

A few of our friends made it. Large amounts of money still seemed to open secret avenues into foreign countries, but sometimes there were traps to find hidden resources and fugitives. One of my cousins, Walter Bloch, tried to escape through his connections with the former Czech army. He was caught and sent to the Mauthausen concentration camp in Austria. A few months later his parents received the customary announcement of his death: "Auf der Flucht erschossen" (Shot on attempt to flee). This was still a time when the death of a person in a concentration camp was at least acknowledged, albeit in a lie.

We were still in our home, we walked on the streets of Prague, we slept in our beds and had a certain routine. Food was very limited, but we were not starving. I lived with my parents in our rented apartment on the outskirts of the city. In the Institute, we still continued the retraining and vocational guidance program preparing people for emigration. Willy

Schönfeld and I were involved in teaching our courses, particularly Rorschach and graphology. I even wrote a textbook on graphology that we printed on a primitive hand press for our students.

The nights were tense. The Gestapo usually picked people up during sleeping hours. Many never came back. We were not allowed to be on the streets without a special permit after 8:00 P.M. Social contacts, dating or meeting for any purpose took place inside a building or under the cover of darkness. My girlfriend, Frieda (Maus), with whom I no longer lived, came to visit in the dark of night. Her father was Jewish while her mother was German and therefore she could leave her house without having to wear a yellow star and was able to move around after the 8:00 P.M. curfew. Her visits could have had detrimental consequences for all of us if we would have been denounced.

Before the occupation we had tried to understand our German contemporaries, their yearning to participate in the burgeoning mass experience connecting German populations all over Europe and beyond. We had lived long enough among them and had seen their outbursts of nationalism when they felt challenged; we had learned history in our youth in their schools, had listened to their heroic epics, operas and fairy tales, and been influenced by their complaints of not being recognized after the defeat of 1918. At moments we were even able to tune into their fanatic, deep feelings of grandiosity. But what we could not grasp was the terrible news about the mass murder of Jews of all ages, including children, women, the sick and old, as the German armed forces seized Poland. Great efforts were made to keep this information secret, but it leaked out through a variety of uncontrolled channels. We desperately doubted the authenticity of those descriptions.

Our small group in the Institute was split in how we coped. Both Willy and I came from similar backgrounds of highly protected childhoods. We were little prepared for life threatening situations like those confronting us. Denial, through both an unconscious defense mechanism and the conscious avoidance of the approaching horror, allowed us to hang on to our activities. Our colleagues recurrently fell into the deep passivity of defeat. It took all our energy to protect ourselves from sinking into this painful depression; too often we were on the margin, struggling to keep our balance. Dr. Hirsch, after the "betrayal" of

Stalin, felt crushed. Only his love for his twelve-year-old son kept him going.

Our life was systematically squeezed by further restrictions. All instructions came from Berlin to the SS commando in charge of Jewish affairs, who was ensconced in a luxurious villa in an elegant area of Prague. They were then transmitted to the Jewish Community Center via a special telephone line. At other times, one of the leading Jewish executives would be called personally to receive them. The SS and Gestapo ordered the progressive restrictions for Jewish groups which would remain secret from the general population so that German violence would remain covered up. Most Czechs and Germans knew little about the steady process that was depriving us of our basic right to exist. Only those who had Jewish friends or relatives were aware of it.

It was the responsibility of the Jewish Center to inform the Jewish community of new prohibitions or regulations. When a new order needed to be disseminated, all available personnel and reserves were mobilized; delivery usually took place after dark. In the middle of the night when the doorbell rang, nightmare and startled response merged into one feeling of panic. One dared take a few breaths of relief only on finding out that it was not the Gestapo but a courier of the Jewish Center. Then came the reaction to whatever news was presented. Announcements were usually about the loss of either another possession or another privilege; the 8:00 P.M. curfew was never officially declared but was strictly enforced.

Step by step in those months, all our possessions and positions were doomed. Jewish professional offices and institutions were taken over by Germans or Czechs, as were businesses, factories and studios. Jewelry and other valuables were collected. Bank accounts were closed or controlled.

When the order came to deliver all animals, including pets, to a place outside the city, many painful scenes proved that we were not prepared for the extent to which the Nazis would go.* For most of us, grieving the loss of a favorite animal was overshadowed by the systematic annihilation of human rights. In those times of daily surprises and new insults, we wondered whether such a concept as "human rights" existed. Had this been merely a theme in our education?

* A moving description of this experience is written as part of a novel, *The Tree of Life*, by Chava Rosenfarb, a Yiddish writer. Adam Rosenberg, a former wealthy industrialist confronts the order to give up the only thing he ever loved, his dog Sutchka, and struggles with this.

Our professional work, which by now had extended into a mental health clinic, was at times interrupted by "special" duties. Once I was ordered to the airport to remove snow under the supervision of the German air force. The voice of one of these young men still resounds in my ears. After a full day of shoveling snow I was slowing down, and he, impelling me to speed up, yelled, "You have not been in a 'concert hall' for a while, have you?" This was a euphemism for concentration camp, an image too terrible to be called by its real name. Psychological terror, even without resistance, was employed to prevent any doubts about the consequences of disobedience.

Our great hope was America. Many of us were registered at the United States Consulate; some, like my parents, even had German passports and emigration visas which were still available from the Gestapo at its discretion. We were told the American immigration quota was indefinitely exhausted and preferential visas were given only to spouses of American citizens and other privileged applicants. We waited for a change in U. S. immigration laws to respond to the existing emergency situation. It never came.

7

HORROR SPREADS

IN THE BEGINNING of 1940, we were quite confused about the world situation. The pact between Stalin and Hitler was the last thing any of us had ever expected. The division of Poland and its absorption by the two powers, Russia and Germany, did not fit into any of our previous political understanding or into the tenor of past official German newspapers and radio propaganda against Russia and communism. Now, in the German news, one could sense careful avoidance of derogatory remarks or denunciations of Russia's attack on Finland and the subsequent absorption of the Baltic States.

We no longer had radios and could get no information from either the BBC or other countries through underground channels sympathetic to Soviet Russia. Two of my co-workers in the Institute, who had in the past proven to be reliable in their reports, became conspicuously silent when I asked any questions about the new alliance. One, a psychology student, still had connections with his former non-Jewish colleagues. One day he did not arrive at work. We never heard from him again and assumed that either he went underground or was caught by the Gestapo. Nobody with whom I had an opportunity to talk could understand Stalin's intention. Devoted communists continued to say that Stalin's move was made to keep his country from being attacked by Germany, that he was saving Soviet Russia and the future of the revolution. We heard about the attempts by Maxim Litvinov, Stalin's foreign minister, to form an alliance of European countries endangered by Hitler's expansion. We could hardly believe rumors about Chamberlain's refusal to cooperate with Litvinov to stop Hitler's bloody onslaught and were shocked to read in German and censored Czech papers that Litvinov had been removed and replaced by Molotov.

There was no opportunity for me to talk with any of my German friends or former colleagues about these events. I was sure, and so were most of my Jewish friends, that the pact between the two former foes, Hitler and Stalin, had only their grandiosity and their fanatic self-interest in common. In our psychological circle, we talked about their each having unconscious fears of failing that contributed to their unpredictable and often erratic actions. Their followers were so enmeshed in the prevailing power systems that a break would have endangered their own existences. Nazi and Soviet masses went with the tide of their leaders; Hitler and Stalin both used terror as an effective instrument against opposition. In 1940 we were primarily interested in what influence this new constellation of power would have on our own increasingly threatened position.

The Gestapo focused its activity on trying to find existing secret underground connections to the Czech government exiled in London. The Czech University (Charles University) was considered to be a suspicious place. Students in both the Czech and the German universities had traditionally been involved politically in nationalistic activities. The German population had been an angry minority. Even in the Parliament of the Old Republic, envy and competition had existed, although disguised and debated in a democratic way, such as dealing selectively with approving or disapproving school budgets. Here was the opportunity to get rid of the Czech rival. The news reported an attempt by Czech students to rebel against the German rulers, which led to the Gestapo closing the Czech university in Prague so that all scientific institutions were taken over by the German university. A number of Czech students were shot and others sent to concentration or work camps. Feelings of panic and distrust mounted. Czechs, as they stood in line in front of stores, would no longer freely express their thoughts and feelings as they once did. Terror had again served its purpose.

The outlook for us was even more grim. The fast fall of Poland, the pact between Hitler and Stalin, and the apparent inactivity of France and England gave us the feeling of hopeless isolation. We heard more about the incredible actions against Jews in Poland, that survivors were concentrated in ghettos where they vegetated under marginal conditions. We tried to forget that we were sitting on top of a volcano. But, when for a few weeks we did not hear any reports from Poland or no one was arrested in our neighborhood, we almost believed we were living a nearly regular life.

Willy and I started a new graphology course. Not only did it occupy us but it also brought us extra income, which allowed a slight improvement in our meals. In the Institute we developed simpler performance tests to screen out applicants who would be unfit for specific tasks or professions; we gave these in groups along with requests for each one's handwritten curriculum vitae which we used for both content and graphological analysis. I worked mostly on early recognition of mental or emotional disturbances. We did not have many treatment facilities but could treat a few under the guidance of Dr. Hirsch, our psychiatrist. Whenever we could get together, Willy Schönfeld, Erwin Hirsch, Nelly, one of our two executive secretaries, and I sorted our material and arranged our manuscripts, which we feared would one day be the only witness of a desperate effort of a small group of people trying to make life functional in a deteriorating society.

The regular communiqués from the headquarters of the German armed forces, OKW (*Oberkommando der Wehrmacht*), talked about England's preparation to invade Norway. We assumed that Hitler was preparing the German people and the world for his next target. Perhaps this time Great Britain might be on the move, which would mean a change in the military situation in Europe. We were excited. For the next few weeks on all the loudspeakers of major roads we heard nothing but marches trumpeting German victories. Then Denmark and Norway were in the hands of the Germans.

We wondered where the Allies were. Even though they seemed not to care what could happen to those already under the power of the Nazis, could they not see ahead? Another glimmer of hope faded. We did not want to believe the Nazi propaganda proclaiming that France and England were not strong enough to fight, but did not know what to believe since in the next months we were cut off from all foreign information. The underground was silent too.

Strident march music continued to roar through the city. Something was brewing on the Western front. Bulletins accused Great Britain and France of starting an offensive. We hoped it was true but feared this was Hitler's rationale for swallowing more countries. In the history books it is written that on May 10, the neutral countries Belgium, Luxembourg and

Holland were invaded. The German papers reported that German troops were jubilantly welcomed in these countries. We knew that could not be true, but it was painful to hear it and to hear it repeated at all hours. I thought of my sister, Hanna, in Holland. Would the Germans dare to treat the Dutch Jews as they treated us or as horrendously as they did in Poland? How would the non-Jewish population in the newly occupied countries react? We were convinced that it was German propaganda that the papers "reported" when they wrote of cooperation of the newly "freed" countries. Hitler's promise was a thousand years of peace and prosperity after the last battle in the west was won.

Our small circle greedily longed for news from the Allies while, at the same time, we felt betrayed by them. We could no longer believe that behind the growing defeat of the Allies lay a planned strategy. We started to succumb to the German propaganda that the military deficiency of the Allies was proof of the decadence of democracy. Hitler's Third Reich was the imperium that would rescue Europe.

In Prague and other cities of the Protectorate of Bohemia and Moravia (the German label for the two western parts of the former Second Republic), they continued to "Aryanize" positions, possessions and work. Businesses formerly held by Jews were taken over by Germans or by Czech trustees. As the livelihood of more Czech Jews was taken away, their roots shaken, they started to think of emigration and finally came to us for advice. Most had hoped to avoid being in the same predicament as the refugees from Germany, Austria and the Sudetenland. If their training and skills were not fit for the country they hoped to go to, they applied for retraining. Our courses were soon flooded and people had to wait for vocational guidance. Other cities had the same problems.

The Jewish Community Centers in the different cities had quickly improvised elementary schools, but the older children and adults were without instruction. Schooling was only permitted under the title "Preparation for Emigration," which, at that stage, was not only tolerated by the Gestapo's Department of Jewish Affairs, but welcomed since it gave them the needed excuse to take over the apartments and possessions of Jewish families. The war situation had made it extremely difficult to reach any destination overseas. Privileged people who had well-to-do family or friends abroad eventually could get a visa to another country after completing all the bureaucratic procedures, leaving all their possessions and paying special fees for an exit permit.

In early June 1940, Willy and I were invited to help organize vocational guidance in other cities. Our first trip was to Olomouc (*Olmuetz* in German). It was the center of the dairy industry in a rich farming area with an old, well established Jewish community. The people were partly educated in German schools, yet knew Czech language and culture. Most people spoke both languages well. Jews were integrated into the bilingual population, represented in most of the professions, crafts, businesses, arts and entertainment.

With passes from the Gestapo to use the train, we felt as if we were in a dream, traveling once again like others and moving freely. We met new and interesting people. Robert Redlich, the head of the community, was a friendly and strong man, his wife an elegant, attractive woman. Other members of the community were also very hospitable and, through us, had an opportunity for contact with life outside the limits of their small town. In spite of war, rations, and additional restrictions for Jews, food in this farmland was not only still available but was better than food in Prague. But people there knew each other and, as they were living in a closer community, they were also much more exposed and under scrutiny. Some members of the secret police (Gestapo) had been recruited from the local Germans who found a welcome opportunity to show their power over Jews who had formerly either been their employers or in other envied positions. I talked with several women whose husbands were picked up one day and had not returned. Not every family was told where the arrested person was kept, whether in a concentration camp or police prison, and hardly was there ever a cause given for the detention. Often it was part of the Gestapo's endeavors to find hidden possessions or connections people had in foreign countries. These common experiences created similar terror in each of the communities we visited.

There was also a need to grab moments of pleasure in order to interrupt the tension. Willy and I observed the voracious longing for passionate experiences. There was rivalry, but not much jealousy. Willy was amused by the flirtatious atmosphere. I was still romantic and sentimental, though wary of any new involvement in order to avoid the subsequent dreaded separation that hung over us. However, I did become friendly with a young woman who had studied psychology until Jewish students were no longer accepted. She had two little children and a husband who seemed more interested in another woman.

Willy and I had come from what seemed like outer space into this closed, somewhat incestuous, circle. They experienced us as a breath of fresh air and we relished being indulged. The contrast between the prevailing high anxiety level and moments of carefree lasciviousness created an ambiance of excitement, different from the heaviness I had experienced in Prague.

At night, when we met for official business meetings, we had to be extremely careful, discussing the political situation only between the items on our agenda. The newspapers hinted that the German attack on France had begun successfully. On our last day in Olomouc, while waiting in the house of our host for the time of our departure, we heard a great commotion outside. The Germans of the area had arranged a victory celebration; the masses sang as they marched through the main streets carrying flags and drums, in an exultant mood. Their headquarters was cheering German victory over France. The fall of France represented the end of our hope of being freed by the Allies; it put us into a desperate state. At the last moment Mussolini entered the war and we heard from the German press that Stalin had marched into Romania. Hitler had not only conquered his western foes but had also made allies of his greatest rivals and former enemies.

The Nazis, as allies of Soviet Russia, could no longer blame communism for the war. Goebbels, the minister of propaganda, turned his full attack against "the international conspiracy of Jews." We were surprised by Mussolini's changing sides, but Stalin's switch was mysterious. The German masses on the street added a new song to their belligerent repertoire: "We are marching toward England." The attack on Britain had begun.

The Battle of Britain, as the next months of the war was called, was fought in the air. The German news described the enormous devastation of London and other important cities of the British Isles; they were preparing the European continent for the pending occupation of England. Hitler's menacing forewarning towards the people of England and Goebbels' mocking of Britain's strength revealed just how insulted these leaders of the Reich were when their request for Britain to surrender was rejected. Winston Churchill became the target of the German smear propaganda. Casualties on both sides of the channel grew in the daily bombardments. German families who had been bombed out were moved into Prague and Jews were removed to clear apartments for them. The narrowed living conditions increased our tension and irritability.

Willy and I were called to two other Jewish centers in Bohemia and Moravia. First we traveled to Moravska Ostrava (Maehrisch Ostrau), the heart of the steel and coal mining industries. Before the German occupation, the city had been known as an important industrial center. Businessmen from other countries visited here, and were involved either with the export of metal, machinery or heavy equipment; they supported an entertaining nightlife that earned it the nickname "Little Paris."

The Jewish population there was different from that of Olomouc, the place of our first visit. Although many Jews had been removed from their positions and the war economy had brought great changes, there remained a residue of affluence. Living was faster and more self indulgent. The city was close to the Polish border, which was thoroughly spied on by the Gestapo and other agencies. A few refugees, mostly younger people, managed to come over. They were hidden and supported by the underground until they could get false identification cards or escape to the border of Slovakia, now a quasi-independent state, a satellite of the German Reich. These refugees were carriers of terrible news. They did indeed report mass executions of Jews. They told of whole families, of old people and children who had been gunned down by special units of the SS. The Jews who survived the massacre were concentrated in restricted spaces, ghettos, sections of cities where they were forced to live, crowded and starving.

8

TERROR FROM A SMUGGLED LETTER

DURING THE SPRING of 1941, the general mood grew even more tense. German editorials and speeches became more belligerent, suspicious and more slurring towards the neutral countries. Since the pact with the Soviets (that led to the carving up of Poland), the big neighbors, Germany and Russia, had muffled their propaganda against each other, but old slogans were warmed up as Jews were blamed for the "imperialistic" moves of Russia in the Baltic and Balkan states as well as into Finland. At night, I heard large formations of airplanes moving eastward and motorized convoys of military units rattled along the roads of Prague. I lay awake wondering, preoccupied.

On June 22, the German offensive against Russia started and changed the general atmosphere. Research documents available after the war revealed that the Soviet intelligence service was informed about the preparation of the German army to invade their country, but that Stalin had refused to accept these reports and had allegedly become enraged when they were mentioned.

The news kept us in great suspense. In the office we tried to exchange information and discuss opinions whenever we were free. A few of us still had marginal connections with the Czech underground, which was in communication with England. We all hoped that any weakening of the German position, like a repeat of a Napoleonic adventure in Russia, would bring an end to the German desire of conquering more countries. However, any frustration occurring in Nazi headquarters predictably triggered an enforced outburst of violence directed against us.

The first time I heard the name Auschwitz was in September of 1941. Robert Redlich, an officer of the Jewish Community Center in Olomouc, came on official business to Prague and brought with him a smuggled letter describing the situation in a newly developed concentration camp in a former Polish village, Osviecim, which the Germans called *Auschwitz*.

The letter described the early days of the camp. Inmates, mainly criminals, were brought there from prisons and concentration camps in Germany and were appointed as KAPOs to supervise work or to act as leaders of camp sectors. The first transports had brought younger people, mainly Poles, who were used for heavy work, as Herman Langbein (1972) reports. Many of these early inmates grew sick or weak after a short time and were "freed from their suffering" by injections of poison. The gas chambers were not yet finished, but there were rumors about the purpose of mysterious buildings being constructed in the countryside adjacent to the first camp. They included structures that were described as crematoriums. The tenor of this letter was a cry of warning, an appeal from a world of deep desperation. It was impossible for us to believe that this camp was being constructed for the purpose of mass killing, as implied in this letter. The anonymous writer felt it a duty to convey the information beyond the electric fences that enclosed that devilish construction site.

Willy Schönfeld and I were sitting in our office listening in silence to the contents of the letter, at times staring at Robert in disbelief. With doors and windows carefully closed, we discussed the terrible news in shaking, low voices. Willy was pale; I was horrified at the news, and recall the sinking feeling in my stomach reaching a nearly unbearable intensity. In closing, the writer of that letter begged the receiver to spread the information so that everybody would know what to expect at the end of a deportation transport. Robert felt it was his duty to discuss this letter with the leaders of the Jewish community of Prague. We were sure it would create an insoluble dilemma. Keeping this information secret was a heavy responsibility while revealing even part of it could lead to an uncontrollable panic. We heard nothing about Robert Redlich's meeting with the management of the community, only that he soon returned to his hometown.

Rumors circulated about pending deportations of Jews from Prague to an unknown destination. Our already severely restricted living conditions seemed to us suddenly quite bearable if only we could remain. The threat of deportation always hung menacingly over us. In September of 1941, I remember walking on the main Boulevard in the center of

Prague early in the evening. Lights were dimmed as part of the anti-aircraft defense. I met a former neighbor, a highly respected lawyer of my hometown. He had been tipped off that his name might be on the first list for resettlement, a glorified title for deportation. The first transport brought panic and desperation to the Jewish population of Prague. Whatever our life had been until now we at least were at home. Now the end of each day meant an uneasy night in which the fateful letter bearing the order to appear for deportation might be delivered.

The first transport of a thousand people left around my birthday, in the middle of October 1941. I do not remember whether we were informed by an official announcement or by a casual remark from the German organizers that this group of Jews would be sent to the newly opened Ghetto of Litzmanstadt, a part of the Polish city of Łódź where a great number of Jews of that area were already crowded together. We had already heard through the underground about the extremely poor living conditions there. More transports were sent to the "east," a destination without further specification. We lived in steady terror waiting for the day of our own deportations. Winter was approaching and we feared that the heavy frost in the east, whatever that vague place represented, would lower our chances of surviving. We still naively thought we knew what to expect, that we would be deprived of all our possessions and would have to enter an already impoverished, congested and starving community. Most of us hardly slept; we were frantic. The number of suicides grew daily. Then came a sudden reprieve. The head of the Jewish center was informed that a model ghetto was being planned south of Prague. Reassuring announcements came from the German authorities that this would be a place where Jewish families could live together, where those who were fit would be given jobs, and where special homes for the elderly and children would be provided.

The transformation of the small Czech town Terezin (Theresienstadt) into a ghetto had started with the evacuation of the Czechs, who had lived there for generations. The first deportations of Jews made a disquieting impression on the Czech population in general. They realized that such an encroachment on one's existence could happen to any group of people. The German propaganda had often blared that this area belonged to the German life-space (Lebensraum). The sudden evacuation of Theresienstadt and the resettling of its population elsewhere shook their trust in the promise of a secure place for Czechs after their land was occupied by Germans.

The newly created ghetto was tightly closed and any contact with the outside was strictly forbidden. During the first weeks a few young men, who were sent with the earliest transports to prepare the barracks, had tried to stay in touch with their families in Prague. Their letters were intercepted and the young men were publicly hanged. It became clear that all statements referring to the ghetto as a Jewish town, where a population could survive the difficult years of the war, were nothing but lies.

The Russian front moved fast at the onset of this campaign but started to slow down with the approach of winter. To attack Russia was, for us and our Czech friends, new proof that the German military leaders themselves were irrational, totally controlled by Hitler. Our hope that the more reasonable German faction would take over dwindled.

Our small group in the Psychotechnic Institute no longer had much opportunity to do any clinical work. However, we still had books and could lose ourselves for short periods in studying. Books on psychoanalysis could not be displayed in bookstores but we had access to some of their storage rooms. We tried to understand what was happening around us. By now we felt convinced that at least part of the German population would have seen through the pretense of the propaganda machine, which camouflaged Germany's substantial losses and military setbacks with doubletalk and ranting against the inner enemy and official scapegoats—the Jews. Official German reports on the eastern front were corrected by underground reports from Radio London, which reinforced our belief in a better future, as doubtful as it seemed that we would have a place in it.

Then came Pearl Harbor and the entrance of Japan and the United States into a full-blown world war. The pact between Germany, Italy and Japan, a coalition called the Axis, was now the focus of German propaganda. Hitler's boisterous speeches attacked Roosevelt and the United States; he presented himself as the savior of the world. During these critical developments we did not know what was really happening. Our hope of salvation through the peaceful intervention of the United States faded after Pearl Harbor.

We tried to encourage each other, embroidering the limited available facts until we could imagine a chance to survive. The military situation had changed. We felt that the Czech population also had become more hopeful and that the underground was growing. The Czech underground was more passive than that of other occupied countries, where the Germans frequently encountered partisans and active resistance. The Czech nation had a long history of oppression, and as a result, had developed a kind of collective pseudo-compliance, which did save lives. It is nowhere better described than in *The Good Soldier Švejk* (1930), a novel by Jaroslav Hašek. Convictions were not expressed in open demonstrations, which would have cost lives and given the enemy more justification for violence.

Reinhard Heydrich, one of the most radical and ruthless of the high SS generals, became the commander of Bohemia and Moravia. As a result, the oppression of the Czech population increased, as did the persecution of Jews. Orders from Berlin scheduled group deportations of about a thousand people each. They were irregular and unpredictable, which only added to the anxiety. Our experience of time depended on our own situations. Each day of living outside the restraint of a camp was an extension of freedom and we regretted the nightfall taking it away. Those heavy hours of waiting for the list of names selected for the next transport moved with painful slowness.

The thousand names were always expanded by reserves to fill in for those not found. A few people, mostly single, went underground. Several people committed suicide on being notified to report to a transport. The full quota of people had to be ready to leave as scheduled.

To our disappointment, Theresienstadt, which we had hoped to be our destiny, soon became only a transit point for deportees going east from Germany, Austria and Czechoslovakia. Rumors about the fate of some of those transports reached us and were still beyond our comprehension. Even though we had heard about them before, they did not fully register. The idea that a transport composed of whole families with members of all ages could be annihilated, was not believable and most of us rejected the information as vicious intimidation. I felt the chilling premonition of total defeat every time hints were circulated about the fate of a transport going east.

To go underground was only possible if one had an opportunity to be covered by others who were willing to risk their lives. Only during the last months of the war did we hear of partisan groups in the eastern area of our former Republic, particularly in the mountains and countryside of Slovakia, where younger people fortunate enough to reach them could be absorbed and organized.

All social contact was diminished. It was difficult to arrange meetings anymore, since nobody knew where they would be a week later. When our names did not appear on a transport list, we felt relieved; we had gained some time, limited as it might be. Each day that passed was a day closer to the next deportation but also closer to the end of the war, which we were convinced, meant the end of Nazi power.

Paradoxically, we wished for time to speed up, but we also wished it to last. Our wishes, of course, had no influence on history. All we could do was wait, hoping that fate would favor us. We had no doubts that the crazy explosiveness of fascism would end in destruction, restrained or wiped out by the reasonable part of the civilized world. But when? Each day found fewer of us left. In the forefront of my attention was the anticipation of the fateful order to leave. When would it reach me, my family, the others who lived in our building? What criteria were used for the choice of deportees selected for a specific date?

Departure became particularly fateful for older people. The Nazis made it very clear that they had no patience or respect for the elderly or disabled. Space and nutrition were wasted on them, the "unproductive" part of the population and they received restricted food rations; for Jews there were additional hardships. The black market was flourishing and Czech grocers did not mind supplying those of us who still had some money. Most of us were running out of savings and had little, if any, income.

Large garrisons of SS and Gestapo were fully occupied with the persecution of Jews; this function provided the excuse that these young, healthy, strong men needed to justify their not being called into the fighting military and probably being sent to the front. As the Jewish population of Prague shrank from deportations, the SS and Gestapo performed the "essential" duty of taking over of what had been Jewish housing, furniture and possessions. These were to supply German families that had either been bombed out or had escaped air raids in other cities for quieter places like Prague.

An enormous system of warehouses was created with what was left in people's homes after the hour of departure. Private houses had been confiscated at the beginning of the occupation for use by the privileged members of the SS, the Nazi Party or other functionaries. The remaining Jewish population was forced to live in the limited available space. Relatives and friends moved in together. Jewish work units were ordered to do the hard work of moving and arranging confiscated possessions after each transport departed. The "bookstore" contained an amazing collection of books of all kinds taken from the homes of the deported. There were rare books in many languages, specialty books in science and literature, journals, updated and enriched with the comments that may have been mental occupation for a reader up to the last moments before leaving.

I was in several different work units. As a member of the Community Center staff, I had so far been excluded from transports. We were seen as privileged and were envied by those who had to leave. We experienced this privilege with relief but mixed with guilt and sadness about the loss of those who left and the anxious anticipation of our own pending departure.

At times there were longer intervals between transports and hopeful rumors spread about a change of policy only to be dissolved in predictable painful disappointment. Some of the "good news" was false news, spread by Nazi propaganda to cloud the enormous process of systematic annihilation of Jewish life throughout the countries controlled by Germany. The population of Prague, as of other occupied cities and Germany itself, had witnessed and heard enough to know or at least suspect what was going on.

In our shrinking circle, we talked about life as we remembered it and fantasized about a possible future, then caught ourselves, and looked at each other with bitter smiles, like embarrassed children observed at play.

Everyone grasped any opportunity that could possibly delay deportation. Most were deceptive promises. There were not many moral or ethical considerations that prohibited an attempt to better one's position or try for an opening to postpone deportation. However, there were also courageous family members, friends and lovers who volunteered to join a transport into the unknown despite warnings that there was little chance of staying together at the destination.

In the middle of this *nowhere* time and space, intimate encounters and sexual experiences were an escape into a strange joyless pleasure. Such moments were rare, precious, and ended in painful awakening. What was missing was the expectation of continuity, belonging and permanence. But a few lovers, well-tuned into each other's dreams, were able to live through episodes of closeness no matter how brief. Couples came to our clinic for guidance. Was there any way out of such a bleak future? "We want to live!" was a much more frequent outcry from couples than the desolate longing of a single individual who, sitting across the desk from me, ended our meeting with a gesture and deep sigh of resignation.

Our psychological work took place only in sporadic sessions. Patients came to the counseling center with impossible requests. Who had the strength to deal with the impact of such a reality? What do you say to a suicidal person who wants, for one last time, to employ the freedom of choice in the course of his life? I would tell him that being alive gave one a chance of seeing the next day; perhaps it would be the day our world would change again. Too often we saw how sadly this next day came and went.

One day a man came to the clinic, a writer, at least twenty years older than I. His wife was having an affair with a younger man, and his teenage children had little respect for him. In his hunger for intellectual contact he had participated in our courses for counselors and became particularly interested and skillful in the handwriting analysis of composers and musicians. He had been a well-known music critic for one of the largest newspapers in Germany. He knew that he and his family would be deported soon. He had nothing to give them anymore, felt betrayed, abandoned and was without hope. He came, as a friend, to talk once more about his wish to die. Others came hoping they would find professional guidance out of their emotional quagmire. I had little more to give than compassion and understanding, but most felt better for the attention and opportunity to talk.

Psychotic patients came reluctantly, often brought by family members. A number of chronic patients who had been barely able to get along before, became unmanageable under the new and restricted living conditions. Melancholics seemed to fit into the environment more easily, but their perceptions were mostly oblivious to the real situation. At times we felt far more comfortable dealing with the psychotics' misinterpretations, their paranoid or melancholic delusions, than we did with the distressed, desperate requests of normal people struggling to cope with an irrational environment. Jewish psychotic patients, who had been in psychiatric hospitals, had to be transferred to one specific institution that was formerly used only for severely retarded and mentally defective patients. It was a hard decision to hospitalize a patient under such conditions.

Each of us was already deeply traumatized and fragmented. It took a strong ego and a great deal of awareness to reject the identity imposed on us, and to maintain what we each had once been. In our clinic we saw people who had been quite successful but had not left the country because they were unable to relinquish position and possessions. Now they had lost everything and had nothing to hold on to. It was crucial for emotional survival to have some flexibility that allowed one to adapt to the new and unstable conditions without total loss of the old values and beliefs. That became increasingly difficult, and the difference in our respective coping strengths became more distinct.

In spring of 1942, we were interrupted in our professional work of teaching and seeing patients because we were needed for more basic labor. I became part of a work unit that was selected for road construction near Karlstejn, an old knight's castle. The road was to lead to a new home for SS General Heydrich, the Reichsprotector. It was heavy work but we received somewhat more food and could buy a few items from farmers or from the Czech foremen. We were still considered free. On most Sundays, we took the train home or had visitors and spent a few hours in the woods around the barracks. Another group of Jewish men worked on the last stretch of this road close to the building where the Heydrichs resided. I was told that Heydrich's wife sometimes stood on one of the balconies watching the work done on the road through her binoculars and that she would summon a guard when she saw somebody taking a moment of rest.

The worst moments were still those of waiting for the list of the next transport. Our work was no protection against deportation, but men who were married to non-Jewish wives were exempt at that time, filling the jobs of those who had to leave. They were envied, but felt isolated and unsure about their temporary privilege.

In May of 1942, Heydrich was gunned down by hidden assailants. A few days later German news reports confirmed the rumor that he was seriously injured. He later died. We understood that the assassination of Heydrich had been instigated in London by Britain in cooperation with the Czech government-in-exile. Obviously, the idea was to demonstrate that the Czech resistance was active and fearless. But most Czechs and many of us Jews believed that the effect did not justify the enormous suffering of the victims of Nazi retaliation. Britain and the Czech government-in-exile showed certain insensitivity to the consequences for the Czechs and Jews remaining to bear the most horrendous persecution by the Germans who, in turn, used the losses of the Czech people as an example of the ruthlessness of the government in exile, which had planned the assassination. Heydrich died in the beginning of June after surgery failed to save him.

The Czech village of Lidice was wiped out in retaliation; the men were shot and the women and children sent to concentration camps. Lidice was chosen because the Gestapo had suspected that paratroopers, sent by the Czech government-in-exile to kill Heydrich, had landed in this village. At the same time, in another punitive gesture, more than two thousand Jews were deported—double the amount of regular train transports. Since the assassination of Heydrich was not a "Jewish act" the destruction of Jews would probably have no influence on future action by the Czech resistance. The deportations after the assassination were an outlet of Nazi rage against the suspected feelings of satisfaction among the Jews, the Czech population, and all those suppressed in the German occupied countries.

The Nazis made great efforts to flush out people who were living underground. These raids took place everywhere, day and night. The death penalty was instituted for anybody caught without identification; the purpose was to catch that part of the population that had become invisible. Some of my friends who had avoided deportation by hiding in cellars or remote places in the country had the roughest time during the frantic search for the hidden foe. The Germans made it quite clear that they would prosecute anybody who helped to hide another person. It became a torturous decision for many to give in and betray the hidden escapee or risk one's own life and that of one's family. Motivations for hiding an endangered person, a family or an orphaned child were, of course, different in each case and often rather complex. Love, loyalty, friendship, as well as political or religious conviction were important factors. Material interest also played a role, but was a much less reliable motive since it lacked commitment. When personal danger increased, as it did during the months after Heydrich's death, it was no longer worth risking one's life just for money or goods. Sometimes former saviors became betrayers.

The winter of 1942 was unusually severe, which made life all the more difficult. Fuel for heating was very limited. Those of us still at home could better tolerate cold and the other limitations on our lives, but we imagined how the people transported in unheated cattle cars without sufficient food and water must have suffered. It was hard to imagine what the end of their journey would be. What if the rumors were true? The thought that this cold winter could become a decisive factor in ending the German campaign against Russia provided little relief in view of the growing danger of annihilation of our already diminished community.

Because of the weather, the road construction that I was working on was interrupted and we were used for other duties. At one time during this cold winter I was ordered, along with another person, to inspect toilets in abandoned homes to prevent damage from freezing. My partner was a young woman, a research chemist. Our tour was surreal. When we entered an apartment, we often had the feeling that people had just left. The dishes from the last breakfast were still on the table since one had to appear at the assembly point for deportation early in the morning before the people of Prague, on their way to their daily workplace, could observe the dramatic scenes of the last goodbye.

The panic of last moments still lay in the air. Food, last notes, forgotten warm pieces of clothing, photos, were lying around, traces of the last minutes of a normal life sharply interrupted. We found evidence of illnesses, medications and surgical instruments. Some beds showed the impression of two bodies in a last embrace. Each of our visits ended in the bathroom, where we drained the last drop of water from the toilet before the frost took over, the official reason for our inspection.

Rumors about the growing misery in the ghettos in Poland became more frightening. We heard about Theresienstadt through the Czech resistance, sad stories of starvation and spreading epidemics. Nothing was known about the destiny of the transports that had left Theresienstadt to go east. We speculated about the extent to which the Western allies were informed about the process of deporting millions of Jews in all the countries that Nazi power reached. (Of course, we knew nothing then about the fateful meeting at Wannsee, where Hitler's plans were organized for the "final solution," the annihilation of all Jews). What we saw around us daily was enough to convey the perilously thin thread on which all our lives hung.

At certain moments the desire to escape the unbearable anxiety became overwhelming. Often it was the reaction to a small insult that made it hardest to control our feelings. We were highly visible, marked by the yellow star on the left side of our shirts. I recall one day riding the tramway with my father, standing on the rear platform, the only place allowed to Jews, when two German soldiers entered. One pushed my father aside with his elbow saying, "*Saujud,* (pig Jew) get out of my way." The other soldier laughed. There were some Czech people on the platform; they turned their heads away. I felt the blood rushing to my face; my fists were clenched in my coat pockets. We got off at the next station and walked silently through the streets of Prague, the beautiful old city that we had enjoyed for many years.

I recall another experience in the post office in Karlin, a section of Prague. There were some Jews standing in line, mostly women. I waited my turn as I was sending yet another letter to a cousin in South America inquiring about a chance to emigrate somewhere. In loud-voiced North German accents, a couple of well-dressed younger women were criticizing the slowness of the Czech clerks behind the counters. Suddenly one of the women turned around, faced me and shrieked, "I am getting crazy, with all these Jews around." I finished my business at the counter and left without any outward reaction. I was boiling with rage. Today, years later, I still see these two women facing me and can hear that unpleasant voice. Obviously, they belonged to the privileged German population, transferred to Prague from cities in Germany visited first by English and then by American bombers. There also were wives of German Gestapo and other bureaucrats living in former Jewish apartments, taking over former Jewish stores and offices along with whatever they wanted from confiscated Jewish possessions. The German government knew that to keep the hatred of Jews hot was the best antidote against any possible guilt. What enraged me most was that these women would have it their way. Soon all Jews would be deported from "their land."

We led a bizarre existence during those last months in Prague. Fall had come, the nights became longer but sleep was shorter. Sleeping pills, when available, were a wonderful escape reserved for a special occasion. I was now able to spend only a few hours in the office. We were ordered to various duties, usually related to liquidating possessions of the deported. I carried furniture and collected books from abandoned apartments. Sometimes I would sit in a corner and read for a few forbidden moments or would take home a book or a can of sardines or, with luck, sleeping pills left on a table.

During these last three years I lived with my parents in a small rented apartment. Along with several Czech families in the building, there were two other Jewish families. One was a Jewish high school teacher and his German wife. The other was Leo Fantl and his family. He had been a well-known music critic in Dresden with a special interest in research of Jewish religious choral music. At night we would meet in one of the flats, drink some ersatz coffee or tea and exchange information that came mostly from Czech and German friends who still had radios and access to English broadcasts.

There had been a slowing down of transports to Theresienstadt and, according to questionable underground communication, none had left there for a few weeks. The rumor was that the German military had protested against the heavy use of the railroads by the SS at a time so crucial for the battle in Russia.*

Shortly before the Christmas and New Year holidays, our family's names, mine and my parents, appeared on the fateful list. We each prepared a pack for ourselves. There was a certain weight allowed, not heavier than one could carry and with specifications as to the contents. The most important items were warm clothes and food. Bread cut into little cubes, dry toasted biscuits and sugar cubes were favored. Cigarettes were not allowed, but if smuggled in, had the value of gold; they could be exchanged for food or medicine. Our Czech friends brought us what was available on the black market. Almost everything was available for a price but our financial resources and those of our friends were meager. Two days before the transport was scheduled to leave, it was canceled. Old rumors were warmed up, new ones circulated. Hope coexisted with

---

* This information was later validated, but so was the fact that they could obtain only a short delay. In the opinion of some authors, for example, Paul Johnson, in *Modern Times* (1987), it is not clear which of the two main goals of World War II was more important to Hitler, the annihilation of Jews or the conquest and decimation of all Slavs.

suspicion and fear of another disappointment. There was hope that the SS, as it had done at times before, would become less active around the holidays. Christmas and the new year were coming and we dared to anticipate a few days of relief.

Willy Schönfeld and I tried to finish a couple of manuscripts. We were able to enlist our former secretaries, both excellent typists, for a few days. Typewriters were still standing around. The classes for reschooling were closed except for a few used as maintenance workshops. Willy finished his manuscript, *Textbook of Scientific Graphology.* He wrote it in German and left it with Paul Eisner, an excellent and well-known writer in both German and Czech, who translated it into Czech and hid it. It was printed in Prague in 1948. I worked on material I had collected for a book on the psychopathology of handwriting. I wrote, printed and published a graphology textbook, *Vorlesungen ZurEinfuehrung In Die Wissenschaftliche Graphology,* which I provided for a class of new students at the Psychotechnic Institute in 1941. It was strange to be in our old offices, which were now mainly used for storage of bundled papers, the residues of the Community Center.

My father, who had been a certified accountant, had participated in our courses for opticians, and now worked in the optical shop. It was extremely important for people who could not function without glasses to have them adjusted and take reserve glasses with them on their trip into the unknown.

My mother spent time scraping together whatever food could be prepared for the inevitable move, whenever it would come. These were the last days of 1942.

On New Year's Eve we "celebrated" with a few friends in our apartment. Were we congratulating each other for still being together, or begrudging the end of a year that moved us closer to the limits? We had some wine, the first alcohol for a long time, and laughed over our dilemma. We decided it was time to open the last can of meat that was hidden down in the cellar, covered with old rags. Staring at the two-pound can, we felt as if we were unearthing a holy treasure to participate in a holiday ritual. Finally the can was open. It was rotten and stank ominously.

The first weeks of the new year were quiet. We anxiously watched for any sign that could be interpreted to our advantage. We had reports from different sources, mainly from those who claimed to have access to foreign news. Listening to the enemies' broadcasts was considered treason. The Czech underground was at that time inactive, except for gathering the news of the free world and spreading it, which was often their most important form of resistance, counteracting the German propaganda. Many lost their lives in this little celebrated and tedious everyday battle.

The German population in Prague steadily increased. We saw them in the streets. We heard their loud, possessive voices and laughter. Their presence made us feel increasingly alienated in our own town; we felt pushed out of our usual environment and were losing our last touch of belonging.

Our anxiety had rapidly increased. We knew by then that our issue was mere survival; everything else was luxurious fantasy. Suicide became more frequent with the spread of rumors about the undefined "east transports." One of my patients said in his last visit, "Doesn't entering the train mean giving up life, anyway?" He was right; only a tiny number of those who left ever returned and for most people the suffering to the final end was not worth the flimsy chance. At that time we did not know the truth and when we seemed to get a glimpse of it we could not perceive it as reality. I talked the patient out of taking his collected sleeping pills. My stand was to postpone the end as long as possible. I saw him in his last hours a few months later when we both knew I had been wrong.

Deportations were resumed. The last list was revived and our family had to appear at the fairgrounds in the early hours of March 6, 1943. As tragic as this moment was for us, I also felt a slight relief that I was not spared from the same fate as many of my friends. Maus helped us prepare for deportation. When we said goodbye, we did not think that we would ever see each other again. She kept some of our family pictures, a few books, a couple of manuscripts and one new suit that had been made by the best tailor in Prague for me to use when I would finally emigrate. On my return after the war, I saw that it had become her best suit.

One of the stories that we had heard was about our family physician, who had left Prague only a few months before and had died of pneumonia. Rumor had it that he had exchanged part of his daily bread ration for the cigarettes he could not bear to be without. He was weak from starvation when the infection set in. I thought of this when we were about to leave and I was determined to stop smoking.

It was early in the morning, a cool foggy day, typical of that time of the year. The streets were empty when we dragged our bags to the station. Those of us who shared this common destiny entered the tramway, some leading children by the hand. Much of the regular traffic had not yet started. At our destination, the station of the fairgrounds, people stood at some distance watching their friends or families leave; a few others stood there observing without involvement, voyeurs of the forced departure.

My parents and I moved slowly towards the entrance of the large building that we had known as the fairgrounds. Bent forward by a heavy backpack, I took a long puff of my cigarette, knowing that it would be my last one, stepped on it and we entered the place. After each group, the iron gate closed loudly. We could not look back, nor did we try. This was the point of no return.

9

THERESIENSTADT, 1943

NOW WE WERE PRISONERS. I did not feel panic nor did I sense much desperation in those around me. I had another feeling, a loss of responsibility, a feeling of being nearly carefree. The feverish effort of the last months to find an escape or at least a delay were over and the strain of waiting and then preparing for the pending deportation were gone. We felt almost as if we were being taken care of. The fairground hall and its adjacent courtyard in a busy sector of Prague was the assembly spot for one thousand people selected for each transport. We entered death row, without judgement and under the lie of resettlement, which we greedily accepted, denying our foreboding.

The group ambience developed fast, the noise even resembled that of a picnic in a campground. Rage took over every time I focused on the terrible reality. Robbed of the freedom of decision making for the first time, I experienced that helpless passivity that would surround me like poisonous air for the next two years.

I threw my luggage on one of the mattresses, lay down and closed my eyes. Through a fog I heard my parents talking with their new neighbors and in the background the undefined mixture of voices of a thousand human beings of all ages. Children cried, some were lost in the big hall, others could not understand why they could not go home. Their perplexity was understandable. It was also cold on this early morning in March and the discomfort of our new situation became painful.

There was some unrest in one corner; I heard anxious cries for medical help. A young man was in convulsion. His parents explained that he was a diabetic in a hypoglycemic condition because he had not gotten his usual meal on time. This was the end of my inactivity. We organized medical and nursing services, which became even more necessary as truckloads of sick people arrived, some on stretchers.

At times, the shrill sounds of the SS commander were heard. He was a small, strong and rude man, always in a great rush to have all orders completed. There was a nervous impatience about this man who would hit before one could even answer a question. I think his name was Fiedler. It did not much matter who he was. He was interchangeable. Day, night, and day again fused into a new kind of perception of dragging time. It was evening twelve hours later when we entered a train to ride for the short distance to a faraway world. When the train stopped, we were in Theresienstadt.

My first impression of this grotesque town was dreadful. Wherever I looked there were masses of people crowded into insufficient space. These crowds were moving as if projected in slow motion. It seemed as if people were trying to conserve energy. I met a few friends, colleagues and relatives. They all showed a certain bitterness toward us as newcomers who had had a normal life until now. Some tried a kind of smile on meeting us. There were enough physicians available but a greater need for nurses. A former teacher from my medical school advised me to seek such service as soon as I would complete my obligatory days of general labor.

The stories of this place would be endless. It was neither a town nor a camp, but a community whose members had only distress in common. They were fatigued, hungry and angry. There was corruption, deceit and favoritism, as well as sacrifice and courage in helping each other. There was a distortion of quantities. Everything was either too much or too little. The children appeared too old in their seriousness, the grownups too child-like in their lack of emotional control. I understood I was not part of them. I was not yet acclimatized. The others who had been there longer felt the difference between us as much as I did; their envy showed in their aggressiveness toward us.

My assigned labor on one of the first days was to clean the yard of a complex for the aged, a courtyard surrounded by little houses, two stories high with broken windows covered with paper. The housemother welcomed me and handed me an old broom. I began to work, slowly. With the slight warming up of the cool drizzly morning, old women appeared for their daily walk in the yard. I realized they did not feel strong enough to leave the crowded compound on their own. Some came closer. They recognized me as a newcomer and hoped I would still have some reserves in my pockets. One of the old women took heart and asked in a shaky voice, "Do you have a piece of sugar?" I took a couple of sugar cubes from my pocket and gave them to her. Hastily, she put them into her mouth as if I might change my mind. Then she burst into tears. The taste of sweetness had become a fantasy. Two cubes of sugar were an important source of energy, perhaps allowing another day of functioning. Later, I learned that old people who could not work had even smaller portions of nourishment than did the average inmate of this strange prison. Many older people, particularly from Germany and Czechoslovakia, were informed prior to being deported from their homes, that old-age homes were being established and they would receive appropriate care in Theresienstadt. On arrival they were outraged, but soon sank into a lethargic passivity.

Both my grandmothers, who were in their eighties, died in Thieresenstadt about two weeks after their arrival, each separately, each unattended and without a familiar face at their side.

On another morning, I was with a small group of men sent out to load heavy bales of straw onto railroad cars that were part of a military transport. Some had volunteered for this job because they received an extra piece of bread and margarine. I had to balance a very heavy load on my back, walk up a narrow ramp and throw it into the car. The army captain in charge swore at everybody who was not running fast enough. I was not up to such strenuous and dangerous work. In the evening, I returned to the barracks exhausted, threw myself on the straw mattress and fell into a deep sleep. In my dreams I continued to balance my load as I walked up the small board and relived the fear of falling over. Once I did fall and woke up. I was shivering with fever and could not swallow.

There were always two people on each floor of the barracks who had the authority to distribute food and make important decisions. In the morning, they would select the most urgent cases to be seen by the visiting physician. When I told the floor elder that I was unable, with such a high fever, to continue that kind of work, he shook his head as if he had to solve a complicated problem. He conferred with his partner; they both shook their heads. They were a funny couple, both men in their sixties who came from a very religious community in Frankfurt, Germany. They and their group were eager to get enough men for prayers at all possible and impossible occasions. After they ended their conference the assistant to the man "in charge" of the floor turned to me and explained in a very soft voice that my request seemed reasonable but that two cigarettes would be helpful in getting me to see the doctor. Cigarettes, like money, were contraband. I had neither. He must have thought he could get something from me. Naively, I gave him two hard boiled eggs that I still had from my last reserves, not understanding that their taking advantage of a newcomer was expected and acceptable in this life.

I did not want to depend on the help of the floor elders and decided that I needed to take charge of protecting myself. Later, I sneaked out of the room and told the clerk, who was arranging the work units in the yard of the barracks, that I was ill and not able to do the work. He sent me back to my room and told me to come back in a couple of days. When I understood that this man was really the one responsible, not the elders, I realized that I had much to learn about the unwritten rules in a system that was so different from my past "normal" life.

When the doctor came he called my name, looked into my mouth, said I had a bad infection and gave me two aspirins and three days sick leave. Nobody ever looked at the piece of paper from the doctor. Nearly every winter during my student years I had had at least one of these painful throat infections with high fever. This time I stayed on my mattress for a day and then walked around. Strangely enough that was the last infectious tonsillitis that I have ever had.

When I was better, I went looking for work in medical services. The chief internist on the hospital floor of a large barrack was glad to accept me as a physician during the day if I would take the night shift as a nurse. This was a heavy schedule but got me back into medicine, the only work that meant anything to me, and as a nurse I was appreciated. The days were busy and interesting. The older doctors, tired and poorly nourished, were glad to save their energy and let me do as much as I wanted—and there was plenty to do. The living conditions, particularly the very poor hygiene, had rapidly lowered the general health of the community.

The nights I was on nursing duty were busier. Running with bedpans, medications and comforting patients in their last hours left little time for thought. There was usually an hour, around three in the morning, when the hall, which had about fifty patients, grew quieter. To the background music of orchestrated snoring, I had a few moments to smell the spring air coming through the open window. Visiting the fruit trees in bloom had been a usual favorite Sunday jaunt during this season. Soon the smell of

65

lilac would sneak over the wall that separated us from normal life. One night, standing at the window, I looked up at the moon and the stars. How familiar a sight they were and yet so different now. The slightly chilly breeze of the spring night used to be exciting, now it was threatening—as any emotion had become.

My place as a newcomer on the nursing staff was not yet secure. One evening, just before starting my nursing shift, I received another work order to appear in the attic of an old building that may once have been a large manor but was now crowded with old people. A steep staircase led up to the empty room under the roof. Men were dragging dirty, worn out straw mattresses up the stairs. These soon covered the whole floor, leaving hardly space to walk between them. A couple of electricians came, inspected the place, but refused to bring power in as they were ordered to do. It would have been against their rules because of the overloaded primitive wiring.

At dawn, a young woman from the transport department arrived with orders to prepare for a special transport of about fifty women from a home for the aged in Berlin. As facilities were already overcrowded, this attic was needed to accommodate them. She said with a bitter expression on her face, which might have been taken for a smile, "There will be places soon enough—old people die fast here."

We improvised a couple of light fixtures that we removed from other rooms and connected them with old cables. That gave us a little bit of light but left some of the older inmates screaming and swearing in their now darkened rooms.

Two women, practical nurses in white uniforms, arrived to assist me during the night. Lights had to be out very early in the sleeping areas and people had to be on their mattresses. A few times we heard the unfriendly voice of the house elder on the lower floor demanding silence. This night, in the beginning of May, was quite chilly. Although the days were now getting more comfortable, the nights were still cold. The roof was defective and the windows, which were not tight, rattled in the wind.

About ten o'clock, we heard the motor of a truck and the sound of anxious voices in front of the building. An endless line of figures moved slowly up the staircase. Some walked on their own, some had to be helped, pushed or dragged and a few needed to be carried on stretchers. From as much as one could see in the dimness, the women were rather well dressed. They were totally perplexed and did not understand what was happening to them. They were thirsty, the most painful of all sensations during those forced moves. We were busy handing out water to all their desperately outstretched hands. In a corner we had an improvised toilet and the women were full of indignation at the imposition of using such a facility. There were hundreds of questions to answer. One of the nurses spoke German; the other was a young girl who spoke only Czech and felt lost and helpless. I spoke enough in both languages.

Between running with bedpans and water I was able to answer a few questions and get some understanding of the situation. Many of these women, all between seventy and ninety, had been living in a home for the aged in Berlin under quite decent conditions. Their children lived abroad, mostly in the United States, and supported them through Jewish organizations while waiting for their families to get visas to join them. One lovely old lady told me that her son was very successful in the movie industry and was impatiently expecting her at the time America entered the war. She was recently informed that he was arranging her exit to a neutral country where she could wait for the end of the war. After a few glasses of water she was very alert and clear. Our conversation was constantly interrupted but I soon learned how outraged these women felt. They had been told that they were moving to a better home in a town with Jewish management away from the hardships of the war. They were also encouraged to write and explain to their respective families about the pending change. They were shocked about the situation. They had not been out of their traveling clothes for some time and were waiting for their luggage, which they would probably never see again.

They had been lied to so much, and yet, to tell them the full truth about their new domicile would have been more than they could have withstood. Some of the members of this group were in poor health and a few seemed to be mentally and physically depleted. After a few hours it became quieter. They were all exhausted; some did not have the strength to crawl to the toilet or wait for our assistance. The air became very heavy. Some cried themselves to sleep. Soon there was only the blurred noise of whimpering and moaning. For a little while nobody asked for help and nobody wanted to be the first to interrupt the break. We divided our shift so that each of us could have a short rest in the dark. Two of us found a corner to sit together under one blanket; my partner sounded and felt like a young woman. We were in a daze, the outcome of extreme fatigue and an irrational environment, and held on to each other in a desperate attempt to find some comfort. About half an hour later I woke up from a mixture of dream and reality. The first light came through a small window in the roof. The new shift came to take over. I had some medical work to do; the two nurses had left before me. I never saw them in the light and probably never met them again. I did not try to find out which one I had felt next to me for those few minutes of warmth during that cold night. The following day I went to find my old ladies in the attic. They were all gone, the room was empty. They had been sent off to other quarters for the aged, integrated into the regular, short span of life allotted to the old in this place.

In June 1943, the elders of the Theresienstadt ghetto were informed that some cottage industry would be established. A giant barracks was built in the middle of the town on a large open lot. A few hundred people were employed in the preparation of belts, probably for uniforms. Anything that could give the town some purpose and occupy people would help to sustain life and increase their chances of avoiding deportation. Willy Schönfeld, who had arrived in a transport soon after mine, had not found a professional activity but now was called upon to administer mass testing in order to choose workers. He asked me to help him. We had our own system, developed to screen out certain characteristics that would be disturbing to efficient production. We utilized a brief evaluation of handwriting, with a focus on pertinent issues. We met with a few friends and former students of our old circle of the psychotechnical department of the Jewish Community Center in Prague to work on the task. Of course, we talked about our situation but now we were without cigarettes or even ersatz coffee and certainly with less hope for rescue. We wondered why the Allies had waited so long; their reluctance had cost so much in human life. Had they not anticipated what we, in our limited way, were seeing of the progressive expansion of the German military machine?

There were always radical opinions among us. A few pressed for more active resistance and attacked the Jewish leadership. It was no better or worse than most management in crisis. The SS command of this camp, in most cases, accepted the functionaries of Jewish communities as the leaders. They were responsible for the management of this community and for carrying out the orders of the SS. In return, they had slightly better living conditions than the rest of us but were under the steady scrutiny and control of the SS. Often they were hated by their own Jewish population because of the power they were given over fateful choices, particularly in preparation of "lists" for transports to the east. Listings of ages, professions, and other characteristics were already required by the SS but the individual names came from the Jewish leaders. My close friends and I held long heated arguments about the moral and ethical dilemma in which these leaders had been placed; however, none of us could think of an alternative. When I had an opportunity to talk with one of the leaders I surmised from him that they realized that they had the least chance of surviving. They had seen too much and the Nazis had always been eager to cover up their actions against Jews by removing witnesses. By avoiding chaos and keeping to some kind of organizational system, the leaders hoped to win time, and even rescue, for some.

In Theresienstadt, people died either from various illnesses, usually infections against which their weakened bodies were defenseless, or they disappeared into the mysterious transports going to the east. To be in active opposition to the system, that is to attempt an escape, hide, or to try to get in touch with people on the outside, meant torture when caught and retaliation against one's family or the rest of the community. I was in accord with the majority, who believed that our only reasonable resistance was to stay alive and help each other as long as possible. This stance has often been condemned as passive compliance, mainly by people who themselves never experienced such an extraordinary situation and who use the framework of normal life as a measure of judging this behavior.

There was a place in the town that substituted for a park. It was really the roof of an old bunker, probably used for storage. Grass grew wild there and I recollect that there were a few bushes or small trees. There I could walk around and, with the right fantasy and company, be reminded of my past enjoyment of nature. The hills in the background were well-known to us. We used to see them north of our hometown. Now we were on the other side of them, separated by prison walls. Several times I walked there with a young woman who worked as an executive secretary to the leaders. We met for only ten or fifteen minutes at a time, but these moments became small islands of relief in the gray mood of the rest of the days.

The summer weather of 1943 was interrupted by rain and cooler days. My double duty as physician and nurse did not leave much time for resting. Occasionally, I met with my friends and colleagues from the institute and frequently with Willy Schönfeld. He had no regular occupation and became depressed but tried to create a place for himself.

A few times I met with a young woman I knew from my earlier life. It is difficult to describe how pairing developed under these crowded and poor conditions. Privacy was not easily available. Couples, when they visited each other, would improvise curtains around their mattresses from all kinds of rags. Sometimes these make-believe *chambres separés* broke down. There were other secret corners and places that could offer moments of cover sometimes leading to comical complications when the wrong people discovered the pair. Marital partners who might have wanted to separate were already separated by their way of living. Others got married as a symbolic gesture. Jealousy could explode into wild rage, controls were weakened and tolerance was low.

My father was again able to work in the optical repair shop. My mother sorted potatoes in a cellar. The work was hard but she received a bonus of a few potatoes at the end of the week, she may also have pocketed two or three more. This was called "organizing," a euphemism for stealing, which was a necessary component of coping with reality and was generally accepted as long as it did not rob some specific person of a rightful possession and, just as in old Sparta, as long as one was not caught. It was possible to make a small fire in a hidden corner of the yard using small pieces of wood. This was enough to boil a little water for the potatoes. It was not easy to ignore the greedy and envious looks of those who watched the three of us dividing one potato, not enough to be generous. We still had some salt, which was also quite valuable on the exchange market. Such small additions of food, usually acquired through the specific kind of work one did, made a great difference in one's well-being. I received an extra meal for night shift nursing. There was extra bread and margarine in the hospital for the personnel, a feeble attempt to strengthen our resistance to the infectious diseases we were exposed to in our close contact with patients.

Sometimes I visited one of my former teachers, Erich Klapp, who had been a doctor assisting the professor in internal medicine at the university in Prague. Now he was in charge of the camp hospital for infectious diseases, one of the most frequented places in the health system. He warned me against working in his hospital. Too many of the medical personnel had succumbed to infections as their general health condition weakened. He himself had a patch over one eye, which he explained had been infected following a bad case of the measles. An unusual number of adults contracted childhood diseases, often with critical complications.

One day Klapp asked, with a strange, joyless smile, whether I wanted to listen to some music. I remembered that he had been an excellent cellist. We had often talked about chamber music. I accepted the offer hesitantly with a strange premonition. I took off for the afternoon. The concert took place in a former theater, mostly empty. On the stage were the musicians, Klapp on the cello and three other strings players. They started to play one of the early Beethoven quartets. I still feel the painful sensation running through my whole body. I had not heard music for at least a couple of years. I suddenly realized that part of me had grown numb. After the first five or ten minutes, which seemed like an enormously long span of time, something changed in me, some frozen feeling started to melt. It was an experience comparable to switching into an altered state of consciousness; I was shaking and felt the blood leave my head. I thought of my grandmother, an excellent musician, who had perished unattended in one of the places for the old and helpless, a few minutes away from this concert hall. She had been highly respected in our city. The music critic of the local newspaper would sometimes watch her face for affirmation of his impressions of a concert; he often found an opportunity to talk with her during the intermission to exchange notes. For some time she had been a member of the City Council of our home town as a music and theater expert, the same city that, a few years later, had permitted her, by then in her eighties, to be loaded onto an open truck and deported to this ghetto. I started to cry for the first time in all these months. I had to leave after the first movement. Erich Klapp looked at me with a painful smile, and an understanding gesture of farewell. I ran to the hospital, took my white coat and threw myself into work. There was no place for delicate feelings, especially not for feelings connected with the beauty of one's former life. That night was a difficult one; I was shaken by the experience and worked mechanically, feeling as if I had been through a heavy strain. The partial numbness returned.

In August of 1943, the camp commander ordered the evacuation of one of the large barracks where I worked in the hospital and clinic, a building which also housed a few hundred women. The building was to become part of SS headquarters. It meant a further aggravation of living conditions accompanied by the concern about deportation. For a few days I wandered around, visiting a few of my former patients who had been transferred to other, now terribly overcrowded, hospital units.

Towards the end of the month rumors circulated that a large transport to the east was in preparation. I tried to get in touch with some of my old friends in the administration. Nobody could be reached except for one friend who had more detailed news. The order was for a transport of five thousand people, supposedly of families of able-bodied men, who were to participate in the construction of a new camp. The ghetto leaders worked feverishly on the list of candidates. We did not quite believe the commander's announcement that these people were really going to construct a new camp but we clung to it anyway. I had the impression that our leaders, in their negotiations with the SS, were trying not to deplete the ghetto of its most productive young people. The outcome was not surprising. The quota of those to be deported needed to be filled. I knew that I was in great danger of being among them.

A few days later, I heard that I was on the list, but was glad to hear that my parents were not. Of course this was not the final version. I tried to get off the list, as did anybody who had an opportunity. My former secretary from the Jewish Community Center, Nelly, who now worked with the ghetto Jewish administration, arranged for me to meet with one of the top executives. He had the power to make reasonable changes. I asked him to take me off the list. He said he would if I could tell him whom to put on to replace me. He looked sad; I smiled. Nelly jumped off her chair and screamed at him, "Then I volunteer to go." She obviously knew that exchanges had been arranged before and did not accept her boss's evasive reply.

On September 5, I received the final order to be at the railroad ramp the next morning. I did not have much that belonged to me anymore but whatever I had, remained in Theresienstadt. The morning of September 6, 1943 was cool and gray as I stood looking at a long row of cattle cars. We were called by name and received a large number to hang over our chests. Suddenly Nelly stood next to me. She said that she had volunteered to go with me. She had freed a sick friend by taking his place. There was little time for conversation. The mass of frightened human beings became even more so when the SS men walked back and forth swinging their whips, their dogs on leashes. Finally the whistles gave the signal. Accompanied by the screaming of the guards to hurry, we had to throw our packages into the car and then climb quickly on board to find a place to sit, either on our backpacks or other improvised suitcases. In a corner there was a bucket that had water and another bucket that would serve as a toilet for fifty people.

The doors closed and I felt trapped. Our train must have remained at the station for a few hours as I recall that gruesome, endless, undefined time. There was no place to stretch one's feet out or stand up, children cried and others moaned. Cries for help and prayers intermingled. There was a smell which increased in intensity every moment. All that, and more, created an atmosphere that was beyond anything one could describe.

Besides Nelly, I do not remember one other person among the other forty-nine in our cattle car, but I do remember a few futile attempts in the beginning to give some medical help. Nelly was next to me, not complaining or expressing any regrets for her decision. She had been an ideal executive secretary, with great skills and a creative mind. I knew that she was devoted to our work and if necessary had been willing to lie and steal for us to keep the office running. I knew that she was married to a pilot who had escaped by plane to join the Czechs in exile in England. I felt somewhat uneasy being so closely in touch with her feelings. But more important to me was having another person, man or woman, to be close to in extreme circumstances, a person whom I could trust and for whom I would be willing to sacrifice if necessary.

The train began to move and soon we passed Prague. There was a small uncovered window high up in the door of the car. If one stood on the shoulders of another person one could peek out for a few moments. The train stopped many times since it was unscheduled and considered less important than military transports that were in movement during that year of intensified battles on all fronts. One time when I looked out, we were stopped on the railroad bridge under which I used to travel by tram daily to and from work. It was only half a year since I had left Prague and my home, but I felt as if I were in a dream sequence from my distant past.

The trip was very long. The first day we moved slowly and spent the dragging hours of the first night waiting somewhere in the countryside. We were relieved when the noise of the wheels indicated movement. It felt as if the narrow space of the car was shrinking with the passing of time. It became very hard to breathe. Our water was gone and our thirst became excruciating. We tried to chew a few bites of our bread ration but could not swallow because of the painful dryness of our throats. Our limbs were stiff. There was not an inch of free space and I did not have the strength to push in any direction. The cars were never opened. At some intersections while we were waiting, we asked our guards for water as they walked beside the long train to stretch their legs after too long a stay in first class cars. Their answers were rude threats.

It became quieter in the car during the next day, when we were without food or water. Most of us were in a state of drowsiness. We could not talk because of the dryness of tongue and lips. We just stared at each other in disbelief. Was this possible or was it a wild delirium in a state of high fever? There must have been another night, or was it still morning after the first night? The last part of the trip was condensed into the one experience of thirst. The excruciating pain of a dried out mouth and throat overshadowed all other suffering.

Gottfried R. Bloch

10

ARRIVAL AT AUSCHWITZ

I must have passed out in a kind of sleep. I was suddenly awakened by the shaking of the train. Then it stopped. The doors were pushed open to a wide vista. I was only half-awake, my limbs were stiff and any movement was a major task. My eye caught a small building, the train station, and its name in large letters—**AUSCHWITZ.** I do not remember whether the Polish name was also there. My recollection of this period is strange. Traces of some hours seem lost, others are vague; then there are very clear pictures in my mind, like my very first recognition of this infamous place. I immediately thought of the smuggled letter we had seen in Prague giving us our first information about this camp.

I clearly recall wondering whether they would give us something to drink before they killed us. This was certainly my only wish at that moment. Nothing was as tormenting as that thirst. The idea of being dead became an attractive fantasy. If only it were quick. Nearby I saw inmates carrying bricks to a construction site. They had blood running down their backs. They were urged on by other prisoners in better looking striped uniforms with "KAPO" (*Kameradschaffspolizei,* inmate police) written on their sleeves and canes that they used to beat the workers on the back when they either did not run fast enough or dropped a brick. These KAPOs had a strange way of using these sticks. The handle was used to catch the neck of the worker, whom they dragged closer, then hit on the back.

That was my first look at Auschwitz. Our poor belongings were thrown onto trucks as we dragged ourselves along, urged to move forward, pushed by guards, some of whom were inmates in uniform. The inmates started to talk to us. They tried to get anything of ours that would be useful. They were interested in good shoes or boots, explaining that we would have to give up everything anyway. They wanted the leather jackets that some people had saved to bring on the journey. They sounded bitter and sarcastic. When we asked about the fate of earlier transports, they pointed to the sky. "Up in smoke."

Among those apparently privileged and experienced younger men, we found a few who spoke Czech. They were from Slovakia, the eastern part of Czechoslovakia, and had come here early in the history of this camp. They told us that only a few of their group were still alive. They mentioned how surprised they had been when they had heard that our full transport of five thousand people, including whole families, were entering what was now called the Czech family camp in the part of Auschwitz called Birkenau (meadow of birches). They tried to explain to us how lucky we were that we all were allowed to enter. Usually only the young and those fit for labor were accepted. They said that they were bewildered by this new development even though one hardly saw any signs of any emotion on their faces. They implied that in many past transports all arrivals had been killed. We did not believe them. Some of us thought that these were horror stories told to make us more compliant. I had heard terrible rumors before, but at that moment of marginal existence, we were compelled to keep any ray of hope alive. Our distortions of an all too obvious reality became as important as morphine becomes for the patient suffering physical agony. We indulged in them and embellished them, thus finding a way to escape for a short time from the actual situation.

The former village was gone except for a few small buildings. On a slight elevation, interrupting the monotony of the scenery, were a few birch trees, revealing the origin of its name. We entered an empty part of that enormous camp subdivided by electric fences. We were told that it would be our choice to touch the power system and commit suicide. On both sides of the camp were the barracks, called blocks. They were prefabricated long wooden cabins reminding one of stables, set in two parallel lines separated by an open space that was the camp road. One side of the road was designated for women; the other for men and one barracks was for women with young children. That did not mean there was any difference in equipment; all were barren primitive housing furnished only with bunks and straw sacks. I do not remember how I got into my cabin. I vaguely recall being dazed, tired and thirsty and falling onto one of the mattresses.

Finally, large barrels were brought very slowly, borne by long wooden poles on the shoulders of two men, a heavy burden, which reminded me of movies about old Rome. From these barrels a liquid was served that they called tea. It was the best drink I had ever tasted. We were given metal mugs that were filled with this wonderful lukewarm liquid. I withstood the temptation to gulp it all down and forced myself to sip it slowly, allowing my dried-out tongue and throat to absorb some of the delicious moisture.

I still had nearly half of my ration saved when a familiar face appeared next to me. It was that of a pediatrician, a man about thirty who I knew from Prague. He begged me to give him some of my tea for his little child who was, he said, in a desperately dehydrated condition. I put part of my saved precious drink into his cup, which he then quickly raised to his lips and emptied, his hands shaking and his face red. I stared at him in disbelief. He wept. I realized in a moment that I had responded with an automatic reflex that belonged to the past, to another world. I felt embarrassed about my naive behavior, which was not appropriate in this life. A while later, when there was enough tea available for all, I began to feel more alive and started to check out my new environment.

About two to three hundred people were housed in each barracks. All of us were now accorded citizenship in this caricature of a community and received proof of identity in the form of a number tattooed on our left forearm. With this procedure we gave up our names.

One of the men working on the registration started to talk with me while doing his work. He was one of the very few survivors of an earlier transport and because we could speak Czech with each other he somehow trusted me enough to open up. He told me that usually only those who were needed for some kind of work had a chance to stay alive longer than a few months. When he heard that I had gone to medical school he thought I might be considered for medical service and my situation would be better. In these first hours, we newcomers tried to get as much information as possible. We also attempted to exchange our impressions, but soon we were confused and disoriented.

The senior population of the camp spoke carefully to us, looking around, obviously afraid to reveal more than hints about the nature of this enormous camp. It felt as if everybody knew a mysterious secret and, if talked about to the wrong person, would lead to dreadful consequences.

We quickly learned that the inmates we met belonged to a silent hierarchy of privileged citizens, either because of their needed skills or because they had seniority as survivors of an earlier transport.

Their remarks implied that most newcomers were condemned to die either immediately on arrival, or soon after from starvation, exhaustion or illness. What happened with us was apparently novel. We were a whole transport entering this camp and were being treated as if we would be staying. Was there a change in the political direction? In March of that year, 1943, a similar settlement had been established in another part of the camp when the Nazis suddenly turned against Gypsies from all over occupied Europe and transported a few thousand Gypsy families into Auschwitz-Birkenau. Life in that sector of the camp was described as chaotic. The very low level of hygiene had resulted in a high rate of mortality, especially among young children and the aged. The different treatment that our transport encountered gave us some hope that there might even be a chance to survive this part of our imprisonment.

It grew warmer during the middle of the day and I felt as if I was recovering from a critical illness. I wandered along the camp road, a lengthy, dusty space in the middle of the narrow sector of Birkenau that was designated as the Czech family camp, B-IIb. Most people from our transport were in their blocks. Exhausted and bewildered, they were stretched out on their straw mattresses, one's only personal space.

The entry from the Auschwitz Archives of September 8, 1943, reads as follows:

5,006 Jews are transferred from Theresienstadt with an RSHA* transport. In the transport are 2,293 men and boys, given Nos. 146694-148986, and 2,713 women and girls, given Nos. 58471-61183.

APMO, D-RF-3/90,91,92
Transport Dl-Dm of September 6, 1943

List of Names; Adler, Theresienstadt 1941–45, pp. 53, 127

(Czech, 1990, p. 483)

* (*RSHA*-Reichssicherheitshauptamt-Reich Central Security Office)

80

I entered an open, apparently empty barracks, and from the little light that came from the small windows under the roof I saw the body of a woman on the ground. Coming closer I recognized Nelly. I had not seen her since we got off the train and had not even thought of her or anybody belonging to the "old world." I realized then how much my conscious mind had been disconnected from my past during those hours of enormous tension. Nelly was not alert. She was red in the face and her breathing was labored. I called for help but nobody reacted. Although she was tall and heavy, I dragged her out of the house to a shady spot by the entrance. By now I knew where to find water and I tried to cool her face. She slowly came to and remembered that she had felt faint while looking for the number of her barracks; she had been very hot and weak, and when she was able to, she crawled into the nearest building, the empty block where I had found her. She recovered quickly after drinking a large amount of tea, which I carried in a thermos, attached to my belt, the very last of my possessions.

I did not have much time to think. The general confusion was interrupted by a shrill whistle calling for attention, the beginning of all announcements, begun by the "elder of the camp" (*lager-älteste*), one of a group of notoriously violent criminals transferred from other prisons in Germany to manage sectors of the concentration camps. Our elder was a tall, slim person, always tense and restless, impulsive and prone to outbursts of rage and violence. His name was Willi. His orders were screamed from one block to another. Special orders were delivered by runners, younger boys, usually handsome pre-teenagers who were the privileged servants of the leader of the camp. Frequently they were sexually used. Most accepted the role, even becoming rude and aggressive towards their former friends. In their behavior, they soon became identified with the miserable, intolerant character of their masters. With the passing of time they became so cruel that even their own families were intimidated by them.

In the early afternoon I heard the whistle and ran out of the barracks. It was too early for the evening roll call. The order came that all physicians were to report in front of the last block. I knew this would be a decisive moment in my life. We all ran to the assembly place where the SDG (*Sanitaetsdienstgrade,* or SS medical corpsman) announced the imminent arrival of the SS physician in charge of our camp. We all had to line up in rows of two and were instructed to stand at attention. The waiting seemed endless. We were still exhausted from the transport and had not changed clothes since we left Theresienstadt. We looked like a bunch of vagabonds. Some of the older doctors could no longer stand up and began to move. The sergeant started to swear and threatened to exclude anybody who would not follow his commands.

I was standing among the physicians when a terrible doubt entered my mind. I had not yet received my doctorate; I had not been able to register to take the final examination in 1938 when the Nazis occupied the Sudets and gained control over the German University in Prague. Now, condemned to stand still for a time that seemed eternal, I became more and more frightened of being considered a fraud and consigned to one of the terrible work gangs that I had observed when we arrived at the station in Auschwitz. I was totally preoccupied with these fears when I suddenly heard the loud order of the sergeant, "Attention!"

A cloud of dust appeared at the far end of the camp road approaching at great speed. The air cleared and a uniformed man on a motorcycle stopped in front of the sergeant who, in strict military tone, gave his report on the number of physicians present. The SS doctor sat stiffly on his seat, head up, looking around at this group of pitiful creatures. I drew a cartoon in my head of this high officer with numerous decorations on his chest as a shining knight sitting on his horse looking down at his conquered enemies who begged for their lives. He was tall and pale; his eyes tested you. My fears rose again and grew. The tension was unbearable. He ordered one physician distributed to each block. When they started to call their numbers I stepped out of the line. Surprised, the man on the motorcycle turned to me for an explanation. I said with shaking voice that I had not yet received my doctorate because of the missing last examination. He smiled and there was something like dim laughter in the group. It was the first and last laughter I ever heard in Auschwitz. The doctor next to me mumbled something that sounded like "idiot" and everybody wondered what would happen next. After the SS physician chose a couple of doctors for the two hospital blocks, one for men and one for women and children, he turned to me and said to the new chief of the hospital and medical service, "Take him to the hospital too so he will not forget his medicine." He swung back on his motorcycle and sped towards the exit gate. I felt enormously relieved about my assignment. I suspected that a decision about work activity was important. I did not know then just how crucial it would be.

That SS doctor, I believe, was Dr. Franz von Bodman, the first commander of the medical unit in the Czech family camp. I had heard that he had been involved in giving lethal injections to sick and weak inmates. He called this process "mercy killing." This was the beginning of the abuse of medicine in annihilating life. It created in patients a terror of asking for medical help. It created in Nazi doctors a *carte blanche* to experiment on people who were considered less than human. It created in other doctors who were ordered to perform such "treatment," or who witnessed these events, feelings that their profession had been smeared by the worst political and racist motives, that the image of healer in this society was destroyed and that their professional ethics would hereafter be compromised.

The first night I was exhausted. So much had happened. Our first food was a soup with some indefinable vegetable matter in it. It was brought, like the tea, in great barrels. The contents became thicker at the bottom of the barrel. These portions were reserved for the privileged, the elder of the block and his helpers. We lapped up every drop of this meal and felt better just feeling hunger again—for days we had been so numbed.

The nights in September were getting quite cold. It was a bitter fight with oneself waking up in the middle of the night with a full bladder to leave the cover of the thin blanket and walk all the way to the latrines that were at the end of the camp. I had a dream on this first night that I was in an elegant English country house. It was a cold night and we, whoever the company, were sitting close to the high flames of a large fireplace. I felt the burning heat on my body and felt an urgent need to empty my bladder, which I did into the flames. I woke up, ran out and did not wait until I reached my destination. Nobody seemed to care.

The next morning we set up the hospital. There was never enough time and most everything had to be improvised. All contact with the SS physician had to be made through the sergeant corpsman. While the SS physicians were not always the same ones, the corpsman was, and was both helpful and protective of our part of the camp, which he considered his realm. At the first meeting, the SS physician selected Otto Heller of our group to head the hospital. He made his decision intuitively, asking only a couple of questions; the choice was made surprisingly well.

Otto was a man of integrity, a well-trained and experienced practitioner. After he was chosen, another man, Hans, stepped out of the group of assembled physicians and claimed to have already been appointed the head of medical services for the whole transport. Nobody knew him. The SS physician patiently turned to him and ordered that duties be divided with Otto. We soon found out that this man had little medical knowledge or skills. Later somebody said that they thought that Hans had owned a medical laboratory in Vienna. He adjusted to the mentality of the camp with ease; his aggressive intrusion probably had been a bluff.

This split of leadership between Otto and Hans was a true division into good and bad, overshadowing our work for the whole time we were together. Hans, the self-appointed administrator of the hospital, built a separate room in a corner of the building where he resided with the block Elder, a young member of our transport, with sharp elbows and a loud voice. Otto slept at the end of the hospital room separated from the patients only by an improvised partition. He invited me to join him. This was a warmer place. Also, I could be available at any time of the day or night. Otto and I became close friends, a relationship that soon included his wife, who worked as a nurse next door in the hospital for women and children. His concern for patients and his creative mind in the practice of medicine kept people alive even under the most primitive and limiting conditions. He earned respect for trying to counteract the often cruel and dictatorial forces controlling our life.

The health condition of the population deteriorated rapidly. Our family camp, in contrast to other divisions of Birkenau-Auschwitz, was treated differently, as was the Gypsy camp. In contrast to the others we were not sent out to work, and were allowed to keep our hair, at least in the beginning. Most of the occupants spent their days in their barracks trying to keep themselves clean, which used up a lot of the time, which they had, as well as energy, which they did not have.

Some, like those of us in the medical service, were lucky enough to find a job in the maintenance of the camp; others created a place for themselves. For example, Fredy Hirsch had been active in Prague as a gymnastic and sports teacher and had been a leading figure in the Zionist youth movement. Children adored him. He was very Prussian in his manners, a handsome, athletic, but somewhat effeminate man, who placed great emphasis on his clothes and appearance. He impressed the leading elements of the camp, even attracted the camp Elder, that criminal psychopath, so that Fredy had easy access to him. He managed to make special arrangements for children, received permission to organize schooling and exercise and gained a slight improvement in their nourishment. Whatever his own interests were and whatever the privileges he attained for himself and his friends, we could still see that his main objective was the well-being of the children.

Anyone skilled, manual workers, electricians, tailors or carpenters, could find better positions. Attractive women used their sexual appeal to gain privileges and position; they felt morally compensated if they were able to bring their children, parents or husband an extra piece of bread.

We worked hard in the hospital, which kept us going. All the familiar diseases became more vicious as our physical resistance was weakened. A common cold could dramatically turn into a fast-progressing pneumonia. Before our deportation, the new sulfonamides had become the treatment of choice for all kinds of bacterial infections. Fresh optimism had revitalized medicine and certainly improved the prognosis for those afflicted with some of the most-feared infectious diseases. But those drugs were not available in the camp and we had to fight the dangerous crises of pneumonia with primitive supportive means, like aspirin and cold compresses, á la Vincent Priessnitz.*

A frequent complication was a meningo-encephalitis, which often followed a pneumonia only a few days after the patient had apparently improved; the high fever came down only to flare up again accompanied by the well-known stiffness of the neck. Nearly all died in coma. We reported our situation to the SS physician. He shook his head without a word, as if he understood and accepted the problem. We tried to appeal to his corpsman, who spent more time in the hospital and who expressed some sympathy for our requests. At times, we did get badly needed medication, but never enough to ensure the complete cure of any patient. The other major problem was getting patients out of the hospital as fast

* Priessnitz was a naturalist born in 1799 in what is now the Czech Republic. He used herbs and cold water as treatments in a sanitarium he had established. The term "Priessnitz compress" is still found in medical books.

as possible to make room for sicker patients who were brought to the preliminary screening for admission. Their block physician, the one living in their barracks, would often be told to take back a patient in critical condition and treat him with whatever was available. Many did not live long enough to reach their turn for an empty bed in the hospital.

Occasionally, the family of a patient would get the needed medication on the black market. The price depended on the supply from the belongings of new arrivals entering neighboring camps.

Scratches or wounds on fingers, toes or legs could quickly develop into malicious, purulent inflammations. The two surgeons who took care of those cases as outpatients were overworked. They were helped by their wives, both trained nurses, who gave this clinic a slightly more tender and comforting touch. The patients were certainly in need of that. They had to stand in line outside the building, poorly clad and hungry, often in rain or cold. They were frightened of surgical treatment. The doctors, frustrated by the deficiencies in supplies and equipment and under the pressure of time, were not always tolerant or patient.

Hans, the self-appointed second chief physician, who thought of himself as commander in charge of the building, demanded order under all circumstances and often had to be reminded of our professional functions. He apparently thought that the more everybody feared and hated him the better his position would be in the power structure. He did not intimidate Otto Heller, who tried to lessen the patients' hardships. Soon the two leaders of this unusual medical organization hated each other fiercely.

After being in this camp just a few weeks, it seemed as if we had been there for a very long time. In the evenings Otto and I would sit with a couple of new doctors who had been added to our staff because of the rapid increase in workload. Occasionally, the doctors who took care of the outpatient activity inside each block joined us to discuss urgent problems as we drank the hot black camp drink that was certainly free of caffeine.

We had a great need to tell each other our impressions and experiences and to exchange rumors and information. We soon learned that an underground network maintained connections between the various camps and the outside world. Of course, during the long journey of whispered communication, the facts often were distorted, some by anxieties, which made the news unacceptable, others by rays of hope that created fantasies. The war seemed far away. When we heard about the progress of the Allies on several fronts it was encouraging but, if true, too slow to guarantee the rescue of the thousands of prisoners around us. We also had been informed soon after our arrival here that knowledge about the nature of this camp could be dangerous for us because of the need by the Nazis to cover up their deeds.

In the next sector of the camp, separated by an electric fence, a group of young men was imprisoned. They spent most of the day standing in formation and were forced to exercise under the direction of a KAPO. Every day they became visibly weaker and fewer and then they were gone. They were Yugoslavian partisans captured by German occupation forces and put into commando units for special punishment. It was an appalling sight; we felt that as the only witnesses we needed to record their slow and cruel execution, to weave it into a human outcry recorded in our memories should any of us return to the free world.

The most painful time of the day was the roll call, when we had to line up in front of each block to be counted. It usually took an hour or longer and seemed nearly endless on cold and rainy days. Often, the number of prisoners reported by the block recorder was incorrect. Some were not there because they were unconscious on their mattresses or had died. Finally, after the dead of the day had been subtracted and the total number of prisoners tallied with the list and given to the SS man in charge we could return to the block, usually frozen and starved. The food of the day would then be dished out—soup, bread and a piece of margarine, salami or marmalade. During the waiting period, when no guard was in sight, we talked mainly about food, of fine menus that we imagined and embellished, helping each other with fancy suggestions. This was done with the same seriousness that children often have in playing a game. There was a vicarious pleasure in talking about food as well as a frustrating teasing in that substitute experience. We called it "food masturbation." However, it may have mobilized our stomach juices to be prepared for digesting the poor quality of bread.

Sometimes, while waiting for the end of the count, we talked about death, with a longing similar to that with which we described the image and taste of a favored dish. Occasionally we even tried to produce sexual fantasies; we went through the words but they were empty. Despite the low level of existence, there was only one suicide during those early weeks in our camp, a formerly successful fifty-year-old family doctor from Prague. He told his friends that he was too tired to live and walked to the electrical fence bordering our camp. The guards, who were watching from the high towers started to shoot, the body fell forward, electrocuted or shot, or both.

11

THE DAY OF ATONEMENT, 1943

THE JEWISH HIGH HOLIDAYS must have been rather late that year. It seems to me that we had already been in the camp for several weeks before that unforgettable Day of Atonement, 1943. The Jewish holidays were special occasions for the Nazis to heighten their hostile measures. It was a gray and cloudy late afternoon, the roll call had not lasted as long as usual and the camps were ghostly quiet. The tension grew when it was announced that gates to all camps would be locked. A prisoner from another camp, who had come to bring materials, insinuated that this was an ominous sign. He had whispered to Larry, the pharmacist, the dreaded word "selection" and ran back to his barracks. In our early days in this camp whenever there were rumors, hints, or direct questions relating to the "great mystery" there was an immediate negation as if it were only a brutal joke. We suspected that closing us into our barracks on that evening was to prevent us from watching the gruesome procedure of "the selection" of those who were to be killed. The SS treated this as if it was a secret but it seemed to be known to anyone who had been there awhile.

The leaders of the camps whistled, the sign to close the gates, screaming crude threats to anyone who remained in sight. I left the hospital door slightly ajar. It was dark in the small anteroom, separated from the main part of the building. I was sure I was unobserved.

I heard the motor of heavy trucks and peeked through the crack. The first truck stopped at one of the barracks in the neighboring female camp. A door opened and the silence of the last minutes was broken by blood-curdling screams mixed with loud, harsh orders. In the half-light of the increasing darkness I saw the beams of headlights directed towards the open door of one of the barracks. The white skin of a naked female body appeared, either jumping or being thrown in the direction of a truck, arms outstretched trying to find a hold somewhere in the air. One body

89

after another went this way. The desperate shrieks, the last appeal to their God for help made me shudder in a way that I had never felt before.

These sounds return to me, even now, accompanied by the same feelings of total helplessness and despair. These women were young; they revealed the beauty of their bodies for a last time, in extreme torture, as they were driven on their last ride.

This episode was the first illustration of what the unbelievable rumors had hinted and what we had been unable to grasp. As I carefully closed the door I felt a shaking body next to mine. A muffled voice said, "Oh, God!" Eric, a young medical student who worked in the hospital as a nurse had also observed the terrible scene. I still remember his pale face.

He was a very sensitive hard-working person whose hope to become a doctor kept him going. When he came to the hospital, he explained that his jaws were deformed from a beating he had received in an anti-Jewish attack in his last days at a German university. A closeness grew between us from these moments in which we were partners to this vision of horror.

I did not sit with the others that night; I was unable to speak. I kept busy trying to make the distressed patients more comfortable. I could not help but think that they might soon become the objects of a similar fate.

The next morning the chimneys of the crematoriums smoked heavily. I recall standing still for a few moments staring at the smoke, visualizing the white bodies of the murdered women ascending skyward. It had a terrible yet almost beautiful, poetic feeling. I no longer regretted having taken the risk of observing the outrageous scene, which I knew would forever stay in my memory to haunt me. I felt it a duty to have been there, to glimpse that terrible reality that could no longer be denied.*

The following day, Eric and I reported our shocking experience to the rest of our group. We had to accept as real what had been until then merely hints from older prisoners and functionaries referring to periodic killings in the camp. They were not exaggerated. The others grew pale, then started to tremble. A young male nurse whimpered. His girlfriend had been deported from a prison in Holland for her participation in the resistance. His last contact implied that she had been transferred to Auschwitz. He mumbled, "She could have been among them, her spirit was strong but she was already rundown from the first prison."

* When I read the collection of poems published in 1967 by Nelly Sachs, *O The Chimneys*, I was reminded of the deep experience of that day in October 1943.

After two or three weeks, the gruesome experience slipped to the edge of my awareness. It felt similar to a past nightmare. I knew what I had witnessed, but it had lost the quality of reality. I also heard many times from others, "It could not have been true!" My colleagues and I escaped again into our work.

12

IN JOSEPH MENGELE'S HOSPITAL

WE DID NOT SEE MUCH of our SS doctor; his visits were short. He seemed to avoid contact with prisoners. All his orders and our requests for additional medication and sanitary material were transferred by the SS corpsman, who spent time in our sector of the camp and would calmly listen to our needs. His main requests to us were for orderliness and the use of chloride of lime to give the impression of disinfecting. We heard from him that another and very different SS doctor of higher rank and importance was soon expected to be in charge of our family camp. His name was Joseph Mengele.

We wondered whether this change in the management of the medical organization of our sector of the camp would influence our chances of survival. All of us had the impression of a tremble in the voice of the medical technician whenever he mentioned the name Mengele, his new superior. A cloud of dread radiated around his name. Our contact with the prisoners from other sectors gradually helped us in our groping toward understanding who this high-ranking SS physician was, this man who was charged with the "selections" of those doomed for immediate execution. Mengele and his staff were the instruments of death based on their impressions or whims about the prisoners' physical or mental conditions. Their new terms "unfit for living" and "selections" supported a political position of the superiority of the Aryan race. Mengele was influential in all experiments on inmates of other prison camps, and there were many. None of us could believe what we heard until we ourselves were witnesses to the horrors. His interest in twins was part of the medical-biological pseudo-scientific "research" in Nazi Germany whose intent was to prove the racial superiority of the Germans.

Mengele appeared in a military vehicle driven by a chauffeur. He was in an immaculate uniform. He had a rather handsome but expressionless face; a hard line around his lips projected a feeling of smugness but was accompanied by a fine quiver at the corners of his mouth, which disclosed tension and suspicious alertness. His eyes were deep set and penetrating. It was rare that he would look at anyone, but when he looked at me I felt stirred up and threatened. He expected short military answers to his questions and was very impatient when he felt a doubt or hesitancy in response to one of his requests. He would then turn to his adjutant with a gesture that unmistakably delegated the issue to him. This description was typical of most of his visits. There was a feeling of relief when he turned briskly to go back to his car, where he sat straight-backed giving orders to his chauffeur with movements of his right hand.

During subsequent rounds, he informed us in his short commando-like way about his interest in twins as objects of scientific observation. His research was in the area of heredity. He ordered special treatment and all possible privileges for twins. He underlined the seriousness of his request, murmuring threats, conveying more through his gestures than by his words. When he spoke of the importance of finding and collecting twins of all ages, his eyes became alive, even fanatic.

In that first evening, we discussed this new development while sipping our black hot water and finishing the last bits of our daily bread. Otto said, "This man would kill for twins." At that time we knew nothing about him.

The corpsman, who had already been with our camp assisting the SS doctors prior to Mengele, was extremely anxious to please him and cautioned us to beware of his quick anger. Whispered reports described him as ruthless and powerful. Old prisoners shuddered when his name was mentioned and some preferred not to talk. One read of what was unspoken between the lines. Our connections with prisoners in other parts of the camp were still limited. Hints were dropped about Mengele's role in the selections. If we asked a second question of senior prisoners we were usually met with cold silence and suspicion.

The first change that occurred was that Mengele arranged for us to have a number of specialists, members of our same transport, for consultations in the hospital. Prior to this, these doctors had been distributed to various barracks to take care of general medical issues as block doctors. This change was related to his special interest in twins. There were a few twins in the camp, some of whom were children. One

93

pair of sisters in their thirties had come with our transport. Mengele ordered these twins thoroughly examined and their medical charts frequently updated. They were tested and checked by every available specialist. Blood tests were sent to the central laboratory for complete work-ups. He was particularly interested in bone structure and the condition and color of eyes and looked painstakingly for identical findings in the pairs. He and his corpsman repeatedly measured size and shape of body parts and entered results and any changes in the charts. The twins profited from their privileged positions since they were given more to eat, were better dressed and were treated cautiously by the camp personnel. Nobody dared to get into trouble with Mengele. The only inconvenience for the twins, at that point, was having to give blood a few times for the laboratory. We wondered about their future. But who of us had a future anyway?

A new problem developed. In one block, a couple of younger men had died; their doctor came to the hospital to talk about his concern. These patients had come down with fever, severe inflammation of the throat and enormous weakness. It was difficult to examine anyone as carefully as we would have liked to do in the poorly lighted, crowded barracks. The doctor of these patients became alarmed by the unusually pernicious infection. The next patient who came down with what we all assumed to be a strep infection was hospitalized and when the bacteriological report was positive we knew we had a case of diphtheria. There were no cases among the children. Apparently, most had been vaccinated.

I do not recall that there were many women suffering from this infection but among the younger men new cases appeared during the next couple of weeks even though many of them were in relatively better general physical condition than the average population of our camp. We were afraid of an epidemic. Any such spread of an infectious disease could jeopardize the existence of a camp.

We were hardly prepared to deal with diphtheria. We separated an area of the hospital using blankets and sheets as partitions. Soon one of our best male nurses came down with the illness. He recovered but a physician, Franzis Polacek, in his late twenties, died due to the complication of an inflammation of the heart muscle. We had been in medical school together. Earlier, when I had found him on duty in one of the barracks, I suggested he be transferred to the hospital to participate with us in the care of the severely ill patients. He gladly accepted. Franzis was the first physician of the hospital to die. We were very concerned about Mengele's reaction.

We talked carefully with the SDG and expressed our need for serum without showing the severity of the situation by the number of cases, pretending that we were treating just a couple of cases of diphtheria. He was not too inquisitive but asked whether we would be able to avoid a spread of the infection. We reassured him. He explained that it was forbidden to put any serum or blood into the hands of Jewish physicians. In addition to the shortage of all medical remedies, there seemed to be some vague paranoid fear or taboo around blood. The handling of blood or parts of it, like serum, was solely restricted to German doctors. This smelled of the mythology surrounding the "purity" of German blood.

Another colleague, Dr. Kosak, came down with the disease when he had contact with an infected patient he had transported to the hospital. Dr. Kosak survived, but for many weeks had great difficulty swallowing and speaking because of a paralysis of the uvula, a common outcome of the disease. He had to relearn both how to swallow and how to vocalize in a normal way.

Otto Heller felt enormous responsibility and the necessity of making swift decisions to limit the spread of the disease. In one of our evening meetings he suggested that we treat new cases with the blood of recovered patients or those still in convalescence, which would carry sufficient immune bodies. Dr. Milek, who had been a physician at the health department in the city of Prague until the Nazis "cleaned" the administration of all Jews, participated in that important meeting. Although he had great experience in dealing with epidemics, he had not seen much of this infection, since with the invention of preventive and therapeutic vaccines, it had not been a great problem in a city like Prague.

We discussed the risks and technical procedures. The next day we started this treatment. Twenty-five cc's of blood of a convalescent patient were taken in a syringe flashed with citrate to avoid coagulation and given intramuscularly to a new patient as soon as he was diagnosed as having the disease. It worked! We did not lose one more patient from diphtheria.

Warned of the constant danger of typhus we were conscientiously and continually trying to exterminate lice, which transmit the microorganism that causes the infection. A couple of months after we had opened the hospital, a patient with very high fever was brought in for observation. We suspected typhus, but none of us had as yet seen a case of this dreadful illness. The SDG, who had some experience with typhus in other camps, talked often of how both the chief commander of Auschwitz and Mengele feared the spread of this infection and fought it rigorously. We had heard through our underground communication that in a neighboring camp patients had been exterminated along with their lice.

Our first typhus patient developed the typical clinical picture, swollen spleen, a severe general condition with signs of dehydration and a characteristic rash. We hunted for lice daily and examined the bodies of all inmates. There were a few isolated cases of typhus but we succeeded in keeping it from developing into an epidemic. We listed the patients with typhus as suffering from pneumonia and neither Mengele nor his helper discovered our cover-up.

We had only one psychotic patient in our camp. He had been in a severe depression when the in-house physician brought him to the hospital because he had not touched his food for a few days. He was dehydrated, non-responsive, and in a melancholic stupor. We fed him intravenously, as limited as our means were, and in a couple of weeks saw him improving. We thought maybe we had been mistaken in our original diagnosis when he taught us otherwise. After an interval of a few days he became manic. He was singing and talking without interruption, ate our miserable food as if it were the finest gourmet cooking and was eager to go on a trip. When his agitation increased we became concerned about his behavior during Mengele's next visit.

The day came and Mengele arrived. He was very pleased about some measurement of twins he had just received and walked through the long room of the hospital barracks passing by the patients who were all quiet and motionless in their beds.

Otto Heller had already mentioned to him that we had a manic patient in the hospital who was improving but needed stronger sedatives. Mengele seemed not to react. We hoped he would cut his visit short as he had done several times before. But he went on. When his rounds reached the end of the row of hospital beds, Mengele was ready to turn around. At this moment the manic patient started to sing. A nurse, whom we had posted next to his bed, whispered to him to be quiet, "Mengele is here."

Now the patient increased his voice and sang over and over in free clang associations, "Mengele, Bengele," (rascal), "Mengele, Bengele." Mengele cringed, his expression was a mixture of surprise and anger and his hand went to his pistol. His posture momentarily revealed fear; then he stretched his head higher, defiantly ignoring Otto, who spoke with a slow but strong voice while his hands moved as if to calm the patient, but really to reassure Mengele that the man was harmless. Mengele turned around and stomped out, ordering his adjutant to transfer the patient to another hospital.

A short while later the ominous military ambulance arrived to pick up the patient who, cheerfully singing, did not seem to care what happened to him. The next day we asked the corpsman about our patient. He stared at us with an expressionless face and the silence of death. This was the first medical killing of someone from our family camp. We had heard about the killing of mentally ill patients, although officially only their sterilization was reported. I worried about Otto. Would Mengele feel ridiculed and need to show his strength? Our slim hope that our sector of the camp would be treated differently from the rest of Auschwitz started to fade.

We did not see Mengele for awhile. A new SS physician came for regular rounds. His name was Dr. Klein. Later I read that his first name was Fritz and that he came from Siebenbuergen, a part of Hungary in which there was a large German population. (Langbein, 1972). The underground warned us, "Don't trust him." He was a man in his fifties, a bit of a caricature in his SS officer's uniform, appearing to be a friendly, concerned family doctor. He talked with patients promising them recovery soon. He listened to our needs and requests and responded with encouraging noncommittal sounds. He spoke broken German with a strong Hungarian accent.

December 1943 had become very cold. The long stove running through the full length of each barracks gave some warmth when wood was available, which was not often. The sleepless nights seemed endless.

During one freezing cold night, while wandering in my thoughts through some of my past experiences, I remembered how one favorite writer of my youth, Jack London, described being a prisoner in winter in the Far North. He had learned that by rolling his body into a narrow ball, leaving as little exposed surface as possible, that he could willfully put his

97

body into a state of numbness until he fell asleep. I did this. If I had been busy in the hospital during the night, I used this position during the day while taking a short rest. I covered myself with a blanket at my sleeping place and all that others saw of me was a hump like a molehill. My colleagues teasingly called me *krtek*, the Czech word for mole, and respected my retreat.

Hans desperately and repeatedly tried to strengthen his position, all the while continuing to prove his incompetence as a physician, if ever he was one. He resented my close friendship with Otto Heller. He also made cynical remarks about our involvement in medicine. He and his woman, wife or mistress we never knew, were the only ones who gained weight, while the rest of us became progressively run down. He picked on me whenever he could find an opportunity and wanted to remove me from the hospital barracks. One day he acquired a special stethoscope from the *kanada*, the warehouse used to store possessions taken from incoming transports. That stethoscope had an amplifier that allowed one to listen to a patient's chest and hear more than the conventional examination would reveal. He called me to a patient I had admitted with the diagnosis of pneumonia. He told me that he clearly heard bronchial breathing indicating that the man was suffering only from bronchitis and need not be in the hospital. This was nonsense medically but I realized he wanted the bed for somebody in exchange for some favor. When I told Otto that perhaps I should leave the hospital, he became very angry and had a hard talk with Hans, who from then on anxiously avoided me. The patient and I both survived one more critical incident.

We had been in this camp for nearly three months. It was frightening to see how people changed. Slowly, irresistibly, we became numbed towards the suffering of others. Our small group around Otto made an effort not to lose all sense of helping and, unlike most other prisoners, we had our professional activity to help us connect with our past and with each other.

We were in a quandary about several men who were brought into the hospital in a semi-comatose condition. There were no similar cases in the women's hospital at that time. We were uncertain about the clinical meaning of their condition. They showed a mild rigidity throughout the body including some stiffness of the neck. All reflexes were weak and became progressively weaker but there were no other neurological findings. The spinal fluid was clear and normal, at least on routine examination. Other laboratory tests were negative. Their body temperatures were below normal, as were their blood pressures and pulse rates. Sometimes the clinical picture reminded us of a mild Parkinson-like syndrome. The patients soon became incontinent, confused, stopped eating and drinking then lost the ability to speak. They slid into death in a few days even when fed intravenously. We registered their death as encephalopathy, our description of a pathological reaction of the organism under the paralyzing effect of extreme stress and deprivation.

One day I saw my friend Leo Fantl, our former neighbor from Prague who had been the well-known music critic from Dresden. He was on the camp road carrying a few red bricks on his outstretched arms. His posture was rigid and his movements slow. He stared at me as the tears were running down his face. He opened his mouth but no sound came. I took the bricks from his hands and led him to the hospital. He had been a brilliant scholar of religious music, highly regarded as a music reviewer for one of the important Dresden newspapers of pre-Nazi Germany. I realized that he was affected by the same unclear, deadly condition. The first day he responded vaguely to me and would swallow only when I spoon fed him. The next day he kept his lips closed. He did not respond to any of our attempts to keep him alive and died the next day.

We found that those with the greatest vulnerability to this condition seemed to be men who had lived and worked by using their minds, particularly intellectuals who could find no rationality in the present and could not deal with it. It seemed that everything in their former life experiences went against their making an adjustment to the marginal crazy existence in this camp. Their demise came speedily after reaching a kind of breaking point. This process was very different from the slower progressive deterioration of the average prisoner who was able to utilize enough coping potential to counteract the fierce conditions until gradually succumbing to starvation and exhaustion. When prisoners reached this latter condition they were called "Musselmen" (Moslems) because of their typical posture, huddled up, covering their heads and body with their blanket, attempting to save energy and heat.

Our position allowed some improvements in our living conditions, like getting a pair of socks, better shoes and underwear. Acquiring something, by whatever means, was called "organizing," which included buying, if one had some hidden money, or trading, when it was even a piece of bread, as well as stealing and embezzling. The most diversified merchandise came from the *kanada,* where the luggage of newcomers, and what possessions remained from those who had died, was sorted, stored and made available for use by the military or needy Germans who had been bombed out of their homes. Prisoners working in this department found ways of taking things and putting them on the black market. Of course, the risk of being found out made it dangerous. Our transport, arriving in the Czech family camp from Theresienstadt, was relatively poor, but we could bring some things that had been smuggled and could then be exchanged for more important items. Our limited luggage was also confiscated on arrival at Auschwitz and taken to *kanada,* so all that one could bring in had to be hidden in a pocket or in another place in one's clothing.

Some in our camp, who had gained special positions, mainly as block-elders, behaved with unnecessary cruelty to their fellow prisoners as if they were insiders in the system. They received satisfaction from beating, insulting and shouting orders to other inmates who, only a short time before, had been their peers, but who then became their subordinates. Of course there were great individual differences. This was equally common among the women.

One of the block leaders, a particularly strong, athletic man, formerly an active and educated member of a circle of younger people in Prague, changed into a most brutal tyrant. I want to forget his name; I cannot forget his face. I shall call him Karel; I will mention him only once more, at his last outburst of rage. Otto tried to talk with him but got a nearly psychotic response.

My resistance to Hans had been dangerous. I refused any encounter with Karel. By then I knew that I had to learn to get along and submit to the hierarchy. The only effective resistance to the murderous system was to survive another day, whatever the price. People used little advantages to gain a step up the ladder of this social order.

Gottfried's Parents
Max and Herta (Birnbaum) Bloch

13

MY PARENTS ARRIVE IN AUSCHWITZ

IN THE MIDDLE of December 1943 we heard that a second transport from Theresienstadt was expected to enter our camp. I hoped that my parents would not be in it; I could not bear the idea of seeing them in this misery. A few days later the transport arrived. People were again led into the camp without selection. At first we were not allowed out. I sneaked into the next barracks of newcomers, found some people I knew from Prague, and received the information that my parents and Willy Schönfeld had arrived on this transport.

I returned to the hospital and asked our block-leader for help. His privileged position had supported getting his parents a better place and I thought he might have had some compassion for me along with the grandiosity of his power. He lent me one of his "elegant" hand-tailored prisoner-jackets and a cap so that I could go out in greater safety. Being better dressed was proof that one was in a privileged position. I found a red-cross band and put it on my sleeve and stormed out, masquerading as some kind of functionary that, in fact, was nonexistent in the camp. When I opened the gates of one block after the other, nobody stopped me and finally I found my mother. She was exhausted and frightened, as were the other women. I had brought some tea, remembering the excruciating thirst on my own arrival in Auschwitz. Her contingent had an even harder trip than mine had because it was winter. She told me how hopeful she was when she entered the transport with promises of reunification with the first transport in a well established new settlement where she could look forward to seeing me. It grew dark. Surrounded by shivering exhausted women I tried to comfort my mother, turning at times to the others too, ignoring all real issues so as not to destroy their last hope. I promised that at daylight everything would look better. My very appearance in her barracks may have secured my mother some better treatment from the block leader, who was screaming for silence, running with a whip in her hand through the barracks crowded with crying, desperate women.

I found my father too. He was very worried about my mother. They were separated on arrival at Auschwitz and horrified by the scene on the ramp. Looking at my "elegant" outfit he seemed somewhat reassured. I tried to calm others who were frightened, mostly for their wives and children. When I told them they would probably meet them the next day they also calmed down.

It was not even three months since my own arrival in Auschwitz yet I was a world apart from those who were going through the initial shock, getting the first glimpse of unexpected hell.

Friends, as well as strangers who recognized me, were encouraged that there was somebody who did not shout at them and anxiously asked about remarks made by the senior prisoners who were directing and pushing them on their arrival at the ramp. They had heard about chimneys and smoke but did not grasp or accept the implications; they also had heard how privileged they were to enter this camp that included older people and children. Their question to the old prisoners and to me now, "If being here is a privilege what would the alternative be?" The usual silent answer had been a move of the arm toward the sky. Somebody asked me directly, "Do those gestures mean death?" No one really wanted an answer.

Soon this newest camp generation, three months younger than mine, would realize that life here was irrational, not following the laws of order as they knew it, more like a bad dream but with no awakening. I recall my qualms about telling the truth. I decided that I would lie to them and avoid saying what they could not yet, if ever, tolerate hearing. My own motivation probably came from not being able to see more desperation.

The next morning the gates were opened and the new members of this "privileged family settlement" could get in touch with the members of the first transport. Some found relatives, often hardly recognizing them; some heard about the death of those whom they had wanted to join. Nelly, whom I saw from time to time, came running. She had found her parents who had volunteered to enter the transport to be with their daughter. On the way, her mother, who suffered from a heart condition, became ill. Her handbag with all her medications was taken by one of the helpers on arrival with the false promise that he would save it for her. We ran to see her. I brought a heart medication, a strophantus injection and a diuretic. Nelly stayed with her and she improved. Nelly, who by now understood the nature of the predicament, wondered why we could not allow her to fall into a peaceful coma. We looked at each other and smiled, still believing in fighting for time.

Our clinic could not cope with all the medical problems of the new transport. This time there were more elderly and sick people who had been selected under the pretext of being united with their families. These deceits were the tranquilizers for the helpless that allowed the transport commando of the SS to manipulate the travelers more smoothly.

My emotional state had changed; I felt the difference strongly. In the last month prior to the arrival of my parents I had slowly acquired a protective shell against feelings. Outside of my involvement with patients I tried to ignore the world around me. I felt disconnected from the past and unemotional about the future. I lived as if I was in a large institution of terminally ill human beings removed from civilization, as if we were in a leper colony of the past. Images such as these were important for me; they gave me a frame of reference for some sort of adjustment.

At night, Otto and I, sometimes with one or two of our colleagues, allowed ourselves to loosen up. To have one intimate friend with whom one could be honest was crucial for emotional survival in this life of lies and pretense. Now that my parents had come, my thin defensive layer of detachment was broken. I was terribly worried about their situation. Every morning I dreaded my visit to their cold barracks and wondered how I would find them. They soon suffered what most people un-avoidably endured, the severe gastrointestinal disorders with diarrhea and inability to take in any of the available food for at least a few days. When I saw my mother getting weaker, I had no scruples about transferring her to the hospital.

My father had some urinary difficulties related to an enlarged prostate. Most patients in our hospital who had to be regularly cath-eterized, died of blood poisoning after a few weeks, even though we tried diligently to ensure the sterilization of the instruments. Using my influence, I arranged for my father to pick up his recently learned skill as an optician making glasses for those prisoners who had lost theirs. He started to repair broken frames and adjust glasses found after the death of their former owners, for those still alive who were often half-blind after the loss of their own spectacles. This way he could be in the somewhat warmer barracks of the clinic and closer to me. Also, the psychological importance of doing something constructive in this organization of systematic disintegration of civil life was enormous.

Willy Schönfeld, who also arrived on this second transport, came down with a high fever. He felt helpless. He had been practically cured of tuberculosis about ten years earlier and lived a sheltered life to prevent a recurrence. The next bed available in the hospital was reserved for him. With our primitive diagnostic means, without x-ray equipment and laboratory, we could not reliably assess his condition. By necessity, we had become quite skilled in primitive methods of examination and observation, but for fine differential diagnostics our resources were insufficient. His fever gradually went down and his old optimism returned. He started to walk around but was not well. A package of swollen lymph nodes above his right clavicle caused discomfort for him and caused us concern. At that time, I did not yet know that this was a frequent development here for patients with a previous history of tuberculosis. Starvation, exhaustion and reduction of resistance due to concurrent infections were probably the main factors in the recurrence of their old illness, which progressively afflicted the lymphatic system. The increasing number of severely ill patients became a growing problem.

A young internist, Franzis, who had first worked as a house physician in one of the blocks, was now instructed to act as liaison between the physicians of the improvised care centers at the various barracks and the hospital. Although Dr. Klein mumbled something about opening a new hospital block to accommodate more patients, he had little credibility and indeed nothing happened.

Most of the physicians around Otto Heller had been trained, as I had been, at the German University in Prague. Its medical school, prior to the annexation of areas of Czechoslovakia by the Nazi government in the fall of 1938, had been one of the top centers of modern medicine in Europe. Our new colleague, Franzis, came from a different background. He grew up in a smaller community near Prague and had studied medicine at the Czech University. His parents were religious Conservative Jews. By the time he reached high school he felt he wanted to get away from any contact with the Jewish religion and was attracted to Catholicism. Even under the great equalizer of a common fate, Franzis felt like a stranger in our group. For many of us, faith and belief were shaken; bitterness and disappointment were often expressed whether religious or philosophical. There were others who had been deeply religious before this breakdown of freedom, and now became fanatic, escaping into a world of devotion to a higher order.

From an early age, Franzis was antagonistic to Judaism, the religion of his family, and was inspired by the solemnity of the Catholic Church. He had believed that his prayers and fantasies would open a new identity for him in the future. He never reached it. Franzis was an intelligent but somewhat naive person, honest and decent, but he thought that my report of seeing the selection of young women for extermination on the last Jewish High Holy Days was a misinterpretation and that we had all lost our judgment. He believed that the Nazis intentionally spread rumors to threaten us into being compliant but he thought that news that we reported receiving from underground connections were also rumors. He saw that many prisoners died from illness, starvation and the hardships of camp life and was willing to accept that the smoking chimneys on the border of the camp were crematoriums, but for the dead. The smell when the wind came from that direction was enough to convince anyone. He argued with us, as well as with himself, trying to preserve his beliefs. He could not fathom what we told him about the existence and use of gas chambers for exterminating humans.

Late one afternoon, I heard the now familiar noise of an arriving train, the click of freight cars hitting each other while being shunted to a sidetrack, the forwards and backwards movements of a long train of cattle cars. Every time I heard these sounds I relived my own moments of arrival at Auschwitz before the opening of the gates. Then came the shrill whistle of the engine, leaving behind the rest of the train, a farewell to the thousands pressed into boxcars. I asked Franzis to come with me to a corner of our camp from where we had a free view of the ramp. Hundreds of people still dressed in their city clothes got out. Our distant view prevented our seeing any details. Having pieced together the process from various bits of information I had heard, I explained to my friend what was now happening before our eyes. He remembered his own shock on arrival, having come with his wife, and the fear that they would be separated as the rude commandos divided the men from their women, some of whom were holding on to their children.

As the cold wind increased it sent the noise and chaotic screaming toward us. Heavy trucks picked up those who could not walk, along with their luggage. Then the whole mass started to move towards the last buildings of the camp. At the end of this unholy procession a military ambulance, with a bright red cross on its sides and roof, moved along at the same slow speed. I explained to Franzis that usually a high-ranking SS physician rode in this medical vehicle with the containers of poisonous gas that would be used to kill most of the new arrivals—a bizarre scene. We both trembled.

Never before had I so clearly put together the detailed steps of that terrible process, even for myself. It was cold as we watched those poor people who had just arrived. Neither of us said one word. I was close to tears; my friend seemed to be in prayer. Any argument about the nature of this scene was silenced.

Sometimes while waiting for the roll call and standing idle in line, Franzis and I would throw our opposing philosophical opinions at each other like ping-pong balls. Neither of us was trying to convince the other but we parried ideas and sometimes even allowed a feeling to slip out.

As a young man, I had developed a comfortable optimistic outlook influenced by a classical humanistic education. I had trusted the natural order into which we were born and accepted human beings as the appropriate inhabitants of such an order. I had not felt the need of an institutional religion; my spiritual experiences were either in the mountains or with music and, of course, in my romantic nature. Franzis needed the order and structure of a religious system. We were both disappointed in what was called our *Weltanschauung*, our philosophy of life, and deeply hurt by the merciless reality. We were both at a loss but were not capable of admitting it.

Mengele came again to visit the hospital to see a pair of twins among the newcomers—two sisters, identical twins, who seemed to interest him the most. They both were teachers and apparently had lived closely parallel lives. I saw him getting involved in an animated conversation for the first time with these two attractive young women and he seemed pleased with his observations.

After he left, we wondered what this ambitious person might have become if he had not found such a powerful place in this terrible system. "But," Willy Schönfeld remarked, "this system was a creation of men like Mengele." We did not see Mengele often during the next few weeks. Our "wireless" communication, transmitted not by radio but by secret meetings on both sides of the wire fence, informed us that Mengele had been very busy performing selections from the thousands of Jews arriving from different countries of Europe. The chimneys were heavy with fumes. We could identify the country of origin of the recent transports through the objects sold on the black market, such as cigarettes and food. We were particularly interested in medical supplies and sometimes were able to do some trading for what we most needed.

Before Christmas it became quiet. No trains had been heard for days, the chimneys were clear and the general mood felt less violent. Willi, the camp leader, the tough criminal who years ago had received a life sentence in a German court for murder, brought a small pine tree to the hospital. Somebody had found a menorah and we lighted candles at Hanukkah; we sang sentimental Czech songs on Christmas Eve accompanied by someone playing a harmonica that Willi supplied. All this felt awkward and absurd but because there had been no transports for awhile we entered into the new year of 1944 somewhat more hopefully.

In the hospital we had some contact with other sections of the camp. The leading pediatrician in the other family camp, the Gypsy camp, was a former teacher of mine at the university in Prague, Doctor Epstein, who had been a renowned expert in his field. After the Nazis took over the university in Prague he moved to Norway, where the Gestapo arrested him soon after they occupied that country and sent him to Auschwitz. When he heard that his sister was in our camp hospital suffering from hepatitis, he asked for a pass to visit her. He had a personal talk with Otto and told him about the terrible hygienic conditions in his own camp. He struggled to prevent an epidemic of noma, a skin affliction that led to severe deformities. It was considered a rare disease found only under the most primitive hygienic condition or as a result of starvation. Dr. Epstein had seen and experienced a great deal and was very pessimistic about the fate of us all.

We still did not understand the reason for the special treatment that our family camp received. Except for the one manic-depressive patient, all deaths so far were "natural," at least as natural as could be expected given the substandard conditions in which we were forced to live. The speculation was that the International Red Cross had planned a visit to Auschwitz for an inspection, which seemed quite likely, since we knew about their visit to Theresienstadt, and how they had been fooled by the commanders of that camp. One area had been open to them, after it had been changed into a clean, pleasant place, like a village, with a small sample of the healthier population. Perhaps we also were to be "shown." Martin Gilbert (1985, p. 658) writes about a visit by a German Red Cross delegation to a section of Auschwitz but I am sure I would have known if they had been to our camp.

The first two months of the new year continued to be very cold. More deaths were reported to the medical center at morning roll call. The population of our group weakened progressively. We had been warned about Mengele's sudden reactions to situations that did not fit into his program. Physicians had been the targets of his rage before. At other times apparently whole sickrooms had been emptied as a response to overcrowding or unacceptable statistics. His unpredictability in deciding about life and death created enormous tension. Franzis still tried to neutralize our fears. He was most stubborn, almost fanatic in his distorting information and turning his attention away from blatant signs of the process of extermination of masses of people.

It was easier to talk to Dr. Klein than to Mengele. Contact with him in the hospital was unavoidable. He always appeared friendly, his words embroidered with artificial sweetness; he would promise to help as much as he could when we were in great need of some medical supply but delivered nothing. Mengele would not often reply favorably, but if he did his accompanying corpsman would make all efforts to respond. Sometimes he would even secretly ask for our help to get whatever it was on the black market. We had the feeling that Klein was afraid of Mengele, who looked at him with contempt. I have a vague recollection of Mengele appearing once while Klein was talking with a patient. Klein respectfully stepped back and gave his military report to Mengele, who left the hospital as fast as he could. Klein was very curious. He had questions for everybody he met and one had to be attentive to catch the fine sarcasm in his remarks. At times, he could barely hide the satisfaction he took in the suffering around him; he would shrug his shoulders and refer without expression to the cruelties of wartime.

Mengele, on the other hand, never entered into any unnecessary conversation. When he discussed his orders with Otto, whom he seemed to respect, his voice at times, softened a little. He trusted him to provide the clinical observations, measurements and tests on twins. He seemed to be convinced that his collection of data would not only help his research on heredity but also contribute to proving the Nazi theory concerning the genetic racial superiority of the German people. We received our information from the corpsman, who had become quite friendly with some of the nursing personnel, particularly the head nurses of the women's block. He would become talkative and say even more than we felt comfortable hearing. When he talked about Mengele, we were afraid that a careless remark by someone could endanger us. At times, Mengele had a strange way of looking through me as if I were not present. I wondered whether Hans had made some poisonous remark. The general attitude of all SS personnel towards prisoners was hostile and sometimes violent, which made it more possible to avoid the normal kind of human emotions that usually develop in people who are in close proximity. When we encountered the SS in a more "normal" setting, such as the hospital, the interaction was apt to be more civilized, particularly when one of the guards or our corpsman needed medical or dental attention.

Willy Schönfeld, still a patient in the hospital, became interested in working, although his energy level was very low. He joined us in the evening or discussed ideas with me about projects for a fantasized future. He wanted to write a popular book on the dynamics of the human psyche. His idea was to describe the structure of mental functioning in concentric circles. The center would be the depth of inborn, primitive drives radiating to interrelated wider circles signifying increasing experience and learning, like the rings in the cross section of a tree.

When we were working in occupational guidance in Prague at the Jewish Community Center, our efforts had been focused on finding a psychological system that could become the basis for counseling people in learning new and modifying old skills. We had used a combination of characterological tests, Rorschach, graphology, and aptitude, relating the findings to the ambitions and experiences of the person. Willy also wanted to develop a psychology of work. His interest was focused on the meaning of activity for the psychological development of a person and the importance of knowing how to choose the most suitable occupational goals when deciding on training. He was impressed with the number of people who were caught in activity that fit neither their talents, nor their ambitions. I had thought of expanding on this theme with a psychopathology of work, applying the same framework for the emotionally or mentally disturbed person and searching for pathogenic elements in inappropriate work situations.

All this occurred with the smoking chimneys in the background! We were aware of the terrible things going on around us but it felt somehow distant, veiled and unreal. Willy and I talked about the need the Nazis had to appear humanitarian and cover up their gradual extermination of the Jewish population. We didn't know if it was to fool a part of the German population that might have reacted to such carnage, or to save face in world opinion.

Larry, a young pharmacist from Prague via Theresienstadt, had joined us. He had grown up in Slovakia and spoke a number of languages, which was very helpful in his communicating with prisoners in neighboring camps. He took care of the small pharmacy in a corner of the hospital building. His function and power was to receive, collect and distribute medical supplies as they became available. Having precious remedies under his control also gave him important privileges. He was a rather reserved person. We savored his contact with a world beyond the fence. He was our best source of important information. Otto and I suspected that he was in touch with the resistance. Of course, at that time we did not know whether such a movement really existed or if it was only our wishful thinking.

The cold days of February brought more illness and death. The children's block, under the leadership of Fredy Hirsch, received better soup and bread; the children adjusted amazingly well. A school was organized and not only tolerated, but frequently visited by ranking SS officers and doctors. Dr. Fritz Klein liked to joke and laugh with the children and complimented their teachers and coaches.

The continuing whistle of the engines, the rattling of the boxcars and the noise of the slow-moving trucks carrying huge numbers of people towards the smoking chimneys created an uncanny air of fear around us and undermined any notion of peace or hope. At the end of February and in the first days of March it turned a little warmer. It looked like an early spring, which inspired us with new courage.

14

DISASTER ON MARCH 7, 1944

DURING THE FIRST DAYS OF MARCH, fresh rumors circulated that a new work camp was supposedly under construction and that some of our people might be transferred there. There were whispers, such as, "This would be the salvation of our people." Larry, the pharmacist, appeared very nervous and distraught. He seemed to know more about it, yet refused to talk. I do not remember exactly when "Heidebreck," the name given the new camp, was first mentioned. The news conveyed by prisoners who worked close to the central offices of the SS was confusing but implied great concern. The underground could get no information.

As miserable as our existence in the family camp had been, we clung to the idea that we had a better chance than the many other transports that we saw arriving and disappearing. We heard confidential descriptions of killing in the gas chambers, we saw the crematoriums smoking and yet even in the hospital, where we had more contact with the other sectors of the camp than most people, we managed to push to the periphery of our reality what might be going on.

Every time some terrible confirmation of the process of annihilation had to be faced, I felt overcome by deep despair and grasped for something to deny the truth. Often I gave words of encouragement to others, until I caught myself nearly believing them. Of course, I knew what was going on. Many of us knew more than we could face but we went on with our lives, involved in the struggle of surviving another day. These rumors of pending change shook our precarious balance.

It became clearer on March 3 or 4, that what was left of my transport into Auschwitz in September 1943 was going to be moved. The rumor, which was intentionally spread, was that we would be going into a new camp called "Heidebreck." We had doubts that there really was another camp. The tension grew. These were the most dramatic days. Willi, our psychopathic camp leader, seemed distraught and irritable. A few of the young men and women, who were usually with him and took his orders, as well as received his privileges, tried to get information. He avoided responding.

Fredy Hirsch, the organizer of the children and youth blocks, held a whispered conversation with Otto Heller, who shrugged his shoulders helplessly. Otto told me that Fredy was worried about the children. If a selection was pending, children would not be spared.

The same day, I found my father and Willy Schönfeld in a corner of the hospital exchanging news. They were nervous and frightened by the disquieting rumors. They had heard that members of the transport that had come first to the Czech family camp, the one I had been in, were to be moved. They were horrified about the prospect of my leaving for "Heidebreck," a destination we knew nothing about. I calmed them, sounding confident and they absorbed my lies gratefully. I found my mother in tears. She was still in the hospital. The fears of the hospitalized patients were magnified by their helplessness. One of the first tips we received on arrival in this camp was never to show illness. Most people usually did not connect such a warning with what they had heard about the crematoriums in the background but on this day the horror showed on their faces. I tried to tell the patients near my mother that some way would be found to take care of them. They believed me.

Otto Heller tried to get in touch with the corpsman, who seemed to be avoiding us on this critical March 5. We hardly slept that night after confirmation of our worst expectations came through the underground connection from the next camp. It was Larry, the pharmacist, who conveyed the message; he talked to Otto, to me and to the other workers in the hospital. He was nearly sure that all of us who had arrived six months earlier were to be killed in the gas chambers. The resistance outside the camp was not ready to help or provide weapons and left it up to us to fight or surrender quietly. Nobody would have a chance to survive either way. We wanted to know if this information was certain and clung to the words "nearly sure."

On the morning of March 6, everybody who had entered this camp with our transport in early September 1943 had to assemble immediately on the camp road. I had a few seconds to say goodbye to my father and Willy Schönfeld but avoided the questioning look on their faces. I ran out of the hospital. I could not enter the next barracks of the women's hospital, where my mother was, as SS guards and KAPOs were running around trying to line us up.

We were pushed, and as usual, this was accompanied by shrill orders and crude curses, as we moved ahead to the gate into a neighboring camp, the "A" camp, which often was used for temporary housing or in SS language, for "quarantine." We had heard this euphemism for the first time shortly after our arrival. This was the camp where we saw young Yugoslav partisans exercising until they collapsed. Now we were on the way towards that same place.

Our hospital was the last building in a long row of barracks. The patients remained in their beds now under the care of physicians and nurses of the second transport from Theresienstadt. We, the medical personnel belonging to the first transport, left our camp as the last of the caravan. Before I went through the gate, I turned around to look once more at our camp, less crowded today but otherwise continuing with regular life. I would never have believed that I could wish to stay in this place. When I looked once more at what felt like home, I saw a military vehicle with Mengele and his corpsman just entering the family camp. I wondered whether he had come to rearrange the hospital after our departure.

On that fateful morning of March 6, 1944, most family members were separated from each other, men on one side, women on the other, as they started to walk on either side of the road from their divided blocks. Everybody was concerned about his own family. Somebody said that a party of women with children was already at the train to go to the new camp. Nobody asked him from where the information came and nobody really believed him, but it felt good nourishing any hope.

We were herded into empty cold barracks. Of the five thousand of us who had arrived six months earlier, about four thousand remained—not a bad record for Auschwitz.

The day moved in slow motion. There was nothing to do. We were locked into the building and I assumed the others were placed in about twenty identical cottages. It was chilly and stuffy. I began to get hungry and thirsty, but it was painful to swallow. My throat seemed to be tied in a knot. Otto walked nervously through the block; he tried to get in touch with his wife and daughter. Eric, the young medic who had witnessed the first selection in the women's camp with me at the beginning of our stay in Auschwitz and had worked since as head nurse with me through the whole time, was now as usual near me, willing to help and assist. Franzis, who up to now had denied the gravity of our destiny, was not arguing any more. He sat motionless; only his lips moved in prayer. I moved around inside the block. I found Nelly, who had made an effort to be in this same cottage. She embraced me. She was relieved to be close to me again in another critical hour of our odyssey.

More rumors surfaced the longer we waited. Those of us from the hospital were better informed than others who had only rare contact with other camps, where people still clung to the idea that they were merely waiting for transfer. Was it our duty to inform them? How would it help? Empty-handed resistance against machine guns and bloodhounds seemed inconceivable with children and older people among us. Several of the prisoners were in a kind of sleep, a degree of somnolence, withdrawn but in touch enough to perceive changes in the scene. Others, fearing the loneliness of sleep, were involved in talking with a neighbor hoping to extract a somewhat more optimistic view of the situation. When the neighbor became hopeless and was close to breaking down, they reversed roles. These fleeting partner relationships were very important and reminded me of the dependency of infants. The boundaries between the two people merged so that it was impossible to know which one felt what. There also was a need to spread rumors and optimistic thoughts that would resonate in a larger group. My neighbor knew me from the hospital. He had a friend whom we had tried to keep alive who suffered from meningitis after pneumonia and then died. "Wasn't he lucky?" We both smiled in mutual understanding.

I must have fallen asleep for a few minutes. I woke up shivering. It was now dark. I got up to move my stiff limbs and asked my neighbor what had happened in my absence. It was on my mind to say, "Please tell me only something good, I am at the most sensitive point of my tolerance. I do not want to wake up unless you can give me some comfort." I do not remember what I really said. He looked at me and said something about my being pale and shaky.

The guards opened the gate and tea and bread were brought. This was confusing but seemed to be a hopeful sign. People selected to die were, as we had heard, written off and usually treated as if they did not exist anymore. We assumed that acting as if people were not there made it easier for the SS guards to cope with the repugnant scenes to follow.

I thought of my last days in Prague. Why hadn't I tried to run away? I contemplated heroic fantasies, hiding in the mountains with others, with weapons ready to fight, determined not to be caught alive. I wondered if I was awake or dreaming.

Eric came over to me and told me that he had overheard two guards outside the barracks saying that we were waiting for a train to "Heidebreck," the promised destination. Had this been done to reassure us and make us more compliant? A nurse from the hospital whispered that he heard that something went wrong at the gas chambers. Maybe the resistance had started to rebel. How could we know what was true? I felt that familiar painful emptiness in my body and wanted to sleep until it was over. I regretted that I had not collected enough barbiturates to make it easier for me to leave this world on my own terms. When I had left Prague, I had carried a syringe and sufficient ampules of narcotics with me in case life became unbearable. Somewhere I had lost my supply and did not replace it even though I could have stolen enough sleeping pills in the hospital. I was never free enough to break old taboos like stealing medication and now faced the consequences of my "maladaptive honesty." It used to be comforting to have the powerful stuff in my pocket and to know that if I lost control over my life I would still have control over my death. Death was not the greatest horror in these hours; it was the imagined vision of what we might have to endure before finding peace.

Franzis had become very quiet. I asked him, very seriously, what he thought happened after death. I could not imagine the thought of nonexistence simply in terms of the comfort of a long sleep. Franzis looked at me with a deep warmth in his eyes and said, "I don't know." Neither his old nor his new religion held the power to comfort him in the face of expected murder.

A young man, skilled as a handyman who had made himself useful to functionaries in and outside the family-camp, had succeeded in bringing his girlfriend with him into our barracks. In passing, on the way to a free corner, he turned to me and whispered, "It looks lousy." She did not hear him and smiling she dragged him into the cozy corner. I walked slowly, deeply distressed, through the building. I was stopped by a man leaning forward from his seat on the edge of the straw mattress. He stretched out his arms to hold on to me. His breathing was labored and he hardly could utter a word, he needed all available air. I recognized him as a former patient who had been brought into the hospital in a severe asthmatic state. He murmured, "Help." He did not realize how helpless I was. In the hospital he had recovered from a life-threatening hunger for air. What irony that he would be choked to death by poisonous gas. He knew that dreadful feeling better than anyone of us could imagine. When I passed him, touching his head lightly, his widened pupils stared at me with an expression of deep disappointment. Strange unclear sounds came from his mouth.

Lights went out. I talked to myself, "Are they saving power on us? The last they have to give us." I felt my way back to my place. The man next to me turned to me with an anxious look. He caught my eye. "No hope?" I turned away and fell, for a timeless span, into a light sleep, numb, weak and empty. Detached, I heard everything that went on around me as if through a damper.

When I woke, my neighbor was sitting up, muttering to himself. It sounded like an argument. Earlier, I had told him in quite pessimistic terms what I had heard. Maybe I wanted him to talk me out of my attitude. He did not. Now he argued with himself. When he realized that I was awake he turned to me. He expressed how difficult it was to accept the closeness of our death. He understood that Nazi power ruled his right to live. But then he exclaimed in a loud voice, "It cannot be!" Eric, who sat by me, gave me a meaningful look. We knew, had seen it already, it could be.

Fatigue took over and I lay down. I had a dream, quite real and convincing, with no trace in it of my present sad plight. Although the fear of death was not present, there was an undefined nagging in the mood of the dream. Although there was no other person in my dream, I heard a voice, loud and distinct, repeatedly calling my name. The voice woke me. I was startled when the same voice came again, screaming my name. It was the block leader of our hospital running through the building, panting and frantic. He had a list of names and mine was on it. He screamed at me to follow him fast. Franzis' name was there also; Eric's was not. With tears in his eyes Eric shook my hand and said, "Don't forget me, maybe there is hope." Nelly tried to hold on to me. I was pushed to the exit of the cottage.

The guard let us pass; outside there were a few other people waiting. I saw Otto and Hans, their wives who were nurses, and other physicians who worked in the hospital. The other physicians from the blocks were not there. We were a small group of about ten people who had been taken out and we were led out of the quarantine camp by an SS guard. It was still dark. An eerie stillness hung over the camp. The only sounds were from the guards up on the watchtowers, who called to each other to prove they were awake. Nothing felt real to me. Was I still dreaming, maybe hallucinating? Maybe already under the influence of the poisonous gas we had heard about through cryptic rumors. The old, nearly extinguished hope crept up—we might be given a chance to live. I walked automatically following the others. Nobody dared speak. Franzis looked up to the sky, as if wanting to pierce the fog to get in touch with his spiritual world. I heard voices from the block we had just left. Our departure must have stirred up new rumors and fantasies. Did they hate us thinking we were being saved or fear for our fate? How were my friends Nelly, Eric, my neighbor in the barracks, making sense of the situation? Did they feel I had deserted them?

The SS guard walked slowly ahead. His being in front was a good sign that he was not concerned that we might try to escape so we probably were not on the way to being killed. We were taken back to our old family camp and, once there, ordered to return to our hospital. It was very early in the morning. Most people were still asleep. Nurses and patients looked at us as if we were ghosts. We may even have looked like ghosts; we certainly felt like we had returned from the dead. I thought at first that we had been called back to transport patients to the quarantine camp. It would have been in Nazi character to eliminate the sick and debilitated first. Nobody gave either explanations or orders.

I threw myself on my bed and immediately fell into a deep sleep, the kind of sleep in which one totally loses contact with the outside world. I had a dream I have never forgotten. I dreamed that I was in the mountains, in a pine forest, far in the background were small farmhouses like those in the Swiss Alps surrounded by meadows of grass and flowers—all this in the most beautiful brilliant colors. There were no people in this dream and no action but it was unusual in its intensity, the intensity of a peak experience that remained in my memory, unlike most other dreams. I had a wonderful euphoric feeling on awakening, which abruptly gave way to deep sadness. The others were still locked in the cottages surrounded by SS guards shrieking commands. The barking of their dogs filled the air. There was no train on the ramp.

My parents were relieved to have me back, as were Willy Schönfeld and my patients. In the evening the fateful curfew was proclaimed. My thoughts were with my friends who were soon, I was convinced, to be driven to their death. I kept the truth from my parents, from the patients and from the personnel in the hospital, but could not hide my deep distress.

We few survivors still did not know why we had been exempt from the fate of our transport. Otto later told me that he had been called to the corpsman in charge of the hospital, Mengele's SDG, who requested from him a list of a few of the most important hospital personnel and then ordered those on the list be returned to work. I knew that some twins were saved, no doubt due to Mengele's interest in them.

The rumor was that our return to the hospital came about through the intervention of Mengele, who had just returned from a vacation in time to defend his territory against the chief commander of the camp. The other physicians who had been distributed among the various cottages and did not live in the hospital, died with the rest of the group.

I recalled the scene of my first encounter with an SS physician in Auschwitz when I, naively, stepped out of the row of doctors to say that I had not yet received my doctorate. He had told Otto to keep me in the hospital so I would not "forget my medicine." Being part of Mengele's hospital staff had also probably saved my life.

Strangely enough, the patients of the two hospital barracks had been spared and were, like us, safe for the moment. Many recovered and had another chance to survive.

The morning after the mass execution, the SS doctor, Fritz Klein, visited our camp. He was smiling and seemed to be at ease as always. He pretended interest in the remaining group of children and disregarded the fact that a large number of them were gone as were some of the teachers, including Fredy Hirsch, with whom he had regularly consulted on his rounds.

When Dr. Klein entered the hospital, he saw my father. He asked him why he was trembling and my father told him that he was excited over the return of his son who had been in the transport to "Heidebreck." Dr.

Klein beamed one of his smiles and said in his broken primitive German, "I am sure your son would have been much better off in the new place, but it is always nice if a family stays together." My father stared at him and was quiet.

It took a few days before underground communication brought us the details of the fateful night of March 7. Our people who had spent six months in this camp and had heard and seen enough, knew by the next day that they were going to be killed. Their awareness caused a tumult that increased every second and grew into an uproar. We heard that Fredy Hirsch had poisoned himself with sleeping pills. Karel, the block elder, who had assumed his role with over-zealousness and cruelty through the months of his career in our camp, attacked one of the SS guards in an outburst of violent rage. He jumped on him and tried to choke him. Other guards gunned him down.

Rudolf Vrba, a clerk whose job was to register newcomers, and Filip Müller, who worked in the crematoriums, describe the gruesome details of the last hours of these people in their interviews in *Shoah*, the movie and the book, (Lanzmann, 1985) and in Müller's book, *Eyewitness Auschwitz* (1981). When the four thousand people condemned to die were forced into the gas chambers, pressed together, crowded tightly against each other awaiting their end they sang the Czech national anthem and "Ha Tikvah" (The Hope), the Hebrew song that later became the Israeli national anthem.

The last messages sent by our friends were to tell the world of their terrible murders; none of us could doubt any longer that what we had heard before about the systematic killing of masses of people in the gas chambers was true. We few, who had been so close to the same fate, could not shake off that icy cold sensation of helplessness, the growing sensation of fading hope that must have reached unbearable dimensions at the final place of execution.

Confused about our miraculous rescue, we still identified with the suffering of our close friends and colleagues who came to such a dreadful end. Why did we all have to struggle for six months only to be condemned to die? There is total depravity in the idea of human beings sent to die on the arbitrary whim of executors of power.

The rest of that month of March was very cold. A mixture of ice and snow covered the camp road. People were constantly being carried into the hospital after having slipped on their way to the latrine; some had broken bones. We tried to arrange care in their own blocks for the older and weaker. At first, people protested that they would appear too frail, which might put them in jeopardy of being selected for the unthinkable. They could still only imagine or listen to rumors while I, on the Day of Atonement, had witnessed what no one else had. I knew it was true. As the weather became too rough to get out, they began to use their own block facilities in order to be protected.

The Jewish prisoners who were transferred on September 8, 1943, from the Theresienstadt ghetto in an RSHA transport and are now in the family camp, B-IIb, are given postcards, are ordered to date these March 25–27, and to write their relatives that they are healthy and that things are going well for them. It is prohibited to write about the transfer to the labor camp in Heydebreck. The completed postcards are brought to the Political Department, which sends them on to the addressees after March 25, 1944.

(Czech, 1990, p. 593)

It is rather unclear why the SS made that great effort to cover up the killings in the gas chambers by sending our postdated cards at a time when the world already had plenty of information about their activities.

With the end of the six month stay of the first group of Jews from the Theresienstadt Family Camp B-IIb and the instruction of the RSHA to kill them, it is decided to liquidate them. To prevent unrest, it should appear that the camp inmates were being transferred to labor camps in the Reich's interior. Consequently, all prisoners who are healthy and able to work are transferred to the Quarantine Camp B-IIa in Birkenau.* First, the men are brought over and put up in special blocks; later the women are also brought over and put in other blocks. They are allowed to take their entire belongings with them, which they brought in boxes or suitcases from Theresienstadt.

For this period the blocks in the quarantine camps are ordered closed.

---

* On September 8, 1943, the day of arrival in Auschwitz, this transport contained 5,006 persons. By March 1944, approximately 1,140 had died. 3,800 deportees were still alive. (Czech, 1990, p. 593)

POSTCARD № 1

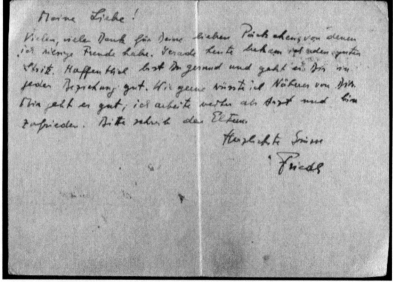

Maus received these cards and gave them to me on my return.

POSTCARD № 2

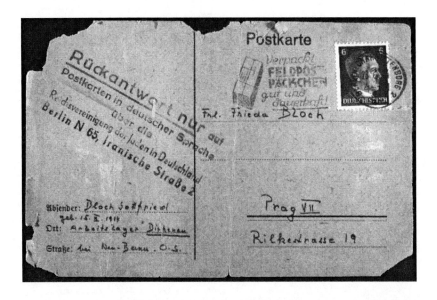

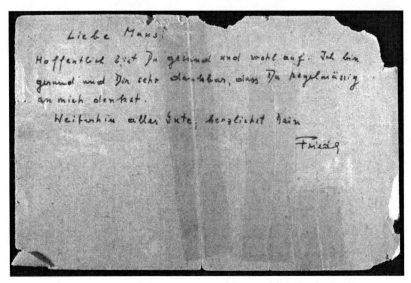

POSTCARD № 1
Translated

My Dear!

Many thanks for your lovely packages * which pleased me very much. Just today I received the good white bread.** Hopefully you are healthy and well off in every way. How I would like to know more about you.

Things go well with me; I work as a physician and am content. Please write to the parents.

Warm greetings,

Friedl

---

* I never received any packages from Maus or anyone else.

** The lie about the white bread was intended to tell her how bad the bread was.

POSTCARD № 2
Translated

Dear Maus!

Hopefully you are healthy and well off. I am healthy and grateful that you think of me regularly.

From here on all the best to you.

Warmly,

Your Friedl

* Written before the destruction of the camp.

15

LIFE AFTER THE MASS MURDER OF MARCH 1944

WHEN ANOTHER transport arrived from Theresienstadt one night, I went to look for friends that I might help. People were totally confused and half-paralyzed from exhaustion, cold, hunger and, above all, thirst. Some got lost on the way to the latrine; a few of the elderly simply lay down on the wet ground, frozen and stiff, giving up. The younger and stronger asked the standard questions, responding with bewildered stares to my careful answers. I avoided much of the truth; I did this for the newcomer as well as for myself. I had already forgotten how, outside of this inferno, people had at one time answered questions truthfully.

The last six months seemed like a lifetime. It was a period in which we dealt with narrowing circles of death, coming closer until they cut deeply into our numbers, touching each of us. None of us were normal any longer, but then it would hardly have been normal to be one's old self in these irrational surroundings.

These newcomers were allowed into the camp with their luggage. I ran into a distant relative who slipped a little package into my hand to save for him. I put it in my pocket and must have lost it later; it was a bit of real tea. We worked the rest of the night to help the sick and injured. When I visited the barracks of the newly arrived the next morning, this same man jumped at me and shouted that I had stolen his tea. He was completely deranged and stopped only after I screamed at him. This was the first time that I had used such an aggressive tone; I heard myself. It sounded very familiar in this environment and I hated it.

A young man of about thirty came to consult with me in the hospital. He handed me a letter that stated that he was a deaf-mute. After a brief period of difficult communication I learned that he was the adopted son of a cousin of my father from Hodonin, a city in Czechoslovakia. He was a strong, good-looking man but frightened and feeling helpless because of his handicap. He was even more concerned about his wife, also deaf and mute, who was being cruelly treated by her block elder. They were both artists who had been known for their fine bookbinding skills. They were a lovely couple, hopeful, uninformed and until now protected by their deafness from the tragic stories to which others were exposed. I talked with their respective block leaders to try to make it easier for them. People in more powerful positions usually showed little tolerance for weakness in others and boosted their own importance by using any vulnerability they sensed in another. I had some degree of influence in the camp since one never knew when a favor from the medical service might be needed. I used my power wherever I could. I never learned the fate of those two people who had coped with their deficiencies so well as long as they were living naturally in a normal environment.

On April 7, the sirens sounded a general alarm, which meant either that enemy planes were approaching or that there had been an escape of a prisoner. We did not know which to wish for more. The next day, April 8, we learned that a Czech Jew from our camp had escaped along with an SS guard. The rumors were that it might have been organized by the British Secret Service. Langbein describes both the successful escape and the tragic ending of the SS guard, who returned to free another prisoner, Renee, with whom he had been in love. (Langbein, 1972, p. 497).

Later, when the Jewish leaders of Theresienstadt were transported to Auschwitz, they explained that the man who had escaped that night from our Czech family camp had secretly entered and talked with them. One of them, a former colleague of mine, told Willy Schönfeld and me about that clandestine encounter and how the Jewish administration did not fully believe the information about the mass killings in gas chambers in Birkenau-Auschwitz. From our own experience we knew how compelling was the need to fend off the unbearable truth, first rejecting it, later arguing about the credibility of the information, finally "protecting" oneself from the reality by a haziness of memory.

After careful discussion, these responsible persons in the administration decided not to act on this information. They reasoned that if the people appearing on the lists to leave the ghetto had known more, even if only based on rumors, that their panic could have jeopardized survival for everyone, including those still remaining. Open resistance without outside support would be senseless.

Those of us in the hospital argued heatedly. Franzis thought it was a betrayal to allow those who were departing on their last ride to do so without a warning. Otto and I were not so sure that informing them would have made it easier for anybody.

We recalled when we had entered the transport at Theresienstadt, that we were told a new camp was somewhere in the east. We were still hopeful and did not think that all was lost. Now, discussing the situation, we speculated about whether the date of our death, that is the death of our whole transport, had been predetermined to take place six months after our arrival. It was more likely a recent decision. Otto asked, "How would we have acted during the first half year in this camp if we had known the time limits?" The leaders of many Jewish communities of victims have too often been unfairly blamed, by those who were not there, for decisions that appeared to be compliance with their oppressors.

I thought, and others agreed, that the meeting between the Elders of Theresienstadt and an escaped prisoner from Auschwitz was a risk to their own lives and could have subjected the rest of the ghetto population to torture and other critical repercussions. The only reasonable resistance in our situation was to help as many people as possible live as easily as possible until the next day.

We all hoped and were nearly convinced that, when the report about Auschwitz would finally reach the Allies, they would feel compelled to act. During that summer, we had been assured by underground rumors that the information about Auschwitz had reached the headquarters of the Allies in London through the Czech government in exile and our hopes for rescue revived a little.*

Our ideas about the risks of resisting proved to be correct. After the escape of the Czech and the SS man, our camp was punished by new security measures. Until that time we had been allowed to keep our hair, our moustaches and beards. After the escape we were all shaved. Not one hair was allowed on the face or on the top of the head. Now we not only looked like each other but also like all the other prisoners in neighboring camps. We received striped prisoner suits, more accurately striped rags, remaining from former inmates. In the hospital, we wore white coats that

* Martin Gilbert has published the summary of two reports that were received at the British Foreign Office on July 4, 1944, just as we had been informed. (Gilbert, 1981, p. 262)

we rarely took off, even outside the block, since it was an advantage to look different from everyone else.

On calmer days, Willy Schönfeld would often join me in a corner of the hospital barracks. Two questions came up in our conversation repeatedly. "Would it be possible for either of us, or anyone like us, to ever again fit into a civilized society?" And the other, "Would we be able to work again, to love, to trust, to share our feelings with another who had not experienced what we had?" Asking the questions implied that we had a future and that we would struggle with the problem of how to tell the world what we had seen. We did not think that statistics alone could ever communicate the horror of this episode in history. Willy thought that only individual biographies describing experiences could give outsiders even an approximate picture of the systematic annihilation of a people. But we also wondered if others would, or even could, tolerate hearing the enormity of the physical and emotional agony and the horrendous losses that we had faced.

Willy had understood the terrible truth about the fate of my transport. He cried when I had returned from the quarantine block, and again as he listened to my description of how people had behaved, particularly our friends. He had known Fredy Hirsch quite well. They had both been involved in educational problems during the first years of the German occupation in Prague. Fredy had always conveyed an impression of strength and control, which he ultimately demonstrated when he killed himself before others could. None of us had understood Karel, who showed his brute strength as a block leader. His last brutal act was to attack the SS guard. Like Fredy, he too used his last chance to resist.

I had avoided telling Willy and most of the others about the scenes of our awaiting the last moments when we recognized without any further doubt or hope that we would be driven into the notorious gas chamber. After I was taken out, I heard, through our sources, that the others had reacted with desperate resistance and were beaten into compliance. The SS troops had known these people—women with children, craftsmen and artists, musicians and physicians—for the last six months. All of them had been functioning as if they had been members of a normal society. The SS, on that day, condemned them as creatures to be exterminated. If there was any conflict in any of the executioners, it was probably transformed into violence. Willy and I discussed how we both had grown up among Germans, although in two different small towns. We had witnessed their need for grouping and for being united by a feeling of mutual strength, how joyously they built a wall of separateness. They created distance in religion, language and politics, at times so radical that whatever else we held in common seemed lost. Many of our German classmates, even some of our intimate friends, had changed under the influence of the political pressures of the thirties. They invested their leaders with enormous credibility and considered deviation from the new political direction tantamount to sinful betrayal.

We both thought that Nazi rule with its hysterical primitive expression, its political intent, and its meticulous bureaucracy, encouraged an impulsive acting out, the ultimate expression of pent up rage, intense and primitive enough to override all other feelings. Their every day world sanctioned and protected these expressions, reinforced by secondary gains. We think of humans as being humane, of having honest desires to live in a fair organization. However, there is another aspect to man's nature and this is what we observed here. It was the more narcissistic and ruthless self-interest that comes from an earlier, more developmentally primitive psychic structure.

The talks that Willy and I had were like short excursions into a past life from which we looked at the present with horror. The Nazis went beyond all boundaries of civil behavior, unleashing rage as a continuing fuel for their henchmen to do what they were ordered to do, each one adding his individual violence. The SS must have hated us just for being there—as if we were the cause of their losing posture as civilized people; as if we, the victims, were responsible for their loss of humanity, for their losing control.

Willy's wife found better work with the carriers of the soup barrels. As she brought him extra food, he gained his strength back. But the tuberculous lymph glands on his neck were slowly spreading. An open fistulae had to be bandaged daily. In spite of the pathetic situation, we were not ready to give up exchanging our ideas, speculations and hope. I joined him whenever I could get away from the heavy patient load. Willy had time, painfully empty time.

In the hospital, we were highly concerned about the future of the patients, especially those people who had been spared the tragedy of the others of my transport. It was not clear to us whether our patients were just forgotten or survived because of a clash of powers. By April, the general health conditions had deteriorated and many of the older and ill people died.

A new transport from Theresienstadt arrived. There was movement on the ramp of masses of people; trucks were loaded and rattled along the main road. The usual mixture of voices and screams could be heard. We followed the scene with great tension. This transport was not directed to our camp. It appeared, from where we were, that the people and cars moved, as we had so often observed before, directly towards the gas chambers.

Finally, a group of younger people came into our camp. They were in the usual panic and exhausted, and were asking for their families from whom they had been separated by the selection.

The next morning, I went walking along the camp road to see if I could meet any of the other new people, still easily recognizable as they were wearing regular clothing. I saw a man standing on the road. He was wearing a dark overcoat and a city hat. He looked around with an expression and posture of bewilderment. In his outfit and behavior he seemed, to me, the more grotesque. I recognized him as docent Bruno Fischer, one of my teachers in psychiatry at the German University in Prague. He stared at the smoking chimneys. Someone had explained to him that "there go the rest" of his transport. He was shaken by the cruelty of such a remark and could not believe my more softened attempt to prepare him for the terrible truth. I still see him walking next to me shaking his head silently. I realized he was trying to separate reality from insanity. In this new environment he could not yet comprehend that they were fused.

It was not quite a year since I had left and Dr. Fischer could not understand my remoteness; he did not know what to believe. We walked a few steps. He stopped and again pointed to the smoking chimneys asking, "You mean this smoke is from burning the dead, the people who came with me, my people? But they were alive!" Otto and others who had known him in Prague spoke with him. He could not understand how so many reliable people, particularly the doctors and students he had once known, could be caught up in the same crazy story. But then, where were the others who did not come into this camp? He was an experienced psychiatrist and thought he could recognize irrational behavior. He felt lost, confused and frightened. After awhile, I saw tears running down his cheeks. I knew then that he had started to give up his resistance to the unbelievable reality.

The cold days were over, which was an appreciated relief. During the day I could enjoy a few moments of leisure in the sunshine. More transports than ever were arriving at the train station. The mass processions moved toward the buildings at the end of the camp; there hardly ever seemed to be an interruption. Heavy clouds of smoke darkened the air above the chimneys and gave witness to the murderous process on the ground. We smelled the sulfur of burning bones even stronger than we had before. (High power dental drills give off a somewhat similar odor.)

We understood that the Nazis must have started an enforced offensive against the remaining Jews in occupied countries of Europe. This battle was evidently more successful than their fighting on the war fronts. For example, the Germans found a way to include Hungary in their totalitarian control. Prior to this date, Hungarian men were sent to work camps but the Germans were not allowed to deport and kill "their Jews." We were quite sure that the war was steadily moving towards a German defeat but we also realized that this was a very slow process and the Axis leaders had nothing to lose by dragging the battle out to its bitter end. Rumors of retreating German troops in the east were very encouraging but the feverish increase of the destruction of the Jews that took place before our eyes eroded hopes of our rescue.

Some of the detailed information about the events outside the fences of our camp came from the SS corpsman. He still spent time drinking coffee with the nurses in the women's barracks of the hospital and talked nostalgically of his family in Germany, insinuating his concern about our future into his remarks. The women told us that they had the impression that he, and probably others around him, expected some changes in the German leadership. At the same time, the German propaganda implied preparation of a powerful new weapon that would soon turn the fortunes of war in Germany's favor.

We received only one newcomer from the next train, a trained psychiatric technician who had accompanied a group of patients from a psychiatric ward at Theresienstadt. All the patients from that train went into the gas chamber. I heard about the grotesque scenes in the anterooms, which were camouflaged as washrooms in order to encourage people to undress. Some psychotic patients with their total ignorance or indifference toward the situation made the SS officers very uneasy. It must have been a strange encounter of different kinds of craziness.

The camps were surrounded by watchtowers. Spending the prescribed time on the narrow platform on top of the tower was a hated duty for the SS guards. They were exposed to the wind, the rain and the snow. Wrapped in heavy coats, only their eyes were free. At times they screamed obscenities to each other; sometimes they shot into the air. They could order us to stop when we walked by to report where we were going. With the beginning of spring more of their faces became visible.

In the late afternoon on a day early in May, I walked along the camp road with one of my colleagues, Bernie, another of Otto Heller's assistants. The guard on the tower stopped us. He wanted to talk and began to ask us all kinds of questions. He wondered about our outlook. We answered him very carefully telling him that we were unsure about the future of our division of the camp, which was treated so differently from the others. We did not expect any answer from him. He said, "We all have the same chance. When Hitler wins, you will have your own state in Palestine. If he loses, all of you are lost." He seemed pleased with his answer, maybe he was making fun of us but he also may have been giving way to a fear for his own future. Who was he anyway? We only saw a uniform, a blur of a face and heard a voice. He only saw two figures similar to all others that filled the camp. We moved on and he became silent up on his tower. The mood was uneasy for everyone.

16

MASSACRE OF THE HUNGARIAN JEWS

OUR CONTACT from the commando unit, which received new prisoners along with their possessions, reported that trains of deportees from Hungary were arriving almost daily. The Nazis had finally succeeded in taking the persecution of the Hungarian Jews into their own bloody hands and during those terrible weeks of spring and summer of 1944, made it a preferred task.

Some Jews in that part of middle Europe were still living under more reasonable conditions. They arrived tired and frightened, but not as worn out as the families who had been transferred from previous camps and ghettos. As we saw them walking in the distance, we noticed that these people differed in their appearance from the others who had come on earlier transports. Some were farmers, while others wore the black attire of Orthodox Jews. At times we had glimpses of city people from Budapest, the capital, elegantly dressed until they reached the washrooms at the end of the road.

The arrival of these transports had changed the economy of the camps. Some of the clothing, food, cigarettes and, of particular importance to us, medications, medical supplies and instruments entered the black market and even reached us. Most merchandise was absorbed by those special units of prisoners whose function it was to deal with arrivals or by those working close enough to the material to steal things. Anything useful could be exchanged. Some person "starving" for a cigarette would give away a piece of bread, somebody else would sacrifice bread for medicine needed for a child. A lost shoe could become an economic disaster. There was not much space left for charity. Probably the hospital was still the last island of a supportive system that kept us in touch with good feelings, a rare and precious privilege.

Close to the end of April and the beginning of May 1944, the area next to our family camp was occupied again. The barracks housed a crowd of young women, their hair shorn, clad in rags of all kinds and colors. When the day grew warmer they came out searching for sunshine. Their barracks projected a noisy mixture of crying, lamenting, and women calling out names, searching for those they had lost. The language spoken was Hungarian, frequently punctuated by loud commands in German or Polish.

After a couple of days, some of these women, the selected survivors of a recent transport, started to interact with us. We were separated only by the chain fence that was charged with power and was deadly on contact. They had learned that our two blocks were hospital units and hoped for some help with their desperate needs. Many of the young women spoke some German; others were originally from Slovakia and spoke Czech. Much communication was by gesture and facial expression. It was amazing how some of the girls managed to improve their appearance. They covered their bald heads and bartered a little piece of lipstick for whatever they had to offer.

In the afternoon, a few women came close to the fence to talk to us. They had seen our white coats and came for medical help. They needed painkillers, mainly aspirin, for all kinds of debilitating conditions. We threw little packages over the fence. The first lesson they received from us was, "Don't admit to illness or weakness." They still did not know, or could not acknowledge, what had happened to the greater part of their transport, including their families and particularly their parents, younger siblings and children. Every day a few newcomers entered their camp, but they represented just a small percentage of the masses that had been unloaded at the ramp of the train station.

A new and ghostly apparition appeared behind the crematoriums. Open fires were burning; flames and smoke rose high in the air. It took us a few days to receive an explanation. The crematoriums could not keep up with the slaughter of those days. Prisoners were ordered to dig large pits, which were then filled with masses of corpses to extend the number of cremations. The usual craziness, structured by rigid Nazi bureaucratic organization, had given way to this wild chaotic orgy of destruction of human life. The killing machine went into its highest gear. The air was full of smoke and the ominous stink covered the whole camp.

During the second week of our good Samaritan services to our Hungarian neighbors, two women came to the fence. One must have been about my age—in her twenties. We had talked with each other before. Her name was something like Nantschi, maybe Nancy in her language. I liked her. She had quickly understood the enormity of the situation but did not panic. Her beautiful face held deep black eyes. On that particular day, she brought a younger girl with her who followed reluctantly and was crying. Nancy explained that while the women were naked in the shower room an SS guard had pushed this young woman into a corner and raped her. She had never been with a man before. Nancy interpreted the girl's words, which were muffled by her tears. The girl was bleeding and had sharp pains; she was afraid that she might have been injured, maybe infected with a venereal disease or might even be pregnant. I talked to her slowly, using my voice carefully. She did not understand much. Nancy translated. She calmed down. I gave her a painkiller. She was afraid the SS man would come back. I convinced her that he probably would be unable to find her. He remembered her as a frightened crying girl among many others. I said, "Stretch up and make yourself tall and stiff and keep your facial expression as empty as possible in critical encounters." I told her to come back the next day; she thanked me and ran back to her barracks but did not return.

I was still able to have some moments to myself behind the hospital. Spring was in the air in spite of the pollution. Bits of grass were growing on this small strip behind the building. On some days Nancy would come to the other side of the fence and sit on the bare ground and we would smile at each other. The shrillness of the whistle that announced roll call broke through these moments and Nancy would wave and run toward her barracks.

One evening, a whole group of women came close to the fence for advice. A very pretty young girl, not more than sixteen years old, asked for help in what she termed a very important decision. She and her family were farmers from a small country village whose residents had been ordered to assemble one morning at a city quite a distance away. They arrived in time, hungry, tired and still totally unaware of the situation. They had immediately been put into a transport to Auschwitz, survived the selection on arrival and now she and her mother were together in this camp. They had been unprepared, had not had any food during the drawn out ride in a cattle car that had been part of a long, slow train and were both very hungry. Her father and the younger children were separated from them and were sent in another direction. She said all this in a somewhat bashful, flirtatious way that made me think she would ask me for bread. But the decision that she had to make was of a more delicate nature. Hesitantly, and sometimes stuttering, she told me that the night before she had been walking close to the fence looking for anything she could chew. Several times she bent forward to pick up pieces of grass. Suddenly, she heard a voice from high up. It was an SS guard who had apparently been observing her for awhile from his post on a watchtower. He told her how excited he was about her and offered her an exchange of favors. He would be on his tower again in two nights and if she would come close to the tower and turn her naked backside to him he would have a large piece of bread for her. She asked me what to do. She thought that what this terrible man asked of her was outrageous and if she would allow him to see her backside exposed she wondered if she would ever again feel good about herself. But she and her mother were very hungry. Her mother did not know of the incident. I told her to think of that man as not real but a ghost up in the clouds and to leave her decision to the last moment. I also had a small piece of old bread, which I threw over the fence. My hope was that she did not make contact with the guard.

During the spring of 1944, we had our first case of malaria. We had heard that this illness was endemic in the area and were alerted to fight the mosquitoes as much as the body lice, the carrier of typhus. The patient, shaking in a fit of shivers, had come to the hospital shortly before one of Mengele's rounds. We had learned how to cover up the few cases of typhus that we'd had but did not know how to deal with this condition. The SDG arrived before Mengele to prepare all requested information and we asked him hesitantly about the extermination of mosquitoes. He promised some spray and did not ask questions.

Mengele was in a great hurry. He looked harder and more tired. His face showed fine twitches. He asked for new admissions but hardly listened to Otto's report. The new patient whom we suspected of having malaria was presented without any special importance as just another case of high fever, probably pneumonia. Mengele moved on and when near the exit turned to Otto and reminded him to continue the measurements of twins. He also mumbled something about possible transfers of more twin siblings to our camp.

None of the effective medications for the treatment of malaria was available to us. The patient, a young man from Bohemia, had a very concerned wife as well as two little children. She tried very hard through all channels to get the needed medication, but in vain.

Mengele was not the only one who was showing the effects of the increased and unbelievable dimensions of the murderous organization of Birkenau. Never before had so many transports arrived. The noise of masses of people moving toward their annihilation was, at times, beyond the limits of endurance. The atmosphere was explosive. The SS guards were irritable and ready to lash out at anyone at the slightest provocation.

My visits at the fence with Nancy became more regular. The contrast between our tender communication and the permanent massacre around us was excruciatingly painful. One night a nurse on duty woke me at about four in the morning saying that Nancy was trying to get in touch with me. She did not dare get too close to the fence at night; the guards in the towers were always willing to use their weapons. I went out; she was somewhere in the dark and yelled, "We are leaving in the morning." Then she was gone. I prepared a little package to give to her, a piece of bread, an old shirt and some aspirin. I waited at the fence for a few hours but she never came back. We heard later that groups of prisoners were being sent away to work. It was an encouraging change to know that some people left Auschwitz alive, even if very few.

We wanted to train a few men for nursing duty in the hospital but the ones who were aggressive in their interest were mainly out for more bread and an opportunity to get their hands on medications for the black market. The turnover was discouraging. Finally, Willy and I decided to use our old skills. We "organized" some paper and a few pencils and asked the applicants to write a few lines about themselves. Willy Schönfeld and I examined the handwritings for signs of honesty and discipline. From that procedure we were able to get the best medical aids that we had yet chosen. I am sure that this was the only "graphological" selection that ever took place in Auschwitz.

Strict honesty was certainly counterproductive to a struggle for survival, but we found that a basically honest person could be trusted to restrain himself sufficiently within the expectable limits of self preservation and still maintain some decency towards fellow prisoners.

As of the beginning of June, six months had gone by since the arrival of the second family transport. We were afraid of a repetition of March 7, which had wiped out my transport. Then something unusual happened. A distraught and exhausted woman entered our camp. She was a psychiatrist with whom I had had some professional contact in Prague. Her story was sad. Her husband, Richard Friedman, officially called Israel Friedman, had been the liaison in Prague between the leaders of the Jewish community and the SS command that dealt with the persecution of Jews. Friedman had been brought from Vienna to Prague and, for the same function, to Holland when the Germans organized a systematic takeover of Jewish possessions and subsequent deportations. He was later involved in the administration of Theresienstadt. When he had come to Prague, we did not trust him since he was sent by Major Guenter, the SS officer who headed the special department for Jewish Affairs. Later we realized that Friedman was trying to be helpful, at times intervening on behalf of an imprisoned person, especially when emigration was still possible. He had attempted to help Professor Starkenstein, an important scientist who was the former department head of the Pharmacology Institute of the German University, and who had created some very successful medications of that era. The Gestapo found Starkenstein in Holland, where he had moved after his exclusion from the university in Prague. The western world was eager to receive him. We wondered whose personal and particular interest had caused his early death.

When I was in Theresienstadt, I had not heard much about Friedman or his position. He and his wife were here in Auschwitz, officially as a punishment for irregularities in his statistical reports about the census of Theresienstadt.

Along with Friedman and his wife there was another man, Jacob Edelstein, also accompanied by his family. Edelstein had been one of the leading figures of the Jewish community in Czechoslovakia. Before the occupation, he had been the director of the Palestine Office of Prague. He was a hard-working and highly gifted political leader. After the German occupation, he remained in his office, refusing to save himself and his family. I remember a conversation that Willy and I had with him on one of his visits to our institute. He made it clear that his position meant a great deal to him; he appreciated the importance and power of directing emigration to Palestine from the center in Prague and enjoyed the trust and respect he had created for himself in the community. Even high-ranking SS officers respected his courage and would get in touch with him at moments that were critical for members of the Jewish community. He could have left earlier but did not. In this intimate conversation with us, he expressed his fears that he did not think that he would have been considered an important person as an émigré himself in Palestine. Many Jews had missed a last opportunity to leave the country for similar considerations.

Edelstein and Friedman were held responsible for discrepancies in reports about the population of Theresienstadt. The two men were shot. Edelstein was taken from his cell but refused to leave before he finished his prayers. The SS officer who came to lead him to his execution waited silently (Gilbert, 1985, p. 690.) Edelstein had always projected strength and courage and this was so even on his way to death. We heard that Edelstein's wife and son were shot before he was executed. We did not learn why the Edelstein family was treated differently from Friedman's wife.

Our extremely primitive existence could not meet even the most elementary needs that our families had known in our civilized environment and had raised us to expect. We lived in steady deprivation, in hunger, with thirst, crowded, harassed, fatigued, bitten by bugs and frightened of the next day's unknown hardships and, even more, of the deadline that would end the reprieve. There were also finer privations. It is hard to communicate what it means not to read or see any printed material for weeks or months. Even an old piece of newspaper, including advertisements, was avidly read. Books came into the storehouse with the confiscated baggage of newcomers who came directly from a regular home. One of the more imaginative entrepreneurs in our camp acquired a cheap edition of Goethe's *Faust* and sold each page for a heavy slice of bread. We bought a few for the hospital. The danger was in the competing use of any piece of paper in the latrine. We had received a small medical-pharmaceutical handbook through our SDG corpsman and we guarded it carefully in the pharmacy next to the rare and dangerous drugs.

We did not know what more to do with existing twins to keep Mengele's interest in them. Some were children, others were older and could easily fall into the group that was considered unfit for work should the time for another selection occur. We also feared that if no more data could be gained from observing them, that Mengele might be more interested in their autopsies. Again, it was a matter of stretching time, but we never knew whether it might be for saving life or for bringing us closer to our end. Otto, who was always the most worried and pessimistic said, "Is it not reasonable to assume that the days of our whole family camp are numbered?" We knew that he might be right but we were still looking for an out. We all really knew the essence of the continuous rhythm of this transitional community. We were part of a population doomed to be annihilated; the destination was clear, the moment was not. And yet, during quiet nights when we heard the far away sounds of heavy artillery, we still hoped. The front was moving, but very, very slowly.

In the beginning of July 1944, rumors were heard about changes in our camp. It finally became official that those of us who were in fit condition and under the age limit of forty-five would be sent out to work. There was no mention of the fate of the rest. Was this another "Heidebreck," like March 7, a lie to make the transfer to the gas chamber smoother? The suspense grew heavier each day. After the insidious manipulation of the events in March, we did not trust any official information.

The first selection of younger people, men and women separately, took place in the early days of July. It was the opposite of the usual selection, which eliminated the sick, and the weak. We were suspicious that this was a trick to avoid open resistance when the time of liquidation approached. We vacillated between suspicion and hope since we had just seen groups of young Hungarian women in the camp next to ours sent out by train as work slaves. I was frightened for the future of my parents. My mother was quite weak from chronic intestinal disturbances and my father, who was active, was clearly not fit for the heavy work that would be required, although he was not yet sixty. My mother was a few years younger. I had no doubt that they would not pass such a selection and the SS physicians could become violent if they discovered that somebody was trying to pass under false pretenses. Only a few people tried and got away unharmed.

Several SS officers took part in this examination of the younger population of the family camp. Some youngsters who had not yet reached the minimum age, which I assume was fifteen, pretended to be older. They were accepted if they were in good physical condition. We had the impression that the SS men were intense in their dedication to find as many of us as fit as possible to become work slaves for their weakening country. Dr. Fritz Klein was active in the selection. He was friendly and smiling, promising good working conditions for those selected and reassuring that older people and mothers with children who remained would be taken care of. One could not trust him; he was the most insidious of all. But people hungrily ate his words and clung desperately to his promises.

The first groups of men left while their wives and children remained in camp. Both groups wondered if they would ever see each other again. Who would have a chance to survive anyway? Was it really lucky to leave this terrible place? We had always thought so but we did not know what was awaiting us elsewhere. We lost our male nurses from the hospital; they were mostly in that younger age group. Some of the doctors left. We called a few of the older doctors from the blocks to help us in the hospital. Then the first group of women, those without children, left. A few had left their teenage children with friends or relatives pretending to be alone and were accepted into a work group. Most nurses in the women's hospital were gone. Now Otto's wife, Hanka, and their daughter, Suzi, did most of the work in that part of the hospital. Both were kind and hard-working women.

The SDG corpsman brought Mengele's orders that Otto and his "regular" staff were to stay with the hospital. Hans, the self-appointed head of the medical center, had left at the first opportunity to enter a work group even before Mengele's orders reached us. We did not miss him. In March, 1944 it had been life saving for both the patients and the personnel to stay with the hospital. We wondered what it would mean for us now. Would they again save two hundred patients in the hospital when the whole camp was to be liquidated? This would be totally contradictory to the history of this camp, as we had come to know it.

We tried to discharge all younger patients in order to give them a chance to leave with a work group. It was not always an easy decision; the patient was the one who had the last word. We felt that we had to be frank and convey our concern about the end of our camp. When patients, or others who were not able to join a work group, pressured me for

144

encouragement, I said that I did not know anything for sure. Our assumption was that leaving with a work group might be the only way to leave alive.

Underground messages from the camp resistance were confusing. There were hints about preparations for an open revolt by the special commandos working at the crematoriums and gas chambers. They seemed to realize that their own extermination was close. Then we heard through the contact from our camp that they wanted to know whether there would be enough people available for an open fight if they would get weapons for us. They made it clear that there was minimal hope for survival. We were not sure that these messages were reliable, so they were very disturbing to us. Our usual underground connection must have already left with a work group. Bernie, Otto and I, the last three physicians remaining in the hospital, debated the situation. I wondered whether the rumors were spread by the SS to provoke the underground network into open action to catch them. Otto thought that the so-called "work transports" might serve to remove younger people from our camp to avoid any resistance before liquidation. Finally, we concluded that the SS had spent so much time in selecting the men and women fit for strenuous work that we could only believe that such effort must be in their own interest of collecting slaves.

On a hot Sunday afternoon in the second week of July 1944, the head of our camp informed us that a last selection of prisoners would take place in the next few days. Otto, Bernie and I went from bed to bed to see whether we could discharge any more patients who might have a prospect of leaving camp. There was still our first, and only, case of malaria. The patient and I had become friends during the weeks he had been hospitalized. I also liked his young wife and their two pre-teen children, who often came to visit him. We convinced him to leave the hospital and supplied him with all the quinine that we had. He met with his family for the last time before he was ready to report for his examination. He passed and left the next day.

17

MOTHERS WITH CHILDREN

THE FOLLOWING NIGHT, the order came that all mothers with children had to line up in the morning for a transport to a special camp. The age limit for children was about fifteen, though nobody stated it exactly. In our family camp, mothers and children had been treated somewhat better than the rest of the people there. The SS doctor, Fritz Klein, and even Mengele had, at times, expressed interest in their well-being. Such behavior was in great contrast to the usual fate of children, who, as a rule, were doomed to die on their arrival at Auschwitz. We sensed that a critical decision was imminent. This was gruesome news. Knowing the merciless politics of power over us, we feared the worst.

The night was very warm when I met with a young woman, Sonia, of whom I had become very fond. Her husband had died of pneumonia in the beginning of the winter and I had helped her and her daughter whenever I could. She knew that she would have to follow this order and leave the next day with her child. The atmosphere of the night was unreal. There was great tension in the camp, everybody was irritable and the anxiety was nearly unbearable. Women with children came to the hospital for information. They tried to reassure each other and spread stories about better care for children awaiting them in the new camp. We expected the worst and did not want to say anything to destroy the last hope. Finally the KAPOs, yelling and cursing, ordered everyone to their barracks. I wondered if anyone slept that night.

My friend Sonia stayed with her child until she was asleep. The children sensed another impending change but trusted their mothers to take care of them. Later Sonia knocked on the wall of the hospital corner where we few remaining staff members sat, unable to sleep. I sneaked out. We found a spot outside the wall of the latrine, protected from the view of the guard at the next tower. It was our first and last intimate encounter.

146

Early in the morning, while sleeping fully dressed on my bed, the shrill whistles of the KAPOs awakened me. All women with children were called to form a line. Most women were young and the children, half-asleep, held hands with their mothers or older siblings. Some chewed on a piece of bread. An unusual number of SS guards were present, rushing in whenever a father or friend tried to have a last contact with one of the women or children.

Then one of the SS officers sent a KAPO forward with a message that spread through the long line of the few hundred women and children. The physically able women were encouraged to give their children into the care of neighbors in line and step out to join work groups. I recall my thoughts, "What a devilish temptation!" It cancelled any remaining hope of mothers being transferred to another camp with their children. It was not clear how official or reliable the offer was, but it was repeated with great emphasis. Perhaps it was the personal initiative of this officer. Somebody screamed a message to a friend who was standing with a little boy in formation, "For God's sake save your life, leave the child." The woman looked at him with great eyes. She seemed to have no concept of living except that of being with her child.

I stood in front of the hospital. These were moments of painful suspense. A couple of women handed their young children to the next in line and ran back to their barracks. Sonia was standing in the group with her little girl holding on to her with one hand, while with the other she waved a goodbye. There was a beautiful smile on her face when our eyes met. Then the column moved forward, walking slowly. Some children could not walk fast. It was the first time that I saw the SS guards patiently adjusting their step. It looked like a funeral procession. The children trusted their mothers and went along. It was their own funeral.

18

END OF OUR CZECH FAMILY CAMP

THE REMAINING POPULATION of five to six thousand people, those above forty or those not yet accepted for a work group, were overwhelmed with fear. Many lay motionless on their beds. The younger and more mobile men of the hospital were gone and we filled our beds with new patients, who felt abandoned in their barracks after their doctors and house elders had left. In some barracks, there was chaos with the strongest reigning over the more helpless; I would not have dared to enter those barracks alone. The order of our world, as unfair and cruel as it had been before, had broken down.

The elder of the camp called for a final selection based on Mengele's order that all those from age sixteen to forty-five appear. We watched the last examinations. An SS officer, whom I had never seen before and did not think was a physician, presided. He was highly impatient and hit people with his truncheon when they tried to join the selection if either their age or physical condition were not appropriate. This all took place inside a now empty barracks but the gates were left open, guarded by a couple of KAPOs.

I discussed the situation with my father as we walked slowly toward the gate to watch the procedure. He shook his head; he knew that he would not pass as fit for heavy work. I wondered if I should try to smuggle him into a group of selected workers or whether it was even possible. It would give him a slim chance to leave this doomed sector of the camp. He refused; he was afraid of endangering me and really his only wish was to stay with my mother to the last moment. He wondered why I wasn't trying to get out. I could have passed this last selection but Mengele could be extremely cruel if his orders were not obeyed and Otto, who was well-known and visible, had been told to remain with his regular staff. Bernie and I were the last two of the regular staff.

The food supply in the camp had been irregular and people were fighting, ready to kill, for their poor rations, although most were too weak to do anything. At least the hospital had enough bread and we could protect those who found shelter there.

After sunset, I met with Willy Schönfeld. We found a cool spot in the shadow of the hospital building, sat down on the dusty ground and talked straight with each other. We knew what was happening and agreed to avoid the usual well-meaning rejections of reality. We had no time to talk of miracles, last moment changes, the sudden end of the war or any of the other soothing expressions of hope we had told each other during our most desperate moments.

Willy had no chance to appear before the selecting physicians. On one side of his neck there was a large package of tuberculous lymph glands protruding and visibly swollen. He was weakened by illness and his movements were slow. This tall man with the large head looked awkward. He wondered why I had not left. It certainly was not clear to me what had moved me to stay at that critical time. Did I not want to leave my parents, Otto, Willy, the hospital? These might all have been factors in my decision. Looking back over that fateful week, I think that I was still following orders, afraid of the consequences if I'd been caught, although it was unlikely that anyone would have cared if I'd appeared at a selection of workers. I told Willy that I felt that I did best when I went with the tide and he seemed to understand me. We were both sure that the end of the family camp was close. We talked about our past work, our hidden manuscripts on graphology, our common interest in the psychological importance of work as well as the pathogenic effects of an unsuitable work situation on one's identity. We discussed the role of work-ideal and how people in various phases of their life idealized certain kinds of work in their fantasies.

Here we were at the bottom of human existence, where the value of people and the only justification for their being allowed to live was measured by their potential for hard labor, yet we still spoke about ideas that could enhance life in a future that we could not expect. We rose and Willy held my hand and said goodbye. His last words were, "If one of us survives and should return to a normal life, he should use all of the hidden materials, tests, and manuscripts to continue our work."

The last small group of workers left the next morning. The rest of the camp was obviously considered worthless for further exploitation. Otto, Bernie and I made rounds in the hospital. When dispositions and orders for the next day were to be made, we did it with the gruesome doubt whether there would be a next day for any of us—patients or doctors.

During rounds, we observed a commotion at the entrance of our camp. To our surprise, kettles of soup were carried in earlier than usual. This was a good sign. Did it mean that another day was to be allowed for this camp? Throughout the camp there was no one who really knew who had given the order for this. Perhaps it was the last help that the underground could provide or a charitable gesture by someone in charge. It was a mystery.

My parents, Willy, Otto, Bernie and I ate this meal together. Somebody, squeezing out the last drop of humor, said, "Is it not grotesque to think that we could be happy if only somebody would promise us such a mug of miserable dark soup every day until the end of the war?"

Early in the afternoon, an SS guard on a bicycle came down the camp road towards the hospital. He called to Otto Heller and conveyed his orders. Otto told us that we were supposedly being transferred to another sector of the camp. Otto's wife and daughter, still in their nurse's uniforms, were to be separately transferred to the women's camp. Our guard was in a hurry and we were rushed to follow him. His face gave away no clue. My father, Willy, a few aids and patients stood in front of the hospital and stared at the scene. A last embrace. Somebody said, "Do not forget us."

The guard said that we were going to the central hospital, which was situated next to the crematoriums and gas chambers close to the hill of birches that gave Birkenau its name. We had been lied to so often that we were not about to trust him. The pale faces of those who remained watched our departure until we reached the gate. I looked back. There was the hospital barracks at the far end of the road and in front were the small figures of the most important people of my life, frozen in the same postures as we had left them.

We were on the road outside of our camp on which we had observed countless columns of people dragging along. Our walking seemed endless; we passed three other sections of this gigantic establishment, all crowded with desperate people. The last one was the Gypsy family camp. The closer we came to the edge of the camp, the heavier our legs felt. Our knees were shaking when we reached the last gate. Beyond this was a short road to the real saunas, to which we had once been sent for cleaning. Then came the false washrooms, the anterooms to the gas chambers. My pulse was fast and booming in my ears. This was the longest walk I had taken in a long time. I felt faint and wished that our route, wherever it was leading, would come to an end. We did not dare talk with each other; we only exchanged fearful glances. Otto, who was the oldest, had obvious difficulties keeping up with us on the last stretch. Our guide got off his bike and made a sharp turn towards the last gate, which was the gate of the main hospital.

19

CENTRAL HOSPITAL CAMP

AT THE GATE, our escort reported our arrival to the guard and we all went into the administration office at the camp entrance. The entry in the Archives reads:

> *The doctors and twins are transferred again . . . in July 1944, to the prisoners' infirmary for men in Camp B-IIf. Among them are the twins . . . and the physicians Dr. Heller (No. 146703), Dr. Bloch (146737), Dr. Julius Samek (No. 147636), and Dr. Pollak (No. 148775).*
>
> (Czech, 1990, p. 594)

The office was in the small barracks in which this lager's (camp's) elder Dr. Senkteller lived; he appeared to be unfriendly, his look bored into you as if he could discover something. We reported by our numbers, he wanted our names. After he left, a prisoner who worked in the office welcomed us. He told us that Dr. Senkteller, a non-Jewish former Polish military physician, had been a prisoner for a long time and tried to have good relations with the SS physicians. Senkteller was said to be dangerous, powerful and hated by everybody except his few friends, who were also former Polish officers.

I was numb and confused and perceived only a part of what I heard. I began to realize that we had received another grace period. I recall these first moments in this new camp in the same way that one remembers a significant dream. I was physically, as well as emotionally, exhausted and my new surroundings appeared unreal. There were prisoners dressed in better uniforms moving around. They seemed to belong to another world than the one from which we had just come. We were sent to a barracks that was also much more comfortable than what we had known in our camp. It was well equipped with real beds, medical appliances and even some furniture. It also had real windows. Everything was clean and orderly.

I was assigned to a surgical department and was told that the patients were there for minor surgery and that the operating rooms for patients in need of major surgery were in the next block. The surgeon, Dr. Goldstein, was a young, pleasant person who had grown up in Poland but had gone to study in France, where he was working when the Germans occupied that country. He told me that the first Jews to be deported from France were foreign citizens, an old trick used by the Gestapo to keep the local Jewish community calm and avoid resistance by the non-Jewish population. Until now he was the only Jew in this building and worked with the clerk who had administrative control, a former Polish officer who had been a teacher in civilian life.

There were no Jews among the patients. Most were Russians; some were Poles. The majority were not regular prisoners of war but political prisoners, either partisans or captured members of the underground resistance. Some of the Poles received packages from their families and gave away or sold parts of their rations, which improved the food situation. A great number of the patients suffered from tuberculous inflammations of the cervical lymph glands. There was not much treatment for them except keeping open wounds clean in order to avoid secondary infections and support drainage. The SS physician in charge, Dr. Koenig, was interested in having this collection of patients accessible for a study he hoped to publish. I assumed he wanted us to do the daily work.

The physician and the administrator in charge had their beds in a separate corner of the barracks, while the rest of the personnel slept and ate in a different building. The soup that we were given later in the afternoon was better than that of our former camp but my throat was closed. The others in our barracks, physicians, nurses, aids and the rest of the staff looked at us with great curiosity. Nobody knew why we had been transferred into this camp. They probably did not understand our confused descriptions of the last hours in the Czech family camp culminating in the sudden order we received to walk out. After awhile they understood our nagging fears about the ones we left behind.

153

The summer evening was warm on July 12, 1944, as we slowly returned to our barracks for our first night. Otto was depressed and concerned about the fate of his wife and daughter. Until now they had not been separated. Supposedly they had been transferred as nurses to the hospital of the women's camp. I was preoccupied with the fate of my parents and Willy. I had little hope for anyone who remained in the family camp. I imagined that they too were concerned about me the moment I was escorted out of the camp. Such special attention often had ominous meaning.

Night came quickly in that area. We climbed into our bunks; Otto was next to me. We lay quietly for what seemed a long time, tortured by worries about the ones from whom we were separated. Neither of us expected to fall asleep easily. The light was turned off and it became very quiet in the building.

It must have been between ten and eleven o'clock when we heard the notorious clatter of the heavy trucks cutting through the silence of the night. It started from far away and as it came nearer, it was close enough for us to hear human voices and screams. That terrible mixture of noises was over swiftly and then the next convoy approached. This time the voices were louder and clearer. I knew that this was the death ride of my parents. It was the end of Willy Schönfeld, my patients and hundreds of other people, the final end of the Czech family camp, which had mysteriously started at the time of my arrival in Auschwitz in September 1943. The rattle of the trucks was our last connection. I was sobbing; Otto extended his arm and held my hand silently. It was a long, desperate night.

In the morning, I was able to see how close we were to the crematoriums; the hospital complex was the last sector in a row of six camps, the most exposed to the revolting smell of burning flesh and bone.

Life in this new camp was quite different from what we had known. In the morning I was half dazed from the gruesome night and although I received a fresh, clean white uniform, I was far from being ready to start my new duties. I dragged myself to the hospital building. Dr. Goldstein, who was sensitive enough to understand that I was in bad shape, shook hands without much talk and sent me to check the pulses and temperatures of patients in preparation for morning rounds.

I had to learn to communicate with people who spoke languages foreign to me. A few Czech words were similar in Polish and Russian; some patients helped by interpreting. The charts were written in German by the administrator of the barracks—in camp jargon he was called "the scribe"—the high school teacher who had taught German and Polish. Dr. Goldstein thought that I would be asked to take over this task.

After a short time Dr. Zenkteller, the camp leader, entered the building and inspected the ward with an intimidating look. He did not answer our greetings nor consider us worthy to talk to. The only person he acknowledged was the Polish clerk. They exchanged some words and Dr. Zenkteller left at a fast military clip. The clerk announced that Dr. Koenig, the SS physician, had arrived. By this time all beds were straightened, patients cleaned, and their possessions hidden. Most patients could take care of themselves; only a few with high fevers had to be nursed.

The door was opened wide and Dr. Koenig entered followed by Dr. Zenkteller. After the military reporting, the SS physician walked slowly through the room. At times he would pick up a day sheet and remark on the vacillation of a fever curve of a tuberculous patient. He asked if there was any surgical procedure scheduled and seemed disappointed that none was planned. He stopped close to the door, ready to leave, and pointed to me, interrupting his conversation with Zenkteller, "He will be in charge of this barracks," turned around and left behind a group of stunned men standing at attention.

Dr. Goldstein became pale. I understood his fears. Did they want to remove him? I turned to him and whispered, "We need to talk," and left the building. Koenig was just coming out of the hospital barracks in which Otto worked and I quickly entered and told him what happened. Otto was bewildered by the fast changes. He stared into empty space and I had to repeat my story to get his attention. He shook his head; the recent events were overwhelming. In the family camp he'd had enormous responsibility that had kept him alert at all times. Now he felt tired and slipped into passivity. He smiled at me and said, "Just go along."

I returned to my ward and asked Dr. Goldstein to accompany me outside for a short talk. I told him that I had very little experience in surgery and knew that he had been quite competent. I remember our conversation as if it took place yesterday. He started to speak in an angry

155

tone. I interrupted him immediately with a forceful gesture. I told him that I wished he would keep all privileges, mainly sleeping and eating in the hospital and that I would respect his professional position. I said, "I have no ambition to make a career in Auschwitz, my only desire is to survive if that is possible."

Dr. Goldstein's usual hard expression melted for a moment. He told me a bit about his desperate maneuvers to stay alive during the long years he spent in this camp; he was one of a few survivors of his transport. The Polish functionaries who controlled the medical center made life difficult for the few Jewish physicians. Both Dr. Goldstein and his colleague and friend Jo, who was the primary surgeon on the ward, were both well-trained and the SS physicians liked to operate while Dr. Goldstein and Jo supervised. Dr. Koenig seemed to be particularly interested in his own surgical training.

We speculated about the reason for his sudden decision to change the situation. Perhaps he thought that I was a skilled surgeon who could bring new techniques to the department. The SS physician-student of the two Jewish surgeons might have wanted to make an impulsive gesture in order to show his power. We also considered that Mengele, his superior, might have given him some direction. Perhaps he had really intended to speak to Otto and not to me.

We never knew the reason for Dr. Koenig's orders. The next day when he made his daily visit and I tried to report the medical status of the ward he interrupted me impatiently and said, "I know that." He called Dr. Goldstein to give the required accounting of the number of living and deceased. I assumed that the old order was reestablished. The intermezzo with Dr. Goldstein held more importance for me several months later and may have been instrumental in my being rescued during another crisis.

Life fell into a routine again. Living conditions were certainly much better. We had enough bread and the soup had more content. I grew closer to my patients in spite of the language difficulties. The Russian prisoners were very careful, often suspicious in their communications. In each barracks there was a leader who acted as liaison to the leaders in other buildings. The Russian prisoners were highly disciplined and resistant to any orders they received unless they had been approved by their own leadership.

The treatment of tuberculous lymph nodes was a tedious job. When the infection broke through the skin, the drainage had to be supported. The fever of these patients was intermittent and frequently recurred after a substantial improvement. No one knew where the greater danger lay for these patients, their illness growing worse or maintaining them in the hospital. Auschwitz had never given chronically ill or fragile prisoners a substantial period of grace. The direction was clear from the "mercy killing" of the disabled by deadly injections to the mass executions of weakened prisoners in the gas chamber. Too early a return of a patient to his work unit, usually to hard work, might mean a new exacerbation of the creeping illness. To keep a patient too long on the ward might make him vulnerable if a selection were to take place for eliminating "useless" inmates. The only hope for the protection of these patients was Dr. Koenig's interest in them.

In the middle of July 1944, the underground news we received contained hints of an attempt to assassinate Hitler. The story spread faster than one could talk. Tension hung over the camp like a bomb ready to explode. Who would be held responsible? How many of us would be killed at once for retribution as had happened in Lidice with the assault and death of Reinhard Heydrich in Prague? At the same time, there were wishes for the fall of the regime.

It was very quiet at the train terminal and the chimneys were not smoking. The suspense was enormous. Then Mengele arrived in his jeep. He was not accompanied by his adjunct. The encounter of that day remains unforgettable. Mengele's posture was changed. His head and shoulders, which were usually held arrogantly upright and straight, hung slightly forward. His voice was softer than ever before. He appeared absent-minded and although he asked the usual questions he missed the answers. He politely turned to Otto and asked him to repeat his report. He collected the charts of the twins that Otto had saved. Whatever was going on in the world outside the electric fences seemed to have shaken him. I did not see him again.

Toward the end of July 1944, we were requested to prepare two beds in the barracks for two adolescent boys who were transferred from the Gypsy family camp. My old teacher, Professor Epstein, the head of the medical service in that camp, had diagnosed tuberculosis of the lungs in both patients. They also suffered from specific pleuritis and needed to be relieved of the pressure of the effusion that accumulated in the pleural cavity. Continuous drainage allowed them to breathe better. Their general health improved and they grew cheerful enough to talk, which they did freely. Every morning while I changed their bandages, they told me bits of their life.

Both boys had grown up in a small German city. They were seniors in a humanistic high school when the war interrupted their education; they spoke German without any other accent. They, in fact, thought that they were German until the sudden persecution and deportation of their families in the spring of 1943. One had a brother who was a German army officer. They were well-educated, extremely polite and grateful for the help that they received in the hospital.

In August 1944, the underground reported that the Gypsy family camp would be liquidated.* The arrival of the feared trucks to transport the members of the Gypsy camp to the gas chambers caused a chaotic turmoil. Their sector was next to the central hospital camp and I observed the pandemonium. Although I can recall that it was terrible, I have no recollection of the scene. There is a rare blank in my memory of that night. The desperate scene must have been unbearably similar to what I had imagined had happened in our Czech family camp after I had left.

We were very concerned about our two Gypsy patients. The next morning an ambulance arrived in front of our hospital. Two SS guards entered the room and ordered us to prepare the two youngsters for transfer to another place. We had to discontinue the draining procedure. Under the steady urging of the two stone faced intruders for us to hurry, I bandaged their oozing puncture wounds. They were put onto stretchers. The boys waved goodbye while they were carried out to the car. It was very quiet on the ward. Only one young patient, who lay next to the now-empty beds, sobbed, his whole body shaking with fever and agitation. I felt faint. I felt that I had reached a saturation point.

The chimneys smoked heavily from the massacre that took place during the night. We had listened to the ambulance stop along the way and heard a shrill scream, a woman's voice, filling the air for a few seconds. Then the ambulance proceeded, driving fast to the exit where it turned left to the gas chambers and crematorium.

* Filip Müller wrote that about three thousand inmates were left in that sector of the camp at the time of its liquidation. (Müller, 1981, p. 149)

Later, we were told of the drama behind this scene. The Queen of the Gypsies, an exquisite beauty who had allegedly been the love of a prominent person, probably a prisoner, had been saved from the mass killing the day before; she had been hidden with the hope of being exempt from the fate of the others. When she saw the ambulance waiting for her, she knew that it was her end. The sound of her voice piercing the air echoed in my mind for years.

I understood that I had reached a dangerous mental condition. Old prisoners had talked about what I now experienced. "You die a bit with every death around you," they had said, "the futility and senselessness of our existence becomes intolerable and you feel the diminishing of your will to survive." I became obsessed with the question of whether I could have done something to help my parents. Would I have given them a handful of sleeping pills if I had possessed them? My father had asked for them.

Willy Schönfeld wanted to survive until the last moment. This had also been my attitude. I remember saying to Willy on the last day I saw him, "I won't believe I am dead before I see it." Willy and I had exchanged the strangest sarcastic wisecracks. It was as if our ignoring the seriousness of the reality might make it go away. "It cannot be true" was repeated with the power of a prayer. It did not help any more than the prayers of our religious friends.

Since I had left our little hospital in which, for a period of a year, we had so desperately tried to save a few lives, I had lost my last bit of feeling of belonging, a strange word to use in such an environment. I felt displaced in the new situation in spite of the better living conditions. I felt as if I had been transferred to a foreign country. Only the chimneys were the same, but now they were much closer. Life felt unreal. There were moments when I felt disoriented and feared losing my sanity. I had a great desire to sleep but spent many hours awake staring into the darkness. To be dead became a tempting fantasy. That thought was a peaceful one for me, but I was haunted by the terrible process of killing and the dehumanizing abuse that all the defenseless victims had to endure before dying. The murder of the two young patients and the wiping out of the neighboring Gypsy camp had shaken my last protective apathy; an excruciating feeling of emptiness replaced it.

The next weeks melted together into a monotonous routine. My friends from the family camp were my only contact with the past. Otto was not with us much. When he was not occupied with patients, he wanted to be alone, involved in his own thoughts while he smoked cigarettes if he could get them. He feverishly awaited a message from his wife and daughter in the women's camp until he finally heard that they too had left with work units. Bernie, who was about my age, seemed to be in better emotional condition. We tried to take our daily walk in the limited space available to us. In our professional functions, we appeared as if we had the strength to take care of others but were highly preoccupied with our losses and waiting for our own unpredictable situation to unfold. Our greatest pretense was that of providing an atmosphere of constancy for patients, which we really did not feel during these last events. There was nothing more important for our patients than knowing that we would be there for them on the following day. That, of course, would have been the most important assurance for us too.

Bernie and I talked a lot on our short walks; we became quite close and open with each other. During September 1944, life went on in the same rhythm. We both tried very hard to bring Otto out of his withdrawn state. Sometimes he would say a few words about his longing for his family. I realized then, more than I had ever realized before, how much one needed the closeness of another person in order to survive the lack of a nurturing environment. I also learned to listen, to acknowledge my interest but not reveal my thoughts and experiences too freely. I was not always able to do this.

One day a new SDG medical aid wearing the uniform of an SS sergeant arrived in the hospital camp. He was about forty. Something about him was different from his colleagues. His posture, demeanor and language distinguished him from the others. I talked about this man with a veteran prisoner, a very friendly gynecologist from Athens who worked as a surgeon on the next block. He shrugged his shoulders and mumbled, "Probably a Gestapo agent sent to ferret out our underground connections." The SS aide had been in our camp for a week or two without anything unusual happening. I saw him walking from barracks to barracks, talking with personnel, sometimes with patients, but rarely was he in the company of any other SS man. In what was described to me as a friendly conversation, he told one of our prisoner-physicians that he had been part of a medical team working on the Russian front, where he had been wounded. He had been sent for several months to a hospital, recovered, was discharged from his combat unit and was told he would be transferred to a quiet hospital in Poland. The address was Auschwitz.

On an afternoon in September when all work was finished and I had already gobbled down my daily soup and bread along with a small piece of margarine, I was stretched out behind my quarters to catch the last rays of the setting autumn sun. The newly arrived SS sergeant turned the corner and looking distraught, saying that he wanted to talk to me. I stood at attention and he motioned me to walk with him. He asked me on which front I had been captured since he wondered about my pure German accent. I told him where I came from and he shook his head in disbelief.

With an anxious expression he pointed to the smoking chimneys. Two days earlier a transport had arrived presumably from France since French cigarettes appeared in the camp. He said that he had heard rumors about people being gassed. I lost all my caution and told him that my parents had been killed in this way. He paled and turned away, repeating many times, "I can't believe it."

I never saw him again, but that evening I was very nervous knowing that I had been extremely careless. I talked with Otto and the rest of my friends. When Otto heard my story, his worried expression of concern for me was the first sign of interest that I had seen since the massacre of our family camp. Seeing me in possible danger broke through his depressing apathy. In fact, nothing happened as a result of my heedlessness. Somebody asked a clerk in the central office what had happened to the new SDG, but a shrug of the shoulders was the only reply.

The days went on as my second year in Auschwitz began. There were longer intervals between transports. When I had a chance to get cigarettes I smoked them whereas before I had exchanged them for bread. Now I had nobody to care for. At times this was a relief; my life was only mine and nobody depended on me.

The first days of October were quiet. The morning fog and the cold nights reminded me of the suffering of the last winter with the endless roll calls and freezing nights. I exchanged some cigarettes for a warmer jacket. The bread had become very bad. I remembered something my father had said. In his last days my father would smile when everybody complained

161

about the rough indigestible bread; he would comfort us by saying, "This is a sign that the war is coming to an end." He said that he had experienced the same signs in the declining morale of the soldiers in the Austrian army in World War I when the food grew poor and the bread rotten.

Occasionally, some dry biscuits came on the market, taken from newcomers from the western countries. Someone sarcastically commented, "When the Nazis take England then the English Jews will finally bring with them the food we have been waiting for." The English government, however, did not accept the reality of an Auschwitz, despite evidence on the aerial maps, intelligence reports, etc. They came at night. We heard their bombers and the sounds of explosions. They must have hit the chemical factories not far from the Auschwitz-Buna camp barracks where prisoners used for hard labor were kept.

My Russian patients started to trust me and informed me of changes in the battle zones. Their news was somewhat different from the reports we received, which were rumored to be English broadcasts, but they matched in the prediction of the pending fall of the German military power. I could never fathom where their radio was hidden.

In quiet sleepless nights I could hear the thunder of the heavy artillery, which seemed to come closer and then would fade again, along with my hopes. Our connections with those inmates of the camp whose work involved contact with the central office gave us access to rumors of the weakening resources in manpower and materials that would certainly influence our future. As a result of the military situation, the annihilation of Jews and others was postponed in order to recruit the strongest of them as work slaves, "new merchandise"—their term for work prisoners selected for export.

20

REBELLION AT THE CREMATORIUM

EARLY IN OCTOBER 1944, the regular routine was suddenly interrupted by sirens. We could not see any attacking airplanes but we were alarmed by an open blaze spreading from one of those ominous buildings just outside the camp. During the next minutes there was the rattle of automatic weapons followed by more gunshots. We also heard the noise of motorcycles and other military vehicles. The dust of the speeding motorcade hung like a cloud over the road. Soon it was quiet again. The flames died down after a few hours. There was activity in the neighboring camp. A group of men passed the gate. When they came closer, we saw a tragic scene. In the middle of the column was a group of prisoners— strong young men with their heads held high as they looked forward with defiant expressions. They were in pairs, locked to each other with heavy iron chains and flanked on both sides by SS men, guns at the ready, fingers on triggers.

We had heard rumors that the special units (*Sonderkommando*), prisoners who worked in the crematoriums, were preparing to break out. They had witnessed so much that they did not expect to leave this camp alive. They must have received some alarming information and made their desperate attempt by setting one of the crematoriums on fire. This happened, according to Herman Langbein, on October 7, 1944 (1972, p. 232).

Hanna

21

MY SISTER ARRIVES

NEW TRANSPORTS were arriving from Theresienstadt, and I was worried about my sister. She had gone for safety to Holland, where she had married, and I knew that she had been in camp Westerbork and from there was taken to Theresienstadt. Her father-in-law, Dr. Benjamin, was a pediatrician in the Gypsy camp here. I had not known him before this time and cannot remember how we ever started to talk to each other over the fence. Somehow we discovered that the man my sister Hanna had married was his son, Carl. He was worried about Carl, who he thought would probably arrive in Auschwitz and he felt helpless at not being able to inform him of the dangers in showing any signs of being weak or sick.

The expected transport arrived in the second week of October. It was to Jo, the Czech Jewish chief surgeon of the next hospital barracks, that I turned for help in looking for my sister. I knew that Jo had some secret way of visiting his wife, a veteran prisoner in a privileged position in the women's camp. If Hanna were to pass the selection she would enter the camp. Of course it was nearly unbearable to think of the alternative. On October 15, my birthday, he once again succeeded in going on his dangerous expedition. When Jo returned a few hours later, he had a note from a woman who had responded to his calling of my sister's name. I recognized her handwriting. The wrinkled little piece of paper, which he had hidden on himself, was a most significant birthday note. After wishing me a happy birthday, Hanna's note asked for advice. She said she was pregnant and that she had succeeded in hiding her condition so far but could not do so much longer. Jo told me that pregnancy in the women's camp meant death. There was no time to lose. He alerted his wife through their secret connection and the camp doctor performed an abortion. I "organized" an old sweater and slacks, collected some bread and waited for an opportunity to get to the sector next to her camp. The only way to do this was to go with the wagon, pushed by prisoners, used for transporting dirty linen and clothes to the laundry. This vehicle had been used before for intra-camp communication and the black market used it for exchange of goods. Most of the time the guards would not interfere, (they probably got their payment in liquor). When the day came, I changed my doctor's coat for the regular striped uniform. I borrowed a good "hand-tailored" one from an orderly to be better dressed. While hardly of consequence by conventional standards such a status symbol was an indication of influence in the camp. The greatest danger in the scheme lay in being caught by the political department, the counterespionage branch of the SS, which was part of the Gestapo. I had heard people say, "In their hands you would wish for the merciful gas chamber."

It was still early in the morning when I heard the squeaking wooden wheels of the wagon long before it reached the hospital. I had heard this noise before but had never given it any importance. The old vehicle, which in its good days was drawn by horses and used to haul hay at harvest time, was now drawn by prisoners. Its horses had probably been first used in combat and then eaten when their strength gave out.

While they loaded linen, Jo informed the leader of my mission. He looked suspiciously at me, I could endanger them all if I was not careful, but apparently he did not want to refuse Jo's request. The journey started uneventfully. We passed the exit gate the guards hardly looked at us. We moved very slowly along the dusty unpaved road, the same road I had many times seen covered with long lines of the damned being pushed towards their unexpected end. Our load was heavy and we feared that the worn out wheels might break down at any moment.

We made a slight detour to get me closer to the camp where my sister was supposed to be. From there, they told me to go on by myself and that they would pick me up in a short time on their way back. They did not want to be caught in a place where they had no business. I crawled as close as I could to the fence of the women's camp. Clinging to my package, I tried to make contact with somebody on the other side of the fence.

A young woman came close enough to hear my voice. When I told her my story, a fine trace of a smile interrupted her hard, lifeless facial expression. She gestured for me to wait and left. I waited endless moments, making myself as inconspicuous as possible. The area was completely flat and the cold October wind caught me unprotected. There was great activity in the camp; many women, all looking alike from the distance, were assembled in front of the barracks. I saw them slowly leaving the camp in the direction of the gate.

It was a hazy morning and everything before me looked ghostly, unreal. To my surprise the woman returned to the fence to look for me. I had been hiding on the ground and got up slightly weak in the knees while holding on to the fence, one of the few that I knew of that was not charged with power. The woman looked around carefully as she walked towards me. My mind raced with thoughts of every conceivable message she might convey to me. Finally, she reached me and said that my sister had left in one of the groups being sent out of the camp; she pointed to the long lines of women passing the gate. I offered her my package, she came closer, and there was a trace of an expression of joy on her face. I unpacked a piece of bread for myself and threw the rest over the fence.

I saw the laundry cart approaching and ran toward it to melt back into the group so that I could get home and climb back into my shell. I returned to the hospital disappointed and tired. The wide empty space around the camp was intimidating, an illusion of free space but full of hidden dangers, not freedom. I felt secure only when the gate of the hospital camp closed behind us signaling our return to the safety of daily routine.

A few days later some new patients arrived, Russian soldiers who had been captured behind the German lines. They were badly wounded but the political department was very interested in getting more information from them when they would recover. The soldiers pretended to be unresponsive; they communicated with their comrades on the ward. We heard that the eastern front was coming closer and that partisans were in the mountains behind the demarcation lines making the retreat of the German army more difficult.

The Germans had gone through ferocious fighting with the Russian army but had to make a slow, constant retreat. After a few days the Russians patients became more comfortable and appreciated our care as well as the concern of the other Russian prisoners. One of the new prisoners talked about some German soldiers in retreat behaving as if they were ready to die, seeming to accept defeat but not allowing themselves to be taken prisoner; they kept fighting senselessly to the death. Others asked to be taken prisoner and then collapsed into total passivity. All they wanted was to stop fighting.

22

END OF AN INTERMINABLE EPOCH

THERE WAS INCREASING restlessness in the camp. The underground was preparing for some last-minute defense against the SS should the Russian army come closer and the camp be liquidated by the Germans. Transports still arrived, selections took place, the "useless" were killed, but it seemed that there were more groups of those fit for work being transported to Germany.

The hospital administration received an order in the last week of October 1944 to prepare a certain number of physicians to leave with a transport of men. I was among the younger ones and found myself next on the list to the senior internist in the camp. This man originally came from Berlin; his name was Fritz Crohn. He had been in charge of one of the hospital barracks and was respected for his knowledge and experience. Now he was among the first to be leaving.

We suspected that this was the beginning of the pending liquidation. We had also seen too much and might have to be removed. I had heard how groups of prisoners who had worked at the crematoriums had been sent away only to be killed on arrival at a different place. It was expected that the SS would want to erase all traces of their activities before leaving the area. We waited for news from the underground. So far they knew only that a large transport of male prisoners would leave for the west. Otto Heller was not on the list. The choices were arbitrary. Otto encouraged me. "Be happy to get out of this place, nothing could be worse." We all believed that the whole maneuver could be one of their tricks to get us to go quietly into the gas chamber. For their own convenience an SS commander and SS physician had once given their "word of honor," lying to a group of people that they would not go to the gas chamber in order to calm the prisoners when they became aware of their fate. (Müller, 1981, p. 78.)

At about the same time there were rumors about a mysterious tunnel under construction in the mountains somewhere in the Thuringian forest where thousands of prisoners from different occupied territories were being used for hard labor. The Germans were overheard boasting about the creation of a gigantic network of buildings inside the mountains that would protect them against enemy bombers, which had already destroyed most of their important military installations and factories. There were also rumors about a new enormously destructive weapon that would be built and deployed from that hidden base inside the tunnels. A sudden reversal of the military situation could be expected as soon as these new weapons reached enemy targets. We assumed that the Germans spread such news as part of their psychological warfare.

Other rumors dealt with the terrible conditions under which the slave laborers worked at those construction sites. It was said that after a month prisoners were worn out and replaced. Whatever happened to the huge numbers of sick, injured and exhausted masses of prisoners was not mentioned. Was there another Auschwitz in the west?

On independence day of old Czechoslovakia, October 28, we left the central hospital camp. We were led to the "sauna"—the notorious area of shower rooms not far from the anterooms of the gas chambers. Somewhat reluctantly we followed the two SS guards who silently escorted our small group of about twenty physicians and other medical personnel. We had all been in this camp long enough to feel the precariousness of this moment and hardly dared look at each other, not wanting to see our own fears mirrored in another's face. While automatically walking towards the mysterious buildings on the end of the camp, I relived the two similar episodes during that last year. I now experienced the same overwhelming sense of helplessness, a feeling of standing on the precipice of my own existence and desperately trying to keep my balance. Was I truly on the road to my execution this time? The last time I walked in this direction was the day the family camp was annihilated and our small group suddenly turned at the gate to the hospital camp where I had spent the last three months. But now we marched farther north. I knew what the end of this road meant. We had seen hundreds of thousands along this path, followed by truckloads of those who were too old, too young or too weak to reach their graves on their own. After the terrible uprooting from their homes and the exhaustion from the trip most believed in the Nazi promises that they were going to a new place to rest, then vanished, as if the ground had swallowed them. The heavy blowing smoke from the chimneys told the end of their stories.

One of the doctors recalled the day he had arrived at Auschwitz. He was among a group of older people and had been separated from his wife who had gone with a group of older women. Suddenly an SS doctor had stopped the group of men and called for physicians to step out. The rest of the men entered the building at the end of the road. When he entered the hospital camp later, he never found a trace of his wife.

Now we entered a building that was cold and humid. We heard water running and prisoners who worked there talked to us. I recognized the familiar face of a man that I had once helped when he'd had a severe hand infection. He had known how to come and go in the Czech family camp and a few times brought us important medications taken from new prisoners before the SS could get them. He reassured us; he knew that we were here in preparation for departure for the west. He envied us. We were shaved, showered and clad in regular striped prisoner uniforms. We all looked alike, similar to the thousands whom we now joined.

When we reached the ramp where a long train of cattle cars waited, I felt euphoric. Once more I had felt the icy panic of near death and slipped out of it. Our group, still consisting only of medical personnel, entered a boxcar, a rather small number of people for a whole car. There was a bucket of water and another for a toilet. We received a ration of bread with margarine and a piece of salami, our last serving in Auschwitz. We regained a bit of our sense of humor. Our car was open; we certainly felt as if we were leaving in first class compared with the way we had arrived. We did not know how the people on the rest of the train were faring. We only heard a lot of commotion when groups of prisoners arrived and the guards whistled; orders were given in the usual rude way.

Finally as the day was ending, guards jumped into position on each car and after a loud whistle from the engine, the long train left the station. There was life after Auschwitz.

We heard while we were traveling west that the Germans intended to erase Auschwitz completely, demolishing the crematorium and attempting to remove traces of what had occurred there. Since Auschwitz was in the east, the Russians reached the camp before this process was completed. Before the camp was abandoned, the SS tried to evacuate the remaining prisoners. In days of freezing temperatures, with minimal food supply, poorly clad and on the edge of total exhaustion, Otto Heller was on one of the death marches to Buchenwald, the concentration camp near Weimar, going west. He would not have made it without the aid of friends. When he arrived, he was recognized by another doctor and taken to the hospital. I was told later, when I came to Buchenwald, that he had passed beyond all help and had died in his sleep aided by strong medication.

23

MY TRIP TO BERLIN

THE LONG TRAIN OF BOXCARS loaded with hundreds of work slaves moved slowly, rattling through the countryside. It was exciting but painful to see open terrain after months of the unrelenting closeness of the camp setting. I felt as if I were waking from a nightmare to a joyful day, as if the passing scenery belonged to me. Seeing the armed guards on both ends of the car abruptly squashed those feelings.

We passed countryside that was similar to that part of Bohemia in which I had grown up. As we moved, we talked about Prague. Since my deportation I had hardly dreamt of Prague, where I had spent the last ten years of my free life, those exciting years at the university that had been most important to me. However, during the long days in Auschwitz we had talked a lot about our life in Prague. All my earlier contacts with Otto Heller and Willy Schönfeld had been in Prague. My dreams in captivity brought me back to Teplitz, my hometown, with its romantic mountain surroundings. Both Willy and I had independently observed that those last few years were fading in our memories, paralleling the progressive numbness of our emotions.

I looked out of the door of the boxcar with a longing to be on the earth that we were crossing. Fields and small farmhouses appeared and disappeared in the gray of the twilight. Several hours had passed. It grew dark outside. There was no light inside the car. I started to feel cold and hungry. At least we had water this time. I made myself as small as possible to preserve my body heat and, leaning against the bench, stared at the lighted window of a small house not far from the railroad tracks. My thoughts were of a normal life in a free situation, which I had taken for granted for my first twenty-four years.

I fell asleep as the light in the window merged with a vivid dream that I cannot recall except for the closeness of a body. On awakening Dr.

173

Crohn, the man we called "Fritz" because of his strong Berliner dialect, who had been a medical officer in the German army in World War I, whispered in my ear that he and another couple of physicians were talking of escape. They had figured out that our train was moving north, deeper into central Germany. They knew the country, had lived there and thought that they could survive in hiding, at least for a short time. We all believed that the war could not last much longer. He and another doctor outlined a plan. The idea was to jump out of the train before daybreak and run into the woods, which, according to their expectations, could be reached in a few hours. Although I was dazed and half-asleep I said that I did not think that there was a chance of surviving in hiding without a contact on the outside. We whispered for awhile without coming to any decision. The train moved on with its usual repetitive noises, the musical score of curves, junctions and brakes hitting the rails. Suddenly, the train stopped. Shots were fired. High-beam searchlights focused on the body of one of the prisoners lying in a ditch next to the tracks. The guards, watching the train from their positions on each car, had reached him with their bullets before he had even hit the ground. His freedom ended in the air. This brought an end to our thoughts of escape. I dozed off again, in and out of a light sleep, never fully losing my awareness of where we were. Fritz, who sat next to me during the ride, became increasingly restless.

Once, we were awakened by sirens howling through the night announcing the approach of enemy planes. By the second alarm we were ordered to prepare for an air raid. The train stopped short, its brakes cutting the night silence. The SS guards, in units accompanying the train, jumped out and looked for cover under the trees on each side of the railroad tracks, their automatic rifles pointed directly at the doors of each car. Then we heard the planes over us. There had been a few alarms in Auschwitz after which I had heard the detonations from nearby factories that were bombed but I had not been close to an actual explosion. We had, however, heard that the German railroad system was one of the frequent targets of the Allies. It was ironic that overhead were our "friends" the rescuers for whom I had been impatiently waiting, who could destroy our chances for survival with their assault on the train. I heard the detonation of the hit and a building not far from us went up in flames. More sirens ended the alarm and the guards again took up their positions on the train as the engine hissed and we began to move. This was the first time we experienced such a raid, and we did not yet know that such episodes would accompany us daily, and even more so, nightly. This first encounter with attacking bombers left me excited and confused. My feelings of confidence in the effectiveness of the Allies were mixed with fears of being hurt. None of us fell back to sleep. Fritz had a great need to talk. He was exhilarated, shaken from his usual apathy by the idea of an escape and then by the air raid. He told me that he felt that his spirit had been broken when he was separated from his wife on arrival at Auschwitz. After he entered the central hospital camp and had seen and heard enough to understand the terrible system, he had given up all hope for the survival of his wife. He had felt isolated in the hospital. His behavior still held the traces of his military training and experience as a German officer; his language was short and succinct and he kept a most orderly ward. He was in his fifties, certainly older than most of the rest of the physicians in our group who were together on this trip into the unknown.

As it grew lighter outside, we passed a highly populated area, a city with houses and gardens. Heaps of rubble were reminders of recent air attacks. At the outskirts there were factories with large chimneys, civilized ones. Our interest in the view diminished under the influence of our growing fatigue and hunger. I ate the last few crumbs of my bread. Fritz was not so tired since he had slept awhile during the night. He talked a great deal about his past. When he had been in his late twenties, he had returned from World War I and found a good position in the *Charité*, the university hospital in Berlin. He became a well-known internist training a new generation of medical students, hoping, as did so many in those years, that never again would there be war. Then came the depression followed by the political turmoil and clashes. He had thought that as a former officer he would be untouchable and respected. He believed that as a university teacher he would always find a place even when, inevitably, political changes would occur. He did not make an effort to emigrate until it was too late. The loss of his wife overshadowed all his other feelings but he also admitted that his sense of identity had been deeply wounded when he no longer had the right to live as any other German. He knew the land we were passing through and recognized a city, some main railroad crossings and said, "If they take the way north they can bring me home." We moved north; direction, Berlin.

Fritz kept talking. He was sure, as were most of us, that Germany would lose the war. He said that rumors about new miraculous weapons had circulated at the end of the last war also and a month later the war was over. However, he wondered where we would go if we survived the war? Another of our colleagues who had entered the conversation mumbled. "Should I go home to my town in the Rhineland and live among the same people after they have lost another war?" A young French doctor reminded us that our worries were highly premature. Someone said, "There is no logical way to return and continue to live where our existence had been broken off." A Polish physician who had been fighting and surviving since the war began and had spent more than three years in camps ended our discussion about the future, "We are already dead in our souls, and our bodies will be gone before this wave of destruction is over." We grew silent. These last words found an echo in all of us. A cold wind blew through the opening of the door and hit me like a knife as we crouched close to each other. All hopeful talk was gone and the familiar dreariness took over.

I dozed off and then I heard Fritz's voice, "We are on the way to Berlin." His observation was soon validated by the sirens, accompanied by German antiaircraft guns. The closer we came to the capital, the slower we moved. Our train stopped frequently to let military transports pass. From what we could observe, most of the heavy equipment was moving west. We assumed that the western front had become the more important and speculated that the German military industry was feverishly constructing new missiles, more powerful than the V-2, which had already been used effectively against England. If such new weapons materialized to terrorize the Allies into signing a separate peace then the Germans might possibly bring the Russian offensive to a standstill. Fritz thought this was Germany's last chance to turn the critical situation around. A young doctor who grew up in Germany at the time of the growing Nazi movement turned to him with words like, "Hitler and his cohorts will never give up, they have nothing to win in peace, their powerful destructiveness will go to the very end and finally swallow them."

We were coming closer to the center and brain of the web in which we were caught. Sirens warned the population of approaching danger but only two ended in full air raid alarms. Our train was switched to a sidetrack and we waited for what seemed like an endless time. We felt like caged animals.

24

A LOST PIECE OF BREAD

IT WAS LATE AFTERNOON when we stopped in the midst of a commotion. We were in an area surrounded by large buildings we thought were part of another type of concentration camp, although it rather resembled a large industrial complex. The boxcars were opened and along with hundreds of other arriving prisoners, we were pushed out into a large hall and allowed to mingle. It was a strange room, poorly lit by naked light bulbs dangling from long cords. It had small windows that were built very high into the walls and heavy cables hung from the even higher ceiling. A few KAPOs in well-fitting prisoner outfits and warm jackets ordered us to be quiet and stand in formation of twos. We learned that we were in the hangar of an aircraft factory. The factory was associated with the Sachsenhausen concentration camp in the town of the same name located north of Berlin. We were further told that we had to stay in this building for quarantine, a term that held a bitter taste for those of us from Auschwitz, although we hoped that here the term would have another meaning since this was a different situation.

During the month that we spent here, no one cared what we did. At night we slept in the large hall on straw mattresses that covered the floor. I cannot even remember whether we had blankets. However, I do remember that it was very cold in that enormous unheated place. Early in the morning we had to leave for the yard; the hangar gate was closed, keeping us in the large outdoor space where we were exposed to cold and rain. We either crouched, leaned against the walls of the building, or paced slowly. Our bread ration was very small since we did not work. Usually we ate that one piece of bread as quickly as we received it. We did not trust each other.

The only breaks from the monotonous empty hours were the frequent howling of the sirens announcing air attacks. The blasts shattered the factory building even though it had never suffered a direct hit. During a full alarm we had to seek cover under surrounding bushes. At night seeking cover meant leaving the building and going into the yard, which was usually cold and wet.

We received information about the outside world from senior prisoners, who were mostly German political and criminal convicts confined in the Oranienburg concentration camp. They brought our rations, bread and the hot liquid they called tea, and told us that the almost daily daytime raids were by the Americans and the nightly raids by the British. At times we were endangered by pieces of metal, parts of anti-aircraft projectiles that hit the ground from high altitude with an impact powerful enough to cause a fatal injury.

Fritz Crohn and I were together most of the time; we thought it was important to walk every day but not spend too much energy without the input of more calories. We talked about the medical and psychological effects of our purposeless daily routine. We were observant of the changes in the people around us and felt that we also were becoming more depressed and irritable each day. There were fights and hostility erupted out of minimal provocation. We were short-tempered and quick to respond aggressively. Our distress and intolerance could only be expressed feebly as if we were laboring under a heavy load. Any movement was a great strain. Inactivity became inertia. I felt the uselessness of my life; I was slipping into a level of existence in which my energy was spent on the burden of just struggling through the day. We had endured hunger and cold before, but not the dreariness of empty days in which time seemed not to move. We both had been fortunate to work as physicians when we were in Auschwitz and I had also worked nearly all the time I was in Theresienstadt.

Sometimes as we talked, we sat or walked slowly, circling the small yard. There was no strength for politeness. Naturally we spoke of our situation. The Nazis had us in quarantine, a military regulation that attempted to eliminate certain illnesses, especially the dreaded typhus, which any one of us might be carrying. The same quarantine, however, was the cause of our being undernourished, which each day made us less valuable for slave labor, the reason we were brought here. With the exception of physicians, many of the weaker and older men had already been eliminated in Auschwitz but some of our own colleagues were older and they were the most vulnerable of our sad group. Fritz Crohn was one of them. I tried to support him in chores like carrying mattresses, washing floors and in latrine duty. He pretended to be all right, complained less than the younger men did and rarely allowed himself anything but straight posture.

Bread was distributed in the afternoon. The few hundred starving prisoners stood waiting in a half-circle around the KAPOs, who with their backs to the wall watched the large basket filled with rectangular loaves of bread. They cut them into the prescribed individual ration, which they then threw a piece at a time into the crowd. Each person retreated as soon as he received his "catch" usually ripping off the first bite immediately. On such a gray afternoon close to the end of November I had been far back in the crowd at feeding time. As was usual, each man pushed, screamed and elbowed to get to the bread. I was as hungry as anyone else but was slow, convinced that I would receive my fair share. When I finally reached the first row and pushed to get my ration the KAPO screamed, "Finished!" I raised my hands, crying out, trying to talk to him. He responded, "Somebody must have two pieces, catch him." The KAPOs left. It was very quiet in the large hall; everyone very carefully chewed the limited bites that one ration of bread could provide. The men with whom I had been friendlier ignored the situation just as much as did those with whom I had had less contact. I looked around; each man was chewing his bread. These moments of the day were the most important; they were the threads that sustained our marginal living. I had a desperate feeling of being lost; I did not think I could withstand the terrible twenty-four hours of waiting until the next feeding. Next to me Fritz Crohn looked visibly disturbed. He had not yet started to eat. He took his spoon, the only utensil we had, cut his bread in two equal halves and gave me one. This was a tremendous sacrifice. I took it, touched his hand and sat down next to him. Each of us ate the reduced meal slowly and silently.

During these times I experienced, in a nearly sensual way, the need to trust and be close to another person. It felt even more intense in these life threatening situations. Nothing seemed worse than the feeling of being lost, alone and detached from those around me.

The last days of November were colder. We had more rain and less sleep because of the air raids. I remember one night the sirens woke us sometime after midnight. I dragged myself out. The KAPOs were screaming and pushing. I heard the noise of attacking British planes as they circled a wide area around the factory. As the FLAK increased, I looked for protection under a bush. The noise was frightening. A few feet away a piece of metal hit the ground with a loud impact. It could have killed me. I wondered how peaceful that would have been. When we returned to the hall, my straw mattress was gone, exchanged for a soaking wet one that had probably been too close to the open gate during the raid. I had my blanket with me and vaguely remember wrapping myself in it and lying down on the plank floor. But I clearly remember a comforting dream that same night. I was walking into a wide open valley, straight ahead, toward an unlimited horizon, with a feeling of freedom. When I woke up I thought of Willy Schönfeld and missed him greatly. In Auschwitz we had often talked about our dreams and I wanted so much to convey the good feeling of my dream to someone, to extend its mood a little longer. The only one was Fritz Crohn whose thinking was physiological, generally directed by a need for accuracy and not receptive to dream interpretation.

One Sunday at the end of November 1944, the chief KAPO called us together by blowing his whistle. He told us that our quarantine was over and we were to be led in a march to the main camp in small groups, under the watchful guard of SS men with automatic rifles. It was a pleasant day with hazy sunshine. Not many people were on the sleepy suburban road and those who were there stared at us. I saw an elderly woman stop on her way as I passed her; she pulled her shawl tighter around her shoulders and shivered. I wondered whether she thought of her son, or her husband. It did not at all occur to me that she would shiver for me.

At this stage of the war we saw older German soldiers as well as very young boys in uniform. When we reached the town, our formation passed a few shops. My eyes became fixed on the window of a bakery; there in the center was one plate with three rolls on it arranged in a pyramid. I had not seen a roll for years. In those few seconds the composition of the plate and the rolls became embedded in my memory like a photograph. I thought of my earliest years and the fresh pastries that were delivered every morning before breakfast, except on Sundays. I closed my eyes and experienced the wonderful taste of a fresh crescent, heard the sound of crispness. When I opened my eyes I saw a woman standing in line in front of a grocery store holding a little boy by the hand while with her other hand she covered his eyes, which were directed at us.

From the center of Berlin there came a discordant interplay of different kinds of sirens. The population of Berlin could not have had many peaceful hours during those weeks at the end of the year. We grew tired and tried to slow down but were pushed forward by the guards. Finally we reached the large gate of the main camp. I had by now seen several gates, entrances to the worst of prisons. Most had the inscription, "Arbeit macht frei." (Work makes free). I don't recall whether this one had the same welcome at its entrance; the image of all gates that I had passed through fused together into one large opening that devoured us.

The main camp that we entered seemed like an enormous military installation. Prisoners moved in orderly units. Barracks all looked alike. SS men noisily stamped their boots as they walked, demonstrating their powerful position. In contrast, we who were at the end of a long march dragged our tired feet creating a shuffle of hundreds. The camp was encircled by a high wall and outside were the familiar watchtowers, a reminder of Auschwitz where I had seen them for the first time. Here they did not overlook an endless flat emptiness but were on the outskirts of Berlin, almost a part of the city. Our guards led us to a building where we entered a large room and were allowed to flop on the cold floor. I used my energy-sparing technique of rolling into a small ball and covered my head with my jacket, laying motionless, hardly breathing.

The next morning we received bread and warm tea made from a different plant than was used in Auschwitz. Then we were led to the cold showers, which were also called "saunas." The long line of thin, naked bodies had to pass a doctor dressed in civilian clothes who asked the passing creatures, in the simplest German, if they were all right. He pointed to me with a short, "All right?" Blue and shivering with cold I looked into his eyes and answered in my best German, "Just a little cold, Herr Doctor." He stepped back in order to see me better, perhaps surprised that a human voice had come from one so wretched looking. He asked if I was German and I answered, "No, I am a Jew." He hesitated for a moment, his expression changed and I thought he wanted to ask more but there was still an interminable line of prisoners waiting, so with a sweep of his hand he ordered me to move forward to the washroom. Awhile later, clad in fresh rags, I huddled in a corner of another hall, still preoccupied with my response to the German doctor who might have been my age, probably just out of medical school.

Before the last few years I had never thought of being Jewish as my major identity. Growing up in a German-speaking environment and studying in German schools, I never doubted that German was my mother tongue. I had felt comfortable as a citizen of old Czechoslovakia, a country that recognized a number of languages. Just a few years earlier this doctor and I could have met as equals in a German medical school. When I stood naked and freezing in front of him trying to gauge his reaction, we no longer even belonged to the same civilization.

I wondered how this doctor and other Germans saw the development of the political situation. While the elusive "new weapons" we had heard rumors of a few months earlier, seemed to not yet exist; we observed that Germany, especially around the Berlin area, remained undefended from the permanent air attacks. While I thought of this, I was alone. The one person I might have spoken to about this was Fritz Crohn and he was in another part of the "sauna."

In the early afternoon our group was directed to another large hall, where thousands of prisoners were either standing around or looking for friends. The mixture of several languages sounded loud and chaotic. I found Fritz in conversation with a group of doctors with whom we had been together in the hospital camp at Auschwitz. I also saw a few other people who seemed familiar but were hard to recognize in their reduced condition.

Some men knew me from Prague and told me of their tragic experiences in other camps where they had suffered great hardships and had lost their families. I met a young physician, Dr. Pick, who was already recognized as a top cardiologist in Prague when I was a student training in internal medicine at the university hospital. He was speaking with a man whom I recognized as Dr. Sinek, first assistant to Dr. Schmidt, who had been the head of internal medicine at the same hospital. Dr. Sinek was a highly competent, brash physician who had been head of a research team involved in cancer treatment using artificially induced high fever. The method followed an earlier model of fever therapy for general paresis and other symptoms of syphilis. There was at that time great hope for the new treatment, which eventually ended in disappointment. Dr. Sinek had been a highly effective and assertive person, always rushing or running, with little patience for students, even for other doctors. When I reminded him of our former contact, he looked through me in the same way he had done five years earlier under more normal circumstances. Just as we ended our conversation an SS physician appeared. He was both older and of higher rank than other physicians I had seen. He seemed to recognize Dr. Sinek, who was soon approached by an SS guard and told to accompany him—that the chief camp doctor wished to see him. Dr. Sinek was very excited; probably he knew the chief doctor in earlier times since he said that he hoped that he had not antagonized him. I wondered if Dr. Sinek was chosen for something revengeful, out of an old unsettled complaint or because the SS physician remembered him as an outstanding physician and needed him for work. Dr. Sinek left but did not return and I never had an answer to my speculation.

During this time Fritz Crohn became quite shaky. It was hard on him to be so close to his home, which for the last few years he had thought would be out of his reach forever. He said, "I can smell Berlin. I want to touch it." But all that we shared with that great city, which had become the deranged brain center of a failing system, was the constant danger of being destroyed by air attack. We knew that we were in an important place because of the number of high-ranking SS officers around.*

Later, as dusk was falling, a number of KAPOs appeared and divided us into different units. Fritz Crohn was sent to one group and I to another. I had no idea whether this was determined by age or by chance and I never saw him again. I was in line with about a hundred others. We were led to a barracks of empty bunks and before we could even find our way about the lights went out and the sirens announced approaching enemy planes. I crawled onto the closest straw mattress where I already found another body; I pushed him to the other side. He complained in a language foreign to me and I answered in Czech. Then we lay quietly together. I fell asleep.

It was still dark the next morning when we were ordered to line up for roll call. We received our bread ration and marched out of camp. My presence in Oranienburg-Sachsenhausen, this central concentration

* Martin Gilbert quotes the summary of reports of Vrba and Wetzler, which had arrived at the British Foreign Office on July 4, 1944, describing the mass killing in Auschwitz-Birkenau, and mentioning the supreme commander of the camp of Oranienburg as the center where all lists of performed executions were sent. (1981, p. 361)

camp on the periphery of Berlin, was short, two days and a night, but it was again decisive for my future as it had been when my number was moved from the list of those in Auschwitz sent to be killed, to the list of slave workers, cleaned and passed through quarantine to be sent out for heavy labor.

We reached a railroad station where a long passenger train awaited us. It was unbelievable to me that once again and at this point in my life I was entering a first class carriage, even one as old and outdated as this one. Although the small compartments had only a limited number of seats they were plushly upholstered in green velvet. We were pushed into a carriage, about five prisoners for each available seat. I was one of the first to discover that we were not alone on the ride. The soft and inviting upholstery was full of lice, the typhus carrier, which an earlier transport must have left behind. In a few minutes we were all scratching. I looked for a more secure spot and climbed up to the empty mesh luggage rack where I stretched out. I saw others trying to do the same, sometimes falling through torn netting onto the people sitting below. There was a good deal of cursing, mostly in Hungarian. I wished then that I had someone with whom I could talk. The situation was ludicrous. We had just gone through this long quarantine, showers, change of clothing and physical examination by a doctor to make sure we were not carriers of any dangerous illnesses. Before the end of this trip we would all certainly be full of lice and possible carriers of typhus. I have no recollection of how long the trip took. We stopped often probably to let more important trains pass. When I left my privileged spot to work my way through the compact mass to get to the toilet somebody else immediately took it and I had to stand for the rest of the trip, squeezed between moaning and smelling bodies.

We arrived at our destination, wherever it was, in darkness and dragged ourselves through the cold night. The wind was painful here; it cut into our skin wherever it was exposed. I had the impression that the new camp was in a forest, perhaps in the mountains. Once again we were divided into units and led to barracks. There was one bunk for two prisoners and each was given a blanket. Compared to our position on the train we felt relieved to be able to stretch out for our first night in the new camp.

25

DEADLY SLAVE WORK IN OHRDRUF

———◆————◆————◆————◆———

EARLY THE NEXT MORNING we were ordered to get up; it was still dark and very cold. The camp ground was crowded with men busily running around to line up in different work groups; many seemed to know already where they preferred to go and pushed their way through. When a unit was complete, the rest were told to look for another formation. The KAPOs, with whistles and loud voices, left no doubt that there was only a limited time to arrange for a work place.

I stayed with those with whom I had shared the barracks the night before, despite not knowing anyone; most of them spoke Hungarian, a few spoke Polish and between the two ethnic groups was an instantly inflammatory antagonism.

The Hungarians, mostly Jews, had recently come from the selections in Auschwitz, where many of their families had been killed. They were the younger and healthier men who had been deported here to the west to be used for slave labor, as was my transport. There were also some Jews among the Polish-speaking men. Most had already suffered in concentration camps in the east. They were experienced and tough, but like many veteran prisoners, were also impatient, tense and irritable from their prolonged exposure to the stresses of imprisonment.

They had witnessed so much violence and had suffered so many losses of people dear to them that they learned how not to take in the pain and misery of others. They sneered at the helplessness and naiveté of the Hungarian newcomers, who had been, only a few weeks earlier, Jews living a normal life. The very sound of their language caused hostile, mocking responses from their Polish or Russian-speaking fellows in misfortune. There were also prisoners from other countries but it was difficult to identify languages, especially when they were spoken in slang or dialect.

Varieties of Yiddish became the bridge for communication among the Jewish prisoners. I spoke German and Czech and learned to understand enough Yiddish to get information from those who had been there longer. They sketched the situation in gloomy terms. The work was hard, living conditions bad, the food poor and getting worse. Only those in privileged positions could last longer than a month while most others were sent to one of the bigger barracks where they vegetated with reduced food rations and no medical care. Many died. Truckloads of sick and debilitated men were sent from there to another camp, which was supposedly a hospital.

Every experienced prisoner knew of the gas chambers in the east. We wondered if there were similar installations here in the west. I understood, as did the others, that for me to continue to live depended upon my usefulness to the German war machine. There was a steady stream of newcomers replacing those eliminated by exhaustion, injury or sickness. We again heard rumors about a tunnel that would be used for the construction of the "new weapon."

We were sent to the hills and into the forests of the Thuringian Woods where our daily units prepared the ground. We worked at hard labor removing rocks and undergrowth, digging ditches for drainage of the water that came down the hills after the heavy rain and melting snows. As we worked, we embroidered pictures in our minds of an elaborate network of factory buildings erected inside these mountains.

One of our foremen, an outspoken fellow claiming to be a Russian, explained to us in his simple broken German the importance of quality and speed in our work. I did not trust him and thought he might be one of the Ukranian collaborators whom we had encountered before. The winter was growing more severe, at times the rain and snow made it nearly impossible to work. On other days it was easier and for a few hours I could even feel the sunshine in the middle of the day. Our daily schedule was rigid and repetitive. We were torn from sleep by whistles early in the morning, still in darkness. I would jump up, ready to leave. If the night had not been very cold, I would have used my jacket as a pillow for my head. My only dressing was to grab it on my way out. It was usually too cold and there was not time enough to go to the washroom, where there were only a few faucets providing a weak stream of water if it hadn't frozen during the night.

We rushed to roll call hoping to join one of the less strenuous work assignments of the day. It took a few days for me to understand the various assignments and to learn how to recognize which were the less horrendous ones. When a unit was filled, we were directed to the next one without being able to make a choice. A few times when this happened I found myself in the work force that removed heavy rocks from the quarry.

Only after all the groups were formed, did we receive our daily ration of bread and a hot liquid, euphemistically called coffee.

Everything had to be done very quickly, running. We would run to the trucks in which we had to stand, squeezed together, unprotected from rain or snow, and there we would wait until the driver arrived to take us to the work site. At the project the foreman would be waiting who then urged us to fetch a tool and run to the spot where we were assigned for the next ten hours. At midday, a cattle car with hot soup arrived and there was a short rest. Usually I ate leaning against a tree or tool shed. Often we were wet and in danger of our bodies freezing to the ground if we did not keep moving.

The days seemed to melt together into one period of hard strain and exertion. At times I felt as if I had reached my breaking point. It was beyond my strength to break into the nearly frozen ground with a pickax. One day my pickax broke when it hit a rock and the guard screamed, "Now, you idiot, dig it out with your fingers." Somehow I continued. The next day I had new tools, the sun came out and I gathered new strength.

Military personnel of all ages were always watching us and directing us. They screamed at us to move faster; they threatened to hit us when we stopped to catch a breath. Once I was hit with a rifle after I talked with the man beside me who was close to breaking down; when he could no longer lift his axe, he began to cry. Another time a soldier stood next to me and stared at me for quite awhile; I expected the usual tirade of swearing. He spoke intelligently in a soft voice, formulating his words carefully so as to make himself clearly understood to someone whose language was not German. He asked me about my former profession. I answered in my clear Prague German that I was a doctor. He responded with bitterness, "And I can't get a doctor for my family!" As we were talking, snow was starting to fall. Slowly he walked away into the nothingness of the mist. I wondered if he had been real. In that environment a friendly voice felt both grotesque and like an unexpected bandage on a bleeding wound. Then it was gone and hard to recall as real.

26

AN APPLE CORE

FEW EXPERIENCES could move me. On one of those milder days that occasionally interrupted the rough winter, I had an experience that did. I was still digging ditches. Our guards were also affected by the spring-like streak in the air; they moved more slowly and did not push us as hard. I was part of a large group of laborers walking through the forest. At a crossroad the unit was divided into smaller groups. My unit was directed to an open field surrounded by pine forests. In summer it undoubtedly was covered with wild flowers. Half of the area was an orchard of young apple trees that had been planted just a few years before, since the start of the war when any opportunity was used to grow what was edible.

I started to work when the man next to me called in a friendly voice to help him move aside a heavy rock so that he could continue the ditch he was working on. We recognized each other; I knew him from Prague. Kurtl had been a jazz pianist in one of the fine bars and I had always enjoyed his playing. We worked hard to release the rock while we exchanged pleasant memories. Later, he managed to get an accordion and succeeded in making a special place for himself in the camp as a musician.

When I returned to my place, I spotted the remains of a dried out apple core lying under a tree. It was rotten and reduced to nearly nothing, a shadow of its glorious fruitful past. I put it in my mouth and even though there was no fresh flesh left on it there remained a faint taste of apple. This was the first "fruit" I had tasted in two years. It brought back the richness of life in the past, of food beyond the daily soup and bread. It also reminded me of my grandmother, who had never missed an opportunity to tell us children that the most important value of the fruit lay in its core. She had impressed upon us the mystery of the potency of the core. As children we did not find it as much a delicacy as the rest of the apple. On that day in the clearing of Thuringia I changed my mind. That rotten apple core was the most delicious taste I had experienced in a long time. I have enjoyed eating the core of the apple since that time.

27

COLD, HUNGER, HARD LABOR

THE FIRST TWO WEEKS in this camp seemed endless. On the second Sunday after we arrived, a blizzard began. The trucks moved slowly on the icy road while we, standing in the back, became a mass of motionless bodies disappearing below the snow cover. To work was futile—no matter how hard we tried it was impossible to break into the frozen soil to dig our ditches. The guards were constantly wiping their eyeglasses, barely able to see us. At midday we were called to the assembly point to wait for the trucks to return us to camp. The temperature had changed and there was a mixture of rain and snow that was relentless. Before this experience I had imagined that there was a certain saturation point of wetness. This was not so. As we stood waiting, I grew wetter by the minute, my clothes grew heavier and my skin began to burn from the irritating roughness of the cloth. The eczema that I had suffered as a result of lice was further irritated. In all of this discomfort, I wondered why the natural cold compresses did not soothe my inflamed skin.

The guard leading our work unit ordered us to march in the direction from which the trucks would come. To keep myself going, I drew a cartoon in my mind. The scene had a certain absurdity. I tried to observe, as if I were an outsider, our bizarre, waddling figures, so miserable in our heavy, soaked clothes, being urged by the SS guard to speed up. They were not too comfortable themselves and did not seem to expect much response to their orders. This kind of playful split allowed me, as observer and object, to tolerate the pain that at times threatened to overwhelm me. During so many of those times of stress, I found it helpful to employ this mental mechanism.

After about half an hour of arduous marching we approached an ironically comic scene on the highway. There were soldiers, low ranking officers and technicians trying to create a convoy from beat up tanks, command cars, confiscated private cars and civilian buses covered in military paint with numbers stamped on them. The officers and military police were driving back and forth along the road in their motorcycles, barely maintaining their balance as their sidecars careened along snow filled ditches. One vehicle had turned over, half of it was in a ditch and the other part was still on half of the two lane road, obstructing the traffic. In one open car there was an elderly gentleman, a commanding officer, impressive, his uniformed chest trembling with medals. His face showed how much he had to strain to project his orders, which became totally lost in the snow and the wind. His gestures expressed his frustration. He stomped out of his car only to get stuck in the snow. The soldiers with him were old, as were the vehicles, which had trouble starting up; if they moved a few feet the motor would die and they would again be stuck in the snow. The technicians, who were growing cold and tired, responding harshly to the drivers who were calling them. When we laboriously marched passed them, they all straightened up.

As we walked, we had to watch not to be hit by a former family sedan now pretending to be a battlewagon in field colors. The uniformed driver had the look of a good-hearted retired schoolteacher. His car moved slowly and finally skidded into the opposite lane where it died. He started to swear. The commanding officer turned to him and reminded him not to show weakness in the presence of prisoners of war. When he saw the slight grin on my dirty, wet face the officer made a gesture with his hand as if to say, according to my translation, "the hell with everything." At such moments I so much missed having a trustworthy friend that I began to talk to myself about how comforting I found this scene I was observing. The prisoners next to me must have felt the same; we all smiled at each other. I thought that if this was the condition of the German army even the advertised "new weapon" could not help them.

Finally, the trucks arrived to take us back to camp. The ride was difficult since visibility was poor, and we moved very slowly. In the open trucks the bumpiness of the road added to our feeling colder and sicker. Suddenly our truck stopped, slid to the side and hit a tree. Fortunately we had been going very slowly so that the impact was not severe. Since we were standing crammed together we had no place to fall; only our heads banged together. I was in a daze; when it cleared, I saw that the tree we had hit stood in front of a small farmhouse. Through the gloom I saw a dim

193

light behind a window. A simple lamp hung over a table. An older couple sat there with a young girl. In the middle of the table was a large dish of steaming potatoes—not a very fancy Sunday *mittagessen* (lunch), usually the main meal of the day. That "still photo" had the quality of a wonderful dream, a warm room, a chair to sit on, hot potatoes, as did the window of the bakery on the march to Camp Oranienburg. Two scenes I have still not forgotten.

We finally arrived in camp by afternoon; this was the first time I had seen the camp in daylight. I was cold, wet and had a pain in my neck but as soon as I lay down, the whistle called us to line up. On this "special" Sunday afternoon there was a thorough roll call, taking a complete inventory of slave workers.

It was still dark the next morning when I woke up feeling miserable. My whole body ached, my neck was stiff and my head felt as if it were on fire. The downpour of Sunday had stopped. There were stars in the sky, the fir trees were enveloped in snow and the ground was frozen. I stood in the doorway of our barracks for a few moments and saw the men, still half asleep, rushing to line up but awkwardly struggling to keep their balance on the ice. A few fell. Somebody who was in pain and could not get up on his own cried out for help. No one responded to him since everyone was trying to get to what they thought would be the easiest work unit. I hesitated to move since my shoes were too big for me and still wet, and were without laces to tighten them. I walked slowly and carefully, stopping at the first group to avoid having to walk one more step than was necessary. I joined the line. The man next to me said good morning to me in German. This was an unusual and pleasant interruption of the harshness of the winter morning. I recognized his accent as Czech and responded in that language. Both of us were hungry to trust someone enough to talk with. I had missed the presence of a friendly person since losing contact with Fritz Crohn in Oranienburg. This new friend, whose name I have since forgotten, had been a tailor in Prague with his own shop and a comfortable life until the German occupation in 1939. We reminisced, griped about our present situation and expressed our intense concern for our immediate future.

My memory plays strange tricks on me as I write these recollections, years after they took place. I never know where a recalled image will lead me; sometimes I am surprised at the details I remember, including names.

At other times I am at a loss to understand why a name, such as the Czech tailor's, is totally erased. It is unfathomable to me why I have retained certain traces and not others.

I had now been in camp Ohrdruf for about three weeks. It grew closer to Christmas. We had a few warmer days and my clothes and shoes were nearly dry. Wounds were beginning to develop around my ankles where the loose edges of the wet shoes had been rubbing and breaking the skin of my naked legs. In Auschwitz, I had treated others for such conditions and had been highly concerned about unavoidable infections spreading. In the state my feet were in, every step was painful and the touch of leather felt like a knife. My new Czech friend and I looked for rags with which to make socks for me.

Whenever we could arrange it, we joined the same work unit, which was not always possible since we slept in different barracks and one could be ordered to line up almost at once by a foreman. The first hour of the day was the worst. The mornings were bitterly cold and the routine began very early.

Anticipating a long and hard workday was grim. We began the day already feeling tired since the sleeping arrangements were so uncomfortable. My bedmate, a tall Hungarian whose limbs seemed to be ever-present, was very restless in sleep and frantically fought off the lice that waited to feed on us each night when our bodies were warm enough. There came a day when I felt a painful itch that I suspected to be an infection of scabies (caused by mites that burrow under the skin). I realized that my general condition had become precarious.

28

A TURNING POINT

IT WAS THE END of our fourth week of being in this camp. A month was usually the deadline of endurance according to our clandestine information. My Czech friend and I were digging the hard soil to build another piece of a drainage network. We looked at each other and obviously both looked abominable. He said, "We have to do something." I agreed. We knew that the camp was lice-ridden so that it was more than likely that any carrier or anyone acutely ill with typhus could become the starting point of an uncontrollable epidemic. We had heard how the SS handled similar situations; their radical solution was to exterminate the lice along with their hosts. It was easier to replace hundreds, even thousands, of slaves than to clean them. Suddenly, I remembered a technique that we used successfully in the Czech family camp in Auschwitz-Birkenau where we had arranged a cleansing of the inmates, one barracks at a time, and ended by treating all clothes with a hot iron. My Czech companion and I were not so much motivated by humanitarian interests as we were trying to save ourselves by establishing a special role, a technique that had saved me before. I was always able to come up with suggestions and possible solutions, but it was more difficult for me to put myself forth to convince the authorities. My friend was not very aggressive either but he had a more practical approach to life as a result of his business experiences. He liked the plan and said he would try to win support for it. That was the last time I saw him.

There was a turning point for me the next night. We were in our barracks just after finishing our soup and bread. Some of the Hungarians had "organized" a few potatoes and started to bake them on the open fire. When there was no more wood, they began to burn the slats from their beds while the more experienced prisoners, myself included, tried to warn them that destruction of military equipment was punishable by hanging.

The Hungarian clique misperceived our intent and thought we were envious and hostile. We were more fearful for ourselves. Some of the straw sacks were, by then, balancing only on one small board, the other boards having gone up in smoke.

Suddenly, the gate was kicked open and we froze in panic. To our surprise we saw two prisoners, nurses, dragging in a young man who looked seriously injured; they threw him on an empty bed. I went to look at him. One of them turned to me and asked me if I could take care of the patient. I said I was a doctor and I would. Immediately some of the Hungarians screamed that they too were doctors. One of the nurses placed a bowl of soup and a piece of bread in my hands saying, "Try to feed him and eat the rest. We will pick him up tomorrow morning. Stay with him." The youngster, probably not yet twenty, was in poor condition. Every move and each attempt to speak caused him pain. I fed him a few spoonfuls of soup; swallowing seemed painful too. He soon gave up and gestured that I should finish his food. After trying again, unsuccessfully, to get him to eat, I did finish his food.

The others observed me with greedy expressions. The young man started to talk. He was the son of a mixed marriage; his father was German and his mother Jewish, living in the neighborhood of our camp. He was in a work unit and hoped to remain free. A short time before this his parents were deported and he was arrested and taken to our camp. His work had been in a unit outside the camp and, since he was familiar with the area, he made an attempt to escape. The guards and their dogs found him at dusk hiding behind some bushes. They had brought him back and beat him mercilessly. I tried to make him more comfortable and gave him the painkiller that the nurse had left for him.

The rest of the soup and the extra bread gave me a feeling of strength that was far more than its actual small caloric value. The next morning I did not go out to work but kept myself occupied with the patient left in my care. When the nurses arrived with a stretcher to pick him up, my duty was terminated. I found myself among the disabled, left behind in the barracks after the able bodied were gone. I had heard about a building where sick and weak prisoners were warehoused and periodically moved by truck to what was called a "hospital camp." We looked upon this arrangement with suspicion; it smelled too much of the "mercy killing" of the sick and the mass exterminations of the undesirable human beings in Auschwitz. We were eternally anxious about being sucked into the circle of uselessness. I never learned the fate of the worn out laborers in Ohrdruf but, that morning as I was left in the barracks, I felt panic. Conditions could deteriorate rapidly and I would not want to be found sitting on my bed or even in the same quarters with damaged beds.*

As I sat there in a panic, the door opened and, for a moment, I considered hiding. Standing in the doorway was Dr. Goldstein, the physician who had been in charge of the surgical block of the central hospital in Birkenau and whom I had not seen since our trip from Auschwitz. He was also surprised to find me. He looked well, clean and wore a special uniform. His greeting to me was very friendly which enabled me to tell him, but with tears in my eyes, that I was close to giving up. He put his arms around me and shook me. I remember with clarity what he said: "You were very decent to me when you could have taken my full position. You even placed yourself in danger by not following the orders of the SS physician. I have not forgotten. I want to help you now." He told me to come to the clinic the following morning to be introduced to the local SS physician since additional prisoner physicians were needed to organize another hospital in a camp in the neighborhood. After advising me to clean myself up, he left.

Why had I not initiated contact with the medical unit before this? I had not even wondered what had happened to the doctors from the central hospital camp in Auschwitz who had arrived here with me. They had obviously learned, during their fight for survival, not to get lost in the mass of anonymous prisoners, but to preserve a privileged position once held. If one was already known in the medical system, it was easier to renew former contacts. Nothing, of course, is always true. The tragic fate of the doctors in the blocks of the Czech family camp at Birkenau-Auschwitz confirmed this. Nothing was reliable in this system run by unpredictable people, not even the rules of destruction. I had again nearly missed this chance by waiting to be rescued and was saved only by the coincidence of being left in the barracks on the day that Dr. Goldstein, for some reason, was walking through the camp. Perhaps he was looking for old colleagues.

---

* Martin Gilbert relates that on General Eisenhower's first visit to a camp he described the "emaciated corpses at Ohrdruf," and was "so shocked" that he telephoned Churchill at once and sent him pictures. (1985, p. 790)

In my life as a prisoner I had absorbed some of the Czech philosophy of passive resistance of *The Good Soldier Švejk* and, until then, this passivity worked for my survival. The inhibition that prevented me from trying to reach the other doctors was, I believe, in part, influenced by my growing up in German "civilization;" some called it a subculture. That society placed an overvaluation on discipline, the following of orders, and "marching in step." These values did not support protecting oneself. In this camp I was assigned to a barracks where I spent each night thereafter until called for work early each morning. And so it went daily for a month, the notorious survival time in Ohrdruf. That morning was an exception to my usual compliance. My infected feet and increasing exhaustion made me realize how endangered I was. The night before when I walked over to look at the beaten escapee, my initiative as a doctor and the additional food I was given allowed me to feel slightly stronger. My awareness of my weakened condition made me decide to remain in the barracks when everyone left for work, but if anyone other than Dr. Goldstein had found me, it could have brought me to a disastrous end.

After Dr. Goldstein left, I feverishly tried to rid myself of the dirt that coated my skin. My thoughts traveled between past and future; back to the days of my encounter with the first SS doctor, Dr. von Wander, in family camp in Auschwitz. A series of lucky coincidences had spared me until now, starting with my naive remark about not having formally graduated from medical school, which sent me to the hospital rather than certain death at Auschwitz.

My unnecessary remark came from the fear of authority and could have endangered my chances. It was an absurdity at a time when there was no proof of anyone's educational qualifications or even of one's identity, only a tattooed number on one's arm. It was my fear of being discovered in a fraud that allowed me to join the hospital staff and kept me back on that tragic March 7 when my transport, including the doctors, had been sent to be killed in Auschwitz. In the grotesqueness of circumstances, my inappropriate honesty was what saved my life. I was on that list of a handful of medical workers of the hospital barracks who were exempt from going to the gas chambers.

Again in July 1944, a few of us doctors were sent to the central hospital camp when the rest of the family camp, including my parents, was liquidated. It was there that I had met Dr. Goldstein and now we were meeting again shortly before Christmas, 1944. Thinking of this chain of events in any magical way was dangerous and also reinforced my passive obedience. I had wanted to become more active in situations, but something I didn't understand held me back, appearing as the way of least resistance. Fear of authority stopped me even when passivity could destroy me, but I felt that there must be other motives I had not yet discovered.

It was an impossible task to remove any of the dirt from my clothes, which I had not changed since we had left Oranienburg a month earlier. I had a beard and looked as run down as the others did after the allotted four weeks of heavy slave labor. In order to perform this cleansing, I had to hide during the day so as not to be sent either to the tent filled with disabled workers or to a work unit. I spent most of the time in the washroom, literally scratching off dirt, trying to free myself from layers of filth. I found a rusty razor blade on the dirty floor of the room and removed part of my bristles. It was a long day, tense with fear intermingled with hope, fantasies and irrational ideas; I played with thoughts that I had helped others enough to feel that I had the right to be rescued—a thought that I needed in order to rationalize the guilt of surviving. I knew better. The hope that I would be saved again at the last moment was mixed with the uneasy feeling: Why me, again?

Time in captivity feels longer and more burdensome than time in free everyday life. There is an additional weight, a heaviness of time, as if it is carried on one's shoulders. The symbolic burden lowers one's head and hurts the neck and back. There are some days that are worse, that seem like one is moving in slow motion, days of expectations or doubts about tomorrow. There are other moments when time itself is threatening because it seems to stand still. The day of my cleansing was one of them. I feared that one wrong step, one move in the wrong direction could destroy my chance to survive, which was so close that I could almost touch it. I felt that if only time would move fast enough I would not lose the opportunity.

In spite of lacking the most fundamental means, such as soap, warm water, a brush and towel, my appearance gradually changed. Carefully, I left the washroom later in the afternoon. A young prisoner on top of a truck of foodstuffs looked at me and said in Czech, "Hey doctor, how are you?" He knew me from Prague. He asked for Willy Schönfeld and was sad when I told him about his end in Auschwitz. This young man's sister was a gifted artisan and had been an instructor in our reschooling courses in Prague. She was an attractive woman and did not fail to get special attention from Willy before he married. The young man seemed happy to offer me a favor and invited me to meet him after the distribution of the evening bread. When I arrived, he had an extra portion of bread and salami for me. That was the coronation of an important day in which I did not work, improved my appearance and received a reward of additional food. Such were the paradoxes of life in the camps. I did not sleep much that night and was up before the official call.

The morning was cold and it was still dark. I wondered if I'd make it. There was the danger that one of the foremen would see me and put me into a work unit so that my appointment at the clinic would be lost. Just in case anyone would confront me, I prepared an explanation that did not sound plausible even to me and probably would not have been heard to the end. I sneaked into the washroom to touch up my beautification and walked toward the clinic, my head higher than it had been for awhile. I tried to appear both serious and sure while my insides were shaking.

There was a male nurse at the door of the clinic screening those in need of medical help. I introduced myself in a confident voice as a doctor and told him I had an appointment with Dr. Goldstein, who heard me and came from the next room. He looked me over and smiled. The change in my appearance was apparent even in the dark waiting room of the clinic. He invited me into his small surgery, where he was treating a patient with wounds around the ankles typically caused by worn out shoes worn with no socks. He had just received some compresses to reduce the inflammation and started to moan.

I thought of the lesions on my own feet, hurting with every step but carefully covered by my pants. I could have been the one lying on this table. The next minutes, I knew, would be decisive as to whether I would be a patient and removed as worthless human trash or accepted again as a doctor. Dr. Goldstein attended his patient and let me sit in a corner. I had not sat on a chair for a number of months.

A small window opening into the place of assembly gave me, for the first time, a total view of the hundreds of shivering figures rushing to their work units. Some were already loaded on trucks, standing close to each other, trying to find enough space to rub their stiffened limbs. At daybreak the trucks started slowly moving out. The place was then empty. I watched while a couple of SS guards walked around, looking for prisoners who had not fallen in for work. Any prisoner who could not stand on his feet was carried to the large tent for the disabled.

A line of patients formed at the entrance to the clinic and was kept in order by the nurse. Some were seriously ill or injured and could not stand up. There were sounds of groaning, whimpering and whispering, which ceased abruptly when the nurse announced the approach of the SS physician. Dr. Goldstein shouted, "Attention!" We all stood up, including some patients, who because of their pain, had contorted facial expressions or were in grotesque positions. The SS physician was a tall, slim young man. He appeared as a uniform on a body, his face an expressionless mask. It was so poorly lighted that I could hardly see. Dr. Goldstein must have already talked to him about me. He said, "This is the physician who worked in the camp hospitals in Auschwitz and would be good for the new camp." The SS officer turned to me and said, "This is a little different from the Schmidt Clinic, isn't it?" He had a slight sarcastic, but not openly hostile tone and I did not know what he meant. He had apparently recognized me as a former fellow student from the same internal medicine department of the university hospital in Prague. I did not think he was anyone with whom I had had any personal contact. My guess was that he might have been a student working in the clinical laboratory with whom we externs had little contact, but I was not sure. I looked him straight in the eye and said, "Yes, sir." My face was motionless. I was uneasy about the development of this encounter and wondered if he had known me at Schmidt and would have feelings that he carried over from earlier times that might end in vindictiveness, or would he demonstrate his power and "generously" accept me. My heart was beating in my neck. I did not move.

"It's all right," he turned to Dr. Goldstein, "take him over to the new camp." I nearly fainted and cannot recall anything about the next few hours although the scene up until that moment is clear with nearly eidetic sharpness. The scene of the grey yard, the assembly of men, the encounter with the SS man, the details of the conversation, word for word, seem like yesterday but nothing beyond. I have tried to complete the memories of such days, to get in touch with what would have been the expectable feelings of liberation, but the tension before the climax must have been so great that all my emotions were exhausted. I just moved mechanically into my new place.

29

I AM A DOCTOR AGAIN

THE NEXT THING I RECALL is being in an improvised shower in a corner of the hospital ward to which I had been transferred after I had been introduced to the camp physician. I never returned to my old barracks or left any trace of personal possessions on my half of the bed. In the shower, a male nurse assisted me in removing all my clothes, handling them carefully so as not to spread any lice. I had not washed my body for many weeks; I felt it as a burning sensation. The nurse called a doctor, an elderly Hungarian who was working as a nurse on the ward. He examined me carefully and was not sure whether my skin reaction was scabies or not, but treated it for that. My clothes were carried out and burned. I was given a clean prison uniform.

The improvised hospital was a former school building that had many rooms, probably former classrooms. I was shown to a small chamber, which I imagined had been the office of the principal, but was now filled with straw mattresses for medical personnel. I fell exhausted onto a free bed. I remember that I had an impressive dream that night, very real, lucid, beautiful and colorful. I remembered nothing of the dream, unlike the dream of being in a beautiful, colorful, environment I recalled in detail of the dream on March 7 in Auschwitz, when, after twenty-four hours, I was rescued from execution. I think of it as another of the dreams of returning to life; Martin Grotjahn thought the opposite, that they were "death dreams" fantasizing the beauty of the realm of death. We have two different views of the intrapsychic field that Masud Khan called "the dream-space" (1974). For me, they represent rescue from the margin of death to the rim of life.

The next morning, I was given hot coffee, ersatz, of course, and a piece of bread with margarine bigger than my ration had been for outdoor work. I felt ready to function. From this new situation, it was difficult to accept the past five weeks of hard labor as a reality and not a nightmare. However, when I looked at myself, I understood that it must have happened. The wrinkles on my body, the uniform hanging loosely from my reduced body were proof of it.

The hospital building was crowded with severely sick patients. I recognized a few. There was a former Polish officer, a teacher in civilian life who had been the clerk of the surgical barracks in which Dr. Goldstein and I had worked. His face was yellow from jaundice and he suffered from a high fever. He probably had one of the strains of infectious hepatitis. In Auschwitz, he had been the best nourished of us all from the food packages he received from relatives who were farmers in Poland. Now he was in very poor shape. He was much less reserved and much less condescending here towards the Jewish doctors than he had been in the Auschwitz central hospital. Dr. Goldstein treated him distantly, which was better than he had treated Dr. Goldstein when he had been the clerk in charge.

There were not many Jews among the patients and I wondered where they were sent when they were sick or disabled. The Jewish prisoners in the camp were from recent Hungarian transports and in relatively good general condition. They were robbed of freedom only during the last year and came from a country where basic food was still available during the late war years. However, only those young and strong enough could pass the screening at the Auschwitz human floodgate. There were exceptions, saved at selections from being discarded as human waste: A few older Hungarian physicians, who were now used as nurses when others were sent to a work unit, a few veteran Jewish prisoners from Poland and Russia, as well as men from France and Greece who had successfully survived early deportations against all odds and who had learned not to get lost in the masses. Their behavior and facial expressions showed high tension, their eyes mirrored suspicion and a readiness to hide or attack, their defensive behavior was that of the hunted animal.

Dr. Goldstein appeared for a short visit and told me that I would be in charge of all medical cases while he would take care of surgical problems. He introduced me to the two Hungarian physicians, who were close in age to my father, and who had survived the selections in Auschwitz when Mengele asked all physicians to step out. When these doctors arrived in Ohrdruf, they were mixed with younger prisoners and sent to hard labor, as I was. Soon they became exhausted and asked for medical help. When they identified themselves as physicians, they were transferred to work as nurses in the hospital.

They were lovely people, well-educated in more than just their specialties; Sandor was an internist, the other was a radiologist. They were friends and talked of each other with great respect. Each would tell me how important the other had been in his work at home; they pleaded to remain in the hospital, willing to do any work. I gladly accepted their help. Sandor reminded me of my father; he was rather short, friendly and supportive to all patients, swift in finding solutions to saving lives at critical moments. We were, of course, short of supplies and many medical interventions had to be improvised. Thermometers were precious instruments and when Sandor broke one during morning rounds he came to me with tears in his eyes, fearing that I might remove him from his position. I succeeded in "organizing" another thermometer.

Sandor was usually at my side, taking over whatever work he could. We became friends. He also became protective of me. He realized how run down I was from the weeks of physical strain, failing strength, injured ankles and the emotional stress of my constant anticipation of doom. During the first days in the hospital, I suffered from the unpleasant sensation of clusters of irregular heartbeats. Sandor examined me and prescribed small doses of phenobarbitrate and rest, which was not possible. The number of patients in our care never diminished. Few were really cured and released to their duties. For each bed freed by the death of a patient there were others waiting. We had fewer medications than we had had in Auschwitz, where our best resources for items such as medicines, shoes and clothing came through the black market. These were items that were confiscated from new prisoners when they entered the camp. We also received items from electricians, laundry workers and others who could move from place to place.

January of 1945 was cold. Patients carried in on stretchers were ill, primarily as a result of being poorly dressed and exposed too long to the low temperatures. Some were comatose. Patients had to remain on stretchers until we could free a bed, if they were still alive by that time. Most were beyond help. The slow pulses and low blood pressures we observed reminded me of conditions we had seen in Auschwitz, which had not been caused only by the weather but what we called encephalopathy.

30

VARIOUS ENCOUNTERS

During my first week in the hospital, a man of about thirty, better dressed than most, entered the hospital and introduced himself in accent-free German. He said, "I am Ernst and I have come to help you get the hospital together." He explained that he was in charge of supplies and would try to get clothes, medication and food. He brought forth a bitter smile, communicating the limitations of his stock. He wanted a list of the most needed medications and seemed to have some knowledge of medicine. While Sandor was working on our request for supplies, Ernst took me aside and touched my jacket. He said, "I shall bring you a warm coat. We have to stay well for the short time before the end." I was puzzled about his chummy, fearless attitude on our first encounter. His behavior seemed to me highly unusual for a KAPO and too obvious even if he were an informer. Ernst was a rather mystical figure.

The next day he brought me a warm coat, a kind of car coat with a fur collar. I thanked him, touched by his generosity but I knew that I could not walk around a German concentration camp in a fur-trimmed coat. I told him this. He looked at me and I grew frightened that I had made an enemy with my straight talk. "You will find a tailor in the hospital who can take the fur off the coat and I'll take it for myself." We went into his office next to the storage room and sat on two wooden crates. He started to talk about himself. He was the son of a steelworker, a union organizer, who was taken away when Hitler seized power. When he tried to find his father's whereabouts by getting in touch with the union, he was arrested. He spent hard times in various prisons and during the last years, like many other German political prisoners, had a variety of functions in the administration of the camps. Nobody even knew anymore why he had been incarcerated and he assumed that no one cared. Despite the years of heavy work that he had endured, he felt more comfortable in his position as a KAPO in a concentration camp than as a soldier in a lost war. I was surprised at his outspokenness and his convictions about the war coming to an end. He said, "Being a prisoner I don't need to argue about the obvious signs of military defeat; I don't believe the fairy tales of new weapons. This is not my war."

When I came back to the hospital with the coat over my arm, a young prisoner, Marek, who was sweeping the floor, turned to me and said something about the fine quality of the car coat. I asked him how he could tell and he said three years earlier when the German army invaded Poland and entered Krakow, he had been a tailor's apprentice. His family, including his younger siblings, was taken to an isolated spot outside the city and shot. Because he had a deformed foot and limped, he could not keep up with the rest and when he fell, an SS guard shot at him then kicked him into a ditch, where he played dead. He had been in hiding for some time, working under a false name in a textile factory until he was discovered to be a Jew and sent to Auschwitz. At the first selection on arrival, he was able to stand on the toes of his crippled foot, which hurt him but enabled him to walk a few steps without limping. From his description of the examining physician, I guessed that it was Mengele who passed him to the side of the healthy newcomers. He soon learned that he could make himself useful in the camp by altering and repairing the uniforms of important people and was therefore saved from heavy work and long walks.

While he was removing the fur collar from my coat, he confessed that he had not yet found a good spot for himself in Ohrdruf; he had swindled his way into the hospital by stepping out of a line while waiting to see a doctor. He scented a chance when he saw an open door. As soon as he stepped out, the line closed smoothly behind him like flowing water and he walked through the door into the hospital proper, took a white coat from a rack and limped slowly, unnoticed, to the end of the room. He was smart and quick and knew that he had to have a function to be here. He opened a closet, took a broom, and pretended to belong to the cleaning crew just as I entered the ward with my coat. I engaged him as an orderly. Marek was reliable and faithful. (The last time I ever saw him was just after the liberation; he was limping along in a group of young men walking up the Wenceslaus Plaza, the central boulevard of Prague. We embraced and I asked him if he needed anything, maybe money. He answered proudly that he had all he needed. The group was waiting for a ship to Palestine to become members of the Hagannah, the forerunner of the Israeli army.)

Our hospital was filled to the last corner. Wherever there was space, we put a straw sack to accommodate another patient. A vicious pneumonia had spread through the camp, hitting not only the emaciated, who were trying to hold on, but also others in more protected positions who were suddenly overcome with chills and high fever despite their better nourishment. Many died in a delirium, others became progressively weakened after the fever subsided and died of cardiac insufficiency. There had been much less fatal encephalo-meningitis here after pneumonia than in the family camp in Auschwitz; perhaps these patients did not live long enough to develop this complication.

There was not much snow during those days but the icy wind made it very difficult to remain outside for very long. The days were short and air raid warnings repeatedly interrupted our work, and at night, our sleep. We heard the detonations in the neighborhood and saw the glare of fire illuminating the sky.

An alarm signaled the closeness of the enemy, our friends. The SS guards were ordered to the shelters. Ernst explained to me that during the day the American air force attacked, while at night the British combined with other Allied planes, led the raids. He hinted about contacts he had with the outside; his information proved to be mostly correct. We could barely see the formations of high-flying planes but the contrails they made in the sky were visible.

During one of these alarms Ernst came through the hospital calling for me. He found me sheltered in a corner with the rest of the personnel and those patients who were mobile. It was late afternoon. A unit working close to the bombing site had been forced to run back to camp in order for the SS guards to return to the protection of their shelter. Three of those prisoners, exhausted and half frozen, had fainted and were carried to the hospital. They were now lying on the ground in front of the entrance. We rushed to give them first aid but it was futile. Then Ernst asked me to make a house call at a barracks at the other end of the camp. The block elder was sick and had finally agreed to see a doctor. Ernst gave me an odd smile, "Be careful, he has a wild temper."

I walked as fast as I could through the camp. The work units had just returned and hundreds of prisoners were standing in line waiting for their bowl of soup. Men were moving from one foot to the other while rubbing their arms to fight the cold. I heard different languages but understood only a few. I was the recipient of envious, hostile, as well as respectful, looks and understood them all; I had been there. Finally, I arrived at the last building, which was larger than most. Here too, prisoners were waiting in front of the building, which made it difficult for me to enter. I told the prisoner who stood guard in front of the block elder's room that I was the doctor who had come to take care of the patient. He shrugged his shoulders as if to indicate that his powerful boss should not need help from anyone. When the door was opened, I observed an unbelievable scene. A lavishly dressed young man directed me, with an ostentatious movement of his hand, to wait. My future patient was busy controlling the distribution of bread to the men entrusted to his care. Through the open door, I saw his silhouette in the big room lighted by only a couple of weak bulbs hanging on cords from the ceiling. The shadowy figure was enormous. The young protégé of the block elder saw my face and responded with a coy smile. The undisputed ruler of this barracks, Max had been a famous heavyweight wrestler in Berlin. He was notorious for both his strength and his temper. Once in a personal fight he had lashed out at a man, killing him. At least this was the story he told me. Max was in prison for life when the SS went looking for tough criminals to become leaders in the concentration camps—which made Max's career.

Finally he came into the room and plunged into his armchair, old and torn but bigger than any chair I had seen in camp. His companion said, "Max has not eaten much for days, he must have lost weight." My guess was that he still weighed over three hundred pounds. His breathing was labored, his skin was gray and he coughed in spells until he became blue in the face. I listened to his chest, whose circumference seemed endless. It appeared that he had diffuse broncho-pneumonic focuses. I told him to come to the hospital. He looked me straight in the eyes and said, "I will not leave." I knew that he was powerful; I had heard rumors about his connections.

I requested a piece of paper and was given the crumpled corner of a paper bag. I wrote down the word "Sulfonamide." I explained that this new drug could help him if there was a way of his getting it. This was a grotesque parody of a prescription and there was no point in either an "Rx" or my signature. I left him tablets of the mixture we had used for years—aspirin, amidopyrin, acetaminophen and caffeine—and told him to stay quiet; he needed to rest and drink a lot. I told his young friend to apply cold compresses if the fever should return. This forceful giant became meek as a lamb. He was afraid to die of illness and to him a hospital seemed to be a dangerous place. He spoke in short, incomplete sentences, filled with slang expressions.

When I left the building, I was bemused. I thought such a type could be seen only in the movies. (Now I think of Rainer Werner Fassbinder's film *Alexanderplatz*). Max's Berliner dialect completed the picture. On my next visit he was already better. His friend told me that Max had done everything I had told him to do, even getting angry when something I ordered was missing. He never did get the "prescribed" medicine but gradually recovered. On my last visit he said that he was sorry not to have something special to give to me so he offered me a piece of bread with marmalade and we drank a kind of tea together.

In the first week of February 1945, Dr. Goldstein came for me wanting to know if I spoke any English. I told him that I could make myself understood. He hardly let me finish the sentence before he told me that I must immediately leave the patient I was examining and accompany him. We proceeded to the SS camp commando. A soldier, a man of about fifty, was waiting and asked if I was a doctor, which I "proved" by holding up my stethoscope. He addressed me with a polite, "Herr Doktor" and explained in his-long winded Saxon dialect that an injured American pilot had been captured after his plane had been shot down. After landing by parachute he had been found hurt but no one could communicate with him.

We went to the local police station. The captain in charge looked at me in my prisoner's outfit and asked me to sign in. I wondered if I should write my number tattooed on my left forearm. I decided to use my name. He asked if I was German. I answered, in effect avoiding the question, "I am from Czechoslovakia." He replied, "Aha," and gave a set of keys to the guard with whom I walked into the police prison.

He opened the iron gate of a small cell used for solitary confinement. There was nothing in the room but a long figure stretched out on the concrete floor. I had to wait until my eyes adjusted to the darkness. The man, wearing the uniform of an American flyer, was black. He was unconscious and his breathing was fast and superficial. He did not react to my voice. I used my stiff fingers to elicit tendon reflexes. I could find no trace of either a wound or any blood on his head. I asked the guard for a flashlight, which he had, but said that lately he was unable to get fresh batteries.

We returned to the captain and I explained that the man was in shock and needed to be immediately transported to a hospital or he would die in the cell. The police officer did not like the outlook; he turned to my escort saying, "Take him back." I no longer existed for him.

On the way back to camp through the village, or small town, I was struck by the sad emptiness. There were a few elderly people, more women than men, standing in front of the stores. They seemed to have a way of hearing when goods were available. They all looked tired and shabby. On their faces one could see the interruption of their sleep by air raids as well as worry. Also, along our way we met troops of teenagers exercising with a new weapon especially made for this last line of defense. On the tip of a broomstick was a small missile connected to a spring that could be triggered by a simple handle. These children were supposed to let the enemy jeep or a tank come close enough and then they were to shoot directly at a particular area of the vehicle.

I could also sense the SS guards' desperation about the turn of the war in the manner in which they denigrated us as prisoners and losers. Previously they gloried in their strength, believing in their power; they now looked angry and responded to the uncertainty of their future with defiance and viciousness toward us. Sandor believed that these were the last days of the Third Reich; his friend, who was a realist, warned us about the fury of "the dying beast."

One morning, Ernst came to the hospital in a very excited state, holding a piece of paper, which he showed me privately. It was a leaflet dropped by a Russian plane during the night. He said that the streets and fields were covered with them. The title of it was "Manifest" and it was written and signed by Ilya Ehrenburg, the Russian novelist and political reporter who had been popular in all of Europe but especially among German readers before Hitler came to power. It started with the words, "Wehe Deutschland" (Woe Germany). Ehrenburg described the atrocities committed by the Gestapo and the SS. The pamphlet warned the German people, telling them to intervene against their malignant ruling system or the total population would suffer disastrous consequences. It also warned that if they, the reasonable part of the nation, would not use this last opportunity to rebel, then all of Germany would have to assume full responsibility. Cadres of civilians were organized in the morning to collect and destroy the leaflets. Ernst asked me what I thought the reaction of the people would be. I said, "Nothing." He disagreed but did not think that any group was either ready or courageous enough to save the country from imminent catastrophe.

I was quite free in expressing myself with Ernst. I explained that I knew and understood the mentality of the Germans. In those last months of the war they must have been deeply disappointed and upset by the condition of their country. Most of the large cities were badly damaged by air attacks against which they had no defense. Most men had been drafted, many were injured and though the number that had been captured and killed in action was not revealed, however, everyone understood that it must have been enormous. The stubbornness of the German military was a combination of ingrained discipline, frenetic rage and enormous fear that led to self-deception and denial. In discussing it with Sandor and a couple of other Hungarian prisoners, I compared the German denial to our unrealistic hope while we were waiting for the last steps to the gas chambers of Auschwitz.

In those early weeks of 1945, we talked a lot about the tactics of the Allies. Most of what we said was speculation since even fragments of news that broke through to us from Radio London were distorted and were more propaganda than information. I recalled a conversation I'd had with Willy Schönfeld while we were sitting in a ditch behind the Auschwitz-Birkenau hospital barracks. I believed that only total defeat along with even more painful suffering than had been experienced after WWI could neutralize the grandiose and violent impulses precipitated in Germany by its military and political leaders. We speculated that only an equally powerful masochistic suffering of total defeat could have turned the tide of history. Small defeats might even have been the beginning of new waves of nationalism with a repetition of the cycle. Willy, with his gallows humor, as we sat behind the barracks in Auschwitz, said, "I would like to read about it in the European and American newspapers sitting in a coffee house in Prague five years from now as we did five years ago."

Ernst was very curious to hear about Auschwitz as were the Hungarian doctors, who had been there only a short time and feared for their families. They could not accept even my carefully worded commentaries, which were far from truly describing the nature of that terrible institution. Those of us who still remained, believed with conviction, that we owed it to our dead friends to convey all that we knew no matter how painful it might be, but at that time I could not tell my friends from the Hungarian transport that their elderly wives and younger women with children had no chance of leaving Auschwitz alive.

Even with Ernst, whose identity was not clear to me, I was selective in my reports. I described my observations and experiences with a kind of "played naïveté." I presented the disappearance of thousands as a mystery, as if I did not know the whole story. He was the one who concluded that the purpose of those camps in the east must have been to provide mechanized facilities for mass killing. I often wondered if he repeated parts of our talks to other Germans, prisoners or soldiers when he went freely in and out of the camp to organize needed supplies.

Rumors about the new weapons had not died but were heard of less frequently. Occasionally we found torn pieces of local newspapers that had articles about the heroic German soldier next to items expressing the need for rearranging the front. We knew that it meant retreat. Our sources of information were foreign workers, foremen and skilled laborers who worked outside the camp; some even lived outside. Their behavior varied according to their convictions. If they were outspoken collaborators, their fears were masked by fanaticism and violent, sadistic behavior toward the slave-workers, mainly Jews. They knew what to expect if the Nazis had to surrender. When I had to be responsible for their medical care, I was carefully aware of every word I uttered.

Outdoor workers who suffered bitterly from the cold continued digging ditches and making way for a future water supply for the tunnel factory, the space planned for the construction of "the new weapons." Progress was so slow on these preliminaries for the tunnel that it was a fantasy to think it would be finished when the allied armies arrived.

Toward the close of 1944 the tension had heightened. Ernst said he was extremely busy with preparations for a change. A few days later, the order came to move out to another camp. It was said that our sector, Ohrdruf II, was needed for injured German soldiers.

We packed again. I don't remember whether we moved instruments and other inventory from the hospital to our new quarters. I took a few thermometers, my white frock and a piece of bread and walked with Marek, who carried the small number of available blankets that we had conscientiously kept free of lice. Patients were moved on a truck, which passed us on our way. We were reassured to see our patients going with us, haunted as we were by the ghosts of "the selections" of the sick and weak in Auschwitz.

In the middle of February, a small transport arrived. Its members were standing in front of the office building. I saw a familiar face among them. He also recognized me and waved me toward him. Fritz was a well-known dental surgeon who had been influential in the organization of health services in the Prague Jewish community. Now he hoped I could help him stay with our clinic. I turned to our SDG corpsman who happened to be looking over the group of newcomers for possible serious medical problems. I asked to talk to him and introduced "Dr. Fritz Berl, a famous dentist from Prague" who was very much needed in our clinic. His facial expression reflected interest. He probably thought of gaining a dentist for himself and other low-rank SS men. Fritz and I celebrated our meeting with a piece of dry bread and "coffee." From that day onward we became the closest of friends.

A short time after we had settled down, we had to move again. We realized then that all arrangements would be provisory, a reflection of the military situation. The move took the whole day. The new camp was large and crowded. Medical personnel were put up in small underground bunkers built of heavy concrete walls. The roof was ground level and was camouflaged with grass interrupted by a small skylight that could be hermetically closed. I could not see how many of those shelters there were, but my first thought was that the heavy doors could be locked behind us and gas sent into the rooms from the openings above. Despite these haunting thoughts of Auschwitz, I was tired enough to stretch out on my bunk and rest, as did the others.

Soon the SS orderly in charge of medical service in these camps entered. We jumped off our beds and were informed that the bunker next to ours was the assigned clinic while the hospital itself was a large wooden barracks at the end of the camp. We went out into the darkness to look for it.

Sandor, the other Hungarian physician, Marek, Fritz Berl and I reached the end of the camp road when a rough voice shouted from a watchtower: "Halt!" We reported that we were doctors looking for the hospital. In an almost indecipherable dialect we were given permission to continue. A few minutes later we stood in front of a simple large wooden building. It looked more like a quickly built storage space than a hospital. It was a one-room bungalow filled with long rows of three tiered bunks. The lower ones were already occupied by patients. New prisoners who were arriving had to climb to the higher beds.

A man in ordinary clothing approached us. He spoke with a Hungarian accent. In a strict voice he announced that he was already in charge of the building. He may have used a title like "chief medic" and we wondered if he was a physician, an orderly, or somebody who was just taking advantage of a situation. He said that he had come with a transport of foreign civilian workers, mainly Hungarian and Rumanian.

My newly found friend Fritz took me aside. He said: "You cannot let this man give you orders. Your patients are here and you must defend your position as the physician, which may even become critical for our surviving." I left without even walking through the large hospital room and silently returned to the clinic. Part of me agreed with Fritz but at that moment I could not be any different. I don't know whether it was good judgement or that I was not ready or courageous enough to assert myself. The conclusion of this encounter took place days later.

I was resting on Fritz's dental chair while he was stretched out on a bunk waiting for the clinic to open for the crowded evening shift when the workers returned to camp. Suddenly the door opened and the SDG entered. We both jumped from our undignified positions; I hit my head on a naked light bulb that hung from a long cord over the old fashioned surgical seat. The bulb exploded into pieces. While the SS medical man protected his eyes we stood at attention. He called us out of the bunker, which was now dark, and, ignoring the awkwardness, ordered me to take over the medical care of the hospital. Later we heard that a few loaves of bread delivered for patients had disappeared, apparently taken by the "chief medic." Stealing large amounts of anything as basic as bread was dangerously greedy; rarely could one get away with it. Such were the unspoken rules in camp. One needed to know the limits as well as realize the importance of good timing; a slight miscalculation could cost one his life. My holding back at the first visit to the hospital worked out for me;

I have not, however, considered it a virtue in the decisive moments of my life. I never saw the Rumanian "chief medic" again.

We were instructed to prepare the severely ill and incapacitated prisoners to be sent to a "real" hospital while we would continue to treat only those who could soon be returned to work. On the first day of my new duty, I took a slow walk through the narrow spaces between the beds of the hospital. Patients had not been undressed since the move. A part of the room was reserved for surgical procedures, including a makeshift operating table, surrounded by medical dressings ready for changing bandages badly needed by patients who had not been attended to for days. The greatest problem was purulent foot wounds, since everyone kept on walking in spite of the penetrating pain created by the poorly fitting shoes. When it became impossible to continue working, a foreman of a work unit would eliminate whoever was lagging. The best we could do was to treat the infection; we hardly ever saw full healing. It seemed impossible to create order since patients spoke different languages and everyone spoke at once. Their needs and complaints were without end. We were told we would have very little nursing or doctoring help since most people were needed to dig the ditches for the planned water supply. Nobody ever told us where the severely ill or injured prisoners were sent. Two worlds were colliding—the one of exhausted prisoner slaves and the other of the Nazis, pushing these slaves to work beyond endurance to finish a fantasized technological project in a futile attempt not to lose the war.

While we were completing our first rounds, I observed a young man hiding between beds. He kept moving while holding on to the bed frames trying to avoid our confronting him. Asking to be left alone for a few minutes I stepped over to look at his face. He was red and shivering. He told me that he had escaped from one of the ghettos in Poland and was caught by SS troops on a patrol looking for hidden youngsters. He somehow succeeded in surviving a concentration camp, I think Auschwitz, and was finally sent on a transport with hundreds of other prisoners to the west of Germany. On the way, they found themselves full of lice. He had been in the camp system long enough to know the danger of body lice. In most instances it does not take long in a lice-ridden group for one typhus-infected louse to meet a susceptible person who then comes down with the disease. The young man who had grown up in hiding and in concentration camps knew that he was very sick; he could hardly stand up. He also knew that being diagnosed as having typhus would mean his being sent away and probably killed in order to remove the danger of infection.

He whispered, "Don't give me away." He described his having been close to death before, avoiding being sent to die and hoping to survive, especially now that the end of the war must be imminent. I hesitated. I told him if he really had typhus he would be a danger for the whole sick room. I could not see any way of keeping the place free of lice. He got to his feet to prove to me that he was not so sick. I examined him. His chest was clear except for a slight bronchitis. He also had the typical rash of typhus, a specific color that by now I clearly recognized. I had seen it for the first time a year earlier in Auschwitz. I ordered him to stay in bed as he could also have had pneumonia. I told one of my Hungarian friends, a doctor whom I had temporarily placed as a nurse, to push liquids as the patient was dehydrated from a high fever. When I left the hospital, I was not sure whether my decision was right. The drama of this young boy was on my mind every day. I wanted to save him. I saw him daily and he slowly improved. Then he was not there anymore.

There was not much we could do for patients in the hospital room. There was no new medication when our supplies came to an end. We gave first aid but our instructions were clear: Those who could not return to work quickly were to be prepared to be sent away.

One morning at roll call, I was ordered into a group of workers for a special task. About twenty or thirty of us were loaded on a truck and driven through the forest. I had tried to get out of it saying that I was expected in the hospital. Nobody listened to me. The SS guards were anxious to leave on time and yelled obscenities that were lost in the rattling of the engine. We got off the truck at a nearby railroad station where a freight train was standing on a sidetrack. We were told to unload the boxcars, which were filled with crates of turnips or some other root plant.

In the middle of the day the sirens began to blow. It was the usual time for the daily attack by American planes, whose targets were mostly railroad stations and industrial buildings. We stood still; I slipped a broken piece of one of the roots into a pocket. An SS guard saw me and pointed with his finger at me. I threw the turnip away. We heard the bombs exploding not far from the terminal and the guards, angry and upset, cursed the Allied air force. The planes climbed higher and then their sound faded. The guard came closer; he was enraged by the attack and shouted at me, "Stealing during an air alarm is punished with death." I did not hear the rest of what he said but I expected to be hung on our return to camp. I was terribly frightened. Any action that could be interpreted as either sabotage or desertion was immediately punished by hanging with few questions asked.

Each successive moment of awaiting my ordeal became longer. I automatically kept doing my work. My arms hurt from the long drawn out process. It grew dark and cold. We went back on the truck and were driven to the camp. I was preoccupied with the threat of the guard. I rushed to the clinic to see Fritz. He tried to comfort me but I insisted that he talk with either the camp leader or if he could to the SDG, both of whom by now were his dental patients. He talked with one and came back laughing and said, "Forget it." But it took me quite a while to recover. My panic had been overwhelming. We all sensed that the war, at least in our region, was coming to an end. Cruel treatment of prisoners and members of the foreign work force increased as the Germans became more frightened. They lashed out at those they felt were causing their defeat. Perhaps it was also a displacement of anger meant for their own leaders for losing the war and betraying their years of sacrifice.

The camp Elder, a criminal most likely transferred from a prison in Germany, ruled with merciless brutality. He was especially suspicious of a group of Russian prisoners who protested against the poor nourishment they received in spite of their heavy work. His only response to them was physical punishment.

One gloomy morning, I saw him limping slowly along the camp road. As other prisoners came out of their barracks, we all stopped to stare at his purposeful stride. He had started from his office at one end of the camp and, with the expression of an enraged animal, was rhythmically twirling a thin metal chain in synchronization with his step. His gesture left no doubt that he was on his way to torture and probably strangle someone. When he reached the last bunker at the other end of the road, he unlocked the door, entered and locked it behind him. No sound was heard. The whole camp was silent. We knew that in those heavy moments, a human being was slowly being put to death. Then he came out and walked back, even slower, radiating his satisfaction while we all watched with fear and hatred.

We were told later that a group of either Russian or Ukrainian prisoners had planned to assassinate him. The plan called for one prisoner to hide behind a tree and jump the elder as he walked from the barracks with his usual slow limp. The others were supposed to come to help. The assailant was apparently overcome by the elder's extreme strength and the others were frightened away.

In March, a new vaccine against typhus arrived. It was not clear to me whether it was an approved vaccine or if we were to be experimented on since some blocks were supposed to be inoculated while others were not and we were to keep statistics. We were sent in pairs to unload the vaccine at night when everyone was available after work. Even knowing the risk of sabotage, my partner, a young Hungarian surgeon, and I decided to fake the procedure since we did not trust the material or the sterility of the instruments. We told no one else. The experiment was soon aborted anyway when the camp was evacuated a few days later because the fighting was coming closer. Some days we had the feeling that we were about to be in the firing line of battle. Then it seemed to move backward for hours or days only to return again with more intensity.

Our connection with the outer world had been mainly through patients who worked in the fields. They talked about thousands, including children and livestock, moving from the west toward the inner country; sometimes creating difficulties for military convoys moving to the front. The workers also described men, clad in rags and tied to trees, who were either prisoner escapees or German army deserters. We soon received another dramatic illustration of the increased effort of the Nazis to fight the disintegration of the system.

One evening late in March 1945, when the other prisoners returned from work, we were ordered to assemble near the entrance gate. As usual, the truckloads of tired and ravenously hungry workers returning at dusk were ready for their soup and rest. The ill and injured lined up as usual in front of the clinic, but everyone had to be sent away until after the mass meeting. It was a mild evening. We heard that the commandant of the chain of camps, Ohrdruf-Krawinkel, would make an important announcement. As our medical personnel group walked slowly towards the meeting place, there was a slight air of hope around us. We knew that the advancing Allied armies were getting closer. We had met prisoners who had been evacuated from camps in the east while others were being moved from the west. The war could not go on this way. We passed the last building and walked through a group of trees separated from the open forest by a high fence. By now it had become dark. Searchlights illuminated a circumscribed area.

We saw before us a scene that resembled an open air theater with the woods as a natural stage. There were hundreds of exhausted men leaning against the gigantic fir trees while others were in a squatting position, probably trying to rest after a day of heavy labor. At the one end of the clearing there were three platforms, each one with a gallows, and on each a man stood with a noose around his neck. One in a torn uniform looked like a teenager. Then a loud voice called: "*Achtung!*" (Attention!). We all stood up silently while our eyes turned in the direction of a high-ranking SS officer who started to speak. He talked about the critical war situation and predicted that anybody who would not uncompromisingly obey an order would hang, as these three would. The first to be hanged was the youngster. His last words still cling to me with frightening vividness. With the high-pitched voice of a child he cried out: "*Mutti, ich bin doch noch so jung*" (Mommy, I am still so young). The trembling of his voice vibrated in the silence around us. The three bodies went up losing their foothold and while they dangled in the mild wind the air was filled with the sound of thousands of tired feet shuffling towards their barracks.

The next weeks were monotonous for us although they must have been crucial in historical terms. We somehow sensed this and made an effort to curb our unrest since we had no factual information about recent strategic or political developments, but only confusingly painful contradictory rumors. Somebody whispered that the SS had started to liquidate prisoners by locking them into the secretly built tunnel. Others who worked at the site denied the existence of any available openings in the rocky hills. Our anxiety charged speculations centered on our future as prisoners; we were also potential accusers as witnesses of terrible crimes.

Work in the hospital had become nearly impossible. Medical supplies were dwindling, and our rounds had become never ending walks through the rows of bunks with the patients on the third deck often not even accessible for close examination. I recognized only a few of the ill prisoners even though I might have hospitalized them myself during previous weeks. Food for the non-working ill was sparse, which contributed to their swift decline.

Fritz Berl and I shared what we could with each other, usually from grateful privileged patients who had special functions or connections. An extra piece of bread played a crucial role in the balance of our meager input of calories. We were also permanently feeding each other with the ever-so-small bits of news from wherever they came from and which were just as important to our emotional balance. Even a found scrap of newspaper hinting at a German retreat was embellished. Some German military leaders must have still been denying the obvious but shifted their descriptions from the grandiose ideas of conquest to acceptance of losses.

Willy Schönfeld and I had speculated about the paranoid rage the Nazis directed toward their victims that we were sure would end in blind self-destructiveness, reducing their own chances of survival.

Fifty years later, as I write about these experiences with the historical information about the last months of the war now available, I can see how correct we were but how greatly we underrated the German irrationality. All I remember of March 1945 is that the Allies' air attacks were more frequent and the noise of their heavy artillery, in waves from the west, came closer. Rumors started again. The SDG medical corpsman informed us that the camp would be evacuated in a few days. Those who were unable to walk would be taken by truck from the hospital. We assumed that those on trucks would not have a great chance of surviving, and talked with those patients we hoped could be put on their feet. Anyone else we were sure would be shot.

I was unsure of what to expect and, thus, unsure of what to advise others. We had heard about the difficult conditions of earlier evacuations in the face of the advancing Allied armies. Weak or sick people could not withstand the situation, but what was the alternative? In Auschwitz we knew with certainty that the feeble and sick were the first to be selected for annihilation in the gas chamber. And yet in March of 1944, we in the hospital and our patients were the only survivors of that unfortunate transport of five thousand. Now, we felt our decision about the sick and weak, an extremely heavy one based on that past experience, as well as the apparent closeness of the war's end. One doctor suggested filling up all beds with ambulatory patients and even finding rescue there ourselves. My colleagues and I, as well as those patients with whom we had frankly discussed the future, concluded that we would not rely on the "welfare" of the SS.

31

A FORCED MARCH

On the following day, the SS commander ordered us to assemble at the gate in readiness to leave the camp. The SDG medical orderly yelled at me, "Get your patients out, nobody is allowed to stay." The KAPOs ran through the camp, driving everybody into lines.

I ran to the hospital. All of the personnel were gone. Some of the patients were very anxious; others were apathetic, stretched out on their beds. There was hysterical crying and calling for help when one patient tried to get out of bed and fell down out of weakness. Outside the hospital, SS guards, with rifles in their hands, shouted threats to prisoners who were not moving fast enough. I picked up a stick, made from a branch, and used as a crutch and with it in my hand, I ran through the room hitting hard at the wooden frames of the bunk beds, screaming at the top of my voice, "Out!" By the time I reached the door I was breathless. My voice was gone as I rushed out of the hospital, not turning back. I joined my friends, who were already standing in line and beginning to worry about me. We moved out through the gate. The camp was closed behind us. By now it was afternoon. When darkness came, we were weary from staying in one place and not moving. Those from the first evacuated blocks had been standing from early in the day; it took hours for this procedure.

A prisoner, whom I had known when he worked in the camp storage clothing room, jumped into the bushes under the trees. A few minutes later, I saw him crawling away dressed in a regular suit. A friend at my side told me that this man had connections in the next town. Somebody asked, "Shouldn't we all run?" But nobody moved. We talked about the alternatives. Without outside connections, one would be lost. The population of Ohrdruf was so frightened of being accused by the SS of being dissident, that they hardly even dared look at us when we finally did march to the train station.

A long train of old, beat-up passenger cars was waiting for us. When our unit arrived, most of the cars were already overfilled. But the SS guards kept stuffing in more prisoners. People were sitting or leaning on each other, fighting for inches, swearing at their neighbors in a variety of languages. Our small group of people from the clinic stayed together trying to help each other. It made a difference in feelings but not in space. The ride was wearing and long.

Early in the morning, we left the train at a small station. Some of the upholstered second-class cars were left with a terrible odor, as well as with a fresh supply of lice and fleas. We were dirty and chilly as we stood outside the station until we were called to line up. Then we waited again. Finally, the long procession of men moved. We walked through the streets of a town whose people looked different from those in other locations we had passed. Their clothes were more formal, although rather worn out.

We were told that we were in the neighborhood of Weimar, the city of Goethe and Schiller, which, for several hundred years, had been the cultural center of Germany, and we knew that the notorious concentration camp of Buchenwald was situated somewhere in a forest in this area.

We walked on a wide, tree-lined road up a hill; I whispered my fantasy to a friend next to me, that it was a sunny spring day and we were walking up the avenue into a forest where we would find a restaurant with a view of the town with its old castles and buildings. My daydream was interrupted by noise two rows behind me. A man with a tall, heavy body was hopping arduously on one leg with the help of two neighbors who had just caught him, preventing him from falling. It could have been one of the Hungarian physicians who had worked with me in the hospital who had a nasty wound around one of his ankles, a legacy from the days of working in the ditches, or someone else of similar stature. He could not progress without the support of two people, his arms around the neck of each. We took turns at this and could go on for awhile, but then we all started to weaken and change at shorter intervals. The guards watched us

225

silently with their fingers on the triggers of their rifles. I do not remember reaching our next resting place.

It was the time of day when people were leaving their homes to go to work in the morning. On the right side of our road was a block of apartment houses. It seemed to be a clean, well-preserved neighborhood with no great damage from air raids. No industrial or military installations were visible. The gate of one of the buildings opened and a man in a dark suit came out carrying a briefcase. This was unusual at a time when one hardly saw a man of any age not in uniform. Before he could quite close the gate, he saw us, was startled and stood stiff, his mouth half-open in horror while he stared at the column of exhausted, worn out prisoners. I carefully turned around to see the cause of the horror expressed on his face. A few rows behind me a prisoner was on the ground on hands and knees. He obviously could not stand on his feet any more. An SS-guard who was accompanying our troop was bending over him digging the end of his rifle into the poor man's ribs; he threatened to kill him if he would not get up. From the door of the next house, a woman stepped out. She seemed puzzled and repelled by the view, as the posture and movement of her body expressed. The man in the dark suit turned to her and by turning his free hand up he expressed his reaction: "What will happen to us?" It was a nonverbal exchange. Then I heard a shot. I did not dare to turn around.

When we reached the top of the hill, I was very tired and put myself into "automatic," a variation of the "hibernation" trick that I had learned from Jack London, which had served me at Auschwitz, when cold became unbearable. Walking or working "in automatic" was a kind of dissociation of my perception and my action, so that I continued mechanically to repeat the same function without fully experiencing my terrible exhaustion.

32

JOINING THE CZECHS IN BUCHENWALD

THERE WAS NO ROMANTIC restaurant awaiting us in an old castle on the top of the hill as in my fantasy, only the entrance gate to Buchenwald. I have no memory of that gate, in sharp contrast to my memories of other entrances to concentration camps. Each was the entrance to unknown horrors, and each I anticipated with fear and little hope.

We were packed into an already overcrowded barracks, but were so tired that all we wanted was to rest. Several of us were on one mattress. The noise of the fighting became louder and more intense. Airplanes buzzed around including small fighters, called in the slang of that time "mosquitos." We assumed that the Allies knew about the camp and we wondered if they would be able to rescue us before the SS succeeded in destroying us.

In this camp there was a strange new fear—the absence of any German SS to keep order. Groups of prisoners of similar backgrounds began to form. Suddenly, two or three strong prisoners dragged in a young emaciated boy who was shaking and whimpering, trying to get away. One of the newly self-appointed leaders yelled at this boy, who was now a prisoner within a prison, "We will hang you, Gypsy, stealing bread!" They pushed him to the extreme end of the building. The wildness and violence in their faces made me cringe. There was a new anarchy of prisoners competing for dominance. The SS stayed in their own buildings as much as possible and gave commands from there. Rumors spread that the camp was to be emptied by sending prisoners to another place before the Allies would reach it.

Honsa, a Czech medical student who had worked in Ohrdruf with Fritz and me, made contact with a group of Czechoslovakian political prisoners in one of the buildings. When the command was given over the loudspeakers that Jews had to assemble at certain barracks, Honsa, who

227

was not Jewish, managed to have the three of us accepted into the Czech block of political prisoners. Fritz and I made our names sound more Czech. My first name had already been translated into Czech on all official documents when I lived in Prague. Now, trying not to be recognized by the SS guards, I marched, as Bohus Bloček, quickly but carefully with my two companions to the block of political prisoners where our countrymen expected us.

The building was different from the usual wooden barracks. From the outside it looked like a real house. Two men hung out of the window of the second floor. Seeing us enter their territory one called out, "Pozor zide prijdou!" (Watch out, Jews are coming!) That was an unexpected welcome! My feeling of security started to crack. I wanted to turn around, but Fritz grabbed me by the sleeve and dragged me through the open door. Two or three of the more important Czech prisoners greeted us. They were all under the tension of the last days. They knew how close the American armies were. They had heard about the pending evacuation and also knew how political prisoners from occupied countries were important as hostages for the SS. What they did not know, and neither did we until many years later, was that Hitler in his last days, hidden in his bunker in Berlin, when asked what to do with those prisoners who might be important for future negotiations, answered, "Shoot them all."

Our new companions gave us a change of clothing so that we would look more like them. We slept in their barracks that night. Sometime during the next day, the order came to assemble. The camp was to be evacuated immediately. On the way to the gate, other groups of prisoners joined us. A long column of people moved towards the train terminal. I think we passed a long row of crowded cars standing on a sidetrack. Through an open window, a voice screamed a message to us that they were Jews of various backgrounds who were being sent from Buchenwald to Theresienstadt.

American fighter planes circled over us while we boarded the train. I had been comforted by the fantasy that they knew all that was going on below. Once more we were pushed into overloaded cars. The whistle announced our departure and, through a window, I saw the next group of prisoners arriving. The speedy little fighter planes followed us. They seemed to dive nearly perpendicularly and turn quickly up after reaching our train. Sometimes our guards would shoot at them. None were hit.

228

We three—Honsa, Fritz and I—stayed close together within the group of Czech prisoners from Buchenwald. In the same car were men from other countries. We all expressed the same thought, but in different languages, that the decisive phase of our imprisonment had begun. We assumed that at this stage the responsible military leaders had to know that they had lost the war. Later, we read how Hitler and his companions still waited for the miraculous switch that would restore their power as predicted by his horoscope readings and in Goebbels' mendacities.

It was the end of the first week of April 1945. Pressed together in a slowly moving train, we were suddenly shook by the thundering noise of attacking planes. The train stopped. The guards jumped out seeking cover. The blast of exploding projectiles was frighteningly close. It took only a few seconds before the planes were gone and the SS returned to continue our trip into the unknown, but the train did not start. The SS guards came out again and moved forward to the engine, which we later saw was riddled with bullet holes. This was the end of our transportation.

Twenty years later, in California, I met a young psychiatrist, Joe, in a hospital where I taught. As we became friends Joe told me that he had been a fighter pilot and during the last weeks of the war had been assigned to strafe train engines to interfere with the remaining German transports. His missions were flown around Weimar and he knew about Camp Buchenwald. We talked about the hope it brought to the prisoners and their chance for survival in those last days of the war to have the trains brought to a standstill. It was strange to think that we might have been in the same place at the same time, albeit in such different positions.

We waited, becoming restless, uncomfortable, stiff and apprehensive. Would they just keep us locked in cars? There was no movement on the tracks around us. We missed the camp routine, our piece of bread and the rumors carried in by the work units returning from the outside; here we had no information at all. A few times, the planes returned and flew low overhead as if to be sure that our locomotive was paralyzed beyond repair. The doors of the cars were opened in the late afternoon. We assembled, flanked again on both sides by SS soldiers, and were ordered to walk. Soon we realized that all Germany was walking. Groups of women and children were moving east to the inner country to get away from the front. The old and ill were on primitive carts. Families moved their possessions in baby carriages. There were few civilian men, other than the old and crippled.

All went in one direction. I remembered the leaflets scattered from airplanes a few months earlier, "Woe Germany," the manifesto signed by Ilya Ehrenburg, a last warning before they too would be uprooted like their victims. It seemed to be coming to pass.

Our guards directed us through a town. We had grown tired and hungry, but mainly thirsty. I knew that torment from earlier times and had hoped that at least we would be given some water. The guards threatened us at gunpoint when we tried to move towards a fountain in the middle of the town.

On the outskirts of the town there was a large meadow with a few trees. Here we were ordered to lie down and rest. The grass was cold and the ground hard but it felt good to get off our aching feet. When I recovered from the painful cramps in my legs, thirst and hunger took over. I stuck a handful of grass in my mouth and chewed on it until I fell asleep. I remember nothing until the next morning when I was awakened by the mixed noises of shouted orders, blowing whistles and endless moaning.

It was quite early in the morning when we were called to form the usual marching lines. At one end of the clearing, next to the trees, was a situation of turmoil. A few prisoners were stretched out and were not able to get up. A couple of SS guards were pushing them. "Nobody stays back alive," one of our guards screamed. I waited to hear shots. We were told to go on, and we did for what seemed a very long time.

Talking had become more difficult because my throat was so dried out, my tongue was like leather, swollen and hard to move and small breaks in my palate burnt when touched. My legs were moving automatically just as they did on long hikes with my father, who would not stop before the predetermined point. I thought of him and others who had been influential in forming the person I had become and who were now gone. I had lots of time to think while my feet became numb and rolled along on their own. On that unending march, the idea of death seemed a fantasy of peace.

Somebody said we were on the road to Jena, but it did not make any difference to us. There were two masses of people on the move; we prisoners with our guards, and the frightened population. We did not see the advancing Allied forces that were announced by the presence of their airplanes and the increasing ferocity of the sounds of battle coming from the front.

We were so dehydrated that we rarely felt the need to urinate. Sandor, the Hungarian doctor in my group, who had worked with me in Ohrdruf, and became my friend, reminded me of my father. He was of the same stature and age as my father, and the same prostate trouble, which caused him to urinate with nasty frequency. He asked the guard next to us if he could step out, got permission and stayed behind the steadily progressing line of marchers. We heard a shot. I saw our guard turning back, his face mirrored what we feared. The next guard, seeing someone outside the column, must have shot him. I did not see this lovely man again. I was close to tears but had none. I was too exhausted.

Our way led us through another small town or village. The main road passed through its center with a now empty marketplace. From there the road narrowed, lined with three story apartment houses. People, mainly women, were on the sidewalks; others looked out of windows. Some of our fellow prisoners put their metal cups out, begging for water. The people turned away and the windows closed. A voice behind me said, "We will come again." The guard looked up for a second and continued his heavy step. It may have sounded like a threat to him, but he was tired too.

33

AWAKENING FROM THE NIGHTMARE

WE CONTINUED WALKING with short interruptions. I was not very alert and remembered nothing until later in the afternoon when, quite suddenly, the front caught up with and engulfed us. The air was full of gunfire. I was too numb to understand what was going on. The noise grew closer. Fireballs flew through the air. I said "If these are our rescuers, they should not kill us in the process." Then it became calm. A guard next to us, whom we had not seen before, started to talk to Fritz and to me about the past in a rather friendly tone. He had been active in the theater of a small town, liked Brecht and Weil, and had been annoyed, so he said, at the changes when Hitler came to power. We did not ask him why he was in the SS but realized that his behavior would have been considered high treason a couple of days earlier, now it demonstrated the turning point.

More fireballs surrounded us, accompanied by whistling sounds. One of my friends shook my arm and screamed, "Look!" The SS guards who had accompanied us were undressing. They could not get rid of their SS uniforms fast enough and beneath them, to our surprise, they already wore regular military uniforms. They had prepared to be captured as regular soldiers. The next moment they were gone and we were on our own in the middle of fire and shrapnel. We cowered and crawled on all fours to the bushes and, covered by them, we ran to a hill with trees. We were free. It had suddenly become very still. There was no more shooting. A few fires were burning. There were no people to be seen anywhere.

Carefully, we moved back towards the main road that we had taken during the last days but we reversed our direction, returning westward hoping to get closer to the front. My perceptions were distorted. With a shout I pointed to another hill where I saw figures in uniform. I yelled, "Get under cover they are shooting." It was an illusion. Fritz looked there and so did the others and could not see any people with guns. I grew more frightened and wanted to hide. They calmed me and we kept walking. My numbness was gone and I realized that we were free, but perhaps we could again be caught or even shot.

We walked until we reached the first houses of a small town through which we had passed as prisoners the day before. White bed sheets were hanging from the windows of private houses and official buildings. After a few American tanks arrived, the town was eager to surrender. The progressing Allied army had bypassed them but the German population was still anxiously awaiting the enemy. As our group of one to two hundred tired and hungry men in rags assembled in front of the city hall, an elderly man with a white handkerchief came out claiming surrender and offering us help. The townspeople offered us food and water if we would leave their town again. The city councilors were still afraid of Nazi retaliation if KZ (concentration camp) prisoners were found in their community.

We were ecstatic over our first meal in freedom. Bread, salami, cheese and wonderful water. Our host told us that a group of teenagers had not gone along with their decision to surrender and locked themselves in the historic town tower. They had special guns, called *panzerfaust* (tank fist), ready to attack the first enemy tanks entering the square. The city fathers were having an ongoing meeting to decide how to convince the kids to give up.

They gave us a letter with the seal of the mayor of the town, saying we were free and yet "ordered" us to walk to the border. It started to grow dark and we wondered where we would spend the night. Looking around for a place, we met a group of French prisoners of war. They had found an empty barn filled with hay where they planned to spend the night. They invited us to stay. We walked there up a slight hill. It was dark inside the barn. I threw myself down, and despite feeling stinging bites all over my body, was asleep in a short time.

I woke at daybreak surrounded by loud, excited voices in a jumble of different languages, mainly French and Czech. All of us stared at the highway a few thousand feet away. An American convoy of heavy military vehicles, including tanks, slowly and steadily moved from the west. The early morning mist lifted and we saw helicopters flying in low over and ahead of the vehicles. We had never seen such planes before. One of us discovered the first American flag. We waved our arms, shouted with joy

233

and cried—finally free to cry. I tried to run down the slight hill to the road but my feet gave out so I walked more slowly. We identified ourselves to an American officer who announced our presence via radio to his command. Soon there was a response. We were advised to march back to Jena towards the "former" Camp Buchenwald. The American soldiers and officers emptied their pockets and gave us chocolate, big cigars, cookies, whatever they had.

We dragged ourselves back while an endless line of American military was moving in the opposite direction. A few from our group were already sick from eating stuff, especially sweets, which they had not had for years. A big cigar as a first smoke after a long abstinence was not easy to tolerate. Finally, we reached the outskirts of Jena. An officer, who apparently belonged to a unit dealing with Buchenwald, led us to an empty camp section. A number of clean barracks awaited us.

I was exhausted. After the enormous overwhelming elation at the first sight of the American army came a reaction of despair. I lay down on the grass outside my new barracks. I don't know why I did not enter and stretch out on my bed but I wanted to avoid the narrowness of a room.

I could not think; I felt my head was empty. Fritz Berl looked for me and found me on the grass, knees on my chest, in a circle, eyes closed and shaking. "Hey Bohus," a shortened version of my Czech first name, "we need to work. One of our people is shaking in fever, I think it is typhus." He had pushed the right button. I got up.

34

THE FIRST WEEKS OF FREEDOM

IN OUR GROUP there were about three hundred former prisoners from Buchenwald, most in relatively good condition. As political prisoners, they were somewhat better nourished than were the Jews, but still fatigued from the last two weeks of marching and the lack of food and water. They recuperated quickly. About two thirds of them were Czechs and the rest were Poles. The local American commander found empty wooden barracks, previously used by the German military, in which we were all housed. Our official address was "East-Camp" Jena, although we hated to use the term "camp."

Fritz had arranged beds in a neighborhood hospital for our more severely ill patients where I visited them daily. He also stayed in contact with the hospital in Buchenwald. With the help of special United States Army units, we desperately tried to save the lives of prisoners who had been found in the most abominable conditions. Others, who had first appeared generally healthier, seemed to become more vulnerable after they were free and eating, often overeating. The young Hungarian physician, who together with me had been ordered to vaccinate prisoners in Ohrdruf, was an athletic and strong person but came down with typhus two weeks after liberation and died.

In the hospital, I had a well-equipped laboratory, which I used for my patients "at home" in the camp. The nurses and technicians, all German women, were very friendly and cooperative. The head technician of the lab, an attractive young woman, was particularly flirtatious and soon became rather seductive. I enjoyed having buried feelings come to life again.

A number of our fellow prisoners, who had not seen women for years, were eager to find company in the city; the German women were equally hungry for male contact. We tried to tolerate each other's adventures and

235

nobody bragged about conquests. Several of my former fellow prisoners were quite at odds with themselves and disturbed by the temptations of their surroundings. Some had wives or girlfriends whom they hoped to find again; others had so much hatred for Germans that they were either unable, or reluctant, to show any affection to those who were available. In the evenings we sat in small groups and talked about the future. We were not really sure where we Jews would go since there was nothing to go back to.

On a warm April Sunday, at the end of the second or the beginning of the third week of my visits to the hospital, I brought a patient's urine specimen to the lab for examination. I took off my jacket in order to analyze it. The young lab technician, who had succeeded in stirring up my fantasies, saw the tattooed number on my bared forearm and asked about its meaning. I told her about Auschwitz. American information services had prepared material to tell the German population what had been happening in their country, so she had already heard or read about it. She asked whether it was true that people were killed in gas chambers. When I explained it, she said, "But those were only Jews, weren't they?" I felt the blood leave my head; the glass with urine in my hand was shaking. I was tempted to splash the contents in her face. I turned around and left the room. I became firm in my decision to avoid any closer contact with the German people in this city.

The incident in the hospital was significant. I realized that it would take both sides lots of time and effort to heal the damage of the past twelve years. Fritz and I talked about it. I had not felt any obvious rage or desire for revenge since liberation. After this incident I felt anger and, even more, disappointment. Certainly I hoped that the responsible leaders and perpetrators who had established the camps would be prosecuted, but I was more interested in finding a peaceful existence for the next stage of my life.

The population of Thuringia was mostly relieved that the war was over. The American forces treated them well, in spite of their orders not to fraternize they were friendly and supportive. In contrast, we heard that the occupying Russians were very different. Their frontline soldiers were aggressive and demanding for women and jewelry, especially watches.

The announcement of the partitioning of Germany hit the population like a bombshell, Germans and foreigners alike. The Allies gave Thuringia, which included Weimar and Jena, to the Russian zone and a date was set for the American occupation forces to withdraw. The honeymoon was over. The German population was frightened; many of the former prisoners and foreign laborers realized that they would have to make a decision they had hoped to postpone. Should they return to their former countries in Eastern Europe, which would now be under Russian control, or move to that part of Germany that would remain under the auspices of the Western Allies? The war was not yet ended, but the pending takeover of Thuringia by Russian troops forced urgent decisions. We did not yet know the exact date of the change. The general atmosphere of insecurity was a painful reminder of Fall 1938 in Prague. Considering all that I had personally gone through during the last seven years, I did not think I would have more obstacles ahead as a result of the current political situation. Not so. The American army had reached the borders of a newly independent Czechoslovakia, but did not enter so that it could be "liberated" by Soviet Russia. We could choose to stay in the western part of Germany as displaced persons until we could arrange for immigration to another country, which was not a tempting idea for either of us. We wanted to return to Prague as soon as we could arrange it.

Fritz was the ultimate organizer, rarely had he been without either a car or a woman. He had managed to find a small German car and a female driver, a local German woman hired by the military, who was educated and came from a fine German family and promptly fell in love with him. The car offered mobility to be in touch with both the German and American administrations to supply our group with clothes, food and finally enable our return to Prague.

Before we left, we had the following experience: Honsa, the Czech medical student in our group, got around the city more than I did since I felt responsible for the medical organization of our quarters and didn't get out much. He knew of a well-known Czech scientist who was a professor of physiology at the University of Jena and contacted him to arrange a meeting. We three were invited to his home. He lived in a comfortable small house, somewhere on the outskirts of the city, along with his housekeeper. Despite the shortage of all food supplies, the housekeeper managed to prepare a fine lunch, which, in most of Europe, was the main meal of the day.

The professor, Emil Drumlig, was a friendly, dignified man in his late fifties. The presence of such a professor in a German university was not clear to us, but we avoided questions that could have been embarrassing for our host. He took us into his wine cellar and opened a bottle of fine red wine, which he said he had reserved for a special occasion. This was my first alcohol since I had left Prague two years earlier. I do not think I fully appreciated the meal and later it made me ill; I no longer could experience fine tastes. We had had enough to eat, thanks to Fritz sending food to our barracks, but this was a real meal. As we parted, Professor Drumlig mentioned he was planning a special treat for us. He had arranged for us to visit a friend of his who was the director of the Goethe Archives.

On the appointed day, we drove with Dr. Drumlig to the Goethe Museum and Archives somewhere outside the city. I clearly recall a modern building, mostly glass, which somehow survived all the bombing. At the entrance we were greeted by a tall, slim man, rather formally dressed in a dark suit. He was introduced as Dr. Goethe, a distant descendent of the great poet and philosopher. He led us through the rooms where original manuscripts of J. W. Goethe were on exhibit. Other papers were kept in drawers. I had been very much taken by Goethe's handwriting, which I had often used in my teaching of graphology to demonstrate the highest degree of rhythm and form. It was a great occasion for me to see the originals, the only way to truly appreciate the stroke and the script-image with all the variances of Goethe's different phases and moods.

When we completed our all-too-short walk through the museum, Dr. Goethe took us into his office and told us about his experiences during the war. During all the air raids in the vicinity, he had feared that the precious material under his care would be damaged. He told us in a lowered voice about an exciting incident that took place in the last days of the war while the city prepared for capitulation. The German army had received orders to remove the coffins of Goethe and Schiller from their crypts so that they would not fall into the hands of the enemy. This order may have come from Berlin, where Hitler, and a very few of the circle still with him, were hiding in his bunker waiting for the end. In Jena, two officers were entrusted with the procedure but, using their own judgement, they ignored the order. Disobedience was certainly unusual behavior in the

German army, but the senselessness of such a command mobilized enough conscience and personal courage for them to justify their action. Their superior officer, perplexed by their behavior, declared them to be irrational and ordered their commitment to the local mental institution for special treatment. That meant being killed by deadly injection, the "merciful" solution for those considered to be deranged. The hospital staff also refused to carry out this order. Meanwhile, the American army entered the city.

When I heard this story of these ordinary men defying orders to save their dead heroes, I wondered what had happened to the courage of the ordinary thousands who, in one way or another, must have known about the irrational mass murders during the years of war. Some had taken an active part in those executions while others had allowed them to take place, if only by turning their heads in order not to be witnesses.

Dr. Goethe also told us a postwar story. One of the first American army vehicles to arrive was a jeep that stopped in front of the Goethe museum. An American officer stepped out and entered the archives. He was the German author and historian, Emil Ludwig, one of the refugees who had left for the United States. He was sent on a mission to see if the manuscripts were intact. His interest was in a particular Goethe manuscript. He came to settle an academic debate with one of his fellow scholars about the location of a comma. We concluded our visit laughing about the grotesque juxtaposition of these two issues; one dead comma and millions who had died.

35

RETURN TO PRAGUE

In May 1945, Fritz Berl, Honsa and I left Jena in the private car that Fritz had procured earlier, but without the chauffeur, and we returned to Prague. We had been informed by the American Repatriation office in Jena that we had to keep moving through the Russian Zone, our papers allowed that, but we could not remain in any one place except for short stops. We were followed by a bus transporting Czech political prisoners from the Buchenwald concentration camp. The trip was long. We soon left the zone occupied by the American army and drove through seemingly endless stretches of bombed-out ruins.

We passed large camps belonging to the Russians that were only improvised stables; thousands of horses and heavy motorized equipment flanked the road, sometimes forcing us to detour. By the end of the day, Fritz had grown very tired and sleepy. Honsa and I could not drive. I was sitting next to the driver's seat, also fighting off sleep but I kept talking and singing in order to keep Fritz awake. When there was no answer from Fritz, I knew he was falling asleep and I would shake him. It was dawn when we entered the outskirts of Prague.

After all that had happened in Prague during the German occupation, the humiliations we had endured, the deportation of Jews, and the emigration of some of my friends, I wondered whether I would experience a feeling of coming home. I did not. I walked through the streets of the city for which I had once had the closest feelings of belonging, but felt estranged. Maybe it was not only me but also the city itself that had been corrupted. The apartment in which I had lived with my parents had twice changed hands. First a German and now a Czech family lived there. Our furniture and the rest of the contents were gone.

In Jena we were told that, as former prisoners from Prague, we could write letters "home" and send them by the special courier bringing diplomatic mail to the U. S. Embassy in Prague. Czech prisoners still had their families to write to. Who could I write to? I spontaneously wrote to Maus, my former girlfriend. I wondered how we would feel toward each other after two years, having lived in different worlds. I assumed she still lived in the same one room flat high up in a building on Rainer Maria Rilke Street. I took the tramway. My badge identifying me as a member of the organization of liberated prisoners gave me a free ride. When I got off the tram a man came up to me, put his hand on my lapel and asked, "What membership is that?" I hated it, took the sign off my suit and put it in a pocket. I did not want to be different from others again.

Slowly, I walked up the hill of Rainer Maria Rilke Street, which had its name changed into a Czech or Russian name, found the house, and entered the building with growing trepidation. I did not know whether Maus had ever received my letter. Slowly, I climbed the steep steps to the third floor. My heart was beating fast. I was short-winded when she opened the door. The meeting was nearly like a dream, unreal, in some way mechanical, but also intense. Nine months later, exactly to the day, our daughter, Ilana, was born.

EPILOGUE

BECAUSE MAUS' MOTHER was German she was able to make slight changes in her identity card and succeed in avoiding both persecution and deportation. She spent the war years giving German lessons to Czech children and taking on tasks that she could do with her hands, like assisting her mother in simple tailoring.

After having withstood the last seven years, from the occupation of the Sudets to the death march in Thuringia, I had tried to reassure myself that nothing more could happen in my life with which I could not cope. But it was an illusion. As a matter of fact, I had become more sensitive than ever to hardship because I was so vulnerable and not resistant to the daily insults and disappointments inherent in the struggle of reestablishing an existence. I was highly sensitive to anything that felt to me like rejection, discrimination, or lack of understanding of my condition. I was impatient and, after waiting only a short while in a store, would often angrily give up my position in line and leave. It was no wonder that we who had returned were categorized as "survivors" and looked upon as a special kind of "demanding" people.

My future brother-in-law, Walter Kohner, who had left Czecho-slovakia before the war, had become an American officer working in psychological warfare, and was stationed at the time in Luxembourg. He came to Prague in late 1945, looking for traces of my sister Hanna, who had also survived, and he found me. Hanna had returned to Amsterdam, the place from which she had been deported along with her husband, who had been killed on arrival at Auschwitz. Walter and I went to visit our hometown of Teplitz. One of the things we saw was the site of the old Jewish temple that Walter had attended as a child. There was nothing but grass, wiped out as if it had never been, like the village of Lidice to which we also made a pilgrimage.

Gottfried Bloch and Walter Kohner at Lidice,
"or what remained of it." — September 1945.
Sign says: "Here was the community of Lidice" (in Czech and Russian)

The struggle with the new Czech bureaucracy made me again feel like a refugee asking for favors, which touched my open wounds. Confirming my citizenship in the new Republic was not easy. Germans had to leave the country and we Jews, who had lived among them and who spoke German or had been educated in German schools, had to go through great efforts to prove our identities. I had to stand in long lines to get forms for all kinds of applications just to be acknowledged as a regular person returning home—there were applications for an apartment, for food stamps and for student financial support. Jewish organizations, mainly the Joint Redistribution Committee, (which we called the Joint), helped me over the first months. After almost a year's delay, I was finally allowed to apply to the Czech University. The German University was closed, as were all other German institutions. To complete my medical studies for my degree, I had to take final examinations in all subjects, this time in Czech, and was finally graduated from medical school January 31, 1947.

I worked in a few different hospitals before I arrived at the neuro-psychiatric department of Vihnoradska Hospital, a university hospital in Prague, where I assisted Professor Šebek in teaching medical students. I loved my work, which was the most important and satisfying part of my life.

However, I considered leaving Czechoslovakia when the opportunity would arise. I was sad to leave my new friends, my colleagues, my acquired position and the country. However, I knew that I could not tolerate the political pressure and felt that I had to leave before I would become too deeply rooted again. After having survived the German terror, I could never live unfree again. Two incidents were decisive.

The university hospital political administration was run by the Czech Communist Party, an agency of the U. S. S. R. One day there was a mass meeting of the total staff at which everyone was urged to express complaints and make suggestions. A maintenance man, a veteran party member, arose and asked why there were so many Jewish doctors at the hospital. Very few had even survived the war or returned to Prague. After a heavy silence, he was referred for further political training.

The second incident involved my being visited by a friendly Party functionary who explained that psychoanalysis was a bourgeois indulgence, outlawed in the U. S. S. R. and my continued interest in it could endanger my career. I understood.

Although I had registered for an American visa in 1938, it was still not accessible. In the beginning of 1948, I had what seemed to be a last chance to leave Czechoslovakia with a transport to Palestine as a volunteer in the Hagannah, the forerunner of what was later the Israeli army. Before all the formalities of leaving were completed, the year 1948 was over. Israel was created and had declared its loyalty to the West. Since Czechoslovakia had increasingly come under the tight control of the Soviet Union, it was very difficult to get an exit permit to go to Israel, particularly for younger people and physicians who were needed by the Czech military. The War of Independence made Israel's need for doctors more urgent. In the early part of March 1949, I left Prague with my family on a transport to Israel, the only chance for a doctor to leave the country.

We did not have individual passports, but were on a collective paper for the whole transport from the Czech government, which had agreed to offer this procedure one last time. In Vienna, Russian soldiers entered the train. With no personal passports, they looked critically at our papers, but finally let us pass. In Naples, Italy, we boarded a boat with hundreds of other emigrants. Later I learned that I had been in the last transport to leave the country. As happened so often before in my life, I had made it by a hairsbreadth.

By the time I arrived in Israel, the first war was over. Almost immediately I was offered a position in a psychiatric hospital, called Geha, belonging to the Kupat Cholim, the worker's health insurance that covered most of the population. It was near Ramat Gan. The head of the hospital, Dr. Hans Winnik, a psychoanalyst trained in Vienna, was very helpful to me. I again had to learn a new language and readjust to a postwar kind of modest living. The hospital had nearly a hundred beds, mainly for acute psychoses and severe borderline patients. An open sanatorium for lighter conditions, particularly depressions, was connected to it but was in a different building.

I was accepted into the Israeli Psychoanalytic Society as a candidate and started my analysis with Dr. Moshe Woolf. He was known for his papers on psychoanalysis and the Russian Revolution. Dr. Woolf met with me in his music room. I had said that I would like to begin analysis as soon as it would be convenient for me. He responded that there is never a favorable time, one just begins when one has the opportunity and he accepted a modest fee considering my hospital salary. At that time, Dr. Woolf was seventy-one and working full time, which for him meant night and day. He was an experienced clinician of the first generation of analysts and was the first person who heard most of the details of my Holocaust experiences. It was only a few years after the war and my emotional reactions to reliving them were strong. A few months after starting analysis, I went through a painfully depressive state, it took me close to half a year to work it through and then I felt better, maybe better than ever before. Often during my analysis, I heard deep moaning coming from behind the couch. Dr. Woolf went through hard times with me. We both agreed that to take care of some of the narcissistic injuries that I had experienced as a result of the interruptions of my life would need more time and distance.

In Israel, I had a small analytic practice along with my hospital work that included all the biological and pharmacological methods of that time, including insulin and convulsive (electroshock) therapy. Dr. Woolf hated bureaucracy and rigidity and understood my desire to apply psychoanalytic principles in therapeutic work where the usual psychoanalytic technique was not appropriate. I worked twelve and fourteen hours a day and was involved in seminars, consultations and teaching. We trained psychiatric residents and nurses. I was involved in research using the Rorschach test and graphology, a carryover of my work with Willy Schönfeld. A group of psychoanalysts wanted to learn more about these methods and asked me to conduct seminars at night. After a few years I became the medical director of the hospital. Winnik became professor at the Hebrew University in Jerusalem and took over that teaching hospital. In addition to being hospital director, I was also on the psychiatric advisory board of the government and a consultant to the air force. I enjoyed my work but hated administrative meetings.

In April 1953, I was in a staff meeting when I received an urgent phone call from a travel agent in Tel Aviv. I did not interrupt the meeting. A day or two later there came another urgent call that he had a ticket for me to visit the United States to appear on a television show. He said, "Your time is running out." I did not know what television was and did not respond. I then received a telex from Paul Kohner. Paul was an important Hollywood agent who had gone to the States before the war and had helped many European actors and theater people emigrate and helped them find work in the entertainment industries. He was the eldest brother of Walter, my sister Hanna's husband. He wrote that I was scheduled to make an appearance on a television show, *This is Your Life*, which would be about my sister Hanna, but it was a surprise for her.

When I tried to get a visitor's visa from American immigration authorities, I was told I was ineligible because I was on a list of applicants to emigrate to the United States, something I had been trying to do since 1938. Through personal intervention by someone in a position of authority at the U. S. State Department, an exemption was granted. It seems that *This is Your Life* was that individual's favorite show. Other complications came about as the result of actions taken by those who feared that I might not return from such a trip. Another personal intervention by a friend, a member of the Israeli High Court, made the trip possible.

I arrived one day before the program was scheduled and spent four, not-quite-real weeks that were emotionally mixed. It was during the McCarthy years and some of the European emigrants whom I met told me that they lived with great insecurity. Symbolically, their luggage was always packed. Others who heard of my intentions to move here as soon as the quota would allow (whenever that would be) encouraged me to stay and see what could be arranged from the States. This was against my feelings of obligation and I returned to Israel as planned. After experiencing some of the luxuries I had not encountered before and hearing about how difficult it was for foreign physicians to receive a license to practice, I felt undecided about what I wanted for my future. When I returned to Israel, my close friends, although happy to see me, thought that I again had followed the letter of the law rather than protect myself.

That experience certainly created mixed feelings. It was ironic that all bureaucratic red tape was cut to get me to America for a television show when, in earlier years, no rules were bent to save my life.

My seven years in Israel were interesting ones—active, exciting, productive and when, in 1955, my application for emigration to the United States finally made the quota and was approved, I felt caught on the horns of a dilemma. I had registered for immigration at the U.S. Consulate in Prague after the German occupation of Czechoslovakia in 1938. It took eighteen years before my turn came. This was my only chance but the Israeli Army again would not give me the OK for an exit visa. I don't know whether I really wanted to leave, but I wanted the freedom to make my own choice. We settled the conflict. I agreed to serve one more year as a psychiatrist in the armed forces and then would be free to go. At the end of August 1956, I left Israel. I was forty-two years of age and longing for a somewhat more comfortable life for myself and for my family. America was the great temptation. My sister, Hanna, was living in Los Angeles with her husband, Walter, her childhood sweetheart who had found her again after the war.

For the most part, I found a very friendly and helpful acceptance into the psychoanalytic community of Los Angeles and met a number of wonderful people. Getting my California license to practice medicine was less friendly and more difficult. One of the conditions of the state of California was that I had to prove that an American trained doctor would have the same chance of acquiring a license to practice in Czechoslovakia as I would here. I had an image of the clerk in the Ministry of Health in Prague reading my letter and laughing with his comrades. Only such current writers as Kundera, Havel, Klima, or Skvorecky could do justice to this scene. No normal person with an American license would apply there under the circumstances that existed then. Of course, I never got a response from Prague and the California board waived the demand but three years later. This was a frustrating span of time during which I regretted having made the move. When I finally was accepted, I had to pass the California written board examination, followed by two years of internship.

When we arrived in Los Angeles in fall, 1956, Noretta, the mother of one of our daughter's classmates, introduced herself as head of the school's welcoming committee and invited our daughter to participate in the Halloween festivities. An important friendship started. In 1971, after twenty-four years of stormy marriage, Maus and I were divorced. Noretta also divorced and we married. She had some background in working with veterans and went back to school for a marriage and family counseling degree and later a Ph.D. in psychology. We had a few intensive years of working, traveling and comfortable living together.

Noretta was a remarkable person. Twice in her life she was seriously ill but continued to work and live, in both instances, a nearly normal life. The first illness occurred when she was in her twenties and she recovered. She could find enjoyment and pleasure in life despite being ill. Her story was dramatic, "never a boring moment," she was fond of saying. In 1975 she was found to have intestinal cancer, This second time she gave up, deciding "that was it." She died in 1977 at the age of fifty-three—another loss in my life.

When Maus no longer felt that she could remain in her apartment, she entered a retirement home, where she met and married an elderly Viennese widower. He died a few years before her. She died in 1996 from a massive heart attack.

My daughter has become a successful painter and art teacher. When she was born on February 12, 1946, neither her mother nor I were ready to provide the comfort and security so important for the beginning of a new life. The first words she learned were in Czech. Her favorite play activity, whenever she could reach a crayon, was scribbling on any surface, including walls. Her stroke was a powerful and expansive movement towards the right margin. She called it, "making A and U," her expression for writing.

When we moved to the newly created state of Israel in 1949, Helena, as she was named at birth in Czechoslovakia, not only changed her language and learned Hebrew in playing with the children of the neighbors and at school, but she also changed her name to the Hebrew, Ilana, meaning "little tree." In 1956, when we moved to Los Angeles, we found ourselves in a very different world and Ilana needed to conquer yet another language. I am sure that the transition was not much easier for her than it was for me.

In those years her hobby was dancing. She responded to any kind of music and would improvise wherever she was, forgetting her surroundings. She watched a ballet class only once but did not want to participate at all. From junior high school her main interests were drawing and painting; dancing became a part of the past. One of her first drawings was of the Charles Bridge in Prague, which she did spontaneously from her memory as a three-year-old. It now hangs on the wall of our library.

Ilana had a Southern California high school life, with girlfriends, proms, and surfer boyfriends. She went on to college to study art and taught art to high school students. Working through the difficulties of her life included a routine job at the telephone company and the additional risks of becoming a working artist. After many daunting adversities, which she has struggled through successfully, she has her own studio and her paintings are shown in some of the most distinguished galleries in Los Angeles and other cities as well as being represented in national publications. All of the places she has lived in her life are present in her paintings.

She now teaches adults, some of who have become good artists in their own right and, many have told us, that she is not only a good teacher but a sensitive and psychological mentor as well. She is an attractive, tactful person and is married to a landscape designer.

Meeting Rosalyn, the woman who has been my wife for the last twenty years, was another stroke of good fortune for me. Something clicked at the first encounter, and a few months later we decided to live together and then married. Many levels of our relationship have allowed pleasure and joy from the most primitive to the most sophisticated and intellectual areas. In addition to our personal life, we share a common philosophical *Weltanshauung* and a similar approach to our professional work. This has led to our successful joint practice in group psychotherapy, couple therapy and teaching, in addition to our own individual work. Rosalyn's background as a highly psychoanalytically trained clinical social worker with a doctorate brought an additional richness to our work in writing and reviewing. Roz was of enormous influence in starting this book, insisting that we buy a computer and that I learn to type. She is poetic, humorous, a talented writer, and an incessant reader. I envy her capacity for pleasurable absorption of literature. It is a lucky turn that the last chapter of my life is such a happy one. Without her, this book would never have been written.

CHRONOLOGY

1912

Marriage of my parents, Max and Herta (Birnbaum) Bloch, July 12.

1914

I was born in Teplitz, then a part of Austria, October 15.
WWI began with the assassination of Prince Rudolph in Sarajevo, Austria, July 28.

1918

Creation of the first Czechoslovak Republic as an independent nation, October 28.
End of WWI. Peace signed at Versailles, France. Hitler said it was unjust to Germany, which became his cause to redress, November 11.

1919

My sister Hanna was born, September 9.

1921

Family visits Frau Leube in Dresden.

1932

My graduation from RealSchule (non classical secondary school), June.

1933

Studied Latin for medical school. Failed for being Jewish, later passed.
Delayed graduation from medical school for seven years (but saving my life).

1933–1934

Beginning medical school at the German University (pre-clinical).

1934

Hiking trip to the Alps with Walter Bajkovsky, summer.
Assassination of Austrian Chancellor, Dollfuss, by Nazis.
Hitler destroyed the organization known as S.A. (Storm Troopers).

1938

Nazi Germany took Austria, March.
Chamberlain acceded to Hitler allowing annexation of Sudetenland to Germany, September.
German University of Prague taken over by Nazis while Prague remained free, September.
My last semester of medical school was unfinished when all Jewish students were expelled, September.
My family came to Prague from Teplitz (part of the Sudet), November.

1938 (continued)

My first registration for a U.S. Visa with American Consulate in Prague, November.

Volunteered at the Jewish Community Center, Prague. Met Willy Schönfeld, November.

Kristallnacht, November 9.

Jews accounted responsible for destruction resulting from Kristallnacht and ordered to pay reparations of one billion Reichsmarks, November 12.

I became an employee of the Institute for Retraining, Jewish Community Center, December.

1939

The Nazi army ("metal circus") invaded Prague, March 14.

Nazi Germany invaded Poland. Allies declared war on Germany. All borders closed. Willy Schönfeld missed his departure, September 1.

1940

Pact between Hitler and Stalin, January.

Construction of concentration camp at Auschwitz begins, February 21.

Hitler took Belgium, Luxemburg and the Netherlands, May 10.

Willy and I traveled to Olomouc and other cities, to organize vocational guidance programs, June.

The fall of France, June.

The Battle of Britain began, June.

1941

Nazi Germany began offensive against Soviet Russia, June 22.

A letter smuggled out of Auschwitz—the first we heard of what went on, September.

The first transport of a thousand people left Prague for the ghetto in Łódź, October 14.

The opening of Theresienstadt after the Czech population was evacuated.

Pearl Harbor attacked by Japanese, America declared war on the Axis powers (Germany, Italy and Japan), December 7.

1942

I began forced labor building a road to the home of Reinhard Heydrich, Commander of all Bohemia and Moravia, Spring.

Heydrich is gunned down and the entire Czech village of Lidice wiped out in retaliation, May.

All Jews held in German concentration camps are ordered to be transported to Auschwitz, October 4.

1943

My family and I were deported from Prague to Theresienstadt March 6.

I entered a transport bound for Auschwitz, September 6.

My arrival at Auschwitz, September 8.

On the Day of Atonement (Yom Kippur) I observed, with Eric, the "selection" of women thrown from the barracks, October.

My parents' transport arrived in Auschwitz, December.

1944

Eleven of our transport from Theresienstadt were saved from the crematorium. Over 3,000 died March 7.

The end of the Czech Family Camp where my parents and Willy were killed and I was transferred to the Central Hospital, July.

1944 (continued)

Liquidation of the Gypsy Camp, August.

Rebellion at the Crematorium in Auschwitz, October 7.

My sister Hanna arrived in Auschwitz on my birthday, October 15.

Himmler ordered the destruction of Auschwitz. Nazis attempted to hide evidence of the exterminations, October 26.

I was in a transport to Berlin for quarantine in preparation for hard labor, October 28.

Hard labor at Ohdruf in the Thuringian Woods, November.

Dr. Goldstein found me and helped me to work again as a doctor, December.

1945

Soviet troops liberate Auschwitz, January 27.

Fritz Berl arrived in Ohrdruf and joined our staff, February.

Forced march to Buchenwald, March.

Liberation from Buchenwald by U.S. Army, April 13.

I returned to Prague, May.

Maus and I were married, July.

My future brother-in-law, Walter Kohner came to Prague. We visited Tepliz and made a pilgrimage to Lidice, December.

1946

My daughter was born, February 12.

I returned to school, this time to the Czech University to finish my medical school, Fall.

1947

I was graduated from Medical School and began to practice in different hospitals, January 31.

1947–1948

Joined Dr. Dosužkov's task force translating Freud into Czech.

1949

I left Prague with my family for Israel. I began to work, at Geha Hospital and began Psychoanalysis with Dr. Moshe Woolf. I learned another language (Hebrew), March.

1953

My first trip to the United States for *This is Your Life* television program, May.

1955

My application to emigrate to the U.S. finally approved. I agreed to remain in Israel for one more year.

1956

I arrived with my family to live in Los Angeles, and another language (English), Labor Day.

1960

I began my internship at Good Samaritan Hospital.

1961

I was accepted into the L.A. Psychoanalytic Society and Institute, February.

I received my California Medical license, November 30.

APPENDICES

APPENDIX I

Psychology of Nazism and the Survivor

I HAVE OFTEN BEEN ASKED how I deal with my traumatic memories and how I could bear the traumas of others in my work. I consider these important issues to address, both from my own background and personality as well as psychoanalytically. Each informs the other.

My own psychoanalysis with Dr. Woolf helped me deal with traumatic memories; my work with those patients who were severely traumatized contributed to my own reparation. New life experiences have been another factor, and the writing of this book has also been a continuing self-analysis, an important process.

When I started to write, I wondered how reliable my memory would be. The process of writing was not easy and often I resisted recalling pain. There was a "warming up" after an interruption, then a hazy picture would come to me, followed by a flood of emotional re-experiencing, leading to a sharp image and a heightened intensity. Anxiety and familiar panic returned and gave the writing an added dimension. My dreams became more involved with old feelings and conflicts. My sleep was less restful. Whenever I finished a section, I felt relieved, especially when it dealt with the most gruesome of times. Not only did I become freer as I let go of my privacy but in reliving events I found that I often gained new insights about my past coping behavior and in understanding others. What I have just described has a great resemblance to the therapeutic process of psychoanalysis.

Another ordeal interrupted my writing, a trauma of the body. In February 1987, I needed bypass surgery. The hours before and after surgery are vague, yet I recall in those free floating spaces, the same familiar wisps of primitive fear that I had felt during the war, a desperate holding on to life, holding on to breathing, on to being. Since I had managed to live through other terrifying experiences, I had expectations of pulling through this one. My omnipotent fantasy of survival was again reinforced. Once more I found myself touching that familiar territory of the margin of existence. After my recovery, I slowly began to write again.

I had a secure, soothing environment in the first years of my life and yet, I was a weak and anxious child. The traumas of my early years arose from my tenuous beginning and from an atmosphere tense with the anxiety of those around me. My mother had already lost one child at birth; then I was born, a "preemie" of doubtful survival. World War I was followed by the fall of the monarchy, the carving out of new countries, and economic worries. The prolonged absences of my father, influential in my early years, led to my being cared for primarily by women, who nourished me with love and attention as well as food.

As a substitute for my father's real presence, I idealized a powerful figure with whom I could identify. The first fantasies and daydreams that I recalled from childhood in my analysis with Woolf involved memories of wishing for the aggressive control of groups of children with whom I played and commanded by ordering military-type exercises, punishing them if they did not comply. Although these were my fantasies in analysis, they gave me some emotional understanding of the Nazi yearning for power and the punitiveness of the Nazi psyche that motivated their behavior toward victims.

The glorification and distance of the father in the German family culture probably led to the yearning for a father-leader for many young Germans. The need for my father translated into my wish for pairing with a capable man with whom I could confide and whom I wanted to care about me, in order for me to gain strength. This is an important theme in my history, including my survival.

Wilfred Bion, an English analyst, (1959) wrote about the concept of pairing in groups, a phenomenon he noticed in his own observations in the military during the war. He described it as the need to feel a connection with another and applied it to psychoanalytic group psychotherapy. Heinz Kohut, an analyst originally from Vienna and later from Chicago, developed the concept of the alter ego or "twinship function" stating that it was a lifelong and normal process to look for another with whom to identify and feel a likeness. It allows one to have feelings of being acceptable. Perhaps the many young Germans, who became Nazis, also needed the masses of their military companions for this reason. It begins with the little boy's wanting a merger with the father but it expands to likeness with others as one matures in order to preserve and extend the development of one's self.

My first twinship relationship, after my idealized and feared father, was with Herbert Hall when we were schoolmates over the years in Teplitz; both were interested in science and planning our futures. We propelled each other into medicine. When his family moved to another city, other friends took over that role. One was Walter Bajkovsky, the friend with whom I traveled to Italy and shared the experiences of seeing the dawning of World War II.

Twinship relationships have been a theme in my life, becoming more intense during critical times. After I was no longer permitted to attend medical school and went to work at the Jewish Community Center, I developed such a relationship with Willy Schönfeld. Willy and I gave each other strength and hope during the years in Prague, Theresientstadt and Auschwitz. The freedom to speak openly was rare and dangerous. To share humor and future plans helped us over the worst moments. Much of this book is the completion of my obligation to report as the surviving one and also to acknowledge his significance beyond his own life.

Otto Heller, the hospital chief in Auschwitz, and I were together twenty-four hours a day and our twinship was a part of that work. Our similar professional philosophies and medical devotion helped each of us maintain our decency, allowing us civilized values in an uncivilized world. This was crucial for our moral survival and preserved the possibility of a future for me. Otto's standing up for me to Hans, even though it might have been dangerous for him, was testament to his loyalty.

Fritz Crohn and I had a similar relationship, brief as it was, starting from our leaving Auschwitz for Berlin. How much more caring could anyone be in such circumstance as to share his meager daily ration with me on the day my bread was stolen? That is something I could not have expected from anyone.

Another step in my survival was my companionship with the tailor from Prague. When in Ohrdruf working on the tunnel, we desperately conspired for a way to rescue ourselves from what we feared would be our imminent collapse. Being all alone among masses of people in Ohrdruf without contact was horrifying. One could fall down in the midst of many and no one would pay attention, as if one had never existed.

Dr. Goldstein, by allowing me to work on a medical team, saved my life. Also being able to work again as a doctor helped my self-image. When Fritz Berl appeared in Ohrdruf as a member of a transport from Auschwitz, I succeeded in getting him into our clinic as the dental surgeon. We were supportive of each other; his mode was one of action and shaping life while I was the more passive. I was able to learn from him. We were close even after our return to Prague, and later in Israel and have been friends ever since.

In Los Angeles, my first real friend, professionally, culturally, linguistically and personally, was Martin Grotjahn, who was a non-Jewish German psychoanalyst originally from Berlin. It is a testimony to individualism that we two, from different parts of a similar culture that had been at war with each other, could become so close. He had an appearance of pride, narcissism and a kind of playful arrogance that at times was charming, sometimes insulting, and at other times alienating. He attracted many of "the beautiful people" of the entertainment industry, who profited from his insight as well as gained from his posture. At times, being with Martin felt like an internal tennis match. Often, I felt enriched in my self-esteem by the attraction of his narcissism, at other times uneasy and inferior.

When Martin became ill and was dying, I again took on the role of helper and healer. My experiences in aiding others meant that I was not helpless, a compensation that could allow me to develop what Matte Blanco calls "conscious asymmetry" with the surround, not to get lost, to be different, to hold on to my self.

Continuing self analysis has been a reparative process for my old wounds. An effective therapeutic relationship serves the patient but in the process of helping the patient the analyst also learns about himself, and often is able to gain insight and repair some of his own traumas. Both persons in the relationship influence each other, knowingly and unknowingly. Each therapeutic relationship of patient and analyst is a created experience that is unique. In the advances and updating of contemporary psychoanalytic theory, this experience is referred to by the term "intersubjectivity," a psychoanalytic version of postmodern thought.

My work as a physician, psychiatrist and analyst has been of prime importance. I felt lost whenever I no longer was allowed to practice. Even disasters can, at times, yield something positive. In 1938, when I could not do my life's work, I looked elsewhere for occupation and found a place in the Jewish Community Center. There I learned graphology, which served to keep my mind active in critical times and has also greatly enriched my psychological knowledge over the years.

Handwriting, as any other intentional, voluntary movement, like one's walk, speech, artistic creation and gestures, contains unique personal characteristics. Scientific graphology studies these elements of expressive movements. It entered psychiatry with Kraepelin in the 1800s, although its own roots go back much earlier.

I cannot look at a signature or a fragment of handwriting without having a response, which may give me important clinical information about changes in a patient, either improvement or sometimes deepening depression and self-destructiveness. It can have an influence on my clinical direction of treatment and my prognosis about a patient. Graphology has not been accepted in the United States as readily as it has been in Europe and is often used here as party entertainment or is viewed as an occult activity.

Regarding the second issue I raised: How, as an analyst and a survivor, can I work to heal others? Often patients who are survivors have said to me, "You cannot even imagine what I am talking about." At that moment I may agree with the patient, because I am not that person, but I might mention that I have had similar experiences. In addition to this being the truth, it prevents a therapeutic stalemate and allows us to go on with the treatment. This particular issue has been a point of controversy in many psychoanalytic discussions; however I have felt more comfortable with this self-disclosure, although I do not usually introduce much of my own life into the treatment process.

Treating patients who have been traumatized in their adult life has been my special interest, including how they deal and cope with aging. One cannot do what patients ultimately wish for—to help them forget. I know from my own experience that one cannot erase memory by "amputation," leaving a vacuum. What the healer can do, to a certain degree, depending on the patient's personality, is to reduce the intensity of feeling by freeing and separating the memories of other traumatic associations, especially earlier ones, by exploring the pre-traumatic developments and disappointments, as well as the losses and narcissistic insults that occur after trauma.

Sandor Ferenczi (1933) describes, particularly well, forgotten "encapsulated" childhood traumas. As an adult, the patient, with the analyst's help, uses associations to revive them as his ego becomes more able to tolerate pain. In contrast, massive and accumulated traumatic experiences in adulthood, such as what we lived through as victims of persecution during the Holocaust, are not sufficiently repressed to be forgotten. These memories are fixed, "unfree" and unable to be altered by the usual defensive process. They are there on the edge of awareness, always ready, due to their intensity, to invade present day life.

I remember the unbearable feeling of pain hearing the quartet playing Beethoven in the nearly empty auditorium in Theresienstadt, and even now when I listen I re-experience much of that feeling. Often I "need" a small piece of bread after a meal, which reassures me after all those times when I did not have enough to eat. Despite the fact that I am not a religious person, when I rise from the table after eating, I say, "Thank you," not to anyone in particular, even when I am alone. When I hear a railroad train and the noise of the tracks, Auschwitz comes immediately and unbidden to my mind. When I am in the midst of nature, I immediately think of and smell the Thuringian woods where I labored; I breathe deeply of the air of freedom. When I hear someone scream, I hear my parents and friends on their way to the crematorium and I want to see if I can help. When I see a young mother with her child in her arms or holding hands, I feel overwhelmed, and recall the day I watched mothers and children leave the Czech family camp, walking toward their death. When I lose someone I am closely attached to, I mourn again out of the scars of those old wounds. It is not easy for me to go to funerals; I have lived so much with death.

Holocaust trauma may be amplified during situations that are life threatening in the later years, particularly when there is illness, risky surgery, shock trauma like fire, earthquake, accident, as well as personal loss.

The therapist has to consider that such patients are vulnerable, highly narcissistically defended, and that any interpretation may be experienced as a criticism, sometimes leading to rage and interruption of the treatment. Patients may go to alternative kinds of treatment or seek compensating life situations, but frequently return to the original therapist. The process of maintaining the thread of continuity of one's sense of self is probably what propelled some patients to return. Kohut's concept of the interrupted *time axis* (1985) helped me better understand those patients and my own traumas of the Holocaust. One needs to understand the work involved in connecting what came before the abrupt interruptions of normal life, to what comes after.

Sometimes survivors react similarly to those who have borderline personality disorders, even though the survivor's emotional arrests occurred later in their psychological development, usually in adolescence or early adulthood. Children and older people had minimal chances of physically surviving the Holocaust at all. Psychologically, there is enormous narcissistic resistance to accepting that emotional pain relates to more than the persecution; but other trauma may have occurred earlier and been repressed. When one has lost family, there is a natural resistance to recalling them as imperfect, it may even feel disloyal to question their past choices or behavior.

The analyst, as a repairing "self-object," is crucial in the treatment of traumatized people. Any "self-object" relationship is important. To foster this, the usual analytic process has to be modified to help the patient tolerate the pain and remain in treatment. The conventional slow development of analytic treatment, unstructured and in the form of free associations, is usually too frustrating for the lowered tolerance of such patients who have experienced near death. In death fearing situations, as we felt in Auschwitz, there was a feeling we called "being lost," an endless falling sensation. The English analyst Dr. Donald Winnicott conceptualizes such anxiety in infants as a baby's sensation of "falling forever" (1965). Kohut's "disintegration anxiety" (1977, p. 104) describes the adult fear of "loss of humaneness as psychological death, the total loss of an empathic environment" (Kohut, 1985, p. 16). Nazi behavior was more than sadistic; it was intended to completely dehumanize a person. I think that the alter ego experience is particularly crucial for the regaining of a sense of being human, being like the other, which supports the extended recovery of the shaken self.

I do not believe that the cruel atmosphere in Auschwitz around the killings was an expression of sadistic pleasure. The cruelty of the executioners, the screaming, swearing and beatings were necessary accompaniments to render the victims nonhuman, and therefore avoid any kind of identification with them. I think of the lab assistant in Jena who said to me, "But they were only Jews." Robert Jay Lifton calls the split in Nazi behavior, "doubling" (1986). The double orientation in their behavior allowed them to be both ordinary feeling men and women with their families and peers and to tolerate not feeling at all in their complicity with destruction and murder.

In the late seventies, a new concept emerged—that of "the aging survivor," a fusion of geriatric and post-traumatic conditions. In my practice I have seen people who had functioned well and seemed reasonably recuperated from their war experiences, but as they grew older, were more limited in their functioning and found themselves unable to cope. The biological persecution of aging evokes a reliving of the earlier persecution.

Many survivors were extremely ambitious and accomplished people in their fields; some were well-to-do, a few even prominent or famous. They had a common addiction; they were driven beyond reasonable boundaries toward work and achievement in order to escape from their unfree associations, which interfered with their ability to enjoy life. On reaching an age or condition that prohibited their fast pace, the narcotic of work that had soothed them was no longer available and they began to feel recurrences of past hopelessness, despair and emptiness.

I have seen other aging survivors who never succeeded in finding work or a position that was more than just enough to provide for them and their families. Such individuals had been waiting passively for years for an opportunity for success and then, when forced to retire, found themselves feeling bitter, disappointed, and unfairly treated by fate.

The earlier conflict between the denial of mortality and the threat of imminent annihilation is sometimes revived in old age. One needs to "relocate" one's own significance in order to survive with any sense of value that can make this stage of life worthwhile. Patients describe their increased suffering, helplessness, passivity, and dependency, which often places demands on their families that are difficult to accept. It may be particularly hard for adult children, who may have idealized a parent as a strong survivor, to observe such decline.

Suicide is a significant issue for the aging survivors. The idea of ending a life that becomes unbearable is, as might be expected, something that many of us, during the war, considered even though we were younger. My own lifestyle was a strong defense against this. I worshipped nature and the rather mystical systems of all life-supporting adaptations. This gave me strength, tolerance and control of self-destructive impulses for quite a long time. More than once, I contemplated the idea that just switching off would be a relief.

Many times I have been asked, "How could you tolerate waiting for your approaching death?" I suspect that in spite of my intellectual logic, in my primitive child-like fantasies, I preconsciously expected rescue. We need to create systems to find explanations for events, for example, bribing one's fate with goodness, prayer, keeping to religious rituals and taboos, or looking for a pseudo-scientific explanation of one's fate through interpreting the constellation of planets and the time of one's birth.

Human belief in a higher power has been symbolized in mythology and carried into superstitions. In the last moments of my own impending death, I permitted myself to imagine the existence of an afterlife, despite my doubts, most likely as a desperate attempt to soothe my fear of the nothingness ahead.

Suicides were expected to occur each time orders were received to report to a transport, and there was always a list of reserves already prepared for replacing those who would be missing. In the camps, suicide was rare, the simplest way to kill oneself was to walk into the electric fence, but usually all energy was exhausted in just surviving the day, hoping for a better next day, unlikely as that was.

Old age is yet another time for survivors when the idea arises again of putting a fast end to a slowly waning life, when the awareness of one's failings become overpowering. Suicide resulting from a fatal fall expresses this symbolically and has occurred with some frequency among survivors. The most well-known of these tragic endings were those of Primo Levi, Bruno Bettelheim, and a science professor I knew, among others. It is a symbolic enactment of falling from the heights of success, from grace. It may represent the infantile wish to finally soar, the grandiose experience of flying that one can have in a dream, or to have the ultimate power over one's own destiny, as well as serve as an escape from the unbearable anxiety and nightmare.

Suicidal thoughts among survivors relate to the heavy burden that we carry forever—we are alive while most of those close to us perished. The fortunate who live on have to cope with the memories, the unfree associations, which haunt us, while the dead are sometimes envied. When those memories are reinforced by new, severe emotional injuries or life-threatening physical impairments, they cast a shadow over one's existence that can become intolerable; to accelerate death in order to escape them seems, for some, the most desirable solution.

"Children of survivors" is a phrase that may imply that members of the next generation all have identical issues dealing with incomprehensible events. There are always multi-generational consequences as a result of extreme changes in social structures. Some offspring of survivors have had more difficulties than others. Whether horrors of the Holocaust were spoken of or kept in mysterious silence, they have had an influence on the relationships of survivors and their children and their grandchildren as well. Recognition of the multi-generation effects has been dealt with in the therapeutic modes of individual, family and groups.

In our global professional psychoanalytic world, we are dealing with another aspect. For many years, the International Psychoanalytic Congresses have had special sessions focusing on treatment of survivors. I recall in the early eighties when the first German analyst courageously presented *her* patient, the son of a Nazi, as a child of a survivor; the atmosphere was chilly. Over the years, there have been more German analysts joining this group; some are young, born after the war. They have conflicts relating their own history to their cultural continuity, but they also have issues about treating persons who were perpetrators. They may themselves be children, or even grandchildren, of perpetrators, truly a struggle for them.

Ursula Hegi, a German writer preoccupied with her own history, has become curious about how other Germans deal with their psychological inheritance. She has found contrasts ranging from total indifference to extreme discomfort in addressing this issue (1997).

Shortly after the end of the war, a former German friend of my high school years located me in Prague and wrote that his family was hungry, asking me for help. I returned a short note telling him that I was still recuperating from my time in the shadow of the crematoriums in Auschwitz.

In 1971, another friend wrote to me in California that he would like to see me and wanted me to visit him and his family in Munich. Shortly thereafter there was an international psychoanalytic meeting in Munich, and I decided to attend since I was very curious about postwar Germans. While in Germany, I took the opportunity to visit my friend. He never asked a question about my time of persecution, but talked freely about his military position building a harbor in occupied Norway and his successful postwar professional life. His adolescent son, however, did have questions.

One evening, while waiting to be served in a restaurant, the waiter did not appear soon enough for my friend. He jokingly said, "I think he has not seen a *Ka Zett* (KZ, a concentration camp) for a long time." His "humorous" way of saying this reminded me of the German air force sergeant, who screamed at me in 1939 when I was shoveling snow at the airport in Prague and grew tired after several hours. However, my friend's untimely use of such German humor, so long after the war, demonstrated how much a part of the German language it had been, perhaps still was.

Meetings that I have had with all my old German friends and schoolmates leave me with the painful realization that they resist hearing about any of my war experiences. They speak to me freely and unself-consciously about their own hardships as soldiers in the German army, their frightening times during the bombings, seemingly not even aware how this would affect me, and have avoided any questions about what had happened to me, my family or other mutual friends. However, the heavy specter of what lies unspoken makes me think they know.

The cardinal question is never approached: How could this have happened? While working on this book, I heard an important news item that was relevant to my description of what occurred in 1939–40, that is, the Soviets blaming the Nazis for the fate of thousands of missing Polish officers. In April 1990, mass graves were discovered in the forest of Katyn, Russia, where the remains of four thousand massacred Polish soldiers were found. The graves of eleven thousand others have allegedly never been found. While the Soviets had blamed the Nazis for the massacre, Russia's former president, Mikhail Gorbachev, in his changed democratic stance, informed the Polish government that Stalin's secret police had performed the executions. Stalin wiped out the core of the Polish army to protect himself from potential attack in the future. The thin layer of civilization can be broken anywhere, individually or by a group. Sympathy for the persecuted depends not only on an alliance with the rationality or irrationality of leaders, but also on the political climate, the needs of various countries and their interests as well as timing.

Time is so crucial a factor. In 1989, while I was writing this book, the strict division between East and West Germany was lifted and the population from the east flocked to the west, many leaving home and family. The psychology of these masses and the situation in Europe was much different from that of World War II, but the events demonstrate how strong the craving for freedom is, and how much stronger when it seems possible to reach it.

During the last forty-five years, since the end of World War II, historians, journalists and others involved in research wondered at the willingness of the military and political personalities, as well as the masses, to switch loyalties, following their dictators who marketed them by seduction, suggestion, temptation and projection. The response of the group-self is dependent upon and often determined by leadership, even the most irrational leadership, motivated by unconscious archaic ambitions and preconscious images of heroism. When the superego is lent to the idealized leader, followers feel enhanced and enact what the leader sanctions. With little consideration of the consequences, their admiration is projected onto him, which in turn strengthens the leader's narcissistic position and propels a self-reproducing cycle of fanaticism.

The years of the Holocaust could too easily be described as a mass psychosis due to a breakdown of rationality. In an illness, the patient truly loses control of reality but in a seduction, which Goethe, in *Faust*, symbolized in the Devil, it is a bargain for omnipotence, a choice to disregard reason for the attainment of a primary process primitive wish. We could also call it the existential choice of the individual. Part of the attraction of the Nazi movement was the promised political gratification of omnipotence as well as the more personal merging with the fantasized, idealized father image. To try to understand the dynamics is a separate issue from the question of responsibility.

Research unearths details to help us understand the historical context, while psychoanalysis can provide a different path of understanding of historical events as enactments of unconscious fantasy life. Psychohistory is a newer offshoot of the two disciplines, sometimes considered a *misalliance* from both sides, but it has brought a rich and new focus to my understanding since ". . . the two disciplines share a common methodology of empathic insight and understanding" (Loewenberg, 1997). The events of those years have been much studied academically as distant history. I experienced them as part of our yesterday that has determined our present and I believe they unfold our future.

In 1930, in his book *Civilization and Its Discontents*, Freud called the struggle between the two human motivating forces Eros and the Instinct of Aggression and Destruction. He said the outcome of the struggle was "a fateful question." In 1931, Freud added, "But who can foresee with what success and with what result." In addition to the instinctual forces, there is also reason and judgement, ego functions that can provide creative and peaceful solutions to conflicts, but they do not always operate successfully.

Freud understood that when we compromise the supervision of our ego's rules and principles in order to avoid frustrating our desires, we also are tormented by mostly unconscious superego guilt, a self-punitive experience. Out of this eternal conflict can come masochistic self-sacrifice or the search for another target, onto whom guilt can be projected, the villain who can be blamed and sacrificed. The term for this is "scapegoat," once a real animal sacrificed as propitiation to avoid sacrificing oneself.

When, in 1938, British Prime Minister Neville Chamberlain allowed Czechoslovakia to be sacrificed in order to avoid imminent war, it was Czechoslovakia that was the scapegoat, followed by all the other countries swallowed up by the German armies. And Hitler tried to unify his European empire using the Jews and other people who were different as scapegoats.

Karel Cåpek, a well-known Czech author, wrote several prophetic books. In one, a satire called, *War With the Newts,* (1936), he describes a species of giant newts that are used by unscrupulous men to take over the world, but then learn to identify with human leadership skills and overrule them. He writes that we have failed in creating one mankind: "Actually we are beginning to realize it; hence those attempts and plans to unite human society in a different way, by making room for *one* nation, *one* class or *one* faith. But who can tell how deeply we are already infected with the incurable disease of differentiation?" (pp. 198–199)

During the last twenty years, a dialectic to the literature on the Holocaust has emerged—responses, laced with hatred, and even envy, perverse as that may seem. A Los Angeles writer, Sam Eisenstein, describes this in a short story called "Holocaust Envy" (1987), in which one of the characters, who was on the outside of this important event, is obsessed with imaginings of what it was like. "It didn't happen to me, but it could have . . ." (p. 218). He feels his history is less significant than that of the other.

A present day illustration of Freud's compromising morality is demonstrated by revisionists who, unable to deal psychologically with this well-documented period, attempt to negate its very existence by rewriting history.

Another term that also illustrates "compromise" is called *deformation,* which describes how changes are made in historic presentations to dramatize events in order to make them more acceptable, especially in literature and film.

There have been other compromise attempts to accept those horrors. The religious explanation that it was "God's will." Another is described in Claude Lanzmann's film *Shoah*. People who were witnesses to atrocities still found justification, from their minimal but negative personal contact with Jews, to explain that it was the Jews' bad behavior that brought it upon themselves.

The most recent and offensive term I have heard used is that of "Holocaust business," referring to the preponderance of material now emerging about this period in history with the purpose of exploiting it as if it were just another sensation. Psychologically, I would think that it represents a need to escape from being overwhelmed and emotionally saturated by the intensity of unimaginable suffering.

I believe that we have not yet completed our mourning of these events and therefore they cannot be laid to rest. There is a natural resistance to completing the process of mourning that begins with the struggle for denial transforming into sadness and accepting the losses.

The Holocaust is the modern technological trauma of everyone's history and therefore it must be internalized individually, digested as it becomes a part of each person, and mourned as a loss of our civilized ideal.

Awareness of the Holocaust becomes everyone's burden since we are the living, and therefore, all survivors. Elie Wiesel wrote that "when we forget, we are guilty, we are accomplices" (1967).

Johann-Gottfried Appy, a German psychoanalyst wrote:

> "Auschwitz is the 'mene tekel' for the destructiveness in us lying daily in wait to force us anew into a psychotic catastrophe, into a *Shoah*, as soon as we succumb to the hypnotic influence of manic fantasies of omnipotence; fantasies which originally served to achieve harmony and order, the preservation of a symbiotic dual union with mother and child, but which are now able to pervert and to lead us to the destruction of ourselves and the world in arrogant self-deception" (1988).

There are also those who say that all this is over and we need to forgive, forget and get on with living. I credit Steven Spielberg for his creating a foundation that has been interviewing survivors on video, of which I was one, and documenting those events in our civilization as a way of conserving our historical memory. Being dead, whether it is Hitler, Mengele, or ten million victims, is seen as the great equalizer. This seems to be the prototype of unfairness. The outcome is the same but the differences in how they died must remain in our memories. The crux of this issue is that the exhausted victim thrown alive and headlong into the ditch anticipates those agonizing moments of demise while his last contact with his "kind" is denial of his whole life by being seen as not human. This robs one of the experience of dying in an empathic human milieu.

In the face of overwhelming danger, the human mind can neither tolerate nor acknowledge unbelievable threat. Distortion of perception during life threatening, catastrophic moments is the mind's attempt to prevent one's own disintegration, the incipient state of losing one's sanity—no longer perceiving reality. A powerful enough traumatic experience can break even the healthy balance of a stable narcissistic equilibrium, and can create a "breakdown" of psychological functions. Misperceiving one's limits may be the greatest menace to survival because it moves one into a delusional world. For example, we heard about

Auschwitz for the first time in Prague from the smuggled letter that Robert Redlich brought. We were stunned, shocked, and speechless, hearing about the creation of gas chambers and crematoriums in Auschwitz-Birkenau. It was unbearable and unbelievable. After a few days, however, we returned to "ordinary" life, carrying this overwhelming knowledge, but defending against it with repression, denial and other defense mechanisms that let us distort the reality. Our grandiose feelings of omnipotence and being untouchable existed alongside our panic.

Docent Hirsch, my first mentor in psychoanalysis, helped me to understand why I hesitated in taking risks to save my life. He thought my childhood experiences of being pampered had influenced my adult fantasies and that my passivity demonstrated my belief that someone would rescue me again.

Most of the historical, psychological and descriptive attempts at explaining what happened to us during the Holocaust are valid; however, I believe not enough importance has been given to both the collective and the individual unconscious response to infantile omnipotence and wishes for superiority, which, in normal times, are sublimated and well-controlled. Our current century's philosophers understand our fears and the responsibility that comes with knowledge, not the fears of ancient man, frightened of the elements, of the mysterious unknown, but those of the modern individual, fearful of acknowledging the potential and consequences of his choices. Again, all attempts to find explanations still leave the question of responsibility unanswered.

This is a book that resounds with coincidence. For most of my adult life I have been intrigued with coincidence and have been in awe of "accidental happenings." These occurrences appear seemingly casual, yet are often connected and sometimes even determine survival. Mathematically fortuitous coincidence seems so unlikely in one's real life but it does occur. Only a few survived Auschwitz and Buchenwald and I am among them—the result of favorable coincidence, that, if written about in a novel, would seem contrived but is as real as I am today.

Those who have been lost have not been left to die forgotten but must be acknowledged in a time past their own. I have chosen to be the bridge for them, the bleeding images in my memory conveying our history.

Auschwitz, and especially Birkenau, with its assembly line, mechanical, dehumanizing technology for mass murder, changed the consciousness of man's trust in civilization. For me it is a ghastly memory, but for the world it has become a symbol and a metaphor that would have seemed incredible prior to this epoch. We, who were there, suffered incredibly, and thought even then that the crescendo of that irrational destruction would have to culminate in self-destruction at its source.

APPENDIX II

Further Notes on Survivors

ON MY RETURN TO PRAGUE, I learned that Otto Heller's wife, Hanka, and daughter Suzi had also returned. Franzis, the man who struggled between religions, did not survive. Hans, the cruel co-administrator of the hospital with Otto, broke down on another march towards the west. Nobody responded to his pleas for help. The last I heard about Bernie Pollack was that he went to Canada and became a specialist in tuberculosis. I saw Dr. Epstein, my former professor of pediatrics, again. He retained his rank as captain in the Czechoslovakian army and became my daughter's first pediatrician.

A few months after my return to Prague, I visited Dr. Dosužkov, the heroic Czech guardian of psychoanalysis, who worked throughout the war officially as a neurologist, while secretly analyzing and training a few carefully chosen professionals in psychoanalysis. I had first heard about him when I was in medical school and tutoring a young Russian girl preparing for her high school finals. She had a learning disorder (today we would call it *adult attention deficit disorder*) and appeared quite anxious and insecure. After she studied with me awhile, she hesitantly told me about her psychoanalytic treatment with Dr. Dosužkov. She mentioned what a kind, comforting man he was and that he spoke Czech with the same Russian accent as her family.

Dr. Dosužkov accepted me with great warmth and said, "It feels as if I know you well," hinting that he had heard about me from some of his patients, one of whom was a friend of mine who had gone underground. I became a part of the task force in 1947–48 that translated Freud's papers into Czech. We sometimes spent hours searching for just the right word and nuance for a term of Freud's. The translation was important for psychology students. Psychoanalysis was also one of the few available treatments for helping people who had gone through terror and persecution, providing a way of dealing with trauma. It was becoming known once more and applied in psychotherapy for the first time since the Nazis had destroyed the literature.

I also participated as a member of Dr. Dosužkov's seminars. In addition he had planned public lectures where one of us would present, in Czech, a review of Freud's basic books. He presented, as the first lecturer, an introduction to Freud's theories. I was next and spoke on *The Ego and the Id*, a book I'd known in German. With some help from a high school professor friend, I prepared a simple Czech paper for an unknown audience. I was uneasy about my accent and the controversial nature of the subject since I was familiar with the xenophobia of the less sophisticated Czechs as well as of the sensitivity to new ideas of those who were educated and intellectual. I actually represented two foreign worlds to them, one, a speaker distorting their Czech language, and the other an interpreter of the human psyche in a new and controversial way. After my talk, a young man approached me and commented, "I understood your German accent better than I understood the first speaker." Though Dr. Dosužkov spoke in fluent Czech he had spoken of theories, of infantile sexuality and instinctual drives—ideas which were more difficult for him to accept than my simple German-accented Czech.

Another teacher, Dr. Kučera, was one of the people that Dr. Dosužkov had analyzed during the war and who later become a close associate of his. This man was the police psychiatrist of the city of Prague. The number of students in the seminars grew and, when professionals and others interested in psychoanalysis joined us, the foundation for a professional society was laid. Dr. Dosužkov urged me to write about my experiences and observations in the camps. In our personal conversations he reacted strongly to my description of the years of imprisonment and was angry when he heard how difficult it was being made for me to reestablish my security and identity after my return to Prague. I was touched by his sensitivity, his ability to grasp the essential and to respond with great tact. He was interested in collecting dreams from those of us who had been in the camps. He was particularly interested in dreams in which there was content related to bodily sensations interwoven with psychic processes.

I worked in a few different hospitals before I arrived at the neuropsychiatric department of Vihnoradska Hospital, a university hospital in Prague, where I assisted Professor Šebek in teaching medical students. I loved my work, which was the most important and satisfying part of my life.

There was hardly anyone in Prague from my past life. On a hot summer day walking along Paris Street in the Old City of Prague, I was overjoyed to run into Franzis Lux, a friend I had not seen since 1939. He had been a lawyer before the German occupation and had participated with great interest in the courses on graphology and industrial psychology with Willy Schönfeld and me as well as in Dr. Hirsch's courses. At the time, he had divorced his Czech, non-Jewish wife, so as not to endanger her. When deportations had started in 1941, he wondered what to do. I recall us walking on a busy street near one of the main railroad stations and listening to the whistle of a departing train with nostalgia for our former freedom. There was no train for us to get out of the trap we were in. We had concluded that we had three choices. Go along and try to survive the war although we considered that likelihood to be very slim. A second option was to join the considerable number of people committing suicide on receiving the order to appear for deportation. The only other choice to avoid the dreaded fate was to go underground. This is what Franzis did. He lived in the cellar of the building in which his divorced wife had her apartment. She took care of him. Being in permanent danger of being discovered was a situation of enormous and prolonged stress for each. They both survived.

After the war, Franzis and I wrote a couple of graphological character analyses of war criminals for popular journals. We had all kinds of ideas for other psychological and graphological papers, but we never got around to writing them because our energies were consumed by the events of the day and the developments in Europe. We were both highly sensitized to political tensions. Czechoslovakia was increasingly coming under the direct influence of Soviet Russia. The Secretary of State, Jan Masaryk, "fell" out of the window of the castle, which was the seat of the government. *Defenestration* had been a traditional way in the past of changing power and we guessed what was coming. All aspects of life, including hospital and clinical work, came under the control of members of the Communist Party, who were often poorly educated but politically acceptable.

Franzis had worked as the Secretary for the liberal Social Democratic Party, but after the war felt more endangered by a new, more rigid dictatorship. I was upset that Dosužkov had to again become protective of his psychoanalytic activity; it did not fit into the Soviet system either. Here we were once again talking about emigration.

Years later we both were living in Los Angeles, where we again worked together. In the eighties we used to meet over a coffee or lunch to talk as we looked out over the Pacific Ocean. He was one of the few links with my past. He died in July 1997 in a nursing home in Santa Monica. His wife, Hilda, died a few weeks later.

Other links were Walter and his oldest brother, Paul Kohner, who were helpful and kind to my family and me. Hanna and Walter wrote a book with Walter's middle brother, Frederick (1984). Frederick and Paul both died in the late eighties, Hanna in 1990 and Walter in 1996. They had one daughter, Julie, who married Steven Greenberg, a space engineer, but Hanna never lived to see her grandson, Daniel.

As an intern, the administration and doctors at Good Samaritan Hospital in Los Angeles treated me with respect. I did some good work there. I liked all medicine but it was another detour from my career as a psychiatrist.

However, I did see analytic patients in my off time. An L. A. analyst, Lawrence Friedman, lent me his office and supervised my cases, so that I was admitted to one of the analytic institutes. There were two more examinations, one for foreign graduates only, the other an oral and clinical one in a hospital. I finally received my California license to practice medicine in January of 1961, more than four years after my arrival. Since then I have been in a comfortable private practice.

SELECTED BIBLIOGRAPHY

Appy, Johann-Gottfried. "The Meaning of 'Auschwitz' Today: Clinical Reflections About the Depletion of a Destructive Symbol." (1988) in Moses, R. ed., *Persistent Shadows of the Holocaust: The Meaning to Those Not Directly Affected.* New York: International University Press, 1993.

Astor, Gerald. *The Last Nazi: The Life and Times of Dr. Joseph Mengele.* New York: Donald Donald I. Fine Inc., 1985.

Bergman, Martin S. and Jacovy, Milton E. *Generations of the Holocaust.* New York: Basic Books Inc., 1982.

Bion, Wilfred. "Selections from Experiences in Groups." 1959.

Bloch, Gottfried R. "Le Perception Des Troubles Psychiques." *L'Encephale*, No. 1 (1951): 114–121.

———. "Traumatic and Post Traumatic Neuroses." presentation to Southern California Psychiatric Society, 1971.

———. "Traumatic and Post Traumatic Neuroses." *Industrial Medicine and Surgery*, 1972.

———. "Post Traumatic Character Changes." W. Regional Psychoanalytic Convention. San Diego, California, 1972.

———. "Group Therapy of Post Traumatic Psychoses." Fifth Analytic Group Therapy Conference. Stelzerreut, Bavaria, 1973.

———. "Therapeutic Interventions in Post Traumatic Neuroses." Sixth International Symposium, German Academy of Psychoanalysis. Munich, Germany, 1974.

———. "Psychotherapeutic Interventions in Post Traumatic Reactions." *Dynamic Psychiatry*, 1974.

———. "Dimensions of Loss." Cedars-Sinai Hospital, Grand Rounds. Los Angeles, California, 1976.

———. "Group Psychotherapy of Post Traumatic Psychoses." New

York: *International J. Group Psychotherapy,* 1976.

———. "The Aging Survivor." Seminar. Cedars-Sinai Hospital, Grand Rounds. Los Angeles, California, 1976.

———. "The Treatment of Traumatic Neuroses." Lecture. University of Hawaii, 1979.

Block, G. and Drucker, M. *Rescuers: Portraits of Moral Courage in the Holocaust.* New York: Holmes and Meier, 1992.

Brauchle, Alfred. *Psychoanalyse und Individualpsychologie.* Leipzig: Philipp Reclam Jun., 1930.

Calic, Edouard. *Reinhard Heydrich.* trans. L. Bair. New York: Wm. Morrow and Co. Inc., 1982.

Cåpek, Karel. *War With the Newts (Valka s mloky).* New York: Putnam and Sons, 1937.

Cocks, Geoffrey. *Psychotherapy in the Third Reich.* New York: Oxford University Press, 1985.

Cocks, Geoffrey. and Crosby, T. L. *Psychohistory: Readings in the Method of Psychology, Psychoanalysis and History.* New York: Oxford University Press, 1987.

Czech, Danuta. *Auschwitz Chronicle: 1939–1945: From the Archives of the Auschwitz Memorial and the German Federal Archives.* New York: Henry Holt and Co., 1990.

Dagan, A., editor in chief, Lewis, G. and W. assoc. eds., *The Jews of Czechoslovakia.* Philadelphia: The Jewish Publication Society of America and New York: The Society for the History of Czechoslovak Jews, 1984.

Eisenstein, Sam. *The Inner Garden.* Los Angeles: Sun and Moon, 1987.

Ferenczi, Sandor. *Final Contributions to the Problems and Methods of Psychoanalysis.* ed. M. Balint. London: Karnac Books, 1933.

Fisher, D. J. "The Suicide of a Survivor: Some Intimate Perceptions of Bettelheim's Suicide." *Psychoanalytic Review.* no. 79 (1992): 592–602.

Friedlander, Saul. *Reflections on Nazism: An Essay on Kitsch and Death.* trans. Weye, T. New York: Avon, 1984.

———. *Nazi Germany and the Jews: Vol. 1: The Years of Persecution, 1933 1939.* New York: Harper Collins, 1997.

Freud, Sigmund. (1927), "Civilization and Its Discontents." *Standard Edition,* no. 21: p. 5. London: Hogarth Press, 1964.

Gilbert, Martin. *Auschwitz and the Allies: A Devastating Account.* New York: Holt, Rinehart and Winston, 1981.

———. *The Holocaust: A History of the Jews of Europe During The Second World War.* New York: Holt, Rinehart and Winston, 1985.

———. *The Second World War: A Complete History.* New York: Henry Holt and Co., 1989.

Hašek, Jaroslav. *The Good Soldier Schweik.* New York: New American Library, 1963 ed. (originally published 1930 as *The Good Soldier Švejk*).

Hegi, Ursula. *Tearing the Silence: On Being German in America.* New York: Simon and Schuster, 1997.

Hellman, Peter. and Meier, Lili. *The Auschwitz Album: A Book Based Upon an Album.* New York: Random House, 1981.

Johnson, Paul. *A History of the Jews.* New York: Harper and Row, 1987.

———. *Modern Times: The World from the Twenties to the Nineties.* New York: HarperPerenial Library, 1992 ed.

Jaffe, R. "Moshe Woolf: Pioneering in Russia and Israel." in *Psychoanalytic Pioneers.* eds. Alexander, F., Eisenstein, E. and Grotjahn, M. New York: Basic Books, 1966.

Khan, Masud. "The Use and Abuse of the Dream in Psychic Experience." in *The Privacy of the Self.* New York: International University Press, 1974.

Klages, Ludwig. *Handschrift und Charakter.* Leipzig: Johann Ambrosius Barth, 1940.

Kohut, Heinz. *The Restoration of the Self.* New York: International University Press, 1977.

———. *Self Psychology and the Humanities: Reflections on a New Psychoanalytic Approach.* New York: W. W. Norton, 1985.

Krystal, Henry. ed. *Massive Psychic Trauma.* New York: International University Press, 1968.

Lanzmann, Claude. *Shoah: An Oral History of the Holocaust.* Text of the film. New York: Pantheon Books, 1985.

Langbein, Herman. *Menschen in Auschwitz.* Frankfurt: Ullstein-Bucher, 1972.

Langer, Lawrence L. *Holocaust Testimonies: The Ruins of Memory.* New Haven: Yale University Press, 1991.

Lifton, Robert Jay. *The Nazi Doctors: Medical Killing and the Psychology of Genocide*. New York: Basic Books, 1986.

————. *The Protean Self: Human Resilience in an Age of Fragmentation*. New York: Basic Books, 1993.

Loewenberg, Peter. *Decoding the Past: The Psychohistorical Approach*. Berkeley: University of California Press, 1969.

————. *Fantasy and Reality in History*. New York: Oxford University Press, 1995.

Lohman, H-M. *Psychoanalyse und National Sozialismus*. Frankfurt: Fischer, 1984.

Miale, Florence R. and Selzer, M. *The Nuremberg Mind: The Psychology of the Nazi Leaders*. New York: The New York Times Book Co., 1975.

Micheels, Louis J. *Doctor 117641*. New Haven: Yale University Press, 1989.

Müller, Filip. *Eyewitness Auschwitz: Three Years in the Gas Chambers*. New York: Stein and Day, 1981.

Munthe, Axel. *The Story of San Michele*. Carroll and Graf Publishers, 1934 ed.

Noakes, Jeremy. and Pridham, Geoffrey. eds. *Nazism: A History in Documents and Eyewitness Accounts*, 1919–1945, Vols 1 and 2. New York: Schocken Books, 1988.

Nyiszli, Miklos. *Auschwitz: An Eyewitness Account of Mengele's Infamous Death Camp*. New York: Seaver Books, 1960.

Pawelczynska, Anna. *Values and Violence in Auschwitz: A Sociological Analaysis*. trans. Leach, C. Berkeley: University of California Press, 1979.

Pisar, Samuel. *Of Blood and Hope*. New York: Macmillan, 1979.

Reitz, E. *Heimat (Homeland): A Chronicle of Germany, 1918–1984*. (film). West Germany, 1984.

Remak, Joachim. ed. *The Nazi Years: A Documentary History*. New York: New York: Simon and Schuster, 1969.

Rosenfarb, Chava. *The Tree of Life*. Melbourne, Australia: Scribe, 1985 (English edition).

Rothschild, Sylvia. ed. *Voices from the Holocaust*. New York: Times Mirror New American Library, 1981.

Sachs, Nelly. *O The Chimneys*. New York: Farrar, Strauss and Giroux, 1967.

Schönfeld, W. and Menzel, Karl. *Handschrift, Tuberkulose und Character*. Prague: Rohrer, 1934.

Shirer, William L. *The Rise and Fall of the Third Reich*. New York: Simon and Schuster, 1960.

Stein Lewinson T. and Zubin, J. *Handwriting Analysis*. New York: King's Crown Press, 1942.

Utitz, E. *Psychologie Zivota v Terezinzkern Concentracnim Tabore*. Praha: Delnicke Nakladatel stviv Praze, 1947.

Weitz, John. *Hitler's Diplomat: The Life and Times of Joachim von Ribbentrop*. New York: Ticknor and Fields, 1992.

———. *Hitler's Banker*. Boston: Little Brown and Co., 1997.

Wiesel, Elie. *Legends of Our Time*. New York: Holt, Rhinehart Winston, 1968.

Winnicott, Donald W. "The Maturational Processes and The Facilitating Environment." *Emotional Development*. Connecticut: International Universities Press, 1965.

GENERAL INDEX

SELECTED INDEX

Psychoanalytic

Selected Index